Essays on George F. Walker

Also available from Blizzard Publishing

Essays on Kushner's Angels
Essays on Caryl Churchill

Essays on
George F. Walker
Playing with
Anxiety

by Chris Johnson

Blizzard Publishing
Winnipeg • Buffalo

First published 1999 by Blizzard Publishing Inc.
73 Furby Street, Winnipeg, Canada R3C 2A2
Distributed in the United States by General Distribution Services,
85 River Rock Dr., Unit 202, Buffalo, NY 14207–2170.

Cover design by Otium Productions.
Printed in Canada by Webcom.

Blizzard Publishing gratefully acknowledges the support of the
Manitoba Arts Council and the Canada Council to its publishing program.

Canadian Cataloguing in Publication Data

Johnson, Chris, 1944–
    Essays on George F. Walker
    ISBN 0-921368-82-8
    1. Walker, George F., 1947– Criticism and interpretation. I. Title.
PS8595.A557 Z75   1998   C812'.54   C98-920222-4
PR9199.3.W342 Z75   1998

This book is dedicated to my son, Zachary,
for whom I too would like a world
with less shit and more justice.

Contents

Acknowledgments

There are many acknowledgements I wish to make, many more, probably, than I can actually acknowledge.

Dean Raymond Currie and the Faculty of Arts at the University of Manitoba for the half-year leave and the financial support which made it possible for me to write this book. Peter Atwood of Blizzard Publishing for his encouragement, patience and good sense. Per Brask, for suggesting the idea of the book, for his friendship, intellectual stimulation and lots of laughs. Ric Knowles for repeatedly asking "When are you going to write your Walker book?" Reading a Knowles article always prompts me to write pages in reply. "Dramaturgy of perversity" was especially helpful to me in writing this book. Ric also supervised two of the three Master's theses which have been written on Walker's work. Denis Johnston for his friendship and encouragement, and for writing the second real and extended article about Walker's work—at last I had someone to talk to and argue with about Walker's work. George Toles, colleague and intellectual *provocateur*. For the excitement of his company and of his work, critical and directorial, over the past twenty years—and, again, a lot of laughs. Margaret Groome, a tireless campaigner for Theory, and while she hasn't converted me entirely, she's certainly made me pay attention. Margaret also held the fort in the Theatre Programme and the Black Hole Theatre at the U of M while I wrote the book.

Raye Anderson, Director of Education at the Prairie Theatre Exchange: Raye's ability to detect bullshit at a great distance is amazing, and she too helps to keep me honest. Libby Mason, director and theatre worker extraordinaire, for sharing her brilliance and her good political and theatrical sense. Marilyn Loat, secretary of the Theatre Programme at the University of Manitoba. For her help and support in countless ways. A woman of great good sense. To my many theatre students at the University of Manitoba, for their provocative company, enthusiasm, and their never-ending questions. Especially Anne Ross and Anna Brierley, whom I quote, and the students and former students who worked with me on the three Walker productions I have directed at the U of M: Bruce Michalski, Guy Stewart, Christine Harapiak, Barb Melnyk, Cynthia Hiebert-Simkin, Lee-Ann Block, Gerald Pauls, Kelli Shinfield, Sylvia Richardson, Tracy Gemmel, Tim Webster, Andrea von Wichert, Holly Longstaff, Leigh-Anne Kehler, and Jock Martin. Also Neil Lawrie who, while he was never a student of mine, was a terrific William.

Lillian Esses, psychologist and my wife, the mother of my child. For a whole lot of things, obviously. I think more than for anyone else, I've written for her over the past few years—she's very bright, very concerned with human thought and emotions, very perceptive, very honest, loves to read, but she's not a literary specialist, and is certainly not inclined to put literature and literary studies on a pedestal. And that, I think, makes her the perfect audience. If it doesn't make sense to her or doesn't engage her, make her think, I've done something wrong. The supreme bullshit detector.

Zak, my son, whose older self is in among my imaginary readership. For showing me again how funny, scary, and wonderful life really is.

And, of course, George F. Walker, whose work has been making me laugh, making me think, giving me pleasure, stimulation, and a great deal of anxiety for nearly thirty years now. For that work, and for his generosity in sharing his thoughts about his plays, theatre, and the "politics of life."

Introduction

I've wanted to write this book for a long time. George F. Walker's plays have been among my favourites, have influenced my thinking about theatre, have been part of my life, and have given me some very good times for twenty-seven years now. There are twenty-six published Walker plays as I write this, a substantial body of work, and for the most part, I think they're very good plays—brash, assertive, perceptive, "genuinely perverse," often wonky, and very, very funny. It's time that someone wrote a book about the accomplishments of this remarkable man, and about his contribution to Canadian drama and theatre, and indeed to world drama and theatre.

As the project evolved, it became clear to me that this book is important to me personally, and that it is therefore more personal and probably less scholarly than are most books about plays and playwrights written by university professors of theatre. Walker and I are of a generation, early baby boomers, and Walker's work taken as a whole is in part a history of that generation, its politics, its early conviction that it could indeed change the world, its subsequent disillusionment, its progress through the stormy and heady latter half of the twentieth century. Furthermore, he and I were both directly involved, in youthful formative years, in a particular manifestation of the "rise of the counter culture," the creation of a new kind of Canadian theatre in Toronto in the early 1970s, and this book attempts to convey some of the excitement of those days—some (self)romanticization is probably inevitable. In a review of Diane Bessai's *Playwrights of Collective Creation* I said that the book

> ... goes beyond analysis in its ability to convey a sense of the excitement, the commitment, and yes, the passion, that animated the Canadian collectives of the early seventies. This is so probably because, one senses, Bessai shared/shares the excitement, commitment, and passion— no "playless theory" for her, and for her, the passing of this era is cause for some regret. (151)

I, too, aspire to that sort of passion in the writing of this book.

Therefore, I don't want to write a book of "theory," although theory, the new critical project, will come into the discussion from time to time, and certainly influences some of the views expressed in this book. I'm sympathetic to the democratizing agenda of much theory, and see much value in valorizing that which was "ex-centric" and peripheral. I've learned much from theory, and have been shown much I didn't know before. Still, I must confess, that much is written in a language in which I am not fluent, and I don't propose to write a "theory book" in large part because I don't think I can.

That said, I also confess that there's more to this decision than the "old dog/new tricks" aversion. While theory's agenda is democratic and inclusive, I think its practice is all too often elitist. I have a nagging suspicion that John Ralston Saul might be very close to the truth (or a provisional truth) when he identifies "theory," recent literary criticism, as a "professional dialect" in *Voltaire's Bastards*:

> What then is to be thought of elites who seek above all to develop private dialects? Who seek to communicate as little as possible? Who actively discourage the general population from understanding them? They are proponents of illiteracy. What [are we to think] of a full professor of English literature who views fiction as an exercise separate from society? Who encourages such ideas as deconstructionism, which render literature inaccessible except to the most intimately initiated? (111)

All too often, it seems to me, theory has frozen into a rigid, heavily-codified, pseudo-scientific and impersonal discourse, appearing to employ an objectivity which it says cannot exist. It says that the "personal is political," but in practice and form excludes the personal and the diverse. While it valorizes playfulness, *jouissance*, it itself seldom plays, and almost never uses play as a form of (provisional) truth-seeking.

Particularly now, given the opportunity to write a book and say some things I think are important, I don't want to speak just to a small group of academic colleagues. I want to talk as well to people who go to George Walker's plays not out of any professional obligation but because they like Walker plays and are challenged, puzzled, and invigorated by them. I want to talk to actors and directors who do Walker or who are thinking about doing Walker, taking a walk in Walkerland. "Sharing an enthusiasm" is a very old-fashioned definition of literary criticism, but I have to admit that sharing my enthusiasm for the plays of George F. Walker is one of the most important motivations for my writing this book, and there's no point in pretending otherwise.

Furthermore, I don't want to abandon and disregard everything theory has decided is irrelevant. In *Producing Marginality*, an excellent and provocative book which has greatly influenced my thinking about theatre, especially about theatre in Canada, Robert Wallace dismisses his earlier book, *The Work: Conversations with Canadian Playwrights*, because of its attention to the writers' intentions. But I don't believe that authorial intention is entirely irrelevant, nor that an examination of social context and cultural politics says everything about a play or a performance text that's worth saying. (Nor do I believe that *The Work* is now a useless piece of Wallace's critical juvenalia.) When I go into the rehearsal hall to direct a play, I have intentions. Needless to say, those intentions are not always entirely realized. Needless to say the reception of those intentions by each individual audience member is equally shaped, perhaps more shaped, by that person's perception of the performance text, and needless to say gender, race, ethnicity, age, all play their parts in influencing that individual's perception. And needless to say the material conditions of theatrical production in the aptly named Black Hole Theatre at the University of Manitoba contribute to the perceptual/cultural/social stew. But somewhere in there, there are still my intentions, and, usually, my interpretation of, informed guess at, the author's intentions, and they are part of the whole, and as such, worthy of some attention. Identifying them by no means explains the whole, but acknowledgement of intention seems to me essential to a comprehensive investigation.

So I plan to talk about Walker's intentions, or at least about what I think about Walker's intentions. Walker writes plays because he has to. He writes plays the way he does, in the forms he does, not because he's made intellectual decisions about how plays ought to be written nor out of allegiance to one school of playwriting or another, but because he's looking for a way to show us the world the way he sees it. To "[share] anxieties," to quote Robert Wallace again, this time in particular reference to Walker's work (*Shared Anxiety* viii). A consideration of Walker's compulsion to share experience in this way, it seems to me, is vital to a discussion of Walker's plays and how they work in the theatre; indeed, I'm convinced that it's a large part of Walker's genius that he has succeeded so fully in putting this compulsion directly on stage. Passion is an important part of Walker's work, and much of his appeal to me (and, I suspect, to many in his audiences) is that he is a very passionate man; what he is trying to say, and trying to say it, are passionately important to him. Here is a playwright who is more concerned with what he is saying than how he is saying it: in conversation, he is more interested in talking about what the plays are about, what they try to mean, than he is in discussing the plays as artifacts, even than as fragments of his own ego.

It's probably clear by now that I'm feeling a little guilty about not writing a more scholarly book than this one is turning out to be. Academic habits die hard, even if one is a full professor and no longer needs the brownie points. Often during the writing of the book, I've comforted myself with the thought that I don't believe for a moment that this will be the only book written about the plays of George F. Walker. This will only be the first of what I confidently expect will be several such books. Therefore, it doesn't have to say everything there is to say about Walker's plays, even if such a thing were possible, which, of course, it isn't. It just has to be my book about Walker. It started, really, in the early seventies, when I took up my first full-time university teaching job.

In the early 1970s, I was teaching theatre at Brock University in St. Catharines, Ontario, on the Niagara Peninsula, around the western end of Lake Ontario from Toronto, about seventy miles more or less south of that city. Close enough to drive in for the evening or the weekend quite often, and it was well worth the drive, because lots of exciting things were happening in Toronto theatre in those days. Theatre Passe Muraille, led by Paul Thompson, who had by then taken over from Jim Garrard as Artistic Director, was developing its highly physical and theatrical docu-drama style, and as some of my colleagues, especially Ted Johns, then teaching at Brock, were friends of Thompson's, ties between Passe Muraille and Brock were quite strong—we often took students into Toronto to see their work, and Brock's Thistle Theatre was included in a Passe Muraille tour of their show, *Doukhobors*. A vivid memory from the time: the Passse Muraille cast rehearsing in Brock's Thistle Theatre, and Thompson, signifying the death of sect leader, Peter Veregin, hurling himself into the air without warning from the top of the vomitorium, about twenty feet above the thrust stage deck, simply trusting that other members of the cast would catch him. They did. Vintage Passe Muraille stuff.

My personal connections, however, were with another fledgling, radical, and "alternative" theatre organization in Toronto, the Factory Theatre Lab. Its founder, incendiary, guiding light and guru, in the way that Thompson was Passe Muraille's guru, was Ken Gass, who had been a classmate of mine in Creative Writing and Theatre at the University of British Columbia in Vancouver, where playwriting instructor, Doug Bankson, busy at the time establishing the New Play Centre, had fired up Ken and I and many other people with the idea that there was no particularly good reason why exciting new plays couldn't be written in Canada, nor that there shouldn't be Canadian theatres to produce this Canadian work, a fairly revolutionary concept at the time. (Ironically, Bankson was a transplanted American.) While I was at Brock, Gass rented and was renovating, in a fairly slapdash manner and with a good deal of volunteer labour, a former candle factory above an autobody shop in an industrial area on Dupont

Street in Toronto. In a move regarded by many as virtually suicidal, Gass declared that his new Factory Theatre Lab would be the "Home of the Canadian Playwright," and announced a "Canadian plays only" policy. Denis Johnston points out in *Up the Mainstream: The Rise of Toronto's Alternative Theatres* that the Factory Lab was not the first Canadian theatre to concentrate exclusively on Canadian plays, but that nonetheless, the Factory and its "Canadian only" policy was "a vital link in the development of new Canadian drama, eventually bringing the Canadian play to the forefront of the 'Toronto movement'" (75). While Ken was still getting his new venture going, in order to get public attention for the new alternative theatre movement, he initiated a Festival of Underground Theatre (FUT) and invited me and a group of my students to bring our production of my one-act play, *Sex, Cold Cans, and a Coffin*, to Toronto for the Festival; Ken knew the play from our days at the University of British Columbia, where it was first produced. Later on, Eric Steiner directed a workshop of one of my other plays at the Factory, and another group of students staged a guest production of a Brock show at the Factory. So one way or another, in capacities including but not restricted to that of audience member, I was in and out of the Factory a lot during those early days. This was my kind of theatre, writer-centred rather than actor-centered, as was Passe Muraille, and *avant garde* and theatricalist in a way that the neo-naturalistic plays that the Tarragon Theatre started to produce a couple of years later were not.

Another vivid memory from those early days: walking into the Factory's dark and grubby performance space, always redolent with the heady fumes of paint solvents and auto lacquer from the body shop below, and on my way to taking my seat being confronted with a "corpse" dangling from a rope tied to the grid overhead. "Far fucking out," I thought (something we said a lot in those days), "what a neat way to start a play." I had been introduced to the work of George F. Walker, the play was *Ambush at Tether's End*. I also vividly remember being as startled as I have ever been in a theatre by the high-voltage, totally unexpected entrance of Shain Jaffe (Walker's current agent) as Jobeo, the dead man's assistant in his posthumous tormenting of Bush and Galt. All in all, it was a riveting evening. Yeah, yeah, yeah, very derivative of Beckett, but *everyone* was trying to imitate Beckett in those days, and this was imitation Beckett with a difference—an energy, a sharpness in the dialogue, a flair for the unexpected and for the often thought but seldom expressed that seemed to belong to this new guy, George Walker, alone. In a sense, then, the book you are reading started in December of 1971, when I was so taken by *Ambush at Tether's End*.

I also remember being a little miffed when Gass appointed Walker the Factory's playwright-inresidence, a post Walker subsequently held for five years. I mean the guy had only written two plays at this point. Who was this upstart crow? But at the same time, jealous though I was, in another part of my brain, I knew what it was that Ken was seeing, and why he was willing to take the chance of committing himself and his new theatre to this relative newcomer. The pay-off is still coming, twenty-seven years later, and Walker has returned the favour on several occasions by coming to the rescue with a hit play when the Factory desperately needed a hit play (or, as in the winter of 1997–98), six hit plays.

Politics and political conviction may have had something to do with Gass deciding to take that chance back in 1971—the place was right and the time was right for a voice from outside the established centres of power, a working-class hero, and working-class voice not unlike that of Billy Brodie in Tom Stoppard's *The Real Thing*. Gass, himself from an unestablishment background, was unlikely to be dissuaded by a lack of educational and "artistic" credentials, was in fact more than usually likely to be attracted by the potential of a diamond in the rough. And Gass definitely had a nose for talent—unlike Stoppard's fictional Brodie, Walker could write—could at that point write startlingly, if sporadically, very well indeed. Furthermore, Gass, himself a passionate, reckless man, doubtless experienced an affinity for the passion he sensed in Walker.

Meanwhile, I had become seriously involved in the academic study of Canadian drama. My experiences at Theatre Passe Muraille and the Factory encouraged me to seek out scripts of other contemporary Canadian plays, and then earlier ones. To my surprise, I found quite a few good ones. There was a conference of Niagara Peninsula high-school drama and English teachers at Brock, and I was asked to do a presentation on Canadian drama., especially on Canadian plays that might be considered for high-school productions—cultural nationalism was an idea very much in the air in Canada from the Centennial year, 1967, on into the early seventies. I met the high-school teachers in the Thistle Theatre green room, carrying a great stack of some of the Canadian scripts I had been unearthing. I was asked almost immediately why there wasn't a bibliography of published Canadian plays. Good question.

The cultural nationalism of the era had a political agenda—the Liberal federal government, then under Prime Minister Pierre Trudeau, was engaged in trying to establish a greater economic independence from the American sphere (the so-called "Third Option" of the day involved increasing trade ties with Europe), and to distance Canada from some U.S. foreign policy, especially in Viet Nam. To these ends, and for its own political advantage, the Liberals encouraged the development of the arts in Canada, which they hoped would lead to a distinct identity and a stronger sense of national self, through funding programs such as Opportunity for Youth (OFY) and Local Initiatives Projects (LIP). The founders of the alternative theatres in Toronto, including Thompson, Gass, and, at one remove, Walker, made extensive use of these financial opportunities; Johnston gives a good and full account of the interaction between politics, funding programs, and the rise of the alternatives.[1]

In 1973, I decided that it was time to get a Ph.D. and I wanted to do more work on Canadian drama. However, I didn't want to concentrate entirely on Canadian work, a practice which seemed to me at the time to be leading to some unfortunate excesses, so decided I would research a dissertation comparing the Canadian and Australian dramas. I went to the University of Leeds in the U.K. to do so. Shortly before I left for England, I was contacted by Ken Chubb, the Canadian artistic director of the Wakefield Tricycle, a small company working out of the King's Head pub in North London; he wanted to produce my play *Sex, Cold Cans, and a Coffin*. Once again I was to be obliquely connected to George Walker, sharing a bill as it were, as the Wakefield Tricycle production of my play was to coincide with the Factory Theatre's English tour of Herschel Hardin's *Esker Mike and His Wife, Agiluk* and Walker's *Bagdad Saloon*. *Sex, Cold Cans, and a Coffin* was tacked on as a sort of a sideshow to what Gass was now grandiosely calling "a festival of Canadian plays." Another vivid memory from the period—an hour or so after getting off the plane finding myself in the King's Head, leaning on the bar, drinking a pint of bitter with luminaries of the London fringe theatre, and trying desperately hard to look as though I did this sort of thing all the time. So that's how I got to see *Bagdad Saloon* at the Bush Theatre in Shepherd's Bush as part of that legendary Factory "English tour," which was a stunning example of both Ken Gass' monumental chutzpah, and the generosity, some might say recklessness, of Canadian government arts funding at the time. We "colonials" were not all that enthusiastically received in the world capital of theatre.

Being in England from 1973 to 1976, then teaching at the University of British Columbia in Vancouver, at the other end of the country, from 1976 to 1979, I missed a good many premières of important Walker plays, to my everlasting regret. For the record, then, I've seen seventeen of Walker's twenty-six published plays produced on stage, although in a couple of cases, the only productions I've seen have been productions I've directed (and in one case, acted in) myself. My readings of these plays are doubtless influenced by these productions and the people who produced them.[2] For the rest (*The Prince of Naples, Sacktown Rag, Beyond Mozambique,*

Ramona and the White Slaves, Gossip, Rumours of Our Death, The Art of War, Science and Madness, and *Escape from Happiness*), I've had to depend on the "theatre of the mind," and Walker being Walker, staging the plays in that particular venue is often quite a challenge.

After *Bagdad Saloon*, I wasn't to see another Walker play on stage again until 1981, when I saw *Theatre of the Film Noir* at the Toronto International Theatre Festival. But he had me hooked. I was eagerly reading Walker plays whenever they were published, and was being dismayed by the often negative critical response. Clearly the reviewers were missing something. In consequence of this conviction, I wrote "George F. Walker: B-Movies Beyond the Absurd," an article first published in the journal *Canadian Literature*, in 1980, and as far as I can tell, the first critical examination of Walker's work (much of this article is reprinted in Chapter Two).

I've since written several articles and reference entries and two book chapters, on Walker's work. I've directed three of his plays here at the University of Manitoba: *Criminals in Love, Better Living,* and *Tough!* In the spring of 1987, I was on sabbatical and living in Toronto. Walker kindly gave me permission to sit in on rehearsals of the Factory Theatre's tenth anniversary revival of *Zastrozzi*, which Walker himself was directing. An article about that experience, "George F. Walker Directs George F. Walker," is reprinted in Chapter Four, and that piece includes material from three interviews with Walker in May of 1987. During the writing of this book, I interviewed Walker twice in Toronto, May 26 and June 29, 1998. I followed up with a couple of telephone calls over the summer to clarify some details. Also during the writing of this book, I was able to get to Toronto three times to see the Factory Theatre productions of all six Suburban Motel plays, all directed by Walker.

My editor dissuaded me from writing a chronological account of Walker's work in favour of approaching the material from a number of different angles, and for that I'm very grateful. Nonetheless, we felt that it would be helpful to provide an overview of Walker's career, and Chapter One does group Walker's work, chronologically, in five "phases." Walker dislikes the idea of "phases" quite intensely, and I'm not that fond of it myself; still, the arrangement does provide a reasonably useful map to orient oneself through this substantial and complex body of work, as well as a sense of the ways in which Walker's vision and work have evolved.

One of the disadvantages of being a major Canadian playwright, rather than, say, a major British or American playwright, is that there is a much greater chance that one's work will go out of print. In Walker's case, the problem was exacerbated a couple of years ago when his main publisher,

Coach House Press in Toronto, went under, the victim of government cutbacks at both federal and provincial levels. Walker's titles, including those originally published by Coach House, are now handled by Talonbooks in Vancouver. The Walker plays currently available are single play editions of *Nothing Sacred* and *Love and Anger*, the six plays in *Suburban Motel*, and the eight plays from throughout Walker's career included in the 1994 anthology, *Shared Anxiety: Beyond Mozambique, Zastrozzi, Theatre of the Film Noir, The Art of War, Criminals in Love, Better Living, Escape from Happiness*, and *Tough!* *Rumours of Our Death* is available in Alan Filewod's *The CTR Anthology*, and *Zastrozzi* is also available in Jerry Wasserman's anthology, *Modern Canadian Plays*, Talonbooks. Where there is a choice, for the most part I cite from the most recent versions of the plays currently in print. Some plays, notably *Criminals in Love, Better Living*, and *Escape from Happiness*, were revised substantially for their appearance in *Shared Anxiety*; on those few occasions when I do cite earlier versions of these plays, *Criminals in Love* and *Better Living* in the 1988 collection, *The East End Plays*, or the 1992 single play edition of *Escape from Happiness*, it is because the earlier versions contain material helpful to the point I am trying to make but which was cut or altered in the 1994 versions. As this book, *Essays on George F. Walker: Playing With Anxiety*, goes to print, Talonbooks is going to print with the first of a series in which that publisher plans to reprint many of Walker's plays.

Notes

1. I, too, took advantage of these programs to hire undergraduate students at Brock to generate bibliographies of published Canadian plays in English, and the result was the *The Brock Bibliography of Published Canadian Stage Plays in English, 1900–1972*, and *The First Supplement to the Brock Bibliography of Published Canadian Plays*, published by Brock University in 1972 and 1973 respectively. Later, Anton Wagner gathered the entries from these two volumes, greatly expanded the range, and produced *The Brock Bibliography of Published Canadian Plays in English, 1766–1978*, which was published by the Playwrights Co-op (now the Playwrights Union of Canada), another organization formed at the time that played a major role in the development of a new Canadian drama. They published, in the bound mimeograph format they employed, most of Walker's early plays, as well as many, many plays by the other playwrights of the alternative movement.

2. *Ambush at Tether's End*, Factory Theatre première (1971); *Bagdad Saloon*, Factory Theatre English tour (1973); *Theatre of the Film Noir*, Factory Theatre at the Toronto International Theatre Festival, première directed by George F. Walker (1982); *Filthy Rich*, Manitoba Theatre Centre (1986), and University of British Columbia Summer Theatre (1989); *Better Living*, CentreStage, Toronto, première (1986) and University of Manitoba, further revised, directed by myself (1990); *Beautiful City*, Popular Theatre Alliance of Manitoba (1989); *Zastrozzi*, Factory Theatre, directed by George F. Walker (1987); *Nothing Sacred*, Vancouver Playhouse; *Criminals in Love*, Great Canadian Theatre Company and University of Manitoba, directed by myself (1988); *Love and Anger*,

Factory Theatre première directed by George F. Walker (1989); *Tough!*, University of Manitoba, directed by myself (1994); *Problem Child*, Factory Theatre, directed by George F. Walker (1997); *Criminal Genius*, Factory Theatre, directed by George F. Walker (1997); *Adult Entertainment*, Factory Theatre première directed by George F. Walker (1997); *The End of Civilization*, Factory Theatre première directed by George F. Walker (1998); *Featuring Loretta*, Factory Theatre première directed by George F. Walker (1998); *Risk Everything*, Factory Theatre, directed by George F. Walker (1998).

Chapter One
A Journey Through Anxiety

Some favourite Walker words: scary, fear, chaos, worry, complex/complexity, pathetic, depressing, shit.

Much has happened since George F. Walker started writing plays in the early seventies. Ronald Reagan became President of the United States. Brian Mulroney became Prime Minister of Canada. The Berlin Wall fell and, some say, "history ended." The former Yugoslavia descended into a blood-bath of revived tribalism and fascism—"blood and soil" to quote Marcuse quoting Nazi theorists. The Gulf video-game War was fought on television. The deficit became a big deal. Right-wing Conservative Mike Harris was elected premier of the province of Ontario, where Walker lives, in Toronto. Everywhere, it seemed, the political middle was moving toward the political right. George F. Walker wrote thirty-odd stage, radio, and television plays, of which twenty-six stage plays have been published. His plays are still very funny, the newer ones possibly even funnier than the early ones. He is undoubtedly the most accomplished comic playwright Canada has ever produced, and one of the most accomplished working in the theatre anywhere today. He is also one of the most anxious human beings on the face of the earth.

Walker started writing for the stage in a period of exciting and liberating expansion in Canadian theatre, especially in Toronto, and of radical experiment in the ways in which Canadian theatre was produced, again especially in Toronto, at least at first, as well as in Montreal (in French of course). The rise of the "alternative theatres" in Toronto generated so much energy and creative activity that in the interim years it has come to be regarded as a sort of "golden age" of Canadian drama and theatre, replete with its own rich and extensive mythology. In his book on this phenomenon, Denis W. Johnston documents the reasons why this movement occurred and why it occurred when it did. There was a precedent and a model in the American radical theatre of the sixties, and in the coffee house theatres of Off-Off Broadway; the Canadian alternative theatres were much influenced by the American example in the first, pre-nationalist phase of their development. Theatre Passe Muraille, first located at and affiliated with Rochdale College, a radical experiment in co-op housing and student self-government at the University of Toronto, staged as its first productions under founder Jim Garrard *Tom Paine* by Paul Foster and a highly controversial production of Rochelle Owen's *Futz*.

At roughly the same time as the Alternatives began to move from their emphasis on imported American radical theatre to the homegrown variety, the Liberal Canadian federal government of Pierre Trudeau viewed it as politically advantageous to encourage the development of an independent and distinctive Canadian culture, and money was available to adventurous young theatre-makers through programs such as "Opportunity for Youth" and the "Local Initiatives Program." The regional theatre system established in most major Canadian cities in the late fifties and early sixties, following the example of the Manitoba Theatre Centre founded in Winnipeg in 1957 by John Hirsch and Tom Hendry, had begun with high ideals, but quickly acquired establishment priorities and values, and resorted to a programming formula which paid little attention to original Canadian plays, or, for that matter, to any sort of non-canonical work. (See my article "Wooing Winnipeg: The Manitoba Theatre Centre and the Community.") A disillusioned generation of would-be theatre artists, many trained in university programs introduced in the post-war period, could see no place for themselves in the theatre world of the *status quo*, the regionals and Stratford, and were prepared to strike out on their own, setting up makeshift theatres in lofts, former factories, vacant power houses.

It was to one of these alternative theatres, the Factory Theatre Lab, that a twenty-two-year-old Walker brought his second script, *The Prince of Naples*. In her Ph.D. thesis, "Parody in the Plays and Productions of George F. Walker," Catherine Smith identifies as Walker's first attempt at writing for the stage *Victims of Movement*, a piece about a rebellious travel agent, played by an actor who "inexplicably" resembled Groucho Marx, and a disembodied voice who bullies him; it was produced and directed by Gino Marrocco at the Backdoor Theatre Workshop, and apparently no copy survives. Walker regards this work as "fooling around," and esteems it so little that he doesn't remember it or the experience of its production very clearly. *The Prince of Naples*, he says, is his first "real play."

It's impossible to over-estimate the Factory's importance to Walker, or his to it. There's an often told story, indeed now part of the mythology of the Toronto alternative scene of the early 1970s, that Walker was working as a cab driver when he saw one of Ken's posters inviting the submission of new plays for the Factory, and that in response to this notice, Walker wrote *The Prince of Naples* (not quite, as the legend has it, his first play).

Walker already knew that he was going to be a writer, was already writing poems and short stories. He knew he was going to be a writer when he was 16 or 17, in Grade Eleven. At that point, thanks to a good high school English teacher at Riverdale Collegiate, Dennis Boulton (since deceased), he had learned that "literature is fun" (an attitude that has never left Walker), and wrote—a lot, easily, and enjoyed it. "Things came," he said. He was going for a walk with a girl he was dating at the time, and they were talking about what they were going to do with their lives. At the time, says Walker, the interests of which he was primarily conscious were "cars and women." He was also very mindful of advice from his father, Malcolm Walker, a labourer employed by the City of Toronto, to get a job with a good pension. There not being many occupations which featured cars and women and which also came with a good pension, he didn't really know what he was going to do for a living after he graduated from high school. His friend quite matter of factly told him that he was going to be a writer. Apparently all his friends had read his stuff, had discussed the matter amongst themselves, and had more or less decided that George was going to be a writer. It was then, Walker said in our interview (June 1998), that "the seed was planted" and that he seriously considered the possibility that writing was indeed going to be his future.

Nonetheless, he added, it was the theatre, the Toronto alternative theatre of the early '70s, that actually made it possible for him to become the writer his high-school friends had decided he was destined to be. He's not a "joiner," Walker says (and indeed, he's quite a private person), and furthermore, the poetry groups and novelists' groups seemed to him to be "closed shops," "the U of T thing" [University of Toronto, very establishment], and certainly not for a "working-class boy from the East End." He says he can't imagine approaching publishers, shopping manuscripts around, doing the socializing work required of a new writer looking for a chance to get published. The theatre, on the other hand, "was just getting started, and they'd take anyone."

So it was that Walker, the script for *The Prince of Naples* in hand, found himself in the long narrow corridor between the two offices at the old Factory on Dupont, meeting Gass. "I hear you're looking for plays," said Walker, handing Ken the script. Intense, charismatic, always hyper, Gass, whom Walker describes as essentially "a farm boy from Abbotsford, B.C.," is on the other hand rather professorial, a bit absent-minded and sometimes abstracted—he started reading the script *immediately*, with Walker still standing there, a bit awkward, trying to get away, say his "good-byes."

Gass kept saying, "uh huh, uh huh," continued to read, and wouldn't let Walker go—Walker says that at one point, Gass actually grabbed him by the sleeve and physically prevented him from leaving, reading all the while.

A week later, Walker heard from Paul Bettis, who was going to direct, that the Factory would produce *The Prince of Naples*. When Walker showed up for the read-through, he saw on the script a note to Paul from John Palmer, who was dramaturge for the production, "This guy is a genuine subversive. We've got to produce him."

Produce him they did, the first several plays he wrote, under circumstances that allowed him, even encouraged him, to be "subversive" in the way that first attracted Factory to him. They gave him the room and the support he needed to teach himself how to write plays. In a recent interview with Carole Corbeil in *Brick: A Literary Journal*, Walker says:

> When I first talked to Ken Gass ... when they made me resident playwright when I was twenty-three years old, all I felt that I wanted to do, even then, was make a body of work. And he said he would protect me so that I could do that—that it wouldn't be about one play or even one phase—so that falling in and out of fashion or having harder times and easier times would never be the issue ... It was a big deal, a big, big deal. He said, You write, we'll protect, and you'll do it. (59)

Walker was the Factory's Resident Playwright until 1976, and during this period, won the first of his five Canada Council grants. From '71 to '76, the Factory produced the first six of his twenty-six published stage plays: *The Prince of Naples, Ambush at Tether's End, Sacktown Rag, Bagdad Saloon, Beyond Mozmbique,* and *Ramona and the White Slaves.* Smith identifies an additional five, unpublished, short plays produced or workshopped during this period, all except the first at Factory: *Victims of Movement* (1971), *Yalser and Enzio* (1973), *Demerit* (1974), *Baseball* (1975–76 season), and *The Extremist* (1976), the latter apparently an early version of *Theatre of the Film Noir.* Walker began a three year affiliation with Toronto Free Theatre starting in 1977, but also returned to Factory as Artistic Director in 1978, a position he held for a year. A small salary from the Factory, the Canada Council grants, and some television and radio work were enough to support Walker and his family, wife Stephanie Staton and daughter, Reni, born in 1967, during this period. He no longer had to drive cab. He was a "professional playwright," meagerly paid and precariously "alternative," but nonetheless, a paid and working writer.

Walker, at first, was a bit suspicious of theatre. It was "elitist and distant," he thought, and certainly far removed from his experience—when he approached Ken Gass with *The Prince of Naples*, he'd only seen one play produced, Shakespeare, and hadn't been impressed. The Factory, on the other hand, was devoid of pretension, free from most of the social trappings of theatre that Walker had found both intimidating and silly, and in Factory's free-wheeling environment, close to the core of the theatre's creative process, he says he was quickly "seduced" by the theatre, especially by the actors and how they do what they do. He was delighted and fascinated by the way the theatre includes other people, the actors, in the creative process. "You write, pass it on to the actors, then they present it back to you," he said. "It's still you, but it's them too." This wide-eyed fascination with acting has never really left him, has in fact apparently been deepened by the experience of directing his own plays, something he has done many times. I think, too, that this respect for actors, and almost obsessive attraction and admiration, is a central aspect of his work as a playwright. It seems to me that throughout his writing career, and through all the changes that have occurred during that time, Walker has striven to write like actors act, and that he's gotten closer and closer to his goal, that his writing for the stage has gotten better and better in this respect. It is this that gives Walker's work as much "presence" and immediacy as it has on stage, and it is this, in combination with an actor's willingness to expose himself and a darkly comic sense of humour, that makes Walker's work so distinctively "Walkeresque."

When discussing Walker's work in a book such as this one, when subjecting his plays to intellectual inquiry and concentrating on the serious issues with which he is concerned, it's quite easy to pay insufficient attention to the fact that Walker is funny. That Walker is funny, that his vision of the world is essentially a comic vision, is extremely important to understanding, appreciating, and producing his work. I don't know when I laugh more and harder, watching his plays or rehearsing them. Time and time again, he surprises me with something that I already knew, in my bones or my gut or from something my Granny told me, but which I hadn't thought of in that way before. Or, which I had, politely, suppressed. Or that I was too embarrassed to admit I knew.

Smith quotes Walker as saying that in his early works, he was trying to create "cerebral farce" (22), which she then goes on to describe as "a serious interplay of ideas within such an improbable context that laughter also results." On many occasions, Walker has spoken of his equal love for high and low comedy, and the actor's resembling Groucho Marx in *Victims of Movement* is not as "inexplicable" as the first reviewer evidently thought, in this context and given Walker's expressed admiration for Marx Brothers comedy. His first Factory plays, *The Prince of Naples* and *Ambush at Tether's End*, are clearly influenced by Walker's reading of plays by Beckett and

Ionesco, but even there, he's subverting his models by introducing elements of popular art and low comedy into the heady world of existential doubt. Through the self-conscious and self-referential borrowing of "cartoon" convention in *Sacktown Rag*, and through his use of the American Western movie, specifically *High Noon*, as a myth which that play's protagonist uses to examine his family's dynamic, Walker expands his use of pop culture convention and energy, a direction he pursues further still in *Bagdad Saloon*, which extends the influence of the Western to the play's form. In *Beyond Mozambique*, the backgrounded form is the Tarzan type B-jungle-movie, as I discuss in Chapter Two, and in *Ramona and the White Slaves*, it is a mixture of the detective film, Charlie Chan, and sixties drug culture.

From the beginning, Walker's work has been anything but conventional—his narratives have never been straightforward, cause and effect constructions. He mixes dramatic styles with abandon, and never confines himself to psychological realism—even when a play may appear to be relatively realistic, the characters always have a "larger than life" quality, driven to extremes by the intensity of their passions, obsessions, and anxieties, and, in the early plays, express those emotions in dialogue simultaneously vernacular and grandiose in a manner similar to the dialogue of the B-movies on which Walker frequently drew at that stage in his career; Stephen Haff calls Walker's work "Spoken Opera" ("The Brave Comedy of Big Emotions" xiii).

From 1971 to 1976, Walker worked at the Factory with three directors Paul Bettis (*The Prince of Naples*), Ken Gass (*Ambush at Tether's End, Sacktown Rag*, and the remount of *The Prince of Naples* with *Demerit*), and Eric Steiner (*Bagdad Saloon* and *Beyond Mozambique*). None of these men were sympathetic to naturalism or the "well-made" play, and none subscribed to Stanislavsky's methods of character development and production preparation, dependent as they are on the stability of psychological states and consistency of realistic theatrical framing. During this period, Walker travelled, really for the first time in his life; *Bagdad Saloon* was written while Walker was living in London in 1972, on one of his Canada Council grants. In 1976, Walker himself directed the première production of *Ramona and the White Slaves* at the Factory. Since then, he has directed ten première productions of his own plays, and many remounts; he has never directed anyone else's work, and, in fact, is somewhat ambivalent about the task of directing (see Chapter Four). He was also writing for CBC radio and television. Smith, using information supplied by Walker's agent, Great North Artists Management Inc., identifies the radio plays from the period as: *The Prince of Naples* (adapted from the stage play), 1973; *The Private Man*, 1973;

Ambush at Tether's End (adapted from the stage play), 1974; and *Quiet Day in Limbo* (1977). Later radio plays were *Curious* (1978) and *The Desert's Revenge* (1984). The three television plays from this period are *Sam, Grace, Doug, and the Dog* (1976), *Capital Punishment* (1977) and *Overlap* (1977). Later, *Filthy Rich* was adapted for television as a "Movie of the Week," and Walker wrote the script for another television play, *Salvation*, produced by Atlantis Films. Walker didn't find work for the electronic media engaging or rewarding (except financially), something of an irony given his fascination with media as source material and structural reference points. He described a later stint in television as "committee work rather than writing," and back in the seventies, felt almost betrayed in that while he was writing for television in the context of a workshop, experimental situation, the scripts were pushed through to full and finished broadcast production of a sort he never intended and for which he thought the work was ill-suited.

Walker also appeared as an actor, for the first and only time, in Raymond Canale's *Jingo Ring* (Factory, 1971), and saw two plays by John Palmer, *A Touch of God in the Golden Age* (1971) and *Memories for My Brother—Part II* (1971), experiences Smith identifies as significant to Walker's development and influential in that Canale and Palmer provided him with models of playwrights who did not work within the codes of "neo-naturalism" then prevalent in Toronto (32–33), and who, I would add, were more ebullient and brash than were his literary models, Beckett and Ionesco. Here in Canale and Palmer, the latter someone who, Walker says, he could really talk to about playwriting and making theatre, was a world that was surreal and fantastic, an unflinching look at serious matters clashing against and amplified by the larger than life, comic, parodic style of the theatrical event.

The unconventionality of Walker's first half dozen or so plays resulted in a good deal of critical hostility; he told me that what kept him going during those years in the face of the apparently uncomprehending response of the critics was the existence of his small but enthusiastic audience—clearly *someone* wanted to listen to what he was saying. Nonetheless, the negative critical response to *Beyond Mozambique* was evidently particularly disheartening. In his introduction to *Three Plays: George F. Walker*, Ken Gass reports that the Canada Council froze its funding to the Factory Lab after *Beyond Mozambique*. He talks about Walker's becoming "more removed and introspective" (13), his toying with the idea of writing a novel "where it seemed easier to work in a vacuum," his writing the first draft of a naturalistic play, "Decades." At this point, Walker, his wife, and daughter, travelled throughout North America. While on the road, Walker tried, unsuccessfully at first, to write *Ramona and the White Slaves*, perhaps the least conventional of the early plays, an experiment in dream image and construction by association which to this day Walker himself says he doesn't entirely understand (but likes anyway). It wasn't until the next play, *Gossip* (1977) and the subsequent *Zastrozzi* (also 1977) that he made any apparent attempt to reach a larger audience. He even talked to reviewers, making himself available to John Fraser of *The Globe and Mail* for the first interview he'd given in six years as a playwright. With *Gossip*, Fraser says, Walker was "trying not only to change the direction of his writing to make it more popular and approachable—'more generous' is his happy phrase— but to accommodate his own perspective to some pressing realities of theatre life in Canada these days" (23). It would seem, then, that Walker was moving into a new "phase" in 1977. Indeed, many would say that the Toronto alternative theatres themselves were moving into a new phase of their development in the mid-seventies.

However much the next set of plays might be more "generous," it would still be going much too far to describe them as "conventional," mainstream, or merely entertaining. From the beginning of his writing career, Walker has avoided closure and "finalizing." The plays are not "monologic" in Bakhtin's sense of the word in that they do not lead to a neat and summarizing conclusions, co-inciding with the author's opinion, but rather, invite a variety of interpretations, indeed often project the questions metatheatrically into the audience. All the cartoon characters of the early plays subvert the stereotypes which they represent, and reveal characteristics that go "against type," thus demanding re-evaluation of the types on stage, indeed of the whole thought process that underlies typing, our compulsion to classify and to see people through pre-determined roles which we then expect them to play, see them playing even when they're not. Beginning with the role transformation experiments of *Sacktown Rag*, *Bagdad Saloon* and *Ramona and the White Slaves*, Walker questions the conventional concept of "identity," and in the more fluid realities of his stage world, there can be no "essential self." Some of his *characters* do hold to essentialist views, but they find that they must alter and order a chaotic world in order to preserve and enforce those views, thus becoming totalitarian tyrants who attempt to seize and control the future by confining it within their predictable definitions. In the political commentary, sometimes oblique, sometimes quite direct, that runs through Walker plays written since 1982, these are the "bad guys," as discussed in Chapter Three. Sometimes, if the essentialists' personalities do not lend themselves to actively controlling and villainous behaviour, those afflicted with the obsessive desire to order chaos merely become "pathetic."

Through Walker's work I don't think we see so much a progress from monologism to Bakhtinian dialogism (as James Earl Baldwin argues in his thesis, "The Space Between Voices"), as a series of adjustments, perhaps compromises, as Walker looks for ways in which to present his worldview, which has always tended to dialogism and heteroglossia, while at the same time involving his audience in the process of the dramatic event, inviting their participation, at a number of levels. It's a continuation and refinement of the "generosity" he suggests *Gossip* contains. I don't think Walker would have been content to pursue the sort of formal experimentation of plays such as *Ramona and the White Slaves* at the cost of confining himself to an audience drawn from the small group of avant garde theatrical *cognoscenti;* quite apart from financial considerations, this would represent a sort of artistic and formal elitism with which Walker is not sympathetic. George Walker does not want to be another Georg Buchner, the mid-nineteenth-century German playwright so ahead of his time that his work was unproduced during his life time, however much Buchner is regarded as a genius and a pioneer today. Much of Walker's creative energy has gone into finding forms which can draw a larger audience into the dialogic worldview to which he has always tended. His democratic values lead him to his attempts to distribute the power of extended vision to that larger audience, rather than hoarding it to himself and to a small group of like-minded individuals. *The Encyclopedia of Canadian Theatre on the WWW* describes Walker as "one of the savviest writers in the land," and as a playwright who "walks a tightrope between pure artistic achievement and commerciality." At the same time, he can't stop being George Walker and seeing the world the way George Walker sees it, and while plays after *Gossip* and *Zastrozzi* in 1977 may, with few exceptions, be somewhat more "generous," they are still far from conventional. "Walkerland" may, in more recent plays, look like a familiar world on the surface, but in the "wonky bits" for which he is famous, the old, surrealist anarchist of the early plays intrudes on any complacent understanding of the "real world" in which we in the audience may seek to take refuge. Walker will never be a Neil Simon, and for that reason, will probably never get the sort of attention he sometimes seems to want from the Canadian regional theatres, more mainstream, conventional, conservative, "realistic" theatre.

Walker himself is suspicious of the idea of "phases" in a writer's career; to Corbeil's question as to whether he sees his work in phases, Walker replies "I think sometimes in interviews you're made to think those things" (Corbeil 59). Nonetheless, "phases" constitute a helpful way of looking at Walker's development as a playwright, at least as a rough guide, as long as we don't take the "phases" too seriously, nor regard them as water-tight with no exceptions nor "wild cards," as that would be highly unlikely in the work of any writer, much less Walker. So, it seems to me that we can think of *The Prince of Naples*, *Ambush at Tether's End*, and, presumably, *Victims of Movement* as very early, "apprentice" work, literary rather than theatrical, written in a state of relative isolation, and arising from Walker's reading rather than from work with other theatre artists and immersion in a theatrical environment. The rest of the early Factory plays, *Sacktown Rag*, *Bagdad Saloon*, *Beyond Mozambique*, and *Ramona and the White Slaves*, are plays in which Walker explores the possibility of theatrical as well as literary expression and develops his own voice within the context of the cartoon and the B-movie. These plays move progressively further into what Smith describes as "parodic satire." The third phase begins in 1977 with the "more generous" plays, *Gossip*, among other things a spoof of the detective movie, and *Zastrozzi*, an unabashed, swashbuckling melodrama retelling the story of Shelley's novella of the same title. The B-movie conventions, tone, and parody (as much as Walker dislikes his work being described as parody) continue, and Walker now also draws on *film noir*.

During this third phase, Walker wrote two more plays featuring investigative-reporter-cum-private eye T. M. Power, the protagonist of *Gossip*: *Filthy Rich* (1979) and *The Art of War* (1982). All three (discussed at length in Chapter Five) are collectively known as the Power Plays. *Zastrozzi*, which proved to be as "generous" and popular as *Gossip*, was followed during this phase by two more plays in a similar vein, *Theatre of the Film Noir* (1982) and *Science and Madness* (also 1982). All three plays explore the nature of evil, and all three engineer collisions between "high art" and vivid and raucous elements of pop art. While none could accurately be described as "adaptations," all three make use of Walker's response to a work of "high art": Shelley's *Zastrozzi*, Genet's *Funeral Rites*, and Mary Shelley's *Frankenstein* respectively. Walker's third phase, then, can be said to consist of a group of "detective plays," The Power Plays trilogy, and a "literary" grouping, the second set of "literary" plays in Walker's body of work. This second set of "literary" plays, however, differs from the first, *The Prince of Naples* and *Ambush at Tether's End*, in that the plays in it are not as obviously derivative, and are informed by a much richer understanding of and love for the theatre. As well, they are distinguished, as might be expected, by a much more assured and distinctive author's "voice."

The "wild card" in this phase would seem to be *Rumours of Our Death* (1980). It seems, at first glance, much less "generous" than the other plays of this phase, much less willing to guide its audience or reader with familiar convention as are the other plays, however much they may subsequently subvert the conventions which at first appear to be helpful and to lead to familiar places. In his introduction to *The CTR Anthology,* which includes *Rumours of Our Death,* Alan Filewod calls it "an ironic fable of colonialism" (xvii) and says of it that it is the "least conventional, the least 'textual'" of Walker's plays (xviii). In a *Maclean's* article on critical reaction to the Factory production, Paul Little describes the piece as a "quasi punk-rock parable that free associates fairy tales with anarchy and the neutron bomb with any other bomb rumoured to be impending" (27). Little contrasts the sour reaction of the "straight" critics, especially Gina Mallet, to the enthusiastic response of the young audience members who "kept coming back in the tradition of the *Rocky Horror Picture Show* cult." Factory's free-wheeling, punk rock treatment, then, did make the piece "generous " in the manner of the other plays of the third phase, although the new audience it brought into the theatre had tastes and expectations with which older critics were not likely to be sympathetic.

It is also, I discovered in interviews with Walker, "literary" and of a piece with the other "literary" plays of that period in a way that I had not recognized. Walker says that *Rumours of Our Death* began as a writer's exercise, an experiment in the style of Gabriel Garcia Marquez, whose *One Hundred Years of Solitude* was very popular at the time; Walker was striving to emulate and work with the "lightness" and pre-logical associations of Marquez' "magic realism." The imaginary kingdom of Walker's play certainly does share some characteristics with Marquez' fictional town, Macondo, including the presence in each of several characters with the same name (and attendant questions of identity), a feature which some of the Toronto reviewers seemed to find particularly irritating. When he began work on the piece, Walker says, he didn't really have production in mind, never really intended that it would be produced.

One way or other, the "generosity" of the third phase succeeded, and took Walker's work to a much larger and broader audience, of one sort or other. *Gossip* was picked up and produced by many theatres, including some important American institutions: The Williamstown Festival and the Empty Space Theater in Seattle in 1978, PAF Playhouse on Long Island and the Cricket Theater in Minneapolis in 1979. *Zastrozzi,* too, was picked up for many other productions, in England, New Zealand, Australia, and Germany, as well as in Canada and the U.S.; in 1981, Andrei Serban directed *Zastrozzi* at the New York Public Theater while Walker was playwright-in-residence there, and in 1984 Walker himself directed a production of the play at the Nimrod Theatre in Sydney, Australia. *Filthy Rich,* too, was given over a hundred productions around the world. In its own, odd way, *Rumours of Our Death* reached a broader audience through running at the Factory for several months, and *Theatre of the Film Noir* was a certifiable hit at the 1981 Toronto International Theatre Festival.

In a relatively short time in the late seventies and the early eighties, then, Walker rose to what passes as prominence in Canadian theatre and drama, became what could be called canonical if there were a dramatic canon in Canada, which I really don't think there is, at least not in the sense that there is a body of work that exerts the sort of power that dramatic canons do in most other countries (see Johnson, "'Wisdome Under a Ragged Coate'"). He also acquired a substantial and often influential following outside Canada. He has won two Governor General's Awards for English-language Drama (*Criminals in Love*, 1984, and *Nothing Sacred*, 1988) and six Chalmer's Awards (*Zastrozzi*, *Criminals in Love*, *Nothing Sacred*, *Love and Anger*, *Escape from Happiness*, *Problem Child*) as well as Dora Mavor Moore Awards for best new Canadian play for *Nothing Sacred*, *Escape from Happiness* and *Problem Child*.

Walker has been playwright-in-residence at Cornell University, the New York Public Theater, and the National Theatre School of Canada, the latter in 1990 when Paul Thompson, formerly of Theatre Passe Muraille, was the School's Director General, and established a playwright's chair. Two of the three anthologies of Canadian plays published in the mid-eighties include his work. With *Nothing Sacred* and *Love and Anger* he had more certifiable "hits," again by Canadian standards, with extended commercial runs. *Nothing Sacred* was produced by many American regional theatres, among them Arena Stage in Washington, the American Conservatory Theatre in San Francisco, and the Seattle Repertory, as well as theatres in Israel, Sweden, Australia, and Hong Kong. He is one of the most widely produced Canadian playwrights, not only in Canada but in the United States and elsewhere. Scott Duchesne identifies Walker, Judith Thompson, and Michel Tremblay as the three Canadian playwrights most often produced outside Canada's borders, and quotes Walker as saying: "About sixty-fiive per cent of my income comes from America ... It's about a seven-to-one ratio in terms of productions there and here" (19). In Canada, success elsewhere means a lot. Walker says that American theatres' wanting to produce his work was a particularly important boost to his confidence, as the U.S. theatres were obviously producing the plays because they valued them and found them interesting and exciting, and were not doing Canadian plays to score points in applications for Canada Council funding, as might be the case in Canada according to Walker's lingering doubts.

Significantly, both historically and symbolically, *Gossip* and *Zastrozzi*, the first two plays of Walker's third and "generous" phase, were the first of Walker's plays not premièred at the Factory. Rather, both plays were first produced at the Toronto Free Theatre, the first directed by John Palmer, with whom Walker already had a close working relationship from the early Factory days, the second by William Lane. The Toronto Free was the last of the "Big Four" Alternatives to be established. It was established in 1972 by Palmer, Tom Hendry (who was previously one of the founders of the Manitoba Theatre Centre) and Martin Kinch. Its work was distinguished by what Johnston calls "the stylish urban tone of its productions" and the "gory decadence" of Kinch's shows (*Up the Mainstream* 172). While still quite wild and definitely "alternative," Toronto Free had a prettier theatre, and paid more attention to production values and "finish" than did the Factory. At the same time, it's important to note that Walker served the Factory as Artistic Director for a year starting in 1978. Walker, then, didn't so much switch allegiances from the Factory to the Toronto Free as expand his operations to include the Free.

At about the same time in the mid-seventies that Walker was becoming more "generous," more general audience friendly, all the Toronto alternatives moved closer to the "mainstream," pressured in part by financial necessity and reduced government subsidies, "the pressing realities of theatre life in Canada these days" to which Fraser refers in his 1977 article. In this accommodation of "pressing realities," the alternatives were led by Bill Glassco's Tarragon Theatre, which always was more mainstream in its outlook, packaging, and preference for the well-made, neo-realistic play. "Through its careful methods and conservative aesthetics," says Johnston, "Tarragon became, in the eyes of the regional theatres, the chief source of readily transplantable new Canadian drama" (*Up the Mainstream* 168). Johnston, whose tastes are relatively conservative, speaks quite approvingly of the changes that were occurring in mid-decade as the alternatives acquired buildings and mortgages, referring to a new "stability" in the Toronto theatre scene.

Even the Factory, after a series of financial crises and last-minute rescues brought on by Factory's rather slapdash artistic process, rushing to production many plays by many untried playwrights, acquired a new and somewhat more upscale venue in 1974 at 207 Adelaide Street, formerly occupied by the Second City comedy troupe. This space was rented, and Factory didn't acquire its own building (125 Bathurst St.), mortgage, and concomitant respectability until well into the eighties. Nonetheless, the Factory did move into a new era (more "stable" or more "cautious," depending on your opinion) in 1978, when Ken Gass resigned as Artistic Director and was replaced by Bob White; simultaneously, Dian English joined the organization as managing director.

Johnston notes the propensity of the Toronto alternative theatres for myth-making, constructing a radical myth fostered by Theatre Passe Muraille's beginnings at Rochdale College, then a nationalist myth, fostered by the inauguration of the Factory and its "Canadian only" policy. The leaders of these developments in Canadian theatre quite consciously recognized the importance of clear mandate and concomitant "cause" in order to establish their presence and win an audience. This, according to Johnston, was followed by a new myth as some of the alternative theatres moved toward respectability and the need to reach a broader audience, in effect becoming the new mainstream as the old mainstream, like the St. Lawrence Centre, was rendered irrelevant. This new myth was "an institutional one, a myth of stability and permanence in an ongoing alternative. At this time, 'Alternative to what?' became the question that had no answer" (*Up the Mainstream* 252).

In *Producing Marginality*, Robert Wallace sees in these developments and in the development of the "hit syndrome" in which the Alternatives needed "hits" in order to meet their new costs and sustain their "new mainstream" status, the means by which the Alternative lost its soul, its ability to "produce marginality." This loss, in turn, forces the old Alternative to become more conventional, hence more imitative of what is successful elsewhere and less likely to produce something genuinely new and unique, which is why, according to Wallace, Quebec theatre has been more successful than English-Canadian theatre in developing a truly innovative art form that speaks not only to its own constituency, but to the wider world as well. Quebec theatre, or enough Quebec theatre to constitute a critical mass, resisted the pull toward the commercial end of the theatrical spectrum, and thus resisted the pressure to produce mainstream theatre like everyone else's mainstream theatre, pale imitations of Broadway and the West End.

Where Walker stands in all this, perpetual rebel or new pillar of a new establishment, canonical or forever alternative, is one of the subjects of Chapter Seven, "Walker and High Art, Walker versus High Art." There are a number of paradoxes involved. Walker himself points out the anomaly of his achieving some stature in world theatre while at the same time, he has never had a hit in New York or London. (One could point out, however, that he has had several "hits" in Toronto, which is the third-largest theatre production centre in the English-speaking world.) As the preceding list of honours and achievements indicates, if there is a canonical playwright in Canada, it's Walker, and he is one of the most produced Canadian playwrights in Canada. At the same time, his work is far more often produced at universities and in alternative theatres and second stages than he is in the big, mainstream theatres of the Canadian regional system. Is this a consequence of the nature of Walker's work, or of the nature of the regionals and the people who run them and go to them? Finally, while he is much more commercially successful than are most Canadian playwrights, as recently as 1997 he worked in television, which he doesn't like, "for the money," to support his family. One would think that by now, in most countries at least, he'd be a rich old fart, but, in fact, he is neither rich, nor, I would point out, an old fart.

If we are to continue identifying "phases" in Walker's work, for the sake of clarity, the next, fourth phase begins in 1982. That year saw the production of the last two plays of the third phase, *The Art of War* and *Science and Madness*, and significantly he has said of the latter play that in it he thinks he was beginning to repeat himself. It was also the year that Cornell University, where Walker was playwright-in-residence, workshopped an early version of *Better Living*, the first of the "East End Plays," or, adopting the phrase Walker used in his 1984 interview with Robert Wallace, the "looking for the light" phase. In these plays, Walker turns for material to the working-class Toronto East End of his boyhood and adolescence, material which he had previously explored only in *Sacktown Rag*, and there only somewhat tentatively and rather awkwardly.

During the last years of the third phase and into the first few years of the fourth phase, there were some big changes in Walker's personal life. In 1980, he married Susan Purdy, an actor who had performed in the premières of *Rumours of Our Death* (1980), as Maria II, and of *Theatre of the Film Noir* (1982), as Lilliane, and in the professional première of *The Art of War*, the 1983 Factory production, as Heather. Their daughter, Courtney, was born in 1985, and their youngest child, Kate, in 1991. I believe that Walker's marriage to Susan has accelerated his understanding of and admiration for actors, and has contributed to his ongoing quest to write like actors act, as well as to his often cited "generosity" to actors in the opportunities his roles give them, to reach into states of extremity seldom encountered in mainstream theatre, and in his scripts' openness to the contribution of the actors' own creative energy. The "looking for the light" of the fourth phase plays, their quest for possibility if not hope, seems to me connected to his own growing into the role of father, while the increased centrality of women in the East End plays, the sympathy for the perspectives of women which a number of critics have noted, is likely connected to his role as the father of three daughters.

While *Better Living* was the first "East End" play on which Walker started work, the first fourth-phase play seen by Canadian audiences was *Criminals in Love*, produced by the Factory with Walker directing in 1986, a big hit that rescued Factory from financial crises brought on by its move to its present home on Bathurst Street, a converted mansion which the company owns. A new version of *Better Living*, much different from the version that had been produced at Cornell, premièred at Toronto's big, regional theatre CentreStage (formerly Toronto Arts Productions and now the Canadian Stage Company), in 1986. The director was CentreStage's artistic director, Bill Glassco, formerly artistic director of the Tarragon Theatre, one of the four major Toronto alternatives initiating the new play explosion of the early seventies, and a long-standing rival of the Factory. *Beautiful City* premièred in 1987 at the Factory, directed by Bob White. These three plays were published together as *The East End* plays by Playwrights Canada Press in 1988, but I would also describe as "East End Plays" three more works, *Love and Anger*, given an almost legendary first production by the Factory in 1989, again directed by Walker; *Escape from Happiness*, first directed by Max Mayer in a New York Stage and Film Company production at the Powerhouse Theater at Vassar College in 1991; and *Tough!*, Walker's only "Theatre for Young Audiences" play, commissioned by Green Thumb Theatre in Vancouver and first produced there in 1993, directed by Patrick McDonald. (Of the last play, Walker says that while it was commissioned by a TYA company, and while it is about teenagers, it isn't just *for* teenagers.)

The odd play out in this phase is *Nothing Sacred*, commissioned by CentreStage and premièred there under the direction of Bill Glassco in 1988. *Nothing Sacred* is "based on" Ivan Turgenev's novel, *Fathers and Sons*, and as such, its affinities are with Walker's "literary" plays. Like Walker's earliest "literary" plays, *Nothing Sacred* is not an adaptation, although a good deal of critical reaction to the many revivals of the play in the U.S. was preoccupied with the issue of adaptation, sometimes faulting the piece for the liberties it takes with the Russian novel. Walker says that when he started work on *Nothing Sacred*, he reread *Fathers and Sons* only once, for the first time since he first encountered the work when he was seventeen, then consulted the novel only twice during the writing of the play, to assist the composition of two passages which stay very close to the original. For the most part, then, the play is not a novel adapted for the stage, but a classical and canonical work of art filtered through Walker's irreverent sensibility, and is therefore itself an original work inspired by the novel's impact on the consciousness of a seventeen-year-old, then thirty-nine-year-old, working-class, urban North American of the late twentieth century. The distinction is important.

The six plays of the East End cycle itself are recognizably located in that working-class neighbourhood of Toronto, and together provide a metaphorical map of the area as physical neighbourhood, and as psychological and emotional state. The plays together constitute an imaginative cityscape, and there are many connections between them. Three, *Criminals in Love*, *Better Living*, and *Escape from Happiness*, concern members of the same family. Characters from *Beautiful City* reappear in *Escape from Happiness*. Even when there is no on-stage interchange, as in *Love and Anger*, Henry Dawson, Junior's Dad from *Criminals in Love,* is identified in *Love and Anger* as one of the off-stage thugs in the employ of the latter play's villain, Babe Conner, as is Rolly Moore from *Beautiful City*. In *Tough!*, too, there is no on-stage interchange, but Tina, Jill and Bobby from that play could well have been classmates of Junior, Gail, and Sandy from *Criminals in Love*—all six characters certainly share an East End youth culture, self-doubt, aspirations, and obstacles much like those experienced by Walker himself in his own East End youth.

In both his use of autobiographical material and the observation of the neighbours to his childhood, working-class home, and in the creation of a linked grouping of plays that constitute a fictional portrait of a community, the Walker of the fourth phase strongly resembles another well-known Canadian playwright, Michel Tremblay, doing for East End Toronto what Tremblay does for East End Montreal. As in Tremblay's juxtaposition of rue Fabre and the Main, there is in Walker's East End plays a tension created by the contrasts and interchanges between a "respectable," working-class neighbourhood, the world of Nora's family and Bargain Harold's, and a seedier, criminal or semi-criminal underworld cohabiting the same city (although Walker's petty crooks, prostitutes, and crooked cops don't have the tawdry, showbiz glamour of many of the inhabitants of Tremblay's Main). This relationship is part friction, part temptation, as members of the respectable working-class are sometimes in conflict with their criminal neighbours, sometimes tempted to marginalize themselves still further by abandoning the mainstream altogether, and entering a world which, while dangerous, also allows them a flamboyance and outlet for violent impulse forbidden in Cabbagetown.

I found that there is even a similarity in the working methods employed by Walker and Tremblay. Both men go for long walks in their home cities (Walker says walking is his "only hobby"), watching, absorbing, thinking, then after a period of creative wandering, go home and write, quickly. Both, too, come from relatively large families and are younger brothers to several sisters (Walker has three older sisters)—both have been acclaimed for their ability to write complex, sharply-observed female characters, and for being able, as male writers, to achieve an unusual degree of sympathy with the women in their plays. Both use selective exaggeration to create a

vibrant stage language from the street language of their working-class neighbourhoods, and both have been criticized for using such a "vulgar" argot
on stage. Both are unconventional nationalists. Both are working-class,
obviously, and maintain working-class sensibilities. Both, despite having
no formal post-secondary education, are extremely well-read. Both have
political sympathies to the left of centre.

   Walker's political opinions are most overtly present in the plays of the
fourth phase, although there have been in his work from the beginnings
clear signs of dissatisfaction with the *status quo*, social as well as perceptual and artistic. In his careful attention to the marginalized inhabitants of
the East End, and through his sympathetic presentation of the problems
and oppressions they encounter, Walker became known as something of
a social critic, with *Love and Anger* in particular becoming as much a political event as a play, credited with catalyzing the anger of many
Torontonians against establishment figures and institutions blamed for de-
spoiling their city. John Coulbourn describes this role as "mere advocate
for the have-nots of our world, bringing their voices to polite society within
the relatively safe confines of the theatre" (a role which, Coulbourn says,
Walker transcends in the Suburban Motel plays); Coulbourn goes on to
say that "it would be easy, in some circles, to dismiss his as the work of an
articulate, even empathetic, left-leaning sob sister" ("Down at the End"
44). Again, Walker was going against the generational tide in a way that
had led John Palmer to describe him as a "genuine subversive." In the
early plays, like *The Prince of Naples*, to which Palmer was specifically
referring, Walker devoted as much energy to satirizing and deflating his
contemporaries and their romantic, pseudo-revolutionary challenges to the
Establishment as he did to attacking the Establishment itself. All young
writers attacked the Establishment in those days, but Walker was one of
the few who also critiqued the attacks. The social criticism of the post-
1982 East End plays seem to me animated not only by class politics, Walker
returning to the East End not only as a locale but as a source of class
loyalties, but also by Walker's sense of betrayal by others of his generation—the "revolutionaries" of the '60s and early '70s had changed sides,
had become the "yuppies" of the '80s, the "Me Decade." "Watching my
generation lose all its moral values and turn to this kind of gross consum-
erism—it's beyond disheartening—it's almost surreal" (Houpt).

   The plays of the fourth phase are also the most "optimistic" in Walker's
corpus, if, given Walker's tendency to dark comedy, "optimistic" cannnot
be considered overstating the case. In the 1984 interview with Wallace,
Walker says that in these plays he is looking not for "hope," a term he
dislikes as excessively sentimental, but "possibility," the chance that the

characters' worlds might be made better, "spiritually" and emotionally if not necessarily materially.

After *Tough!* premièred in 1993, there was a gap of about four years in Walker's stage output. Some people (among them, me) were wondering what had happened to George, and Walker, going through one of his periods of disenchantment with the theatre, had thought "in some part of [his] brain" that he had given up the theatre. During this period he wrote four radio plays for CBC's *Sunday Showcase: The Favour; How to Make Love to an Actor; How to Make Love to an Actor, Part 2: The Green Room*; and *How to Make Love to an Actor, Part 3: Opening Night*. He was working "for the money" in television, as a "consultant" for Ken Finkleman's self-parodying CBC-TV series, *The Newsroom* and *More Tears*, and for *Due South*, the Paul Gross CTV/Alliance series about a Mountie, surrealistically attired in full dress scarlets and stereotyped "Canadian" boy scoutish attitudes and good manners while on loan to the Chicago police department; the series is shot in Toronto, posing as Chicago. I see some resemblance, on the surface at least, between the central character and Corporal Lance in *Beyond Mozambique*. It is significant that if Walker is to become involved in the bureaucratic world of network television at all, it should be with off-beat TV shows that make fun of Canadian icons: the CBC and the RCMP.

Then, all at once, the six plays of the "Suburban Motel" cycle appeared: *Problem Child, Criminal Genius, Adult Entertainment, The End of Civilization, Featuring Loretta,* and *Risk Everything,* and the "fifth phase" began. Three of the motel plays (*Problem Child, Criminal Genius,* and *Risk Everything*) were given what Walker describes as "workshop like" production by Rattlestick Productions at Theater Off Park in New York in May and June of 1997 under the direction of Daniel De Raey, and all six were produced by the Factory Theatre in rep in the 97/98 season, with Walker himself directing. All six plays were written in a period of "about ten months," some in Toronto, some in Vancouver, where Walker and his family lived during 1996/97. All are set in the same, rundown motel room on the outskirts of a large North American city, and all six concern society's marginalized and disenfranchised, although Walker describes his attitude to the characters as more neutral than was the case in the East End plays, as he found himself more concerned with letting the characters tell their own stories, without his trying to attach to those stories any political message or somewhat optimistic search for the light. These, Walker's most recent plays, I would say, constitute his "fifth phase."

Walker is currently working on a play commissioned by the Canadian Stage Company in Toronto, a "play about divorce" and a play in which Walker sees the possibility of touching a middle-class audience in the same immediate and intimate way as he was able to with *The End of Civilization*. Walker will be directing a revival of *Better Living* at the Factory in the spring of 1999, and there are plans to revive *Escape from Happiness* to start off the 1999/2000 season, bring back the revived *Better Living*, and run the two East End, "Nora's family" plays in rep. An American company, Golden Heart Productions, made a film version of *Better Living*, set in the Bronx. The film premièred at the Hampton Film Festival on Long Island on October 15, 1998, and has been invited to the Sao Paolo Film Festival in Brazil. A film based on *Beyond Mozambique* has just been shot in Montreal. Three of the Suburban Motel plays, *Problem Child*, *The End of Civilization*, and *Criminal Genius* have been revived to start off Factory's 1998/99 season, and productions of plays from the cycle are scheduled all over North America; in Vancouver, three plays from the suite are being produced simultaneously by three different theatre companies. In February of 1998, the birth of Reni's first child made Walker a grandfather. "Scary," "fear," "chaos," "worry," "complex/complexity," "pathetic," "depressing" and "shit" are still favourite Walker words.

The "shit of the world" has if anything deepened since Walker started writing plays, and the Walkerland of the latest plays reflects our deteriorating if laughable dilemma. Anxiety remains the sanest response, and laughter the surest defence.

Chapter Two
B-Movies Beyond the Absurd

For all that the Factory Theatre Lab of the early seventies proclaimed itself "the home of the Canadian playwright," for all that it took advantage of the political popularity of the cultural nationalism of the era, and for all the ferocity with which Gass and his co-workers kept the faith with the theatre's "Canadian only" policy (a policy generous enough to accommodate recently converted Canadians, especially American draft dodgers and avoiders of the Viet Nam War), the Factory was in many respects very *un*Canadian. It was reckless, bold, and put a high premium on originality and spontaneity. It was gritty, grotty, avant garde, and urban. It cheerfully ignored a great many rules. It was decidedly impolite. And in all these respects, of course, Walker was in the vanguard.

Walker's flaunting of convention is most startling in contrast to those realistic works of rural angst, "man against the wilderness" epics, which are so prominent in Canadian literature, including drama, and amply documented and discussed in Margaret Atwood's *Survival* and in Northrop Frye's essay, "Garden in the Wilderness." Gwen Pharis Ringwood's *Still Stands the House* (1938) and *Dark Harvest* (1945) epitomize this sort of Canadian play. Even in the Toronto alternative theatre of the early '70s, neo-realism and rural roots plays, like David French's *Leaving Home*, drew the biggest audiences and garnered the most favourable critical responses. Walker (and Palmer and Canale) saw themselves as odd men out. "Not many prairie landscapes in George Walker's plays," Ken Gass remarks wryly in his introduction to a collection of Walker's plays (3). Indeed not. Or as Walker himself puts it:

> It would be very dishonest of me to attempt to write any sort of rural play. I had been surrounded by things like movies, television—you know The World at Six, that sort of thing—theatre and literature of all kinds all my life. What did I know about the farmer and his wife? And yet I was criticized. Everyone kept telling me I should go to the grass roots and that Canadian plays should be naturalistic or historical. Natural-

ism was very big in Toronto for a long time. I couldn't help thinking that was one kind of theatre, but there other types of theatre as well. (Galloway 18)

The Prince of Naples concerns a relationship familiar to every North American, that of student and teacher, and draws extensively on the perspectives of a contemporary urban world, simultaneously literate and electronic. The work shows its literary ancestry through its form; in its use of language, transforming pat phrases into extended and volcanic passages of nonsense, in its heavy dependence on a central theatrical image, and in its concerted effort to include the audience within the emotional event the characters are experiencing, the play models itself after the Theatre of the Absurd in general and after Ionesco's *The Lesson* in particular. Walker reverses the usual power structure in the educational process, making the young the instructor of the old, to examine a social phenomenon, the cult of the young and the supposedly liberated, associated with the '60s, and in the process questions the new credo of superficial relativity and romantic, anti-establishment inversion:

> Now the word insane has been reapproached by the wide-eyed armies of time and given a new meaning. The word has been dragged out of the dampness of our mental basement and placed high on the clouds of our consciousness. (*The Prince of Naples* 76)

The method of employing a form to question ironically the ideas underlying the form became characteristic of Walker's work.

Ambush at Tether's End was Walker's second exercise in the theatrical techniques of the Absurd: this time, the most important model appears to be Samuel Beckett's *Waiting for Godot*. The central character in the play is a corpse (an echo of Ionesco's *Amedee, or How to Get Rid of It?*), a poet-philosopher who has hanged himself and who has left a series of notes attacking the values of his friends, challenging them to confront "reality" as he has with a "definitive act" equal to his. While there are similarities linking the friends to Beckett's tramps (Mullaly correctly identifies rhythmic similarities in their speech [53]), Walker has localized the situation, and has made the dichotomy depicted by Vladimir and Estragon a more North American opposition of obsessions, those of the ambitious businessman and the sexual athlete. If those who wait are diminished, so too is that for which they wait. Max, the moralizing corpse, endangers his own authenticity through his posthumous showmanship, and the philosophical life is discredited by the dead man's petty rivalry with a colleague. While Galt and Bush are, predictably, destroyed by the dilemma in which they find themselves, there is little to recommend an alternative to their views if Max is the representative of that alternative. Walker sees both the society he satirizes and the modish and pseudo-romantic challenge to that society as inadequate, and in the play constructs a theatrical model of the intellectual quandary in which many of his generation found themselves.

The influence of the Theatre of the Absurd can be seen in many of the plays produced in the Factory Lab's first few seasons, and several critics were quick to identify their derivative nature. In his review of *The Factory Lab Anthology*, in which *Ambush at Tether's End* appeared, Edward Mullaly writes:

> Twenty-five years ago the enunciation of man's absurd situation might have constituted a positive statement. But a similar inability to discover or point out shapes and structures today no longer constitutes experimental, or even interesting, drama regardless of the country in which it is written. (51)

Of Walker's play itself he questions "why Walker has spent his time on a script Beckett had already written with much greater discipline, intelligence, and skill" (53). While Walker's early efforts are in many respects undergraduate exercises, few saw at the time that they are superior undergraduate exercises, and that in turning the form against its content, Walker avoided slavish imitation.

The Theatre of the Absurd has remained largely a European phenomenon: American playwrights have had as much difficulty transplanting its insights and techniques to a North American *milieu* and audience as have had the Canadians Mullaly criticizes. Martin Esslin attributes the difficulty to history:

> The convention of the Absurd springs from a feeling of deep disillusionment, the draining away of the sense of meaning and purpose in life, which has been characteristic of countries like France and Britain in the years after the Second World War. In the United States there has been no corresponding loss of meaning and purpose. (266)

While the statement is undoubtedly less true than it was when it was first written, it is significant that most of the American playwrights whose work had close affinities to the European avant-garde of the fifties and early sixties have subsequently developed in different directions. Thomas Porter advances a more commercial explanation in *Myth and Modern American Drama*. While mainstream American drama consistently portrays the failure of the American Dream, which maintains the illusion of "meaning and purpose," the American theatre-going public has an aversion to the next step, a dramatic form which not only discusses but reflects the disintegration of the Dream. In consequence, American attempts to transfer the technique as well as the message have been stillborn (Porter 255). The American playwrights who have most successfully communicated to an American audience those insights usually associated with the Theatre of the Absurd have been those, like Jean-Claude van Itallie or Sam Shepard, who have taken particular care to couch these insights in an American idiom, who have employed the disjointed nature of American popular culture to display a fragmented theatrical vision of lost "meaning and purpose." Shepard, whose work is most clearly relevant to a consideration of Walker's, has proven particularly adept at employing the trivia of American society as a means of both celebrating the vulgar vitality of that society and suggesting an emptiness beyond.

In Walker's third play, *Sacktown Rag*, he draws on North American pop culture in a manner somewhat similar to Shepard's, and in turning to more autobiographical subject matter, discards some of the literary self-consciousness which intrudes in the earlier plays. The structural technique is that of the cartoon: the working-class schoolboy protagonist experiences the traumas of growing up in a world dominated by middle-class values; the world of the play is sometimes realistic and sometimes drawn in the lurid colours of the comic strip. While the caricatures of parents and teachers sometimes have the gleeful and scatological energy of schoolboy graffiti, Walker does not entirely trust his conventions and chooses to explain them away with a memory frame that weakens through too much qualification the integrity of the cartoon vision. At the same time, the device does make *Sacktown Rag* more than a proletarian diatribe, as even in a work this early, Walker displays his anti-romanticism. Brick's conversation, as an adult, with a friend, recalling his boyhood, interrogates some of the cartoon's class iconoclasm and satire of authority-figures, strongly suggesting that the protagonist's story-telling may be more than a little coloured by self-pity and working-class mythologizing. It seems to me, too, that we may have here a self-portrait of Walker of the time, a working-class boy suddenly transplanted to an "artistic environment" and wondering whether, in this context, stories of an East End boyhood and of the slights and insults suffered in such a childhood, might not be self-dramatizing—ever the "subversive," Walker here subverts his own "otherness." In subsequent works, Walker learned how to achieve this sort of double vision much more effectively.

In *Bagdad Saloon*, first produced in 1973 and subtitled "a cartoon," Walker does not dilute his pop art conventions: the result is a bawdy, sprawling collage of short scenes, music, and *coups de théâtre*. The cartoon figures are less personal than the graffiti of *Sacktown Rag*; characters drawn from American high and low culture, Gertrude Stein, Henry Miller, Doc

Halliday, have greater resonance, and extend the implications of the piece beyond itself.

The incident which precipitates the action of the play is the kidnapping of the American legends by a pair of improbable Arabs who want to learn the secret of mythic immortality. The attempt, of course, is futile: Halliday and Miller are frauds, and Stein, while she has visions, proves incapable of communicating what she sees. The American saloon is grafted onto fabled Bagdad, and Aladdin decks himself out as a dime store cowboy in pursuit of a new and neon mythology, even while the efficacy of any myth in staving off the chaos is put in question:

> AHRUN: Fame is a fickle commodity. Not bad, mind you. Just fickle.
> DOC: So what?
> STEIN: Exactly.
> AHRUN: It needs to be guided, so to speak. And if it's guided in the right direction, it can create things. Purpose. Glamour. Mystique. (*Pause.*) Artists. Or folk heroes. All things which we find very scarce around here.
> STEIN: What happens then?
> AHRUN: Folk-lore.
> STEIN: And then?
> AHRUN: More folk-lore.
> STEIN: And then?
> AHRUN: And then ... and you can—and then there's always ...
> STEIN: Yes?
> DOC: What?
> (*AHRUN shakes his head violently. Turns. Leaves ...*)
> (*Bagdad Saloon* 55)

So much for identity, Arab, Canadian, or otherwise.

As Gass points out in his introduction, the first movement of the play constructs the saloon and decorates it in all its crass glory, while the second movement destroys and discredits the structure. Unfortunately, the process is unduly protracted and Walker is often distracted by his fascination with the decoration; the piece is theatrically inefficient, its meanderings sometimes irritating. Still, in *Bagdad Saloon*, Walker shows increased control of his new medium, and develops further the talent for stage metaphor revealed in the earlier plays: the image of the all-American hero, sportsman, and pop singer as pathetic, speechless grotesque is an image that lingers long.

It is a commonplace that, particularly in matters of structural convention, theatre has been drawing for the last two or three decades on popular electronic forms, especially film, reclaiming the debt that art form owes theatre in general and August Strindberg in particular. Walker has not been the first Canadian playwright to borrow from cinema: George Ryga's "liquid dramaturgy" owes as much to film as it does to the folk song (Hay 6), and James Reaney cites Walt Disney as an important influence. These older playwrights, however, use cinematic devices to shape the presentation of their vision of the world whereas for playwrights of Walker's generation, the vision itself is frequently filmic.

> Like so many of my generation, my mind is sort of a media garbage bag sometimes. We're all so heavily influenced by television and movies and you don't have to be very perceptive to see it coming out in new plays. The dilemma for me was not to rebel against the problem—it is, after all, a fairly central reality—but to assimilate it and make something of it. (Fraser 23)

As Walker suggests, the influence is to a certain extent involuntary, the result of a lifetime's exposure for the generation which grew up with television and whose dreams are, in effect, movies. The process of "making something of it" has involved becoming aware of this mode of thought as just that, an artificial construct rather than part of the natural order (Esslin identifies the post-war generation's frequent inability to make that distinction in the postscript to the revised *The Theatre of the Absurd*): it has also meant exploiting the dramatic possibilities of a contemporary pool of shared understanding, which becomes the basis of a coherent (if not necessarily logical) set of social assumptions to which the social act of theatre can be addressed.

Obviously film is a richer source of theatrical convention than is the cartoon, and provides fuller access to the popular pool of understanding. It also provides, especially through the so-called B-movies, a rich source of images, plot models, and a set of stock characters not unlike those used in melodrama or Commedia dell'Arte, an iconography available to the contemporary playwright to be employed as he sees fit. *Beyond Mozambique* (1974) marks the beginning of extensive recourse to the raw material of the B-movie. In employing stock characters and situations as the vehicles for insights and ideas beyond the capacity of the popular form from which they were drawn, Shepard in *Mad Dog Blues* or *Angel City* and Walker in *Beyond Mozambique* and *Ramona and the White Slaves* follow well-established theatrical practice: Beckett and Ionesco draw from music hall and film comedy; Pirandello, Chekhov, and Ibsen drew from melodrama; and, of course, Molière made use of the characters and conventions of Commedia dell'Arte.

The B-movie also provides an ironic mode, an element acquired through the almost accidental manner in which the older B-movies were reintroduced into the mainstream of popular art through late-night movies on television and hence into the imaginations of the generation shaped by television. In this way, trivial works which would otherwise have perished, as do novels unworthy of reprinting or plays not worth reviving, lead an extended life; the extension, the survival of artifacts mean to be disposable, frequently leads to levels of meaning not intended by their creators. The B-movies of the forties and fifties present a vision of life so simple and naive that the effect is comic, while the rapidity of shifts in popular taste gives the films a quaintness which emphasizes the naivete and heightens the comic effect.

In adapting the world of the B-movie for the stage there are two dangers. The first is that an audience might accept that world at face value, despite the integral irony of a topical perspective out of context. The second pitfall is the temptation to revel in the exuberant awfulness of it all: the result, here, is usually described as "camp." Tom Cone's *Shot Glass* and Hrant Alianak's *The Blues* are examples of plays which duplicate the mood and rhythms of old B-movies very accurately indeed, but which offer almost no perspective from outside the worlds they depict, which remain satisfied with accidental irony, and which therefore succeed as anachronistic replicas, camp artifacts, rather than as original works of art. In *Beyond Mozambique* and subsequent plays, Walker circumvents the perils through the addition of elements from other modes, hyperbole, and explicit comment on the theatrical context.

Beyond Mozambique is a jungle movie, but contrary to the opinions of several first-night critics, it is not just a jungle movie. Set on the porch of a decaying colonial mansion in the jungle, the play throws together six disparate characters in the best "ship of fools" tradition, and allows these figures, or "masks" as Richard Horenblas describes them (8), to enact for us the decline and disintegration of western civilization; while its mode is that of the B-movie, its content is not: technology does not triumph over nature, white heroines are not pure, white heroes are not all-powerful, and while the embattled whites are not overwhelmed by the forces of "savagery" drumming in the bush, they do succumb to the chaos within, and it is the drumming of that threat which provides the play's rhythm and central theatrical metaphor.

The play's central character, played by Donald Davis in the original production in 1974, is that most twentieth-century of archetypes, the mad scientist. Rocco combines the familiar B-movie archetype and hints of concentration camp "medical experiments," sadism disguised as a quest for knowledge, or, perhaps, the quest for knowledge undisguised; he is both the historical nightmare and the popular rendition of the obsessions in part responsible for those nightmares: in the face of impending disintegration, he can think only of pressing on with his experiments and of acquiring the necessary subjects. While he is horrifying, Rocco is, in Walker's wry view, the most positive character in the play; he has a Kurtz-like integrity which compels him to define, to defy chaos even if in a perverse way, a drive often expressed in gloriously B-movie lines: "There's something about committing crimes against humanity that puts you in touch with the purpose of the universe." Parody makes the line funny; history, and the terrifying possibility that Rocco may be right, given an Absurdist vision of the universe, make it not funny.

Rocco is accompanied by the requisite hunch-backed assistant, Tomas, who is primarily responsible for acquiring the experimental subjects and initiating a one-man crime wave. Tomas says very little, and much of that in Greek (a sardonic combination of classical heritage and bestiality personified), but his presence brings onstage a manifestation of the savagery by which the central characters feel themselves threatened, and makes explicit the erotic and racist implications of all those glistening dark bodies in B-jungle-movies. As the whites decline, non-white (or "othered") Tomas ascends, expropriating for himself the style and trappings of power. Later in the play, we encounter a third B-movie personage, the failed priest; again the element of parody is present, as Liduc does not go to the ends of the earth to redeem himself, but has been sent by a Church which sincerely hopes he will never be heard from again. His presence makes possible the introduction of the pseudo-philosophical observations so characteristic of the B-movie as a form, and which Walker gleefully deflates and redirects: "Jesus doesn't mind losers but he has no patience for idiots."

To these refugees from a jungle movie, Walker adds figures from other worlds, but worlds no less threatened by the surrounding chaos. Olga, Rocco's wife, is obsessed with the world of Chekhov's plays to the point where she believes that she is the character of the same name from *The Three Sisters*, complete with a sentimental attachment to the artistic traditions of the *ancien regime* (represented in the play by a treasured Renoir which she employs as a talisman against the forces of the jungle), a determination to preserve social form at all costs, and the obligatory yearning for Moscow. In the original production, the part was played by Frances Hyland, further heightening the effect created by introducing high culture into flamboyant pop. The introduction of a Chekhovian character points out the pattern of non-communication and obsession in the piece, gives an added significance to the manner in which characters are isolated from each other, and adds a dream-like memory of bitter-sweet against which Walker can contrast his more garish effects.

Corporal Lance, formerly of the RCMP, brings a distinctly Canadian contribution to the model apocalypse; we Canadians, too, get a share in the fall of the West. The Corporal is one of the very few explicitly Canadian characters in Walker's work and it is a reflection of Walker's views on what Canadian theatre ought to be that the character is a very crafty parody: the Corporal is inept (natives have dismantled his motorcyle and he can't put it together again), naive, apparently clean-living, and very Canadian—in the grip of malarial hallucinations, he sees wheat (a sly dig at the "rural angst" plays mentioned at the outset of this chapter). The character is a good example of Walker's growing ability to manipulate audience expectations. The Corporal is at first merely a comic Mountie, who, as we would expect, fails to understand what is happening in the sophisticated world of decadent allusion, worries about not having anything formal to wear but his scarlets ("Am I over-dressed?"), and gives his wholesome all to the battle against subversion. But this quintessentially Canadian joke—which makes possibly the uniquely Canadian pleasure of being self-deprecatory and self-congratulatory simultaneously and which therefore neatly disarms a Canadian audience's defence mechanisms—acquires an uglier, more sinister quality as the play progresses: he is so distressed by misery that he puts to death all who suffer, hence making his Canadian wholesomeness an agent of the final destruction. The acute but unkind comment about our national personality is administered while we are still distracted by the reassuring cartoon.

The last of this stranded crew of expatriate whites is both of the world of B-movies and not of that world, thus providing a bridging device and a means of comment. Rita is a porn-movie star engaged in jungle smuggling operations in an attempt to raise the money to finance a legitimate movie and realize her dreams of respectable stardom: "This one is going to be a classic. It'll have sex. But it'll be sex with class." A classic definition of the romantic B-movie, or, for that matter, B-jungle-movies. Rita is the character most fully aware of the theatrical and cinematic elements of their plight, and the one most given to consciously dramatizing the situation; through her, Walker adds to the devices of hyperbole and film the technique of explicit comment which makes *Beyond Mozambique* more than an exercise in nostalgia and parody:

> Sometimes I just pour myself a stiff gin and lean against that big tree outside my tent and just let that sun sink slowly down into the ground

> while I shake the ice cubes around in the glass. And when I do that I
> get so deeply into Rita Hayworth I could just about die. (22)

We all play our roles to the death. Rita also prepares the way for the
final moments of the play in which the characters become aware of the
audience, either making us the drummers or including us within the cir-
cle surrounded by the drummers, and so involving us in this last moving
picture show just before the final darkness descends.

Beyond Mozambique is a much more disciplined play than is *Bagdad
Saloon*, evidence that Factory Lab's policies were paying off; some of the
original writers were dropping away while others, like Walker, pushed
doggedly on, learning the language of the theatre. *Beyond Mozambique* has
tighter focus, and a clearer sense of direction, in part created by Walker's
continued progress in the creation of the single, unifying stage image, the
device which gives Theatre of the Absurd much of its trenchant force. The
split between Walker's manic sense of humour and his more serious concerns is effectively healed; *Beyond Mozambique* is splendid black comedy,
combining the comic and the grotesque to produce Jonsonesque social
comment. And Walker completed, in this play, an important step toward
developing an efficient personal style. In his perceptive discussion of James
Reaney's plays, Ross Woodman notes that in order to progress from the
early pastoral comedies, Reaney needed to develop a "lens" through which
his personal vision could be viewed by an audience (48–49); in Reaney's
case, the necessary "lens" was provided by childhood games, rituals, and
rhymes. Walker, too, needed a "lens," and in *Beyond Mozambique* he discovered that his lens was the B-movie. When watching a Walker play, we,
like Leonard Cohen's Nancy, see "the late late show / through a semi-pre-
cious stone" (Cohen). The world revealed is eerie, often beautiful, the
ordinary made extraordinary by the unnatural hues and the lateness of
the hour.

Having used this lens to bring social comment into focus in *Beyond
Mozambique*, in *Ramona and the White Slaves* (1976) Walker uses the B-
movie lens again, this time to explore multiple realities, versions of "truth,"
and aberrant psychology. Set in what is apparently a brothel in a turn of
the century, impossibly decadent and chaotic Hong Kong, the play shows
us the Madam/Mother, Ramona, and her convoluted relationships with
her daughters, their lovers, her crippled son, and a man who may be her
pimp, her missing husband, or both. Two frameworks are provided: the
piece begins with Ramona's opium dream in which she is raped by a lizard—and there is a strong possibility that the entire play is an opium dream
(a drug induced state of mind is another "lens" to which Walker some-

times resorts)—while commentary is provided by a detective ostensibly attempting to solve a murder, one of many, which occurred in the street outside the brothel. The detective (a device Walker also employs in *Gossip*, 1977, *Filthy Rich* 1979, *Theatre of the Film Noir*, 1981, and *The Art of War*, 1982) has a long history as a useful dramatic device, and in addition provides the B-movie lens. Cook's inquiries do not produce the answers he sets out to find, nor do they reveal much biographical information about Ramona, for most spectators guess early in the play the bizarre secret of the ex-nun's history. The search, however, takes us through a tour of Ramona's psyche, the obsessions which compel her to devour her children and which make her, simultaneously, a powerful and compelling figure, a B-movie Medea, and a striking presentation of the mother/whore dichotomy so central to Western, male erotic fantasy.

After a period of personal crisis and discouragement, which Ken Gass documents in his introduction to *Three Plays*, Walker began with *Gossip* to alter his tactics somewhat, to make his plays "more generous." *Zastrozzi* is certainly more accessible than all but his earliest plays, and *Zastrozzi* is one of his most popular works. The play is, unabashedly, a melodrama, and is subtitled as such. It pits good against evil in a plot taken from Shelley's novel, but a note in the Playwrights Co-op edition of the play informs the reader that Walker worked from a description of the novel: therefore the play is not really an adaptation of the original work. In the context of this discussion, it is important to note that there is certainly as much Errol Flynn as there is Percy Bysshe Shelley in Walker's play, and that Walker is continuing to make use of his B-movie lens.

As William Lane, the director of the original production, implies in his introduction, *Zastrozzi* is, in addition to being a melodrama, a contemporary (and tongue-in-cheek) morality play; Walker evidently believes that morality plays are rare in contemporary theatre and ought to be supplied, but is also aware that a contemporary audience is unlikely to accept a naked statement of central propositions: our defensive objectivity or superficiality or materialist disbelief must be circumvented through giving us the opportunity to laugh. "The moral centre of the play is Zastrozzi himself—the very one who never has a moral crisis" (Lane, Introduction to *Zastrozzi* 5). Zastrozzi, in fact, constitutes the moral centre through his implacable desire to follow the dictates of a kind of morality to that point where morality annihilates itself. "Mankind is weak," he says. "The world is ugly. The only way to save them from each other is to destroy them both" (*Zastrozzi* 56). This is a logical extension of the thinking of both fundamentalist Protestantism and the playwrights of the Absurd. In the plot, Zastrozzi is the play's villain, the master criminal of Europe, and the adamant pursuer of his mother's murderer, a man turned saint or fool by the magnitude of the act. Within the play's metaphorical structure, Zastrozzi is the principle of order, standing as the last bastion against the coming of a new, liberal, "pleasantly vague" world being born at the turn of the century, the time of the play's events and the beginning of our own era. As William Lane observes:

> Zastrozzi is already a figure out of his time. He comes on like some medieval nightmare, wielding his sword and dagger as though they were still the most lethal weapons on earth … Zastrozzi's attitude is mercilessly aristocratic. His foe is the new middle-class with its shiny new liberal education and its fancy for art. (Introduction to *Zastrozzi* 5)

He is, in short, "the master of discipline," the one who takes it upon himself to supply an absolute, a means of assuring that everyone is answerable.

Evil has great stage presence, and given the theatrical advantages ever afforded the villain, it is inevitable that the eponym seizes and holds the attention, and in some ways, the sympathy of the audience. Walker himself has expressed some concern over the implications of the attraction a figure such as Zastrozzi commands, compared to the evidently pallid alternative, Verezzi the guilty saint:

> There's been a tendency to think of him [Verezzi] as moronic. I think that's just a reflection of our own age. We cannot accept God, obsession or goodliness, when in fact, a Verezzi has his own power … It's a sign of our times that we tend to think of Verezzi as a fool, and Zastrozzi as a charming evil villain who's more in touch with reality. Well, maybe he is, but I still think there's room in this world for people like Verezzi. At least I hope so. (Hallgren 24)

Nonetheless, Walker presents the B-movie-hero-in-white in such a way that contemporary cynicism cannot fail to judge the character a fool. The man whom Zastrozzi has pursued for three years cannot recognize the danger he is in, choosing instead to fantasize that he is a sort of messiah, complete with invisible followers; most telling stroke of all, he is a sexual flop, and we certainly don't want to identify with that. At the same time, Walker puts into the mind and mouth of a character we are sometimes invited to despise sentiments with which we know we ought to agree. At first glance, *Zastrozzi* seems to run contrary to Walker's usual practice of using a form to undermine the mode of thought behind the form: for the play, like melodrama and melodramatic B-movies, makes a clear distinction between good and evil, and gives each side the formalized statements of faith or anti-faith. However, by giving to the villain a passion for order and definition in some respects attractive to the inhabitants of chaotic times, as well as many of the best lines, and by giving to the putative hero qualities which we know cannot stand up to current events or intellectual trends, Walker encourages the wry and condescending smile with which we customarily respond to melodrama (unless it has been updated with the contemporary trappings of T.V. social drama) and with which we reject the melodramatic world of good and evil revealed. Walker's skilled evocation of the double response leads us into an old fashioned examination of the nature of good and evil; again, the theatrical hand is quicker than the eye of the audience, who thought they were just watching swashbuckling melodrama and parody of swashbuckling melodrama.

Melodramatic simplicities are further complicated by Victor. In some ways, Zastrozzi and Verezzi are opposites: Zastrozzi is a realist, and Verezzi is an idealist. In other ways, they are similar; both shape their lives with absolutes. In this respect, and others, both find their opposite in Victor, servant to Verezzi and failed priest, who, in order to keep a promise does his utmost to protect the victim from the destroyer. Realistic, materialistic, pragmatic, Victor commands respect for his decency, resourcefulness, and courage. It is here that Walker's growing powers of characterization are most impressive, for despite all his decencies (and decency is notoriously boring on stage), Victor is an interesting character; he is the one who, as Lane points out, has the moral dilemma, and he responds to it in a manner with which most members of the audience would agree. He calls a madman a madman, acts instead of hypothesizing, and, alone among the characters, is possessed himself of a sense of humour. We identify with him; he is like us. In the final sword-fight in a play full of sword-fights, Victor at first, against all odds, survives Zastrozzi's attacks, because his inept swordsmanship is improvised, hence unpredictable. The audience is tempted into believing that our surrogate will win. Victor, however, succumbs to his own glee, and himself falls into the temptation of believing in absolutism, proclaims that he has found God again, calls himself "an emissary of goodness" and, while he is thus distracted, is killed.

We therefore agree intellectually with one character, feel we ought to respond spiritually to a second, and identify most closely with a third. While B-movie conventions would lead us to expect an either/or proposition, we are given three poles, and ambivalent poles at that. Walker uses the rest of the cast of stock characters to extend the central issue, and to comment upon it. An assistant villain is present not only to facilitate the plot in the usual manner, but to demonstrate the difference between ideological evil and mere thuggery. The presence of a villainess and a purer-than-white heroine gives a sexual shape to the contest, reducing the cosmic struggle to "naughty" vs "nice," and at the same time adding a strong strain of eroticism to help bring the point home, to bed. Zastrozzi's imaginary seduction of Julia is a very compelling scene indeed.

In some respects in the early plays, Walker seems to be a "small c" conservative. *Zastrozzi* ultimately asserts that evil does exist, is not the product of environment, and must be confronted. In *The Prince of Naples*, the easy assumptions based on a facile acceptance of relative values are pilloried, and *Bagdad Saloon* dismantles a system of values based on the publicizing of subjective fantasy. Walker is a champion of language and definition, a concern that has increased as his career progressed, and he rejects naturalism, in part, because it has forgotten how to reach areas of human experience accessible to older dramatic forms. In this, he resembles Eugene Ionesco, who claims not to be of the *avant-garde* at all; Ionesco dismisses much recent drama, finding "Ibsen heavy, Strindberg clumsy, Pirandello out-moded," and wants in his own work to return to the theatre of the Greeks and the Elizabethans, a larger than life theatre "concerned with the human condition in all its brutal absurdity" (Esslin 164–165). That is what we are left with at the end of *Zastrozzi* as the villain surveys a positively Jacobean heap of corpses, enjoying his impersonal Greek blood revenge. The form is contemporary but the clash of forces therein depicted is an old and vital one.

Since first writing about Walker's work, I've changed my mind about Walker being a "small 'c' conservative," or maybe Walker has changed his mind about being a small "c" conservative. To be sure, there is to be found in later work some elements which could be associated with a conservative or traditionalist mindset. He has, for example, remained suspicious of fads, and there is little sense in any of his play that Walker is much influenced by or interested in that which is merely theatrically fashionable. He is still suspicious of imprecision and sloppy thinking. He is still a champion of language, and among the most fastidious of Canadian playwrights in his attention to putting the right words in the right order, although his vocabulary and linguistic palette are enriched by recourse to vernacular sources which many conservatives would avoid. He still has little use for small "l" liberals, and is very fond of challenging liberal values and characters (although at the same time he has emerged as an implacable foe of the neo-conservative, the far right, and the "New World Order"). He still believes in the existence of evil. And he is certainly consistent in being dissatisfied with simple, pat answers to complex questions, and in despising sentimental optimism. With increasing frequency and persistence, Walker has privileged "family values" in his plays, and old-fashioned qualities like love, friendship, and loyalty, although what

Walker has in mind is quite different from the devalued Coutts-Hallmark versions sold by the televangelists, the Promise Keepers, and others on the religious right.

While one can still see in Walker's accumulated work some traces of aesthetic, even political, conservatism, there is much more evidence of the social reformer and critic. Indeed, in the ever darkening depiction of social and political corruption in "The Power Plays," and in the sympathetic attention to what William in *Criminals in Love* calls "the great underclass of our society, the doomed, the forgotten, the outcasts," in "The East End Plays," we see Walker the subversive. Finally, it is as difficult to place Walker on a left/right political spectrum as it is to pigeon-hole him within any specific "school" of playwriting: in 1984, Denis Johnston described Walker as a "playwright in progress," and in some important respects, I would say that this is still true, even though Walker now has twenty-six published plays behind him. There is in all Walker's work evidence of a suspicion of all organized politics (and organized religion and organized law, not to mention organized sports): "My ideological position has always been one of not understanding ideology, of just trying to come to grips with what I think are the moral injustices of the world. I generally distrust ideology as a limited road to a limited truth" (Qtd. in Wallace, "Looking for the Light" 29). In later work, oppositional protest itself is seen as more likely to reinforce the status quo than effect any meaningful social revolution, and is no longer regarded as sufficient by itself—what is needed, says Walker, is a new way of looking, thinking, and knowing.

In a 1988 interview with Robert Wallace, published in the journal *Canadian Drama*, Walker identified a shift that occurred in his work in the early eighties:

> … it was a matter of letting more light into my plays; just naturally, I felt I had to do that, see what sort of hope—that's not a good word; "possibility" might be better—I could find. More than anything, that's the major change I think: I'm getting more possibility, more future, into the work. The early plays don't have much hope for the future; their essential concern is "what is the world?"—what is the nature of the chaos there? Now it's more a question of how to deal with it, how to fight through it. And, if anything, it's a stronger question. ("Looking for the Light" 22)

Now, this is still far from Marxist, utopian belief in the perfectability of man, but it does move away from the pessimism of the earlier plays toward the possibility that change can occur, perhaps even toward an activist conviction that one ought to try to make changes occur, to try to change an audience's mind about how the world operates, or could operate, or should operate.

The "B-movie lens" about which I first wrote in 1980, and which I still believe is extremely important to the early plays, is much less important to those plays written after 1982. Walker still draws extensively on electronic media, pop culture, street slang, but the way in which these sources are incorporated into Walker's work has shifted dramatically from the plays of the seventies to the plays of the eighties and nineties. Discussing the early plays in her Ph.D. Thesis, "Parody in the Plays and Productions of George F. Walker," Catherine Smith uses as one of her starting points Linda Hutcheon's *Theory of Parody*:

> Hutcheon suggests three main reasons why a parodist draws on past art forms: to imitate a subject in order to create a ridiculous effect (which is the way that parody is usually defined); conversely, to pay homage to a past tradition or work of art; or, more neutrally, to look at old things in new ways and, in the process, effect a dialectic between old and new. In reference to this third reason, she defines parody as "repetition with a critical difference;" that is, "in the background of an author's work will stand another text against which the new creation will be measured. It is not that one text fares better or worse than the other; it is the fact that they differ that the act of parody dramatizes." (3)

Smith goes on to explain that Walker uses all three of these types of parody, sometimes all within the same play, but that as he progressed through the '70s and into the '80s, he increasingly moved from the first two to the third: "He is trying to be a social critic by using aspects of our culture as a vehicle to make his audience look at the culture in a new, more critical way" (5). She then quotes as an example of Hutcheon's third type of satire my contention in "B-movies Beyond the Absurd" that "artifacts meant to be disposable" acquire "levels of meaning not intended by the creators" when placed in a new context, with reference to Walker's use of B-movies and *film noir* as backgrounded texts to foregrounded plays such as *Beyond Mozambique*, *Gossip*, *Filthy Rich*, and of course, *Theatre of the Film Noir*.

> Walker's works can be seen as being what Hutcheon terms "parodic satire" because he aims at criticizing something outside the text but employs parody as a vehicle to achieve his satiric or corrective aim. He draws on the style of the B-movie not at all to attack this form, but rather, to use it for a social, ethical or politically satirical purpose ... As a satirist, Walker is trying to make his audience look at social problems in new ways through the vehicle of parody, which begins by making us look at established forms of art in new ways. In this sense, parody and

satire have similar purpose: both contrast the old and the new; and this contrast is heightened when the two genres are combined. (Smith 8)

I think I would still argue that some of the assumptions embedded in the B-movie form, especially the excessively simplistic worldview in which good is easily distinguished from evil and in which good almost invariably triumphs, are attacked, interrogated, and subverted by Walker's early plays, but Smith is right when she says that Walker uses the tension between the backgrounded work and his own creations to investigate much broader cultural concerns. Walker is often made uneasy by popularly fashionable opinions, as in *The Prince of Naples*, and by popular art, particularly by its sheer quantity, a deluge which threatens to overwhelm individual thought and which contributes to the "chaos" with which virtually all his characters in all his plays contend. Further, he is made very anxious by the way in which popular art shapes thought, by the possibility that it is no longer possible for anyone to have original thoughts, by its erasure of difference which he intuits as integral to individual experience. Nonetheless, his anxiety is much larger than the deleterious effects of pop art, and even than his own ambivalent response to pop art, part fear, part celebration. While his "parodic satire" is often in the first instance directed at the "popular art/individual thought" nexus, the ultimate target, the real source of anxiety, of which popular art is merely a component, perhaps a symptom, is Western culture itself, perhaps even the human condition. In both Western culture and the human condition, or so we Westerners think and feel, there is a need to order chaos so desperate, so compelling, that it often makes us do and say ridiculous things, and think ridiculous thoughts. It is often Walker's purpose to demonstrate just how ridiculous those actions and thoughts are, and that goes far beyond ridiculing any particular work of art, high or popular, or even any literary or media genre and the thought processes that go with it.

Smith pursues Walker's use of the B-movie and *film noir* much further and more thoroughly than I did in "B-Movies Beyond the Absurd," often identifying particular novels and films as backgrounded works and as "reference points" for specific Walker plays. Thus, for example, she sees Evelyn Waugh as well as B-jungle-movies, and, of course, Chekhov, as contributors to the parodic tensions in *Beyond Mozambique*. She discusses movies such as *The Maltese Falcon*, *Murder, My Sweet*, *The Thin Man* and *The Big Sleep* to establish the source and ancestry of some of the stock characters, like the *femme fatale* and the hard-boiled detective, as well as the tone, the worldview, and the style of dialogue Walker both employs and parodies in plays like *Ramona and the White Slaves*, *Gossip*, *Filthy Rich*, and *Theatre of the Film Noir.* I'm less convinced when she applies the argument to the "third phase" plays after 1982. For example, she sees the social protest play, such as Elmer Rice's *Street Scene* and Clifford Odets' *Awake and Sing,* as models for *Criminals in Love,* and draws links between William and a somewhat similar character in the film, *My Man Godfrey.* She identifies Tom in *Better Living* as the "intruder-redeemer" figure who often appears in 1950s family melodramas, such as those directed by Douglas Sirk, and Nora as the "widow-divorcee" type found in the genre. *Scarface* is present in *Beautiful City* through the family name, Raft, and through the conflict between "families" for the control of a city. Hardy Boys adventures provide the parodic tension, she contends, in *The Art of War.* I would add to the list of references and foreground-background tensions and contrasts in these plays. I agree with the reviewer who saw in *Better Living* echoes of Ibsen's *A Doll's House*; Walker says, in fact, that naming the character Nora was a "playful tip of the hat to Ibsen" (interview, June 1998). I think I see some Ibsen too in *Beautiful City,* this time *The Master Builder.* I'm quite convinced that Kafka is present in *Criminals in Love,* and Tom's final, enigmatic reappearance at the end of *Better Living,* after he has apparently been killed, reminds me of the slasher-movie villain who refuses to die.

Smith amply and proficiently demonstrates Walker's movement from the "overt parody" of the early plays, where characters quite self-consciously refer to their theatrical context and to the genre being referenced, with many "reference points" where Walker deliberately links background and foreground for the audience so that they are consciously aware of that which is being parodied, to the much more "covert parody" of later plays of the seventies and very early eighties, where reference is much more oblique and submerged. But I think there's a shift in kind as well as of degree in Walker's move back to the relatively realistic environment of the "East End," the working-class neighbourhood where Walker grew up and which he had left artistically unexplored since *Sacktown Rag.* I think *The Art of War* too is on the near side of this significant border, less abstract, more politically focussed, less dependent on the "B Movie lens," or any kind of tension provided by literary or media reference. Through the work of his first decade as a playwright, Walker developed his own very distinctive voice, and at the end of that decade came to rely on that voice more confidently and moved to a dramaturgy that no longer relied as heavily on parodic tension as do the first dozen or so plays, counting the unpublished ones. The "voice" Walker had established in the cartoon and cinematic plays carried over into the more biographical territory of the East End, without becoming naturalistic in the process; Walker says of the Walker style carrying over into the more personal subject matter: "… I think part of the reason that I had avoided this material earlier was that I was afraid that it would affect the voice. But when I shifted I felt that the voice was intact, and that it would go to this new work and that whatever happened to it would just be natural" (Qtd. in Wallace, "Looking for the Light" 31). So while an audience may be aware of the "young lovers doomed" motif in *Criminals in Love* or the roles of William in *Criminals in Love* and Gina Mae Sabatini in *Beautiful City* as fairy-tale "wise guide" figures, these references are much less particular than were earlier genre references, and the later plays are much less dependent for their effect, especially for their comic effect, on an audience's holding two artistic/cultural visions in their minds simultaneously; the Walker voice alone (increasingly, a web of Walker voices) is enough to establish a doubleness, an alienation, seeing both the familiarity and the strangeness of our world at once.

Increasingly, it seems to me, as I've argued elsewhere ("'I put it in terms that cover the spectrum'") if parodic tension exists in Walker plays written from 1982 onward, it is often the *characters* who reference an antecedent, background form, rather than Walker directly, and because different characters in the same play can be referencing different artifacts, the Walker play in which the characters appear does not and cannot relate to an external work in a one to one, direct manner, as was often the case with the early plays. Obviously R.J. in *Problem Child* and *Risk Everything* confuses the realities of life and television, and obviously there is a reason why he does so, avoiding the anguish of his own life by projecting his anxieties into the suffering and humiliation of the talk show participants, their being subjected to injustices parallel to those he himself is experiencing. When he complains to the talk show producer over the phone about going too far, in effect he's talking to God, or to whomever, R.J. thinks, creates his own circumstances and shapes his own destiny.

Here the referencing is part of R.J.'s character rather than a characteristic of the work as a whole; it is not the "engine" central to the experience of the play in performance to the degree that an awareness of B-movie conventions is central to the reception of *Beyond Mozambique*, or that an awareness of the conventions of melodrama is central to the reception of *Zastrozzi*. I think Henry Dawson Sr. in *Criminals in Love* has seen too many crime movies and cop shows on TV; as in R.J.'s case, realities have merged, and Henry speaks, thinks, and conducts his life as though he were a fictional character, a dime novel criminal; one of his biggest problems is that he is intellectually and constitutionally unsuited to the role. I think William is quite conscious of his "outsider philosopher" role, and of the Kafkaesque nature of the dilemma in which he and his protegees find themselves; he enjoys playing it, and plays it to the hilt. Tom in *Better Living* doubtless reads *Soldier of Fortune*; he certainly reads newspapers and watches television news through the paranoid eyes of the right-wing survivalist, as Walker makes clear. Mary-Ann, in *Better Living* and even more so in *Escape from Happiness,* has been reading many feminist, pop psychology, self-help books, and these artifacts interact with her own characteristic anxieties and neuroses. Again, the *character* makes the reference for his or her individual reasons and lives his or her life according to his or her obsession with that reference, which is different from the dynamic of a work in which characters function within a referential framework established *a priori*, and whose effectiveness depends in large part on the audience being aware of that framework. This is also different from those occasions in the early plays when an individual character is obsessed with a backgrounded work, as is Olga with *Three Sisters* in *Beyond Mozambique,* for there the individual obsession is contained within and played out in the context of the overarching, parodic genre reference, in this case the jungle movie. In these later plays, the characters collaborate, at varying degrees of consciousness, with external, cultural constructs in order to construct for themselves a subject position which mediates, or which they hope will mediate, between their imaginative lives and the "real" world within which they live, and which usually threatens and oppresses them.

Walker no longer collaborates and mediates in the same way. So even if Walker intends references to "redeemer-intruders," or family melodrama, or Ibsen, the individual audience member doesn't need to be aware of the reference to appreciate *Better Living*, or of the Hardy Boys to experience *The Art of War*; we have moved fully into Walkerland. Particularly with the growing tendency of characters from one Walker play to reappear in another, the reference, if there is one, is to another Walker play or plays, to Walkerland itself, a tendency which reaches its climax, thus far, in "Suburban Motel."

Chapter Three
Who Controls the Future?
Power, Class and "The Politics of Life"

In the midst of writing this book, I had a nightmare. I'd been hired to teach at McGill, and went to Montreal only to find that Montreal was now a single building thousands of stories high—"the university is on the 1,439th floor, this room is the English Department." The rest of the city had been abandoned, a wasteland of derelict buildings around the base of the monolith. Once inside the building, you could not go outside again.

I was very upset by this state of affairs, and could not hide the fact that I was upset. This made me a dissident. So I was tricked into getting onto an express elevator that never stopped. It just kept going back and forth between the top floor and the bottom, and if you didn't have a legitimate reason to get off at either, and papers to prove it, you had to stay on the elevator. Presumably forever. That's what the inhabitants of the building of Montreal did with dissidents. Even while dreaming, I recognized that this form of penal servitude did have its comic side. Somehow I managed to escape from the elevator, and after crawling through miles and miles of maintenance tunnels and pipes, ended up on the roof where I experienced a mixture of relief, release, and terror—I'm frightened of heights. The dream ended.

I suppose this could be described as "shared anxiety." I also have very strange dreams when I direct a production of a Walker play, for then too, as in writing this book, I become immersed in Walker's world where the air crackles with anxiety, as it does in the stage spaces created by the plays. One of the primary sources of the anxiety is the question posed again and again by Walker's plays: "Who controls the future?" Is our future and that of our children ours, or is it, as our present often seems to be, a construct produced by other people and by huge organizations whose shape we can barely see? Control and ownership of the future is often explicitly the focus and objective of class and political conflict in Walker's work.

In *Better Living*, Nora excuses the extremely ordered, indeed fascist, plans her husband has for the family because his plans seem preferable to a future which makes her even more anxious. Tom knows about this even more awful future because he has a letter:

> A highly official letter. A government letter. Written to someone in the government from someone else in the government. Someone who has access to information about the future. You see the future isn't really the thing we think it is. To people like us the future is an open space filling up with things we can't see until we get there. But for certain other people high up in the government the future is something you make. And these people have decided to make it bad … They've got their reasons. High-up reasons. Over-population. The impurity of the social system, and big deficits, very big deficits. Also it's possible they're just mean. It's all in the letter. (315)

The reference to "big deficits," and to big deficits as the excuse for ideologically driven social engineering, proved positively prophetic.

Petie Maxwell, the crusading lawyer in *Love and Anger*, says of a right-wing newspaper publisher that he's "An investor in the future. But I've looked through the hole in my head and seen his idea of the future. It's a nasty stupid place" (61). All the right-wing totalitarians in Walker's plays justify their positions through their ability to impose order, to make things clear, on their terms of course, and, as I pointed out when discussing *Zastrozzi* in Chapter Two, there is a part of our minds that responds to this and longs for simplicity and easy answers, which, in turns, draws us to Walker's villains. Sometimes, this longing for order, stasis, peace, extends to a Wagnerian-Hitlerian vision of apocalyptic annihilation, Zastrozzi's ultimate destruction of both the world and mankind, or, in *The Art of War*, Hackman's "vast darkness": "Let's call it war. The new war. The inevitable destruction of everything. Life-ending war. But even without war, it ends. Everything we build now will be ruins in, what, a thousand years, anyway … War is a way of taking temporary control, that's all" (179). Walker's bad guys are against complexity and confusion, against "impurity of the social system," change; the worst of them want the stasis of annihilation.

The characters who most qualify as "good guys" in Walker plays, on the other hand, want like Nora to live the future rather than control it, and accept as the nature of life and its future, complexity and diversity. Jane, the daughter of the earth-mother figure in *Beautiful City*, says to the sick and confused architect protagonist:

> You've been living like a fool … You've lost touch with the genuinely complex nature of reality. All your friends think alike, talk alike, want the same things … .. You're dying from a kind of simplicity … It's like

you've taken the huge throbbing life force and turned it into a piece of
thread ... and it's not enough to hold you together. (266)

Sarah in *Love and Anger* talks about "the commonality of complex pain.
That makes sense. It's the thing that ties us all together" (36). While Petie
Maxwell in the same play says "I'm expressing the complexity before I
attempt the clarification. Any fool could rob the situation of complexity
and then clarify an essentially fraudulent simplicity" (14). In *The Art of
War*, the apparent protagonist, Power, says to the fascist Hackman: "Any
asshole can get the trains running on time!! Any asshole can do that, but
it takes something more to get the people on the trains for any reason
other than the fact that they're scared shitless of the asshole who got them
running on time" (204–205).

In Walker's plays, anxieties often arise from power imbalances and struggles, ways in which characters are deprived of control over their own lives,
often of their futures both immediate and distant. Often the anxiety comes
from a suspicion that power derives not just from the obvious and clearly
identifiable sources of social and economic power, but from an organiza-
tional network so remote from the lives of ordinary people, so secret and
mysterious, that its existence can be glimpsed only through its effects. Its
amorphousness, ambiguities, even the doubts around whether it actually
exists at all, lead to a fear and a state of anxiety far beyond any caused by
identifiable threats. Beyond even that, in Walker's work politics merge with
theology and metaphysics, issues of social hierarchy and class conflict
mingling with an almost Greek sense of fate and a universe that is not
only potentially hostile, but more hostile to some than to others. Those to
whom the universe directs more than their share of hostility are almost
always those who are already socially, economically, and politically disad-
vantaged. When Walker raises the stakes, and gives these characters insight into the true nature of the universe and hence of their dilemma, theirs
is the most intense anxiety and fear of all.

Walker's understanding of power imbalance and resulting anxiety is
visceral and of long-standing, as is his attention to luck, good or bad.
Walker's background is working-class. The son of a municipal labourer,
he was raised in Toronto's working-class East End, first in a Cabbagetown
neighbourhood before his house was bulldozed for a housing development, and the whole area "gentrified," then on Pape Avenue, then on the
Danforth. Walker is frequently referred to as a working-class writer. In
trying to come to grips with the question of why Walker and Walker's
work resist assimilation into the dominant culture, despite canonizing and
commercial forces pushing in that direction, and which I sometimes think

includes Walker's own efforts, certainly those of his agent, I've come to the conclusion that the resistance is generated in large part by those working-class origins. His primary source, his early and formative experience, is "ex-centric" in that early on, he saw himself as part of a group of people distanced from the established centres of power. But while he is often referred to as a working-class playwright, no-one follows through on the possible implications with regard to the work; this fact is indeed assimilated, tacked on to the nationalist myth of the '70s Alternatives as our very own Horatio Alger story. In this, I've certainly been as remiss as everyone else.

I would say that there's evidence of working-class origins and outlook in Walker's irreverence with regard to what is proper, acceptable, polite, and in his irreverence for middle-class institutions: high art, law, religion, the professions, capitalism, Marxism. It's there in his love for low comedy and rude jokes, his ear for the language of the streets, his conviction that what you have to say takes precedence over how you say it, in his impatience with pretentiousness and his own lack of pretension, his contempt for "taste," his attention to "ordinary" people, his passionate anger.

One of the advantages of a working-class background is that it confers on the recipient a sensitive and efficient bullshit detection system. The working-class writer and thinker is relatively free from the restrictions of respectability and appearances, the need to show off and to compete in the intellectual realm. Academic fashions are irrelevant. This is not to say that the working-class perspective is immune from its own romanticisms, or from the systems of illusion directed to it: the blandishments of the Reform party, white supremacism, the NRA, the WWF, *Hustler*, the militia movement, and so on. But it does mean the individualist and independent working-class perspective and sensibility is almost entirely free from pretension, the only operable pretension being the compulsion to avoid pretension. Ken Finkleman says something like this when he talks about class and perception as components of their working relationship when he and Walker worked on Finkleman's television series, *The Newsroom*:

> George is a smart, tough, working-class mother ... and I'm fundamentally the other side, an upper middle-class, Hollywood, spoiled Jew. I was as intimidated by everything that was real about him as I think he was intimidated by everything that was false about me. (Posner 1997, D4)

Furthermore, in content as well as in the way he puts it, Walker's work is often class iconoclastic. The official myth is that while there may be the odd regrettable racial or ethnic tension in Canada, there really are no social classes, and no class struggle in Canada. Walker disagrees. As a country we pay lip service to the ideals of the classless society, and like Americans, we base our national mythologies in large part on the assumption of unlimited social mobility, upward of course, for every individual. Nonetheless, we all know what is meant by "working-class" or "blue collar" in Canada, and have a pretty good idea of who can be so classified. Further "down" the class system that supposedly doesn't exist in this country, we know what is meant by the imported American term, "white trash," and we all understand the permeability of the boundaries between respectable, working-class and working poor and the underclasses beneath. We recognize that the characters in Judith Thompson's *The Crackwalker* are Canadian and that they also belong to an identifiable lower social class, and that some of the cruelties chronicled in her play *Lion in the Streets* are cruelties inflicted by one class on another. At some level, most of us know that it is possible to fall right off the bottom of the scale completely, like William in Walker's *Criminals in Love*, or as almost happens to Paul in *Beautiful City*, become a "homeless person"—although we'd like to think that these are personal catastrophes, rather than an indictment of our society as a whole. We all understand the classist assumptions embedded in phrases like "trailer park," "demolition derby," "East End." Or in tatoos, or junked cars in the yard (as in *Better Living*). Prostitution. Criminal behaviour, unless it's white collar. Welfare. Poverty.

Lately, "official" denial of the existence of a class system has been exacerbated by identity politics' relegation of class differences to insignificance relative to differences of gender, race, and sexual orientation. Loss of power and identity, displacement, the anxiety created by technological and geopolitical and infrastructural job loss, and the ongoing effects of a culture of denial with regard to class, seems to be contributing to a working-class, white male rage, all too often manipulated by the likes of Howard Stern and Babe Conner, the publisher of a right-wing newspaper in *Love and Anger*, and directed into "big beefy white guy" movements. This white guy rage makes several appearances in the plays of the Suburban Motel cycle, especially *The End of Civilization*.

Relatively few Canadian playwrights pay attention to issues of class. Some, like Arthur Milner or David Fennario, George Ryga of course, refer to the Canadian class system explicitly. A very few, Walker, Tremblay, Judith Thompson, a few others, incorporate class, class distinction, class consciousness, class conflict, into the very fabric of their work. Walker and Tremblay from the vantage point of their working-class origins, Thompson from the other side of the class divide. Constance Penley's examination of various working-class and "white trash" pop art forms in North America, primarily working-class pornography, notes their tendency to flaunt their trashiness "which, after all, is nothing but an aggressively in-your-face reminder of stark class differences, a fierce fuck-you to anyone trying to maintain a belief in an America whose only class demarcations are the seemingly obvious ones of race" (90). I think there's a good deal of this "fierce fuck-you" in Walker's work, a conscious exploitation of the "trashy," whether it be the liberal use of verbal obscenity, colloquial humour and insult, "gratuitous sex," pop art references, "trashy" characters and settings, or violence. He breaks rules on purpose, whether they are the structural rules of the naturalistic, well-made play, or the unspoken rules governing the conduct of "artistic" discourse in polite society, decorum. These aspects of his work simultaneously attract and titillate a mainstream, middle-class audience, and repel it. They, and related strategies, also make Walker's work "political" even when he is not explicitly discussing politics.

There is little overt attention to political issues in the early, cartoon and B-movie plays, but there is a good deal of energetic rebellion against the status quo. In *Sacktown Rag* most of the schoolboy satire is directed at authority figures, especially the teacher, Miss Missus, the school principal and the priest: the working-class protagonist says of the corporal punishment inflicted at his school, "it wasn't the pain, though, it was the degradation" (I.17). In *Beyond Mozambique*, science, religion, legal authority, and culture are all revealed to be empty, futile, and founded on illusion and self-deception. The society whose nature is exposed through the investigations of T. M. Power in "The Power Plays" is a society riddled with corruption, deception and power games: in *Gossip*, so many are implicated in the political wrongdoings, including almost anyone who could be described as a friend of Power, that the play ends with the crusading Power isolated and drinking by himself. The corrupting power of money in *Filthy Rich* is so pervasive that Power can't find a "good guys" side to join, and ends up allying himself with the "slightly less bad guys."

While it's clear that Walker's position is anti-establishment, often to the point of cynicism in the plays of the seventies, it's impossible to contain Walker's political views neatly within any political doctrine, or even explain them as entirely the consequence of external, materialist oppression: even in *Sacktown Rag*, Max's recollections of a powerless and humiliating working-class childhood are interrogated within the play itself, coloured with the possibility that they may be exaggerations or self-romanticizing or the results of internalized oppression. As I've pointed out elsewhere, "At various times in various Walker plays, the political right, small-L liberalism, and the revolutionary left have all been attacked by Walker, evidently with equal satirical glee and political conviction" ("George F. Walker" 84). In "Looking for the Light," Walker tells the story of a New Democratic Party (social democratic, slightly left of centre) city councillor who attended the première of *Criminals in Love* and was made uneasy by the play, by the difficulty he had in determining what "the play's politics were":

> I said to myself, well, of course, cause he's trying to slot the play into his socialist ideology and I'm just writing about the politics of life. I suppose you could probably find a socialist critique in the play, but it wouldn't cohere finally because at some point … the play starts to talk about bad luck, which is more than being oppressed. (Wallace, "Looking for the Light" 28)

While Walker's politics aren't doctrinaire nor clear-cut, and while his good guys are often confused and inept, in many of the plays, the enemy, the bad guys, are very clearly identified. Right-wing villains and authoritarian power figures abound in Walker's work. Some, like Rocco in *Beyond Mozambique*, are out and out fascists, and unapologetic about it: "There's something about committing crimes against humanity that puts you in touch with the purpose of the universe." The attention to "evil," power, and various forms of oppression is one of the earliest manifestations in Walker's work of a political sensibility.

Born in 1947, Walker belongs to the generation to whom the Nazi is still an extraordinarily powerful and evil figure, part of the parental/family mythology of "The War," frequently the comic book villain of choice. German-accented bad guys appear in countless B-movies, urbane, sophisticated, unspeakably sadistic, in the late forties and early fifties. Through his fascist characters, Walker can avail himself of the iconic power of the Nazi, the twentieth century personification of evil almost universally recognized and accepted, especially among those of his generation or older, an image as powerful and menacing as medieval demons, and as useful in the construction of twentieth century "morality plays."

Like the medieval "Vice," Walker's Nazi is often comic in his grotesque outrageousness, the danger somewhat mitigated because the evil is so obvious, and comedy arises from the completely blasé manner in which the fascist beast accepts as perfectly normal and unsurprising his own depravity. Like morality plays, the melodramatic separation of good and evil into black hats and white hats is rather comforting in its simplicity, but as Walker's plays became more sophisticated, so did his moral barometer and his exploration of evil. The villains become more dangerous as they become more persuasive, and more attractive. The binary opposition of right-wing versus left-wing politics, or melodrama's pitting good guys against bad guys, or the morality play's opposition of good and evil, are all further subverted by Walker's qualifying and interrogating the goodness of the angels: often, as in *Filthy Rich*, it's difficult to tell the sides apart, and often, as in *Zastrozzi*, *Theatre of the Film Noir*, *The Art of War*, and *Adult Entertainment*, the purported hero engaging in the struggle against evil is in danger of assuming attributes of the villain.

While the Nazi is in pop-art a figure of unmitigated evil, there is nonetheless something compelling, even attractive, at least aesthetically attractive, about the Fascist villain, especially to the sort of mind that produces and consumes comic books. Good clean lines, no ambiguity. There is in a number of respects, a strong resemblance to that other "attractive villain" of pop culture, Dracula, and vampires in general. As Susan Sontag points out in her essay, "Fascinating Fascism," an essay to which Walker refers in the souvenir-edition program of *Theatre of the Film Noir* produced for the 1993 revival of the play, Nazi uniforms are better cut, more stylish, "sexier" than the uniforms of the good guys, dramatic and menacing. Elsewhere in the essay, Sontag suggests that for people of Walker's generation, curiosity adds to the attraction: "For those born after the early 1940s, bludgeoned by a lifetime's palaver, pro and con, about communism, it is fascism—the great conversation piece of their parents' generation—which represents the exotic, the unknown." (323). Certainly Walker wasn't alone among the young playwrights of the Toronto Alternative in making use of recent history, and pop art depiction of recent history, the good guy/bad guy mythologies of their adolescence, by putting Nazis on stage, and in exploring the iconic meanings of the Third Reich and of ways in which that epoch redefined concepts of good and evil for post-war generations. (Ken Gass' *Hurray for Johnny Canuck* and *Winter Offensive*, and Bryan Wade's *Blitzkrieg* come quickly to mind.)

As well, it seems likely to me that the young playwrights of the Alternative used the iconography of Nazism, in part, to shock, and to make use of the great morality play of the Second World War for reasons similar to those Linda Hutcheon cites:

> It is this very familiarity that enables certain cultural texts (performances, paintings, photographs, music compositions, literature, as well as critical discourses), to call upon public memories of National Socialism's history in order to provide a shared discursive context for many in Europe and North America even today. And it is the still potent emotional force unleashed by those memories that makes irony's edge so tempting for both ironists and interpreters. (6)

One of the first writers to investigate the sexual power of the Nazi was Jean Genet in *Funeral Rites*, a work to which Walker also refers in the preliminary material to the souvenir edition of *Theatre of the Film Noir* published to commemorate the Factory Theatre/Shared Anxiety revival of the play in 1993.

> This play was inspired by Jean Genet's *Funeral Rites*, several other French novels of the period, a movie or two, a conversation between two distraught lovers I once overheard on a subway, and an acquaintance who lived a lonely "abstract" life and worked for the Ontario government for over twenty years. His job was to keep the scrap paper in neat piles. I would like to dedicate this production to him … wherever he may be. (inside cover)

The play, like Genet's somewhat autobiographical novel (Genet's biographer, Edmund White, describes four of the five Genet novels as "autofiction"), is set in Paris shortly after its liberation by the Allies, a time and place where the status quo, the order of things, had apparently been completely inverted. In actuality, however, such momentous historical events do not occur overnight, whatever the uniforms of the soldiers marching through the streets, with a neat clean line demarcating German occupation from American occupation, because the values, or lack of values, of one era leak into the other, creating a moral no-man's land, especially in the minds of those who are occupied. Significantly, Bernard, the Walker character equivalent to Genet's first-person narrator, identified by the writer as "Jean Genet," is as afraid of the American soldiers as he was of the Nazis, as he fears that the Americans will beat him because he is a homosexual; he can tell by the way they chew their gum. (Walker's character shares his Christian name with Bernard Frechtman, Genet's American translator.)

The Nazi in this play is Eric, like the character of the same name in Genet's novel a German soldier in hiding from the liberators, and like Genet's character, Walker's Eric generates both fear and sexual desire—when Eric confronts Bernard in the graveyard (Nazi/Vampire visual and atmospheric parallels are very strong here) and removes his civilian disguise of loose overcoat to reveal the German uniform underneath, the effect is both chilling and thrilling—we both fear for Bernard, and relish his terror, enjoy the sexual *frisson* generated by the terror.

Genet, in his principled anti-social criminality, sides instinctively with the outcast and the underdog; thus when the social order is inverted, Genet identifies with those who are hunted in the new scheme of things, the Nazi stragglers and the collaborators. Mourning the death of another "Jean," his young lover killed by the pro-Fascist militia in the street-fighting preceding the arrival of the American and Free French armies, Genet's protagonist becomes obsessed with the equally young and beautiful militiaman who killed his lover, and perversely makes the killer the object of his sexual desire—"perversely" unless one is Genet, and doing the despicable, becoming the despised, is the principled thing to do, and, like sharing lice, a way of maintaining a connection with the dead beloved. Walker's play follows Genet's work in that it goes beyond the "democracy versus fascism" conflict which inheres in the large historical events framing and precipitating the personal stories to a consideration of whether society can accommodate an outcast such as Bernard, or his model, Genet, or whether it is more likely to exterminate such outcasts rather than risk "infection"— according to Walker, at least in this play, democracy is as likely to resort to extermination as is fascism, and in this respect at least, Walker's play goes even further than Genet's profoundly disturbing novel.

While he predates historical National Socialism, Zastrozzi in the play of the same name is brought into Walker's Nazi *gestalt* by his absolutist beliefs, his assumptions of superiority, his German ethnicity, his ruthlessness, and the leather and weaponry with which he is associated, and it is in this play that the attraction/repulsion dance between audience and villainy is at its most intricate..

As Walker's plays present settings closer and closer to our own time, the Nazis and the villains are less willing to proclaim their fascism and their villainy. Hackman, the right-wing power broker and arms dealer who does battle with Tyrone M. Power in *The Art of War*, has friendly relations with South American dictators, raises mercenary armies to fight for rightwing causes, and engages an ex-commando as his personal assistant and hired killer. Nonethless, he is a Canadian of the late twentieth century, a retired Canadian general, and cannot publically revel in his extremism as do the monsters of the early plays. He has a cover, significantly as adviser to the federal Minister of Culture, cultivates a garden and the arts, and has made a point of developing a persuasive, smooth, apparently reasonable persona, for all that he is a Nazi underneath. Jamie, Power's young sidekick, says of the first encounter between Power and Hackman: "He sounded perfectly rational. You [Power] sounded perfectly obnoxious" (*The Art of War* 183). Significantly, I would place *The Art of War*, along with the early version of *Better Living*, as the first of the "closer to home" plays of Walker's career, not "realistic" *per se*, but more firmly grounded in a more familiar reality, and, I would argue, more overtly political than the earlier work: we are now more concerned with fascist powers at work in contemporary society than with the more symbolic Nazis of the cartoon plays.

The Power plays, *Gossip*, *Filthy Rich*, and *The Art of War*, are so named for the central character of the trilogy, Tyrone Power (his mother was a romantic, Power tells us to explain his name; Walker was probably attracted by the resonance of the surname). Unlike the romantic film hero for whom he was named, who among other things played Zorro in the '40s, Walker's Power is a balding, middle-aged, progressively isolated figure. In *Gossip* he is an investigative reporter, assigned by his editor to find the murderer of a society woman killed at a gallery opening: the investigation is so complex, the social and political corruption it uncovers so pervasive, that the original question is all but lost along the way towards a dramatic conclusion in which Power is successful, but even more isolated than he was at the beginning of the play. In *Gossip*, the character of Power amalgamates the two cinematic stereotypes of the reporter developed in thirties and forties films like *The Front Page*, *Five Star Final*, *I Cover the Waterfront*, and *Deadline U.S.A.*: "the witty, irreverent, but essentially likable guy" and "the more melodramatic image of the unfeeling muckraker or the fearless crime solver" (Barris 18). In *Filthy Rich*, Power has descended the social ladder, lives and works on a novel doomed to failure in a squalid office "in a dirty old building in a dirty old part of the city"; he is dragged unwillingly, as a sort of unofficial private investigator, into a *film noir* world of murder and political intrigue in which, as I said, it is difficult to distinguish the good guys from the bad guys. He drinks more than he did in the previous play. In *The Art of War*, Power drinks still more again, and is obsessed with pursuing the Nazi, Hackman; it becomes difficult to tell whether, in fact, Power is really the good guy. His goodness is certainly qualified, and its efficacy, at the very least, questioned.

In his fine essay "George F. Walker: Liberal Idealism and the 'Power Plays'," Denis Johnston sees in Power's disintegration through the three plays an extended metaphor for the failures of liberalism:

> If there is any sense of progression in the content of these three plays, it is in the progressive seediness of the fruits of liberal idealism. In *Gossip*, Power is an influential political columnist, taken off his regular assignment because, in Baxter's opinion, his superior intelligence would enable him to succeed where the police had failed. He wins the battle with relative ease, and presumably regains his position in the newspaper. In *Filthy Rich*, he is an alienated and deteriorating ex- journalist, who is dragged unwillingly into a political power-game, but plays it wonderfully well. His victory here is less clear-cut, however: some guilty people are punished, some are made mayor, and Power himself squanders all his money on a futile gesture, failing even to recoup his expenses. In a more recent play, *The Art of War*, Power returns as an obsessed and pathetic pauper, by his own admission "a freelance writer

with diminishing talent." In *Filthy Rich* he was a reclaimed drunk, heroically fighting the forces of evil; in *The Art of War* he's just a drunk,
retreating to his bottle whenever he becomes too overwhelmed by the
futility of his struggle. (202)

There are some striking parallels between the political conflict of left
and right in *The Art of War*, and the more metaphysical albeit tongue-in-
cheek struggle between good and evil in *Zastrozzi*. As in the earlier play,
the opposing sides in *The Art of War* are symmetrical reflections of each
other, like pieces in a chess game. In *The Art of War*, the principle opponents, Power and Hackman, are each supported by a "side kick," Jamie
and the ex-commando thug, Brownie, respectively, and by a female ally,
Heather, a young crusading journalist not unlike the Power we saw in
Gossip, and Karla Mendez, daughter of a South American would-be fascist
dictator. This is the same symmetrical arrangement of principal opponents
and supporting cast of assistants that we see in *Zastrozzi*. Like Zastrozzi,
Hackman is attractive in his smooth stylishness, his capacity for irony and
wit (although unlike Zastrozzi, Hackman reveals no vulnerability at all).
As in *Zastrozzi*, the opponents are alike in some ways, as Power is as
unbending in his obsession with destroying Hackman as Hackman is in
his determination to impose order. As we are in the case of the melodrama,
our response to the political parable is probably to identify with the pragmatist, Victor in the former, Jamie in the latter. Significantly, in *Zastrozzi*,
Victor is defeated only when he abandons the pragmatism which characterizes his actions throughout the play up until his sword fight with
Zastrozzi, when, gloating that he is succeeding in surviving and thus "neutralizing" Zastrozzi, he succumbs to self-righteousness: "I am the emissary
of goodness in the battle between good and evil. I have found God again.
*VICTOR lunges forward wildly. ZASTROZZI plunges his sabre through VIC-
TOR's heart*" (108). Jamie, on the other hand, is pragmatic to the end and
this, his youth, and his class, in combination with Power's disintegration,
suggest that it is he who will carry on the fight against the Hackmans of
the world, at least to the point of neutralizing evil by surviving.

There is a striking similarity, too, between the endings of the plays.
Zastrozzi, after subduing Verezzi, and forcing him to acknowledge his sanity
by acknowledging that the fear he now experiences is justified, releases
him, allows him to escape, gives him a day's head start, because he,
Zastrozzi, wishes to remain "occupied"—"evil" needs "good" in order to
exist. Hackman, although he could kill the wounded Power at the end of
The Art of War, does not, but instead, escapes, gloating: "Don't die. Try to
live. It would be more interesting if you lived and we met again. There's
so much I could teach you … No. Please. No need to stand on my ac-

count. Besides, I want to remember you just as you are" (216). The political right, like Zastrozzi's "negative spirituality," needs an opponent.

As neither Power nor Hackman deserve the audience's sympathy, Johnston argues, the audience's sympathy and identification goes to Jamie. "… Jamie emerges as the play's most attractive character. He tackles the stronger forces of evil in the certain knowledge that he will be beaten up for his presumption. While both Power and Hackman resort to devious and violent strategems, Jamie believes that protecting his friends is more important than winning the game" (Johnston, "George F. Walker: Liberal Idealism" 204). If each side in the contest between fascism and degraded liberalism resembles the other, and if they are, in fact, part of the same dynamic, which sustains them both, perhaps the most reasonable thing to do is distance oneself from both, or so *The Art of War* would seem to imply. Jamie says:

> War. Yes. I'm seeing it all now … This is a battle between two men. One of them, Power, wants the world to work properly with justice and equality and all those things. The other one, Hackman, just wants the world to work. Period. I figured all that out a while ago but I couldn't figure out my part in it all. But I learned. Experience taught me. I'm a pacifist. (214)

Johnston concludes from this:

> Jamie is beginning to understand this bizarre game, and he has no wish to play. Through him, the audience is made aware that non-involvement in political issues need not be a sign of cowardice; when both sides have lost their original positive differences in a maelstrom of rhetoric and revenge, Jamie's may be the only rational position. ("George F. Walker: Liberal Idealism" 204)

Nonetheless, in the action following his speech, Jamie does in fact align himself with Power, regardless of his misgivings regarding Power's ideology, competence, and sanity, and regardless of ongoing differences of opinion with Power regarding politics and political motivation, and Jamie does take physical action, although he proves almost as inept as Power—his failing to tie Karla up properly results in her escape, Power's being wounded, and the ultimate defeat of the "good guys." Jamie remains neither neutral nor pacifist. I would disagree with Johnston's contention that Power is almost as culpable as Hackman, for he is not a killer; in the end, the pragmatic, working-class boy (and on more than one occasion, critics, including Johnston, have noted the similarity between Jamie and Walker) remains on Power's side, promises to do better in the future.

In *The Art of War*, the liberal loses through a classic liberal dilemma: because of his beliefs, values and respect for human life, he is not prepared to kill, whereas his opponent is obviously more than willing to kill. Hackman tells Power:

> You're indignant. You're outraged. You just don't understand, do you. Anger is a weapon. Allowing you to be brutal. Brutality is another weapon. Allowing you to take action. In this way, you build your arsenal. Until you have the ultimate weapon. Immorality. Which allows you to take any action in any way at any time. Immorality is a great weapon. And you don't have it. (215)

This is a dilemma to which Walker returns again and again in subsequent plays, and more often than not, he raises the stakes and tests the liberal's values to the point where the liberal does in fact conclude that there are circumstances in which taking violent action is morally justified, and does take violent action. This occurs as Walker concerns himself more and more in the East End plays with the dramatic reality of East End Toronto, the here and now rather than the exotic locales of earlier plays, and I would argue, as Walker, formerly disgruntled and rebellious but relatively apolitical, becomes more politically active and definitive in response to the circumstances of his own upbringing and background, and in response to the social and political changes he sees occurring in his own country and in his own city. These subsequent East End plays lead me to question whether we should be as dismissive of Power in *The Art of War* as Johnston says we are, although in all fairness to Johnston, the context provided by the East End plays appeared subsequent to his writing "George F. Walker: Liberal Idealism and the 'Power Plays'."

At the same time that Walker's villains become more concerned with concealing their identity as villains, and with hiding the nature of their villainy, the "good guys"—the proponents of change and of what Walker in "Looking for the Light" calls "possibility"—encounter progressively complex and "realistic" questions regarding the nature of "goodness," as Power does with his liberalism in *The Art of War*. For example, the decision to resort to violence, to fight power with power, however necessary it seems at the time, comes with danger and with cost:

> If a worshiper of power decides to extend his power over your society, your choices are between surrendering and mounting an equal and opposite power. In either case, the power worshiper wins—he had converted your society into a people who understand that power is the highest good. (French 19)

This is the dilemma confronted by the liberal hero in *Love and Anger* (which I would place among the East End plays). Having suffered a stroke, Peter (Petie) Maxwell, formerly a corporate lawyer, sets up a "grimy office

in the basement of an old building on the fringe of the downtown area";
the stroke effected a profound transformation and now he turns against
the establishment and takes on the cases of the dispossessed and the
marginalized, with the ultimate goal of "undermin[ing] the entire institutional bias of our culture." In this he is aided by his loyal but somewhat
staid and reluctant secretary, Eleanor, and, much more enthusiastically, by
Eleanor's schizophrenic sister, Sarah, recently released from an institution,
and, eventually, by Gail, a young woman of colour, the centrifugal forces
in this play. While investigating the case of Gail's husband, who is in prison
for a crime which he was coerced into committing, Petie, as he now prefers to call himself, comes into conflict with John "Babe" Conner, powerful publisher of a right-wing tabloid newspaper, much like the Toronto
Sun, and Conner's legal adviser, Sean Harris, formerly Maxwell's legal partner. These two represent the status quo, the establishment, centripetal
forces, while the "good guys" are the centrifugal forces trying to disperse
power, working against established, hegemonizing centres of power. In
the course of the play, the "good guys" kidnap Conner, and put him on
trial, with Sarah presiding as judge, for the crime of "Being ... Consciously ... Evil," for advocating the law of the jungle, survival of the fittest.

On the level of the "political convictions" expressed by the characters,
the politics of *Love and Anger* would seem to be pretty simple and straightforward. As Walker says of this political aspect of the play:

> One critic in Washington said that the politics in *Love and Anger* were
> naive, and I remember thinking, well they would be—if they were
> politics! What they are are desperate emotions! ... They're not a cool,
> political view of the world. This is what happens to people when they
> get frustrated—they go nuts! [Maxwell] is *nuts*. That's what I think is
> important about that—you're marginalized and you get desperate. (Qtd.
> in Corbeil 60)

In his rage, Petie is determined to do whatever it takes to "get the enemy"—he will blackmail judges, falsify evidence, whatever it takes, because, for him, "this is the age of getting even."

In this play, the contemporary Nazi is Conner, and while he is a good
deal less likable than Zastrozzi, and a good deal less smooth than Hackman,
he too is concerned with appearances, with rationalizing his political views
and making them palatable. Conner is extremely sensitive to the word
"Nazi," and becomes very upset when it is employed against him. (Similarly, Hackman rejects the term "fascist" in one of his arguments with Power
in *The Art of War*: "An unfortunate choice of words, in the modern context, I mean. I'm someone who just wants to rid the world of chaos, get
the economy moving again, and restore order." [204].)

In current political debate, the left and non-mainstream social critics are often accused of using the terms "fascist" and "Nazi" too loosely, thus devaluing the experience of those who suffered at the hands of the German Nazis in the '30s and '40s; while this is sometimes the case, it is nonetheless true that the argument is often used by those with extreme right-wing views in order to derail legitimate comparisons: it is important to them, and to their agenda, that an appearance of political respectability be maintained. In the Western democracies, it is no longer politically feasible or advisable to call your policies "fascist" even if that, in fact, is what they are. Petie puts things into an historical context when he tells Conner:

> Your particular place in the historical corridor allows you to modify your behaviour for appearances, but you are still a Nazi. If you were put in a position of power in any society desperate for a violent purging you'd buy yourself a uniform—and you'd be a Nazi. (*Love and Anger* 22)

Following his stroke, Petie sees the world through the "hole in his head" and through an awareness of impending death: he has promised himself a new kind of honesty, and honesty compels him to honestly describe the nature of men like Conner: "If it looks like a Nazi, call it a Nazi" (22).

Good advice, and neither hysterical nor paranoid as some reviewers implied. This is Canada after all, where the Fraser Institute, a respectable, respected, and often quoted conservative think-tank supported by more than half of Canada's hundred most profitable corporations employed as its senior economist from 1979 to 1991 Walter Block, who is quoted as having said in 1986, "Why does it follow that we should have an equal right to vote in the political process? Voting in a political process is not a negative freedom, it is a positive freedom, and it is an aspect of wealth" (Russell A12). On another occasion, Mr. Block remarked "poverty is simply a reflection of the fact that the sufferers were dealt an unlucky intellectual or physical allocation from the roulette wheel of genetic inheritance." This sounds like a Walker villain, like Babe Conner:

> Fuck the people living on the fucking street. I've heard enough about the fucking people on the street. I mean you'd think there were thousands of them, the kind of press they get. I mean Jesus man this has got to be a place for winners. We've got to keep the momentum going. Let the slower people pick up the jet stream. That's our only choice. We've got to get richer. The only alternative is to get poorer. (*Love and Anger* 81)

Now, could we not follow Petie Maxwell's advice, and point out that Block's remarks are not just "right wing," conservative relative to centrist and left-wing political opinions? They go even beyond oligarchy. They're off the map, in fact, fascist. "If it looks like a Nazi, call it a Nazi." (And they say George Walker exaggerates!)

The schizophrenic Sarah Downey is another character in the play who describes precisely what she sees, and while sometimes what she sees is wonderfully "wonky," as when she washes her pizza in an attempt to separate the different ingredients, it is often startlingly penetrating, voicing what many in the audience see too, but are too fearful or too confused or too co-opted to say. Like Maxwell, she sees the parallel between Babe's politics and methods of manipulation, and those of Nazi Germany; when she encounters Conner and his lawyer, Sean Harris, both dressed in formal evening attire, she says: "You look like you've come from a dinner at the Reichstag" (*Love and Anger* 43).

Earlier in the play, Sarah opens scene three with one of Walker's extended arias of anxiety, the celebrated "big beefy white guys" speech about the guys who buy white tractor trailers, run in packs, take over towns, and kill everyone they don't like, the skinny people, the brown people, the black people, anyone who isn't beefy and white. I think Mary Pat Mombourquette is mistaken when she describes the "big beefy white guys" of the speech as representatives of the "dominant class" in her M.A. Dissertation, "Walker's Women in the East End Plays"; rather, they are embodiments of misdirected working-class male rage, the dupes of the dominant classes. The speech identifies as a contemporary source of rightwing power the redneck, "white trash" working-class whose resentment and anger are often instigated and channeled by media such as Conner's newspaper, which pander to the lowest common denominator and exploit the basest of instincts and most unreasonable of anxieties:

> They're free to be themselves. Free to be the one thing that's been hidden all these years. The big beefy white guys full of hate. Because some of them, most of them, aren't really big, don't look big, only have the big guy *inside* them. The big beefy white guy inside them has been talking to them for years. Telling them to let him out. To do his thing. His necessary thing. (*Love and Anger* 34)

At the conclusion of the speech, Sarah identifies one of the most frightening aspects of her vision, the extent to which the "big beefy white guy" philosophy had become normalized in the 1980s, accepted, like Rush Limbaugh or the Fraser Institute, as "respectable": "It's a movement. It's happening everywhere. It's out in the open. It's an accepted thing. It's the way it is" (34). Sarah and Walker persist in disagreeing with the "greedy pricks," Conner and Harris, in the play, and with those in society whom the characters represent.

In the climactic final act of *Love and Anger*, the "good guys" put Conner on trial "for his public stands on all the major issues of the day, on his contributions to making this city a place which is only satisfying to base-ball fans and real estate agents! For his endless manipulative use of the lowest common denominator and his lack of respect for the essential mysteries of life!" (68). Sarah sums up the charges as "Being ... Con-sciously ... Evil" (i.e., being a Nazi). Elsewhere, Petie identifies as the principal evil of the enemy the belief in the maxim "Might is right":

> ... what *upsets* me about his newspaper is that it promotes the theory of the survival of the fittest. The law of the jungle. And the problem with that is actually very simple to understand. This is not a jungle! It's a civilization! Get it? Get the difference? Well your buddy [Conner] doesn't, or for some very cynical reason he chooses not to. And that is why I *despise* him from the bottom of my soul. (*Love and Anger* 74)

As in *The Art of War*, Walker in *Love and Anger* first encourages neo-Aristotelian identification with the protagonist, then disrupts that identi-fication by switching heroes part way through the play. Power appears, at first, to be the hero of *The Art of War*; in the previous Power plays, after all, he assumed the roles which serve the heroic function in the backgrounded pop art forms which *Gossip* and *Filthy Rich* employ: the investigative reporter of crime melodramatic films, and the hardboiled private investigator of *film noir* respectively. He concludes each of these plays "heroically," turning in friends when honour and justice require, and nobly throwing away the "filthy" money, even though Walker qualifies the heroism a great deal more than is usually the case in the source forms. In *The Art of War*, he pursues Hackman not because he has been hired to do so, not for monetary gain, but as a matter of principle, or so, at least, he thinks, although as Johnston points out, there's a lot of ego involved. In *Love and Anger*, Petie appears, at first, to be the hero: he is the crusading lawyer parallel to Power as crusading reporter, a rebel with a cause who fights with style and humour: we cheer Petie's spirited attacks on the sys-tem. He even dies at the end (maybe) like a tragic hero.

In the cases of both men, their qualifications as anti-establishment heroes have been enhanced by movement in their lives away from suspect cen-tres of power towards the periphery, by their becoming more like the marginalized on whose behalf they think they fight. In Power's descent from career truth-seeker to common if pretentious drunk, as Johnston says, and in Petie's post-stroke epiphany and legal establishment apostasy, they themselves embrace marginalization, Petie more consciously and deliber-ately than Power: while Petie's marginalization as "disabled" (due to his stroke) is involuntary, his embracing that marginalization and putting it to use in the manner he does is voluntary. Middle-class, middle-aged, white, heterosexual males (the assumed audience for dramatic realism, the perpetrators of the "gaze") can, at the beginnings of both plays, have it both ways—Power and Petie are like us and are powerful like us, or have been. But, like each of us, Power and Petie each harbours a rebel within. We aren't really like all those other middle-class, middle-aged, white, heterosexual males because we really *do* sympathize with the marginalized, and fight for them, in our own ways, and would, if we were in the same position as Power or Petie, do so openly. *Love and Anger*, the later play and the one more sophisticated in its techniques for co-opting then ambushing the audience, goes a step further, and encourages us white guys to identify with Petie as hero by default: he is the only male in the play who's on the side of the angels, and besides the other potential candidates for hero are ineligible not only by virtue of their gender but on other counts as well: Gail is black, Eleanor is timid, and Sarah is crazy. That little "snick" you just heard was the door of Walker's trap closing behind you (assuming, just for the moment, that you are a middle-class, middle-aged, white, heterosexual male, like me).

Power and Petie lose, and do so in not particularly heroic ways: we are denied even the romanticism of the lost cause gamely defended against insurmountable odds. Furthermore, each in the course of the struggle begins to resemble his opponent: in rigidity, in the assumption of righteousness, and in the degree to which ego rather than principle becomes the issue (it is not accidental that Petie lost his wife to Harris, nor that Power feels his competence and manhood threatened by Hackman). Perhaps most significantly, or so Marilyn French would have it, in each case the hero comes to resemble the villain (the "worshiper of power") through his reliance on traditional and establishment means of exerting (patriarchal) power.

In a 1982 Walker play, *Science and Madness*, a character explicitly recognizes the dangers of speaking the language and using the methods of the "enemy." In a variation on the Frankenstein story, Lilliane, a poet, tries to compose a letter that will dissuade her scientist brother from pursuing experiments she believes are evil. Being a poet, she would write a poem, but "fear is clouding my mind." Furthermore, "your heart is clouded by your mind, so you wouldn't understand it anyway!" There is a struggle between her poetic and her assumed voice:

> ... I will try to reach you in the language of the heartless mind. The language of reason. Ben ... I have an intuition ... No I believe ... No I deduce ... that you are trying to destroy the mystery of life. [An act of

which Maxwell accuses Conner] I mean ... you ... think science is ... pure knowledge. But science is a raven on the shoulder of the anti-Christ! No! Stop it! Science is ... a device in a person's hand, like anything else. And your science will destroy the human soul, I mean the spirit of romance, and replace the mystery of our existence with rationality, and that in turn will create an even larger mystery which has no romance to it at all, only emptiness. And the need for more science. More knowledge. More ... emptiness! No!! He won't listen. I can't save him this way. This is the evil way. The rational way. I need another. I need to do it ... God's way. (17)

In both *The Art of War* and *Love and Anger*, the role of hero is assumed part way through the performance by another character, one whose marginalization is integral, by the standards of mainstream society, rather than voluntarily assumed, as is the case with Power and Maxwell, and whose marginalization at the beginning of each play seems to disqualify that character from serious consideration as protagonist hero. Jamie is marginalized by his class, his youth, and by his structural function as "sidekick," although it is he in the later scenes of the play who undertakes genuinely heroic actions while at the same time resisting the oversimplifications of rigid political classification: "Liberals, conservatives, communists, fascists. Who cares. Not me. I'm a working-class pragmatist. I believe in the politics of staying alive" (*The Art of War* 197). (Granted, Jamie says this while Hackman is threatening him with death.) Sarah, of course, is marginalized by her gender and by her schizophrenia, and it is she, primarily, who demonstrates subversive or "perverse" heroism by, to quote Richard Paul Knowles, opening "fissures ... in the legal and philosphical systems based on binary opposition and 'objectivity'" ("Dramaturgy of the Perverse" 227). To employ one of Knowles' important distinctions between "subversive" and "perverse" postmodernist plays, Power and Maxwell are oppositionally subversive, while Jamie and Sarah, by, among other things, assuming different subject positions in the course of each play, pervert the social and political modes of thought that oppress them, which goes much further than debating or playing a game with or engaging in a contest against those who hold views further down the continuum. As I suggest in "'I put it in terms that cover the spectrum'," it is through Sarah's eyes, not Petie's, that the world, and justice and law in particular, are re/visioned in the trial scene of *Love and Anger*. In the content of the play and in the way in which he fractures our conventional responses to his characters, as well as in the dramaturgical perversions of neo-Aristotelian form and thought to which Knowles refers, Walker seems to be agreeing with Tina Turner, "we don't need another hero"—oppositional heroism is no longer enough.

While Johnston may well be right in seeing in Power's progress through the Power trilogy a critique of liberal humanism, I think there's more to the process than that. There is also a progressive perversion of the response of identification and of the Western constructs of "hero," "heroism" and "heroic"—maybe "tragic vision" isn't a very healthy way of looking at the world, at least not here and now (and in that respect and in that conclusion, Walker's plays resemble Anne-Marie Macdonald's *Goodnight Desdemona [Good Morning Juliet]*). Again, *Love and Anger* goes further than the earlier play, shifting our identification and concomitant subject position not only from dominant (relatively) to peripheral/marginalized character, but from individual to collective. At the end of *Love and Anger*, after losing the trial in which he functioned as prosecutor, Petie suffers another stroke and dies; Sarah attempts to revive the dead hero with "positive energy," but the real hope for resurrection here is not in her attempt to revivify Petie (the play ends before we discover whether she succeeds) but in Sarah's awareness of her friendship with Gail, another marginalized woman. In the last moments of the play, then, the focus and heroic function shift from Sarah to the community of marginalized women which gives her access to a future that is enriched but not controlled by others, and in that context, the death of the old-fashioned hero and the possibility of his resurrection are less at issue, less the point, than they would be in an old-fashioned play. Because Sarah is a character who "makes it up as she goes along," regards the future as an "open space," is not unified, does not maintain a consistent subject position, does not have a through-line or a superobjective in the usual sense, self-discovery does not occur in the usual, neo-Aristotelian sense; as she rather than the original protagonist now moves the play forward, there is no "final or permanent recognition of an essential self" (Knowles, "Dramaturgy of the Perverse" 227). Furthermore, as is usually the case with a Walker play, there is no closure.

While many of the same things can be said of Jamie in *The Art of War*, there, I think, the transfer of "heroic" function is incomplete: Power remains alive, if wounded, and while the earlier play does project a future, any element of "possibility" in that future is tenuous at best; it seems more likely that the future struggles predicted by the conclusion of this play will result in future defeats for the "good guys." Jamie promises to do better the next time he ties someone up, but Power still has the last line, "I'm tired of losing. It's so … depressing" (184). The final image is that of the bad guys waving triumphantly from the top of the cliff. *Love and Anger*, on the other hand, while the bad guys still win the central debate, projects a future in which "possibility" is much stronger and much richer, much more open to the control of the marginalized, still without toppling over into sentimentality.

It's important to note that in these plays Walker moves the focus, the weight, our sympathy away from characters, heroes, who are like him toward characters who are not. True, Jamie is, like Walker, working-class in origin, but he is also younger than Walker, of quite a different generation. Johnston sees in Power a strong generational link between the character and the playwright, and a clear metaphor for the political history of that generation:

> Walker is writing about the loss of political innocence experienced by his contemporaries, the children of the baby boom, at the same time as their loss of youth. In the 1960s, this generation believed they were able to change the values of society by virtue of their own liberal ideals, a rather naive faith sustained by their youth and their disproportionately large numbers. As the decade ended, this faith was shattered by violence, the certain knowledge gained on the grounds of Kent State University that the forces of reaction would shoot to kill. In the 1970s this generation backed away from their social causes and turned inward, establishing an alternative lifestyle outside the system or a career within it, turning the Age of Aquarius to the Me Decade. These stages are recapitulated in Power's circumstances in *Gossip* and *Filthy Rich*: he is an equally sympathetic character as a career truth-seeker of the '60s or as an embittered dropout of the '70s. But when Power takes up the old crusading postures again in *The Art of War*, he looks ridiculous. ("George F. Walker: Liberal Idealism" 205)

With increasing frequency in his later plays as well as in *The Art of War*, it seems to me, Walker turns to generations younger than his, not for "answers" or for "hope," but for what he has called "possibility." Similarly, in *Love and Anger* it is not the character most like Walker (and the one who has the most Walkeresque lines) but the marginalized, schizophrenic woman, or, more accurately, the community of marginalized women, who take the play beyond containment into the possibilities, into the unenclosed future. With increasing frequency in his later plays, then, Walker also turns to a gender other than his own, not for "heroes" or even "heroines," for that would take us back to oppositional polarities, but for people, perhaps even role models, capable of holding new worldviews less dependent on deceptive simplicities, more open to polyphony and dialogism.

Generational conflict, generational politics, in a Walker play is perhaps at its sharpest and most intense in *Nothing Sacred*, "adapted" from Ivan

Turgenev's *Fathers and Sons* (1862). Bill Glassco, artistic director of CentreStage in 1988, originally asked Walker to adapt Chekhov's *Platonov*, but Walker, "after experimenting with several different approaches to the story, got bogged down" (Glassco 9). Walker proposed instead a stage adaptation of Turgenev's book, "a seminal Russian novel in its manifest distrust of reason and logic" (Lowe 139), and Lowe's description is in itself a possible explanation for much of Walker's abiding interest in this novel.

The events in *Fathers and Sons* are precipitated by two university students visiting their homes in the country; the slightly younger and certainly less worldly Arkady Nikolayevich Kirsanov is much influenced by the radical politics of his friend, Yevgeny Vassilyich Bazarov, described as a "nihilist" (and Turgenev's novel contains one of the first occurrences of the word). Arkady, nonetheless, still loves and admires his father, Nikolai Petrovich Kirsanov, and is thus torn between old and new values. The elder Kirsanov is somewhat sympathetic to the reformist tenor of the time, and now sees himself as the manager of his estate rather than the aristocratic landlord; still, his attempts to manage the land according to new, scientific methods of farming and organize the serfs as tenants are largely unsuccessful. Nikolai Kirsanov is a gradualist rather than a radical, like his son's friend, but nonetheless much more liberal than his older brother, Pavel, an unrepentant aristocrat and representative of the *ancien regime*.

As is often the case when a novel is "adapted" for the stage, Walker finds it necessary to simplify the action—many side journeys are deleted, so, for example, we do not see Bazarov visiting his own parents, and the focus is on events and debates transpiring in the Kirsanov household. In an exchange central to both novel and play, and here Walker stays very close to Turgenev, Pavel asks Bazarov "what you are planning to do after you have torn everything down." Bazarov replies:

> Nothing ... I'll do nothing. The tearing down is sufficient. In fact an entire life's work. The next generation can do the building. As for your earlier comments. Principles mean nothing to me. Neither as an idea nor a word. Other words. Aristocratism, liberalism, progress. Just empty words. Useless words. And foreign words to boot. I simply base my conduct on what is useful ... Oh a few years ago we "young people" were saying that our officials took bribes, that we had no roads, no trade, no impartial courts of justice— ... *Then* we realized that just to keep on talking about our social diseases was a waste of time, and merely led to a trivial doctrinaire attitude. We saw that our clever men, our so-called progressives and reformers never accomplished anything, that we were concerning ourselves with a lot of nonsense, discussing art, abstract creative work, parliamentarianism, the law and the devil knows

what, while all the while the real question was getting daily bread to eat, stopping the vulgar superstitions of our church, prevent our fledgling industries from coming to grief because of the crooks who run them, and realizing that the government's so-called emancipation of the serfs will do us no good because the serfs are so without pride that they spend most of their time robbing each other and drinking themselves into oblivion. (*Nothing Sacred* 33–34)

Much of the preceding speech, while in effect written by Turgenev, sounds like Walker himself (the early Walker, at any rate), and it's clear that Walker is strongly attracted to the nihilist, Bazarov. Remarks he has made in conversation suggest that there is a good deal of identification with Turgenev's character, and some, like Ronald Bryden, have suggested (in conversation) that Walker has sided too much with the sons and too little with the fathers. Nonetheless, Walker himself, while he still relates strongly to the nihilist, recognizes a connection to the other side of this particular generation gap.

It's funny that I'm writing about Bazarov at this time because I read *Fathers and Sons* when I was seventeen years old, and I related so strongly to that character then. That I should get around to writing about him when I'm forty, and still relate to him so strongly, is odd because I'm no longer just a son; I'm a father, too, and I have to come to grips with that, to understand that as well. (Preface, *Nothing Sacred* 8)

Walker's affinities and origins, then, cross two of the dialectical boundaries within the play, that of generation and that of class. There are two salient points about Walker's version of the Turgenev character with whom he apparently most strongly identifies. The first is that Walker's Bazarov, like William in *Criminals in Love* and Petie in *Love and Anger*, must move closer to the marginalized for whom he purports to speak and fight. At the beginning of the play, Bazarov cannot look or speak directly to the peasant whom he saves from a beating at the hands of a bailiff, but must speak to him instead through Arkady as intermediary, even though he claims, perhaps in jest, to love the hapless victim. When the peasant later fails in an attempt to rob the friends at gun point, Bazarov takes Gregor, an invention of Walker's, under his wing and attempts to educate him. Bazarov must move from a position of abstract principle to personal action in the course of the play, and must open himself to a relationship with a real individual among the hundred million oppressed before the principles acquire any social reality. Thus Walker's Bazarov, unlike Turgenev's, moves beyond nihilism, and the shift in Walker's character parallels in important respects the shift between Walker's early plays and his later ones.

The second important thing to say about Bazarov is that Walker kills him. True, Turgenev kills off his central character too. But Walker so drastically alters the circumstances of Bazarov's death from those we find in the novel—he dies accidentally in a duel rather than from a random, unrelated infection—and *Nothing Sacred* departs from *Fathers and Sons* in so many other respects that one can conclude that Walker didn't have to follow Turgenev in killing this character; he chose to do so. With Bazarov gone, the cause requires that someone else take over, as Jamie does from Power, as Sarah does from Petie, and the most likely candidate would seem to be Gregor. Again, the mobility of heroism, indeed, an interrogation of just what constitutes heroism, raises the possibility that dualistic opposition may no longer suffice. The antagonist is fairly easy to identify, as the nail polish, the affected mannerisms, aristocractic pretentiousness, and self-indulgent, destructive romanticism mark Pavel out as a character likely to be antipathetic not only to Bazarov but to Walker; even so, Walker does give the representative of the old order some sympathetic characteristics, and the other representative of the older generation, Kirsanov, Pavel's brother and Arkady's father, is definitely sympathetic, well-meaning if confused and possibly inept. Identifying the hero, the protagonist, is not quite so easy. Bazarov certainly thinks he's the protagonist in all the dramas in which he involves himself, but Walker, like Turgenev, undermines the "positive hero." Bazarov, like the aristocrats, is given to excessive simplification, and while Walker may see some merit to Bazarov's contention that it is his job to tear down, someone else's to decide what will take the place of the *ancien regime*, Bazarov's arrogance and aloofness, while somewhat reduced by the lessons of life he learns in the play, nonetheless contribute to his ultimate destruction. Is his death the end of the struggle? Walker's ending, like Turgenev's, suggests maybe not, although in Turgenev it is the moderate Arkady who seems the most likely to carry on, less rashly. In Walker, as in Turgenev, it is Arkady who experiences the greatest internal conflict, drawn by his youth and his friendship toward Bazarov, drawn by filial love and history to his father. Whose story is this? To whom does the future belong? Arkady, progressive but not an extremist? The politicially radical, proto-feminist *femme fatale*, Anna Odintsov? Gregor, who is not only from the peasantry, but "young" according to the list of characters? The baby, traditional receptacle of hopes for the future and as son of an aristocratic father and a peasant mother, representative of a humanity transcending class division? As is the case with most of Walker's plays written since 1982, there is no simple, single answer to either question.

While *Nothing Sacred* is clearly inspired by *Fathers and Sons*, the changes effected by Walker go far beyond "adaptation"—he once said to me that "nothing sacred" is a warning as well as a title—a fact that dismayed reviewers of some of the several American productions of the play, and that clearly upsets die hard lovers of the Russian novelist. Glassco says that in rehearsal, Walker frequently reminded the CentreStage cast "This is a Canadian comedy, not a Russian tragedy" (11). One of the biggest changes, it seemed to me when I first wrote about this play, is the way in which Walker gives the peasants a louder and more prominent voice, chiefly through the invention of two new characters, Gregor, Bazarov's protégé, and Sergei, Odintsov's huge and superstitious bodyguard.

> Differences between social classes, which in the novel were alluded to in the abstract or were the subject of conversation between aristocratic characters, are objectified for the stage through the addition of these peasant characters. As a result, Walker's play is even more clearly political than is the novel. In fact, it is the peasants, not Turgenev's eternal reconciliation and life without end, which are given the last words. They are the ones who are left to try to make sense of Bazarov's enigmatic and interrupted death-bed prophecy, Bazarov dying—in perhaps the most radical and significant departure from the novel—not from an accidental infection, but somewhat accidentally in the duel with a much dandified Pavel. (Johnson, "George F. Walker" 92–93)

Gust Olson calls me to task for saying that Walker brings Turgenev's "off-stage" peasants on stage, pointing out that through Dunyasha (a character Walker cuts), "the boys who fished with Bazarov, and the peasants in Bazarov's parents' district," the serfs are neither "off-stage" nor voiceless in Turgenev (40). Olson is correct of course, but I still stand by my contention that the presence of peasant characters is much more central and significant, the emphasis on the direct presentation of class conflict much greater in Walker than it is in Turgenev. Actually, Olson makes a similar point, approaching the question from a different direction, when he says "*Nothing Sacred* is George F. Walker's exploration of the personal relationship between the champion of society's victims and the victims themselves, with an emphasis on the political rather than the psychological aspect" (37). Olson's essay is a very good one, and I think he's right on the money when he points out that Walker's Bazarov differs from Turgenev's in that Walker's "has fun, learns, and grows. He is not a dark, inscrutable, prideful 'man of principle'" (38). It is this difference, Olson says, that makes it possible for the play to "[preach] the principle of dismantling and rebuilding. That is one of the biggest differences between the two and one of the greatest strengths of Walker's *Nothing Sacred*." And, it seems to me worth repeating, this is one of the biggest differences between early Walker and later Walker. It's also worth repeating, however, that Walker isn't about to romanticize "hope"—"possibility" is about as far as he can honestly go. I think both Olson and James Earl Baldwin see the ending of *Nothing Sacred* as both clearer and more "hopeful," Baldwin with disapproval, than it actually is.

Baldwin's M.A. dissertation, "The Space Between Voices: Dialogics in the late plays of George F. Walker," is among several recent critical examinations of Walker's work which use approaches associated with literary theory to illuminate the political implications of the plays as reflected in structure, rather than in content alone. Baldwin applies Bakhtin's concept of the dialogic to *Nothing Sacred*, *Love and Anger* and *Escape from Happiness*, and sees in the three plays progressive movement toward expanded use of the three elements of the dialogic: polyphony, the plurality of voices and consciousnesses neither contained nor unified by authorial intent; novelization, in which "voices are treated as being specific to certain contexts rather than transcontextual signifiers of meaning or character"; and unfinalizability, in which characters seek "to destroy the framework of other people's words about him that may finalize and deaden him." In dialogic, as opposed to monologic, structure, voices are placed between centripetal forces that contain meaning, and centrifugal forces which "subvert this tendency by challenging or 'opening up' meaning" (Baldwin 2).

Baldwin describes his initial readings of the plays in terms which recall the difficulties already discussed in "placing" either Walker's "style" as a playwright or his politics: "When reading the texts, I continually felt conflicted. I could not decide whether I was reading the characters as 'over the top' or 'real'; whether Walker was being political or apolitical; or whether the action of the play was resolved or unresolved" (8). Through examining the plays, and by applying to them the concepts of dialogism, however, he finds that they "constitute a dialogism that critiques monologic systems such as aristocracy, law, patriarchy, logocentrism, and other hierarchical forms of social organization."

In *Nothing Sacred*, for example, Baldwin says Walker sets up a dialectic at the outset of the play: "the thesis (a need to change Russia), the antithesis (a resistance to changing the old ways) and the projected synthesis (a new Russia)" (11). However, the dialectic breaks down when neither party in the debate, the "fathers" nor the "sons," is able to maintain a unified, essentialist position. Kirsanov, for example, is divided between the habitual outlook of his class and his desire for reform, his desire to treat former serfs as tenants, between his social position and his love for the young house-keeper and mother of his illegitimate child, Fenichka. Bazarov, says Baldwin, is in Walker's play "an inconsistent man, the only consistency he displays being his advocacy of change. In fact he is almost an anti-hero since the only thing that really matters to him is wide-sweeping change of almost any kind" (22). In the play, Baldwin says, Bazarov is finally killed by his own inconsistency: while he is opposed to the tradition of duelling, he is attracted by the novelty of the experience, accepts the challenge of the effete arch-aristocrat, Pavel, and is subsequently, accidentally killed. (Pavel wasn't aiming to hit Bazarov.)

At the end of the play, Bazarov dies telling the peasant characters in the play, whom he has asked to come into the room, "You are the ..." but expires before he is able to finish the sentence. The peasants argue whether he was about to say "the future" or "the dirt under his shoe." Gregor tries to explain "the future" to one of the others, who says, when asked if he will listen, "I'll try," the last line in the play. Anna Odintsov, the bomb-throwing revolutionary and object of Pavel's obsessive love, laughs, sadly at first, "then with a kind of light joyful recognition." Short blackout. Then Walker calls for "a dazzling white light which throws people into silhouette" (*Nothing Sacred* 99). Bazarov has left the stage. The others watch the two peasants walk off, Gregor gesturing, the other just listening. End of play. Baldwin refers to this ending as a "symbolic epilogue."

> Bazarov's climactic death, in the play, implies that his own desire for change is too rash, too extreme. In the drama no resolution (but the symbolic epilogue) is proferred. The death merely infers that different voices will continue to articulate different positions, but will do so in their own directions. While individuals may team up (Anna and Arkady, Kirsanov and Fenichka, Gregor and Sergei), there is no collective movement that would suggest a revolution. (23)

Despite all the movement toward the dialogic in the play proper, Baldwin sees in this sequence "the monologic control of the playwright [asserting] itself" as the "action moves towards a synthesizing abstraction." "Having the play begin in darkness and end in light re-establishes authorial intent and it appears that Walker is suggesting, somewhat monologically, that where there was once ignorance, now there is hope" (24).

I agree with Baldwin that the ending of the play hints at the optimistic, but agree with Walker that "possibility" is more accurately descriptive than "hope," and I'm not sure the ending is quite as monologic as Baldwin suggests it is. "I'll try," says Sergei in response to Gregor's asking whether he will listen to the message about the future that Bazarov is apparently passing on, but what we've seen of these two characters previously casts doubt on whether Gregor has in fact understood the message, or whether he's passing on a garbled version; "He's my future" Bazarov says of Gregor in an earlier scene, but Gregor is as yet a frail vessel. There's also some doubt as to Sergei's ability to either listen or understand. Maybe this transaction will work and eventually lead to a new society, a new Russia, but maybe it won't. The change in Odintsov's laugh suggests that the character sees cause for optimism, but it doesn't necessarily follow that we have to agree with her, nor that we welcome the society whose birth she apparently thinks she sees—this does seem to me one of those moments where Walker leaves the interpretation to us, and that once again closure has been thwarted. The other characters in the play, minus Bazarov, watch Gregor and Sergei leave, but this suggests to me that they are waiting to see what will happen, not that they know what will happen—the stage composition here is not necessarily celebratory. Finally, it seems to me that there's a strong possibility that the visual irony of the moment undercuts any authorial and monologic statement about ignorance yielding to light; the stage picture of the conclusion, peasants in earnest conversation exiting into the blinding light, is to me strongly reminiscent of those Soviet posters in the style of socialist realism, with agricultural and industrial workers, arms linked, staring resolutely towards the rising sun, the dawn of a new age of which they will be the masters. Certainly, a contemporary audience cannot help but bring to the moment, and to their reading of the moment, their knowledge of subsequent Russian and Soviet history, which further augments the irony, and openness, of the ending of the play. At this point, one is reminded of temporal and historical contextualization— a stage adaptation of *Fathers and Sons*, no matter how faithful (and Walker's is not), can't possibly mean in Canada in 1988 what it meant in Russia in 1862.

Some meanings, however, meanings associated with nationalism, imperialism and colonialism, do carry over. In addition to the generational politics of "fathers and sons," and the left wing/right wing politics of anarchism and reform versus the established order, *Nothing Sacred* concerns a third political dimension, that revolving around the states of "nationalism," "imperialism," "colonialism," and "post-colonialism," a dimension that appears in a number of Walker's plays. In *Nothing Sacred*, Pavel's aristocratic and establishment stance is to a significant degree based on fashions, attitudes, and values he has imported from elsewhere. This "colonial" allegiance to other centers of power has its parallel both in Turgenev and in history, for the Russian aristocracy after all preferred French, a language of "civilized" Western Europe, to the Russian of their Slavic and "barbaric" homeland. In an interview with Ray Conlogue, Walker said of his adaptation of Turgenev that he weights the story more "to a Russian aristocracy that doesn't know it's Russian; it thinks it's French" (Conlogue, Sep 1987 C1).

From its own colonial days, from the anglophile period extending up to World War II, to the post-war period in which American political and economic power was seen to be the most important threat to Canadian independence, Canada too, has often been thought to occupy colonial and post-colonial states of mind, and here in Canada, as in Turgenev's Russia, it is often suspected that the loyalties of the upper-classes lie elsewhere, with "Mother England" in the past, with the "New World Order" of transnational corporations and capital in the present. As Walker says, "There's definitely a parallel with ourselves. I worry about questions of identity. Why? Because I don't want my kids to have to go somewhere else" (Conlogue, Sep 1987 C1).

Thus a Canadian audience is likely to be reminded of its own position, part resentment of and part intimidation by non-Canadian centers of power, on hearing some of Pavel's sentiments regarding the superiority of English fashion and foreign values:

> At this moment in our history we could learn much from the English. The aristocracy in particular ... The English aristocracy never yields one iota of their rights. And for that reason they respect the rights of others. They demand the fulfilment of obligations due to them, and therefore they fulfill their own obligations to others. (*Nothing Sacred* 27)

What Pavel is looking for here is foreign, i.e. English, i.e. superior, affirmation of his own nostalgia for a feudalism in which everyone knew his place. Later in the play, Pavel attempts to instruct his servant, Piotr, in the ways of the Parisian salon:

> PAVEL: You are at my side. You are always at my side ... in the European fashion. Not so close! (*PIOTR backs up a step*) Good. Our relationship is formal but cordial. Your attitude is one of muted insouciance. Mine, of amused tolerance. I banter with the guests. The topic of conversation changes quickly and often, without warning. I follow easily. And you in your own way do the same. And even if you don't you appear to. You accomplish this with the eyebrows ... (*PAVEL demonstrates. PIOTR copies him badly*) I'll teach you later. In the European fashion I occasionally ask you to remark. For example, I am asked about my home. I say it is comfortable but simple and quaint in the style of my country. Isn't that right, Pierre? You say something appropriate.
>
> PIOTR: Home is where the sheep graze. But the heart ... stays?
>
> PAVEL: Too much. But the tone is right. (*Nothing Sacred* 57)

To Canadians, and to Walker, the rigid rules of order and of social hierarchy of the "Old World" are bad enough, but the "unspoken rules," the etiquette and codes of conduct which one is to heed while appearing never to have learned them or to which one never pays conscious attention, seem especially irksome and silly.

In Chapter Two, I pointed out that Walker uses his subversion of the Mountie stereotype, Corporal Lance, to include Canada and Canadians in his parable about the decline of Western civilization, what he once said "jungle movies were really all about" (Wallace & Zimmerman 218). Ken Gass describes *Bagdad Saloon* as "Canadian as moose meat" in its depiction of the post-colonial phenomenon of self-consciously trying to construct a new culture, but doing so relative to the culture of others: "What is tragic about Ahrun and pathetic about his associate, Aladdin, is that they can never achieve fame because they worry too much, because they stare at themselves through other people's eyes" (11).

The Walker play probably most concerned with the post-colonial state of mind, and with Canada's position as a peripheral player in twentieth-century global politics, is *Rumours of Our Death*, tantalizingly subtitled "a parable" and first produced as a punk-rock musical in 1980 at the Factory Theatre, where it became something of a cult fixture, running for months with many audience-members returning repeatedly in a sort of *Rocky Horror Picture Show* celebration. The play is a strange one, even by Walker standards. Filewod says of it that it is "the least conventional, the least 'textual' of [Walker's] plays—so much so that the published text can only provide a glimpse of the play as seen on stage" (xviii). This is clearly a case where not having seen a production of the play puts me at a distinct disadvantage.

Rumours of Our Death is set in an imaginary country, not, in some respects, unlike the Ruritania that provided the settings for the usually romantic, political parable films of the forties and fifties set in obscure, and imaginary, European principalities. References sometimes seem to point to Canada, the "peacable kingdom," and other times, not. The King, whom many suspect of being a machine because his mouth moves very little during his recurring speeches and because "you can look through his eyes and see little sparkling blue lights" (109), might be Trudeau, but maybe not. The Queen, Maria I, who has visions which get published in popular magazines, might be Margaret Trudeau. But maybe not. The foreign takeover which occurs throughout the play certainly echoes the Canadian situation and Canadian concerns. In the play, all civil rights are suddenly suspended, without explanation—is this a reference to the October crisis in Quebec in the early '70s, and the subsequent imposition of the War Measures Act by the Trudeau Liberals? There is an hilarious scene in which the terrorists apply for government grants to finance the revolution—the Canada Council, a major source of funding for the supposedly "subversive" alternative theatres? There is even some similarity between Walker himself and Raymond the novelist who is "well respected in other countries" but regarded as "silly" at home. *Rumours of Our Death* is a lot of fun in this *roman a clef* way.

Throughout the play, the King says, in speeches, that there is about to be a war, but the war never quite happens, in a way that resembles the Cold War, in 1980 still very much on. Throughout the play, there are rumours about a bomb that does selective damage: "I heard a rumour about a new bomb that only kills machines" (110). "I've heard rumours about a new bomb that only kills children under the age of twelve" (113). "... someone had invented a new bomb which killed nothing but which caused all the water in the rivers and lakes to evaporate" (119). "Now here are today's rumours. Someone has invented a bomb which kills nothing and evaporates no water but which causes people to disappear into another dimension. This is either a truly remarkable bomb or a truly remarkable rumour" (124). The neutron bomb, rumoured to kill people but leave the infrastructure of the attacked country intact, was very much in the news at the time.

Maria II, daughter of the King and Maria I, is kidnapped by terrorists, but then joins the movement and urges them on to even greater violence, reminiscent of Patty Hearst—Hearst was released from prison in 1979. The apathy with which the populace responds to these various rumours and reports of catastrophe seems characteristics of all who live in the age of "information overload." Walker has said of the play:

> Rumours ... came out of my reading too many newspapers. I'd gotten overloaded on that stuff—the neutron bomb and other obscene information. I mentioned all that bad stuff to friends, and they'd just shrug. Somehow we're overloaded, so that kind of appalling, obscene information gets only a shrug. (Milliken 45)

In his interviews with me, Walker said that actually, when he first began work on the piece, he did not have production in mind, but rather it was a "writing exercise." He was trying to write in the style of Gabriel Garcia Marquez, to capture the "lightness" with which Marquez' characters speak, and presumably, to create an imaginary place, like Marquez' Macondo, where realities collide and intersect, and where kinds of magic are possible. In the interview in *The Work*, which took place shortly after Walker directed the Factory production of *Rumours of Our Death*, he linked the frenzied comedy of the piece and his concept of humour as survival mechanism, as a means of preserving sanity:

I try to put evil at arm's length, somehow. And the letters—some lovely letters we got from people on *Rumours*—were just about that. Because it was a play about the neutron bomb, as much as about anything. And people would write us letters saying thank you for writing a play about the madness, the utter madness of the neutron bomb, and allowing us to put it at arms' length—all this political, and economic and potentially cataclysmic stuff. Thanks for helping us laugh, not giggle, but laugh. I guess that's what I'm trying to do. Do it for myself. It's not therapy. I'm not trying to purge. It's a survival mechanism. One of the ways of making the world less chaotic, I guess, is to show that it *is* chaotic. (Wallace & Zimmerman 220)

The play has had an extended life at colleges and universities, where it is a favourite of young directors: it gives them the opportunity to create an entire world on stage. I think it is popular on campuses also because it is political in flavour and politically provocative without being didactic or explicit; elsewhere in the 1982 interview, Walker speaks of using borrowed forms to "write, say, a political play which is not obviously a political play but which makes people think about politics" (Wallace & Zimmerman 219).

"The personal is political." The East End plays are political in that there is a larger outside world with which the depicted families must contend, but they are more centrally political in their attention to domestic politics. *Better Living* is about family politics and male–female power conflict; Tom is the "Father" as Nazi, and the play is Walker's most explicit critique of patriarchy; in Walker's words: "*Better Living* ... is political about the family; it's about patriarchy, and that's political. I mean that's the essential question of life on this planet: who's gonna run these things and must it always be that kind of pressurized male soul?" (Wallace, "Looking for the Light" 29). Again, who controls the future? Tom brings to this examination of family politics a political dimension beyond the domestic through the right-wing affiliations and values embodied in the survivalist mentality he uses to subjugate the family he deserted ten years previously. The survivalist movement is another contemporary social force dominated by white supremacists, the "big beefy white guys" of Sarah Downey's speech in *Love and Anger*: the fear of the outside world which Tom inculcates diminishes the significance of any fear his family may have of him, and by isolating his wife and daughters, he makes accepting his authority seem inevitable—the strategy is commonly employed by abusers. The domestic tyrant, and the militia mentality and paranoia he represents and exploits, are linked to global fascism through the name he gives to the new household regime, "consumer socialism" obviously echoing "National Socialism," and through his self-justification: he, like Mussolini, makes things work:

> Things are improving around here. Life is improving. Life is organized. Things are working again. The back burner on the stove is working. The light in the refrigerator is working. The broken faucet is working. The broken stairs are repaired. All of them. Front. Back. Basement. The shower doesn't leak. The toilet flushes the first time. The windows have been caulked. The doors all have locks. There are 500 cans of stewed tomatoes in the root cellar … And work on the basement sanctuary is right on schedule. Is there anything that shouldn't be trusted in any of that. Speak. (*Better Living* 323)

This is an ordered and systematic household in sharp contrast to the family as it was shaped before Tom's arrival, by Nora's improvisational, relatively democratic approach. As in the case of *Zastrozzi*, Tom's ability to take charge and impose order in a chaotic world is, in part, attractive to those frightened by the chaos, and all succumb to this seductiveness, Nora, Mary Ann, and eventually even the strong-willed Elizabeth. Gail, the daughter who has escaped the household and distanced herself from the seductiveness of power and authority, is the one who recovers the memory of the brutality at the core of this paternal authority and who finally confronts domestic fascism. The same daughter, Gail, is the first to forgive Tom and to try to re-establish a relationship with him when we next see the family in *Escape from Happiness*, but that reconciliation and restoration of balances seems to me to belong more to the area of sexual politics.

Walker subverts left-wing–right-wing, good–evil binary oppositions in the entirety of his work as well as in individual plays. Being a woman, or working-class in origin (like Babe Conner) doesn't necessarily make you a good guy, and nor does being left-wing, as the failures of Power and of Jack, the disillusioned priest and Nora's brother in *Better Living*, would seem to demonstrate. As extended and as virulent as Walker's attacks on the proponents of a totalitarian, right-wing future are, he doesn't align himself with all attacks on that future, and at times dissociates himself from some of his enemy's enemies, especially the social romantics. Whether one is a reactionary in Walker's world, whether the character is a "blocking" figure for the protagonists, for life force, for unenclosed future, for Walker's "possibility," depends not just on one's position on a right–left political continuum, but on a matrix of characteristics and affiliations, a matrix which involves political beliefs, class, gender, and age.

Wineva Dawson, in *Criminals in Love*, is an unsympathetic Walker character, despite her being a woman (and most women in the later Walker plays are sympathetic) and despite her politics. Clearly identified as left-wing, at least by herself, she pronounces her crime spree a "revolution," bombs a bank, and has conversations with an imaginary Che Guevara. But however much Wineva purports to be an enemy of the status quo, she is still one of the biggest threats to Junior and Gail, the central characters of the play, the working-class hero and heroine whose love we want to triumph. The integrity and sincerity of Wineva's revolutionary views are undercut by her mental instability (in contrast to Sarah Downey, whose disability contributes to her clear-sightedness), and by her class, far removed from the east-end and working-class origins of the youngsters whose interests she purports to represent. William, philosophical bum and friend of—and wise-man Jungian guide to—the young lovers, says of Wineva:

> This for sure is a child of the middle-class. Some grandmother's favourite. Daddy takes her shopping. A good university is selected. She skis. Occasionally reads a book. Then one day. Bingo. It strikes. The consciousness. Maybe she meets someone who instructs her. Teaches her the phrases. Maybe she sees a documentary about torture. A feeling comes. Not too deep. It goes only this far under the skin. But she's got a temper. The world makes her mad. Madder than Mother ever made her. This is a classic case here. And there's a plus. She's insane. Perhaps that feeling made her insane. Perhaps she got insane from too much skiing ... (*Criminals In Love* 1988, 99)

Wineva's revolution is fraudulent because it confuses personal grievance with social cause, and arises from personal pathology (the world makes her madder than Mother ever did), and this pathology traps her in a highly romantic binary opposition. Also, her class completely insulates her from the realities of deprivation and limited choice: she belongs to what William elsewhere identifies as "the skiing class, the long-outdoor-summer-class" (*Criminals In Love* 278), who "have forgotten anything they might have known about life" (*Criminals In Love* 266). Wineva herself betrays her misplaced and condescending social romanticism when she tells Junior and Gail, "I love you people. You're the people I do my work for. You're the working-class. The peasant class ... I've got some books for you to read. If you don't know how to read, I'll teach you" (*Criminals In Love* 271–272). The class sympathy to which she appeals is as self-centered and fake as are the claims of family loyalty and Mafia-like kisses with which she enforced obedience earlier in the play.

Finally Wineva is divorced from the realities and dreams of the young people whose lives she helps to ruin by her belonging to an older generation (Walker's, as it happens, and Power's), and by clinging to that generation's myth of youth and its personal social rebellion as the golden age: "If you'd been in Chicago in '68 you'd understand," to which Gail responds,

"I was only two years old in 1968" (*Criminals In Love* 1988, 100). In Walker's work, all recourse to the past, no matter how appealing myths of that past might be, are futile and often obstructive or destructive. Wineva's final attempt to play out the apocalyptic myth of confrontation with the police and of political martyrdom, taking the others with her of course, is her ultimate attempt to act out her political romanticism, and, like Walker's right-wing villains, to control the future by annihilating it. As in *Rumours of Our Death*, there seems to be a reference here to Patty Hearst, and in Wineva's shoot-out fantasy, an echo of the LAPD's show-down with the SLA (Simbionese Liberation Army), a television image embedded in the electronic text of the era. Walker almost always takes the side of the younger characters in his plays (with obvious exceptions, like Stevie Moore), even when that means casting as the villains characters his own age, or questioning the integrity of characters of his own generation.

Wineva is not the only self-proclaimed revolutionary in *Criminals in Love*, nor even the only character prone to romanticizing revolution. William's extraordinarily colourful past, revealed to Junior off-stage but never made clear to us, apparently includes incidents of youthful anti-establishment activity; confronted with Wineva's bomb, he is caught between the idea of the bomb and its actuality: "In my youth I too, well let us say I am aware of the injustice ... the institutional ... the need for a counter measure to—" (*Criminals In Love* 1988, 94). Finally William can't condone bombing the bank because unlike Wineva, he does feel for Junior and Gail, and does understand the impact the symbolic act will have in their real world. William is like Wineva in that apparently he comes from a middle- or upper-class background, certainly an intellectual one, but differs from her in that his attachment, while he does artistically and consciously romanticize and poeticize it, has had real material and emotional consequences. Like Power and Petie Maxwell, his right to speak for the marginalized has been enhanced by his voluntary move from the centre to the margin: "I have great sympathy for the truly sad cases of our world. The victims. I have felt so badly that I fell amongst them" (*Criminals In Love* 258). When William speaks for the oppressed ("I speak of the great underclass of our society, the doomed, the forgotten, the outcasts" [*Criminals In Love* 239]), he does so with the authority of experience and authenticity; like Sarah Downey, who thinks she is black, William's feelings for the oppressed are so strong and authentic that the identification becomes reality. I believe that Walker would like us to accept him as a serious spokesman for the dispossessed, possibly even, as I have argued elsewhere, for Walker himself ("'I put it in terms that cover the spectrum'"). In the context of the play, William can not only identify with the positions of the young lovers, but attributes to that love a value and a restorative power that almost equals the importance they themselves attach to it.

At the same time, it is important to note that in this case too, Walker qualifies and subverts. Like many other liberal crusaders in Walker plays, William is finally compelled to examine the morality of violence, and actually does take violent action: he really does try to kill Wineva and he really does try to kill Henry. But it is too late, and like Power and Petie Maxwell, William finally loses: if there is a possibility that the future may be liberated from the oppressors, left-wing or right-wing, the socio-economically marginalized young lovers, who have been trying to avoid heroism throughout the play, will have to take responsibility for doing so.

It is clear that Walker writes plays not just to entertain, that he writes in large part out of a passionately held conviction that there is more injustice in the world than there need be, and anger that this is so. He once described his experience of writing for the theatre as "like being a cross between a crazed missionary and a dancing bear" (Wagner, "Curse of the Shopping Class" E1). Presumably, then, he hopes that things will change, and that we, and especially our children, will be able to avoid some of the horrifying futures of which his work provides glimpses. If we are sufficiently frightened, or if our anxieties are reinforced by being connected with his and those of his characters and thus demonstrated to be more than personal and individual neuroses, and if we can be sufficiently dislocated so that we can see that that which is preposterous and outrageous on stage isn't really all that preposterous and outrageous at all, but has its parallels in absurdities in our own society, perhaps we can be moved to make changes. In these regards, then, Walker seems to want what Baz Kershaw calls a theatre of efficacy; Kershaw's "possibility" amplifies and makes efficacious Walker's "possibility":

> ... the possibility that the immediate and local effects of particular performances might—individually and collectively—contribute to changes of this kind [widespread and lasting modifications in culture and society as a whole]; that the micro-level of individual shows and the macro-level of the socio-political order might somehow productively interact. Hence, by efficacy I mean the potential that theatre may have to make the immediate effects of performance influence, however minutely, the general historical evolution of wider social and political realities. (1)

There are some parallels between Walker's work and that of the alternative theatre companies in Britain that Kershaw examines, and in both cases, the goal seems to be "cultural intervention," attempts to influence the collective future.

Walker doesn't confine his social critique to direct statement; he encourages reformation, radically reappraises society by making us like, admire and agree with the characters who want change, "to undermine the entire cultural bias of our culture" as Petie has it, then by shifting our identification even further from the centre out into the mindset of those most marginalized by North American consumer capitalism. But in Walker's work, nothing is simple or black and white. Politics, economics and social hierarchy do not, in themselves, explain all the bad things that happen to his protagonists. There is always bad luck.

In *Criminals in Love* the formality of William's speech and manners, his intellectualism, his fondness for debate, his middle European origins and accent, all suggest the "old Left"; these same qualities, and his missing last name, which begins with "K," bring Kafka to mind. William occupies a position alienated from the mainstream not only by political conviction but also by a visceral understanding of the absurdity of that which others accept as "natural" or "normal." William's opposition to the status quo is not limited to the material nor to doctrinaire socialist positions, but takes into account "bad luck," what he calls "the hanging shadow": "Other people would want to talk in terms of social patterns. Real things, like economic reform. Re-education. They'd dismiss the theory of the hanging shadow with a sneer" (*Criminals In Love* 113). He goes on to attribute these opinions to "the skiing class"; whether members of that class adopt rightwing views, like the "pull yourself up by the boot straps" school, or leftwing, like Wineva, they can't accept the reality of the "hanging shadow" because the privileges of their class usually protect them from its effects. In this respect, I think, William's views resemble those of his creator.

In *Escape from Happiness*, Mary Ann, like William, attributes her family's misfortune to a version of the "shadow":

> Is this family doomed. I used to ask myself that question all the time. Are we forever doomed. Forever on the brink of destruction. Under some enormous shadow. Has God constructed a gigantic, mean-spirited shadow full of noxious, evil vibrations emanating poisonous, soul-killing rays, that has one job and one job only. To hover over this family and keep us doomed. (342)

In *Criminal Genius*, Phillie, searching for the thing that he and the hapless Rolly and Stevie Moore have in common, rules out stupidity and settles on "Bad luck. I think bad lucks binds all the unfortunate of the earth … and makes us … unfortunate" (136). At the end of the play, sitting on a toilet and waiting to be shot by the gangsters whom he has almost accidentally angered, the alcoholic Phillie delivers an hilarious and heart-wrenching aria of self-pity and acknowledgment of bad luck:

Sure kill me for any old reason. Who am I. No one. Nothing. Fuck all. Phillie Fuck-all … You can kill him anytime you want. Kill him, fuck him, kill him fuck him, kill him. Who cares. He's just a pathetic asshole … Well isn't that a sad commentary on our society … I mean really. I blame society for producing that kind of callous indifference to fucked-up individuals … I really do … I really really do. *(Long pause.)* Looking back I never had a chance. My parents were idiots, my teachers were idiots, all my friends were idiots, everyone, every single person I ever met in my whole life was a mean-spirited, demented idiot. And I never complained. Never. Not once … Not until now. I've been a fucking saint! *(A noise from the bathroom.)* Oh look. Great. Someone's at the window in here. He's trying to climb in. No he changed his mind. He's happy just looking at me. Mean-looking prick is just staring at me. Oh great, he's got a gun. Yeah here he is, some other demented idiot in my life for no good reason and this one is going to shoot me. Well go ahead, asshole. Shoot me. Why not. Who cares. *(A gunshot.)* Great. *(Sound of a body falling.)* (156)

When I was directing a production of *Better Living* here at the University of Manitoba, I was on the phone with Walker a number of times—we were trying out a new version of the script, and there were things I wanted to check out. I was confused by a stage direction that occurs when Gail, having remembered the severe beatings inflicted on her by Tom when she was a child, confronts her father, and eventually pulls a revolver out of her shoulder bag. Her Uncle Jack apparently intends to kill Tom, and "Staring at TOM he reaches out his hand to GAIL for the gun. She looks at him oddly. Hands him the sandwich [she is eating at the time]" (*Better Living* 343). I wanted to know why this happens, more particularly "What Does It Mean?" Walker's reply was that it doesn't mean anything in particular, but that "wonky bits" are part of life, that in life absolutely absurd things do happen at very serious moments, which more conventional art would depict very seriously and dramatically. Of course. Expecting the moment to "make sense" in a particular (conventionalized) way, wanting logic and a logical explanation, I was missing the obvious. Gail thinks Jack wants the sandwich and reacts accordingly. People (mis)communicate in this fashion all the time, but this aspect of "reality," this wonkiness, is not allowed for in the conventions of the well-made, realistic play, nor in Stanislavsky. There is, then, a larger meaning in such moments, and that meaning is that life is larger, more complex, less predictable, more inclusive, sloppier, than we've been led to believe it is, and especially more so than Western art has led us to believe it is. One of the simplifications that have misled us is that which holds that the comic and the serious can easily be detached, each from the other, or even that they are mutually exclusive. "Wonky bits" pervade Walker's work as a constant reminder that this, in his opinion, is not so, from small-scale moments, like Gail's handing Jack the half-eaten sandwich to the introduction of "bad luck" into situations which rational thought would like to investigate in terms of measurable, socioeconomic factors, as in *Criminals in Love*, *Criminal Genius* and *Problem Child*.

Walker catches us unaware, slips through our defences to convince us that that which we take to be "normal," "the way things are," is really absurd, effecting a kind of "alienation," which, like Brecht's, "makes the familiar strange," thus affecting how we receive "Walkerland" on stage, and also setting us at an objective distance from the social world the plays depict and to which they respond. Walker's politics are found not just in what the characters say, nor even in the events narrated, but in the form and anti-forms of the plays themselves, the "Walker twists" and "wonky bits" that fracture the modes of perception and thought which our culture has made habitual in us, hence unquestioned until someone like Walker comes along.

Richard Paul Knowles' "The Dramaturgy of the Perverse," referred to earlier in this chapter, is the best account I've encountered of "structure as politics" in Walker's work, of ways in which Walker's altering of perception has political implications with regard to current structures of society, current structures of "knowing." In the essay Knowles discusses plays by Walker, Margaret Hollingsworth, Judith Thompson, and Beverley Simons as examples of a Canadian theatrical postmodernism based on the "perverse." Knowles starts from one of the O.E.D. definitions of the verb "pervert": "to misapply, misconstrue, wrest the purport of." Theatre of the perverse, argues Knowles, goes further than the more familiar postmodern concept of subversion (like the parodic satire Smith and Hutcheon discuss) in that it is not "simply arranged in an oppositional (and therefore affirming) relationship to the dominant" Aristotelian, lineal, cause and effect structure based on reversal and recognition.

> Perversion is dialogic in Bakhtin's sense, more variously disruptive and less simply reactive than the concept of subversion suggests ... As a structural device, the perverse revisions the romantic and post-romantic conceptions of a unified subject and of unified character and action. It focuses rather on the constructed nature of identity; it displaces the symbolic authority of such structural principles as reversal and recognition and, while acknowledging and employing engagement with character, plot, and dramatic ritual, it disrupts the complacent and voyeuristic satisfactions and containments provided by dramatic catharsis. ("Dramaturgy of the Perverse" 226)

In Walker's plays, Knowles says, "the Walker twist" (Walker's term) replaces reversal

> so that recognition is at the very least a more complex and less comfortable concept than in more traditionally linear structures; and … the satisfaction of closure is rarely provided. Indeed, if Walker follows any tradition it is that of dramaturgical perversity as established by Christopher Marlowe, that most 'wayward, petulant, crossgrained' and unsettling of the Elizabethans. ("Dramaturgy of the Perverse" 227)

Here Knowles quotes another O.E.D. definition of "perverse." Knowles then examines the manner in which *Love and Anger* perverts the conventions of the trial it depicts in its final scene:

> The trial is inconclusive, there is no reversal in the play's action, and, in spite of the central character Petie Maxwell's best intentions, no revolution in the play's plot. But there *are* fissures opened in the legal and philosophical systems based on binary opposition and "objectivity"; there is the beginning of a new community among the play's variously marginalized characters; and there is a "twist" to the proceedings that is characteristic of Walker and of the dramaturgy of the perverse, which as I see it typically *foregrounds* the expectations of its audience in order to disappoint, disrupt, or fracture them. There is, too, an implied rejection of the concept of "recognition" as the self-discovery of a unified subject, especially in the characterization of the schizophrenic Sarah, who emerges as the unlikely hero of the play. "Character" in this play comes to mean something closer to a series of temporarily adopted subject positions that are continually subject to reversal but allow for no final or permanent recognition of an essential self. (227)

I think I agree, and that I was trying to get at something similar when I was discussing the manner in which Walker works against ("disappoints, disrupts, or fractures") audience expectation through his use ("perversion") of the conventions of melodrama and melodramatic cinema in *Zastrozzi*. He doesn't simply argue against or satirize (and thus reflect in opposition) the conventions and values of melodrama, or even remain content with the implicitly broader critique of parodic satire, but uses the conventions for purposes other than those for which they were intended ("wrest[ing] the purport of") and thus sets the conventions and values at cross-purposes to the point where they self-destruct, as in, for example, his use not of two moral poles ("binary opposition"), the white hats and black hats of melodrama, but three. At least.

The night before I wrote these few preceding paragraphs, I was down at the Prairie Theatre Exchange watching University of Manitoba theatre students in a PTE stage-fighting workshop presenting some year-end projects. One group worked on part of the final scene of *Zastrozzi*, Bernardo's killing of Julia, and the subsequent fight between Bernardo and Zastrozzi. I was struck once again by just how fractured an audience's expectations are through that sequence, and consequently how "fractured" the audible and visible response is. This stuff is truly hilarious, but at the same time, truly horrifying, especially if the violence is extreme and well executed. Either one is torn violently back and forth between laughing and wincing, or one contorts body and mind together by doing both at once. Thus critics like Frank Rich who take moral offence at lines like Bernardo's "I'm going to rape and murder you. Not necessarily in that order" miss the point (Qtd. in Conolly 216). The binary opposition of good and evil is irrelevant at points like these in Walker's plays. Rather such moments are "Walkeresque," "perverse" (and here the meanings of the word as Knowles uses it, and as it is commonly used, with regard to sex, come very close together).

I think that what happens during the eighties, as Walker moves away from the exotic locales and backgrounded pop art forms of the first (roughly) dozen plays and into the world of the East End plays, is that the component of parodic satire goes down, while the proportion of the "perverse" as Knowles defines and explains it, goes up. At the same time, I think the "perverse" was always present in Walker's work, and that parodic satire is still present, to some degree, in some recent work. In the East End and later plays, though, we don't need reference points and aren't invited to experience memories of earlier works and pop art genres as we were in the seventies, as I argued earlier (with the possible exception of *Nothing Sacred*). We are thus denied the illusion of satisfied expectations that is sometimes generated by the earlier plays: we are no longer comforted by being able to share the knowing smile (related to but not quite the same thing as condescension) in response to the naivety of the wonderful old pop art forms, however perverted by Walker in the play we are watching. There is no longer any nostalgia to fall back on; the perverse is more immediate, confusing, unsettling, threatening (and consequently and paradoxically, funnier). As Knowles says in one of his footnotes: "Hutcheon's 'parody' is related to what I am calling 'perversion': however I am focusing on intertexts that operate on the level of structure and semiotics without conjuring any conscious reflections of specific texts" ("Dramaturgy of the Perverse" 234). The conventions and values perverted in the later Walker plays are closer to us than are the conventions and values of melodrama or B-movies. They are more internal, more embedded, more likely to be taken by us not as attributes of a discrete and by-gone art form, but as the natural order of things, the "way things are." In short, Walker is perverting cultural constructs basic and central to Western thought and culture, the larger construct at which he used to take pot shots through targetting specific cultural artifacts. He's cut out the middle-man.

Or, as Ed Nyman says, "perversity is a pro-active strategy designed not just to subvert, but to take control of a system of representation. A perversion goes beyond the boundaries of what is recognisable within the traditional ways of seeing" (57).

Or, as Walker says, "life is wonky." Or, "the traditional ways of seeing" were never particularly relevant or helpful anyway. Walker, who has never been very interested in or impressed by established forms and their embedded perspectives, "invisible editing," sees life in a way that many would describe as "perverse."

In content, Walker's perversity, obviously, is anti-authoritarian. To the question, "Who controls the future?", he responds, "Not us," and adds, "That's not the way it should be." The powerful control the future, and like the old Greek gods, the powerful are not powerful because they are good, but because they are strong. The future they are busy constructing is a future designed to serve their ends. So far there's nothing particularly surprising in Walker's analysis of power, class, and the "politics of life." What is surprising is the degree to which he includes the element of "bad luck," and the attention he gives to ways in which the flaws of the "good guys" play into the hands of the "bad guys." Furthermore, his plays not only discuss the dangers of succumbing to established power, the power of the establishment, but in the way they are written and put on the stage, themselves attempt to deconstruct, subvert, and pervert established ways of thinking and of looking at the world.

B-movies, parodic satire, Bakhtinian dialogics, a dramaturgy of perversity, all this and more. "We're not in Kansas [Toronto] any more, Toto." And yet, in a strange way, we are, and for all the weirdness (relative to Neil Simon or most television); the large-scale wonkiness in structure, like Knowles' "dramaturgy of perversity"; and the introduction of "bad luck" into situations which rational thought would like to investigate in terms of measurable, socioeconomic factors, as in *Criminals in Love,* this place is not only familiar, but extremely familiar. I've begun to think of this place, state of mind, way of looking at things as "Walkerland," borrowing from Ross Woodman's "Reaneyland." The "rules" which we have been trained to believe govern our lives are suspended and/or perverted; we get off the elevator and escape from the building onto the roof where we feel simultaneously liberated and terrified.

Chapter Four
Cops, Robbers, and the Carnivalesque

> Maybe I'm supposed to repent … or something … Offer my apology or
> a reason … I've been living in hell so I know I should be trying to get
> out … Get out of hell … Become a good guy again. Stop hanging out
> with low-lifes. Stop fucking whores. Maybe get some counselling. Shit
> like that. But … I don't know … The thing is, Pam. It's shit. The world
> is shit. It truly is … And somehow I feel better when I'm not pretend-
> ing it isn't. When I'm with you and Emma and I'm pretending every-
> thing is more or less fine … it's like bullshit in the extreme. (Donny in
> *Adult Entertainment* 70)

A cop trying to explain to his estranged wife why he behaves like the crooks
he's hired and sworn to pursue. Good guys who act like bad guys, like
Donny and Max in *Adult Entertainment*, Donny and Henry in *The End of
Civilization*, Power, Maxwell, and maybe Bazarov. Bad guys who think
they're good guys, like Conner and Harris in *Love and Anger*, Wineva in
Criminals in Love, Tom in *Better Living*. Bad guys who fear they may harbour a good guy within, like Zastrozzi. Good guys who fear they may
harbour a bad guy within, like Jack in *Better Living*. Little crooks, like Rolly
Moore in *Beautiful City*, who almost look like good guys relative to big
crooks, like Mary Raft in the same play. A good-cop–bad-cop team, Dian
Black and Mike Dixon in *Escape from Happiness*, who turn out to be a
good-cop–bad-cop duo all right, but in the order opposite to that we initially believed. Mothers who behave like whores, and vice versa. If the
"world is shit," as it often seems to be in Walker plays, or if it contains a
very high shit quotient, who's the cop and who's the robber? According to
whose rules and definitions? Who gave the rule-makers the authority to
make the rules? How do the good guys, or the putative good guys, like
Power, Maxwell, or Donny, avoid getting swallowed by the shit? Right from
the earliest plays, with the confusion of white hats and black hats, this has
been one of the central questions in Walker's work, and leads to a fasci-
natingly complex and fluid depiction of order and chaos, arising from

Walker's ambivalence towards authority and order, and fascination with that ambivalence and the issues it raises.

Jerry Wasserman notes the prevalence of the "justicer" figure in early Walker plays, the figure, good guy or bad, who tries to impose a kind of order on the chaos that threatens to overwhelm both him and the world. Thus Zastrozzi is a justicer of the Jacobean, revenge tragedy sort (much like Bosola in Webster's *The Duchess of Malfi*), a morally ambiguous enforcer of order for whose unwilling accomplices the play recruits the audience members. Power in *Gossip* and *Filthy Rich*, Inspector Clair in *Theatre of the Film Noir* (the three plays Wasserman is reviewing) are "archetypal cinematic justicers": "Here we are at the thematic centre of Walker's recent work. Chaos and meaninglessness—but chaos in particular rule the day. The hero is he who, because he cannot forget, must restore order, impose justice or, if necessary, invent meaning" (Wasserman 99).

Stephen Haff points out the irony to which this drive to impose order on chaos leads: the justicers, whether good guys or bad guys, are so obsessive in their pursuit of their kind of order that ultimately they contribute to the chaos against which they strive:

> … speech is the arena where the characters fight the very basic human battle against arbitrariness, against accident and chaos. Their self-conscious cleverness, awareness of their own form, is part of the definition, and hence control, which the speakers crave. This craving, the urgency for definition and passion for exactitude, is Walker's signature. Language is more than an instrument of definition and self-definition: the characters articulate to survive.
>
> Walker's characters, as independent entities or absolutes who do not so much interact as collide, rule out the possibility of harmony, and in struggling to shield themselves against disorder, contribute to it, create it anew. ("Slashing the Pleasantly Vague" 63)

Looked at from a thematic approach, a quick survey of Walker's plays reveals some striking facts: of the twenty-six published plays, nineteen are explicitly concerned with issues of making, enforcing, and breaking the law; fifteen of these include characters specifically identified as policemen, policewomen, criminals, or lawyers, often two of the three groups, sometimes all three. From *Beyond Mozambique* on, and Corporal Lance, the bumbling ex-Mountie who kills out of pity, most Walker plays concern themselves with legal issues, investigation, attempts to identify the bad guys within a framework of law, bringings to justice of one sort or another.

Twice in the earlier plays, Walker uses the *film noir* convention of the investigator-narrator framing the story of a criminal investigation, Inspector Cook in *Ramona and the White Slaves*, Inspector Clair in *Theatre of the Film Noir*. Cook fails, Clair succeeds, if not in clarifying events and solving the murder he set out to investigate, then in re-establishing order in a very revealing way. In *film noir*, the investigator is in continual danger of being absorbed by the sordid world he inhabits, and one of the central conflicts of such films is the central character's struggle against giving up, a test of his very individualistic integrity, often expressed as a tough and hard-bitten cynicism. Cook is closely identified throughout the play with the decadence he is purportedly investigating, doubled with the pimp, Mr. Sebastian. In a crucial scene, Cook trades costumes and roles with Ramona, much to the confusion of first production audiences and critics, and even to some reservations on the part of Ken Gass: "Personally, I find this scene glib and overextended, detracting from the rhythm of a cascading series of horrific revelations" (14). Smith points out that this role exchange follows a series of relatively minor and temporary role exchanges, and seems to be another step in Walker's experimentation with role transformation, which Smith says he began with *Sacktown Rag* and *Bagdad Saloon* (69). Cook, like Lance in *Beyond Mozambique*, is progressively "infected" by the chaos he attempts to set in order, to the point where he becomes a version of that which he investigates. Recent science has it that that which is observed is affected by the very act of observation; according to Walker (and to a good deal of anecdotal evidence) it would seem that the process operates in reverse as well, and that the observer can well be affected by that which he observes. This issue of "infection," law enforcers corrupted by lawlessness, overwhelmed by the "shit of the world," arises in many of Walker's subsequent plays, perhaps most strikingly in *Adult Entertainment*.

As Clair investigates the murder of Bernard's lover, Jean, in *Theatre of the Film Noir*, and becomes progressively aware of just what an outsider Bernard is, how dangerous both his "perversions" and fears are to the ordered society Clair wishes to restore, Clair also becomes aware of the danger of "infection" and, as Ed Nyman suggests in his article, "Out With the Queers: Moral triage in George F. Walker's *Theatre of the Film Noir*," kills Bernard because doing so is necessary to the preservation of a patriarchal order which Clair represents.

> I have decided that the murder I was investigating was just something that happened because of the war. Truth is, I don't know if Bernard killed Jean. Or if Lilliane killed him to protect her lover. Or if the Communists killed him because he was stupid … I have decided that none of that matters … because Bernard had to die. He was just a part of what we have become. But it was the saddest most unpredictable part. (*Theatre of the Film Noir* 159)

We've already seen, in some ways, how Power in the Power plays, serving as the investigator figure, the "justicer," becomes more and more damaged as his investigation reveals that the "world is shit" and, according to Johnston's reading of the plays, becomes progressively like the villains. His incorruptibility, which he hugs to himself with great determination, becomes his obsession, his vice.

Stackhouse, the detective in *Filthy Rich*, is infected from two directions. Even though he's apparently an honest, straight-arrow cop, he becomes involved in the scandal involving the disappearance of a mayoralty candidate, blackmail, and the murder of Power's friend, Whittaker, by acting unofficially, on the quiet, "on special assignment," to try to stop the bad guys before they kill more of the slightly less bad guys in order to hush up the whole business, stop it before prosecution and public disclosure are necessary. "Crooks protecting crooks protecting crooks. We live in troubled times" (*Filthy Rich* 104). He's caught up, he says, in

> ... a story about a bad smell. About a bunch of rich powerful people pushing and screwing each other and everyone else to get a whole lot more money and power that they don't really need in the first place. It's about the way the cities in this country were first formed. Through pay-offs and favours and double-plays and connections between a select handful who never let go and who can't be gotten rid of because they were in there from day one. (*Filthy Rich* 103)

From the other direction, Stackhouse is infected because he identifies himself completely with the abstraction he serves, the law, and people who think they are the law often think they're above the law. "I'm the law," he tells Power. "Oh. You mean you're a policeman." "That's what I said." "No. You said 'I'm the law.' Which is sort of like saying I'm the truth. Or I'm wisdom. Or I'm the god of the Bountiful Harvest" (*Filthy Rich* 84). Often in Walker, an institutional abstraction, like law, often law, but sometimes science, as in *Beyond Mozambique* and *Science and Madness*, or "the nation," as in *Theatre of the Film Noir* and *Rumours of Our Death*, or a "prosperous society" in *Love and Anger*, or "civilized society," as in *Problem Child*, is used by an individual in order to protect himself or herself from individual, human responsibility for his or her actions. As a general rule, people who claim to speak for a larger group of people, or worse, for a set of ideas, are dangerous in Walker's world. Often such people are policemen.

Tom, the father and domestic tyrant in *Better Living*, is, significantly, an ex-policeman. His work has contributed to who he is now; in the revised version of the play, published in *Shared Anxiety* (1994), he says: "I used to be messed up. I know that. It was my work. I saw a lot of anxious people.

A lot of scum too. Messed me up after awhile" (318). Like Nora, he has a horrifying vision of the future, sees himself as the "soldier of the total shit future" in which society, his family, needs a soldier, a policeman, prepared to kill. Chaos has infected him:

> I've got a mission. Why won't you trust my mission. I've seen the flames of destruction. Battles raging. Societies crumble. Men women children dying in the street. Everything I tell these people is the truth. I saw the future. It changed me. I had to come back. To help these people get ready. (*Better Living* 1988, 208)

He has come to believe that through his experience he has learned what's best for his family, better than they know it themselves. The infection is now so complete that the remedy is as bad as if not worse than the disease, as Jack, Tom's brother-in-law, sees when he says:

> ... it seems there's this army of strange men wandering around out there. Men who let the pressure blow their minds out of their skulls. Heart breakers. Baby beaters. Family killers. (*Better Living* 1988, 212)

Mary Ann, who fills the family role of worrier, sees the sort of authority and danger Tom has become, the means of regulation more threatening than the chaos it purportedly regulates:

> Until we're murdered in our sleep. Until we accidentally break a rule, fail to meet our work quota, eat more than our share of canned pears. Then we'll see. Punishment will come. Death will come. The tyrant will come. The commissar. The dictator. The chairman. In our sleep. Slit our throats ... The policeman, the principal, the crossing-guard, the première, the president, the executive director, the person with the key, the one who signs the cheques, gives you an allowance, gives you advice, helps you grow up, makes you understand, makes you better, makes you over, makes you from scratch, the maker—(*Better Living* 1988, 214)

To which, in the version published in *The East End Plays* (1988), Elizabeth ironically adds, "The giver of life, the creator—" God is the ultimate policeman.

The family from *Better Living* reappears in *Escape from Happiness*, and the complex and scary world with which they have to contend in the sequel includes both cops and robbers; the groups are sometimes hard to tell apart. The cops who arrive to investigate the beating of Junior present the good-cop–bad-cop pairing familiar from so many crime movies. Mike Dixon, an old time tough cop and an old friend of Tom's from their days on the fraud squad together, seems to be the bad cop. He's taciturn most of the time, blunt, abrasive, and bullying when he does speak. He's bigoted, and automatically assumes that the perps were "black guys" or "Oriental guys." Assumes that Nora's information is suspect because she was once hospitalized for psychiatric problems. (Tom had her committed in the action antecedent to *Better Living*.) He jumps to the conclusion that Junior was involved in organized crime, "drug-related activities," "prostitution-related activities, pornography-related activities, money-laundering-activities," and was beaten up as a payback for a deal that went wrong. He thinks his partner, Dian Black, was too friendly in her interrogation of Nora, and says of Nora, whom we like, "She's a fuckin' flake. They'll be putting a net around her any day. When she talks, my skin crawls. I get a headache" (*Escape from Happiness* 366).

Dian, on the other hand, is young, a female in a predominantly male occupation, apparently up to date and professional, educated. She seems to be sympathetic to Nora, and sensitive to her distress. She says Mike reminds her of her father, and smartly puts him in his place. When the police find drugs stored in the basement, and arrest Nora, it is Dian who insists that Mike not handcuff her. Obviously a good cop. A nice cop.

Wrong. It turns out that Dian arranged to have the drugs planted in the basement, so she'd have an excuse to arrest Nora, so she could intimidate and blackmail Nora's oldest daughter, Elizabeth, a lawyer waging a campaign to expose corruption and brutality in the police force. When her guilt is revealed, Dian explains her actions to Elizabeth:

> You were planning to do serious damage to something to which I owe a high degree of loyalty. You understand loyalty. Think of the police force as my family and you'll understand better. (*Escape from Happiness* 438)

Elizabeth points out that her loyalty is to human beings, whereas Dian's is to an institution. In this play, to our surprise, Dian is the Walker villain who has lost her soul, and lost her ability to function as a human being to an institutional abstraction.

Mike, on the other hand, while he originally intended to participate in what he suspected was a cover up of police wrongdoing, decides to help Elizabeth in exposing Dian's plot, not to try to pervert and stand outside the law.

> MIKE: … I came here to try and cover up your crazy scheme. But now what I want is for you to leave these people alone. Let Elizabeth make all the fuss she wants. And let the police force deal with her any way, any goddamn legal way it can.
>
> DIAN: Damn you! Damn you guys. Cut me some slack here. I'm the kind of cop this city needs now. I'm creative. I can arrange solutions to difficult problems in non-linear ways. I am the future! You big dumb jerk. And I'm tough. I'm tough, too. I'm that rarest of human

beings. A caring, sensitive, intelligent adult who also happens to love law and order! (*Escape from Happiness* 440)

This time we agree with Mike when he calls crazy talk crazy talk. Mike goes by hunches, like an old fashioned, uneducated policeman. Sometimes he's wrong, but sometimes, as in his suspicions of Dian, he's right. He functions not as an instrument of an abstraction but as a human being—his coming to the aid of the family is motivated in part by his old friendship with Tom. He has integrity. He doesn't put himself above the law (except when he beats up crooks). We don't agree with his prejudices. We probably still don't like him very much. But he's closer to being the good cop than Dian is. In Walker's world, it's not easy to tell the white hats from the black hats, and that's the point.

The crooks whom Dian hires to plant the drugs, and who are responsible for beating up Junior, are a father and son team, Rolly and Stevie Moore. Rolly and Stevie also appear in an earlier Walker play, *Beautiful City* (1987) and—their ineptitude and stupidity in full and glorious flight—in one of the plays of the Suburban Motel suite, *Criminal Genius* (1997). Rolly and Stevie are small time crooks, and Rolly in particular seems to be more a person who has chosen devious and shady ways of surviving than an evil person. The Moores do have feelings and they do have scruples. And their ineptitude prevents us from taking them too, too seriously as bad guys. At the end of scene two in *Beautiful City*, after the cops have left, Rolly and Stevie, who have been hiding nearby, hold Nora and two of her three daughters, Elizabeth and Mary Ann, at gun-point. They say they want their "thing" and they're ready to kill. But then the youngest daughter, Gail, enters carrying her infant daughter. A long pause. Gail sees the gunmen.

GAIL: Great. Just great.
STEVIE: Oh, man. Dad, she's got a baby.
ROLLY: I can see that.
STEVIE: I can't do bad things to a baby. No way.
ROLLY: Yeah. Okay. No one ever asked you to hurt a baby. Stay calm. Everyone! Stay calm.
GAIL: I know you guys. You're the guys who put my husband in the hospital.
NORA: Gail. We don't have any opinion about the identity of these two men. These two men could leave now, and it would be like they were never here.
ROLLY: Except we need something you've got. And the thing is—the thing is—
STEVIE: I can't, Dad. Not in front of a baby. We might have to use maximum force here. And I don't know. I just don't know.

ROLLY: Hey, stay relaxed. You know. Calm down. Okay. Okay. This is
   the thing … We're … leaving. (*Beautiful City* 379–380)

They flee, empty handed.

Later in the play, after Nora and Elizabeth kidnap Rolly in an attempt
to get to the bottom of just what is going on, Nora has a little chat with
Rolly, and acknowledges that there may be reasons behind his criminal
activity, and sets out to help him:

> Don't let yourself believe I'm saying these things about someone else.
> Someone neither of us knows. For example. If I say you feel worthless
> and afraid, you can't say to yourself that's not true. And then not listen
> when I suggest all the reasons you feel worthless and afraid. Because if
> you do, you won't understand when I get to the part when I talk about
> all the ways you can maybe stop feeling worthless and afraid. (*Beautiful
> City* 408)

Rolly may, in part, be a criminal because he feels worthless and afraid, but
Rolly can, according to Nora, do something about it.

We might expect from the nature of power politics as they appear in
Walker's plays, and as those dynamics of power and class are discussed in
Chapter Three, that criminal behaviour would be explained by social
oppression. Sometimes, in fact, criminal behaviour is the result of social
oppression. Gail's off-stage husband in *Love and Anger* is coerced into
committing a crime by people much more powerful than he is. Gregor in
Nothing Sacred attempts highway robbery, extremely ineptly, because he is
poor and desperate. One of the reasons that Wineva is able to coerce Junior into a life of crime in *Criminals in Love* is that Junior is sociopolitically
vulnerable. But just as "bad luck" intrudes in Walker's consideration of
class structure, and makes it more than simple politics, so there is something else at work which distinguishes crooks who are criminals out of
desperation from crooks who are something worse, what Walker usually
calls "scum," even though both may be from the lower classes, what those
in the upper classes sometimes refer to as the "criminal class."

In *Criminals in Love*, hearing that Henry has betrayed his son, William,
who has posed as a psychiatrist in order to get into the prison, tells Henry:
"You are a big stupid shit-spewing asshole. One of the world's truly pathetic empty spaces. An enormous nothingness on legs. A total waste of
time. Vomit. If I had a gun I'd shoot you." Henry replies, "I want another
doctor" (256). While William feels "great sympathy for the truly sad cases
of the world," for Henry William feels nothing. Henry has chosen to be
worse than he has to be. Of dealing with Henry's brother, Junior's Uncle
Ritchie, William says that "… threats don't work. Neither will reason, nor

compassion, obviously. No normal social dialogue. The logic is not there. The mind bent from years of repression." When Gail expresses disbelief that repression is the problem, William explains "The class is repressed. When the class is repressed, it produces a certain percentage of moronic immoral slimey offspring" (247–248). A certain percentage. The something else, something again like "bad luck." Gina Mae makes a similar point about Rolly and Stevie in *Beautiful City*: "We're dealing with pure slime. Social sexual single-celled creations of a cruel God" (260). Later, she takes Rolly in with the intention of trying to reform him—he may be salvageable, as he's getting on in years and his legs are no longer up to a life of crime. In this play, however, Stevie seems beyond redemption.

Thus in Walker criminality is explained, but not excused nor romanticized. We cheer, at least inwardly, when Elizabeth tells Mike Dixon that she's going to continue her campaign against police brutality. But we know that Mike has a point when he replies:

> Did you say something about police brutality? Well, you just keep right on complaining. I hate it when those awful police get brutal. I mean, who the hell are they to get brutal. All the nice people they get to deal with. All that love and affection they get from that wonderful scum out there. Why the fuck would anyone want to get brutal with that fucking, wonderful, goddamn scum. (*Escape From Happiness* 440)

The issue of infection again, and Walker is flipping our sympathies back and forth again. Mike Dixon's position, the policeman's position, between "normal" people and the "fucking, wonderful, goddamn scum" is an important part of Walker's treatment of the cops, Max and Donny, in the Suburban Motel plays, *Adult Entertainment* and *The End of Civilization*; so is "infection," and the technique of sympathy flipping. I'll talk about those policemen and those plays in the chapter on the Motel plays.

Ed Nyman quite correctly includes "carnivalesque" in a list of terms inadequate to describe Walker's work (57). Nonetheless, Mikhail Bakhtin's idea of the carnivalesque is, I think, important to an exploration of Walker's work and world, and a very useful tool. The idea is developed in Bakhtin's study of François Rabelais, 1494–1553, author of the five comic and ribald books about the giants Gargantua and Pantagruel. One is struck by the marked similarity between what Bakhtin has to say about Rabelais in his introduction, and what many people have been saying about Walker for some time now.

> There is ... no doubt that he is the most democratic among these initiators of new literatures. He is more closely and essentially linked to popular sources ...

It is precisely this specific and radical popular character of Rabelais' images which explains their exceptional saturation with the future ... It also explains Rabelais' "nonliterary" nature, that is the nonconformity of his images to the literary norms and canons predominating in the sixteenth century and still prevailing in our times, whatever the changes undergone by their contents ... Rabelais' images have a certain undestroyable nonofficial nature. No dogma, no authoritarianism, no narrow-minded seriousness can coexist with Rabelaisian images; these images are opposed to all that is finished and polished, to all pomposity, to every ready-made solution in the sphere of thought and world outlook ... To be understood he requires an essential reconstruction of our entire artistic and ideological perception, the renunciation of many deeply rooted demands of literary taste, and the revision of many concepts. Above all, he requires an exploration in depth of a sphere as yet little and superficially studied, the tradition of folk humour. (3)

In many respects, this is what I discussed in Chapter Two, what Smith says about Walker in "Parody in the Plays and Productions of George F. Walker." Walker's sources and spirit come for the most part from popular art, and the way in which he uses the energy of popular art goes far beyond simple reflection and distortion of first level parody. At the beginning of his essay, Nyman presents some Walkeresque images:

A doctor rips a severed human foot from around another man's neck and throws it into the audience. As he does so he says, "What's wrong with you. Have you no respect for human life?"

A drunken young man sits beside the coffin of his recently murdered lover whose grave and corpse he has just desecrated.

A woman narrates a dream of being raped by the tongue of a lizard and lapses into describing the rape of a Catholic school girl by a priest.

A lady proposes a toast and falls dead through a suspended tire.

When the curtain rises, a corpse is suspended above the stage. It remains throughout the play. (57)

Obviously, forms of expression on which Walker draws are much broader and even more "nonofficial" than the B-movie. This partially explains the "undestroyable nonofficial nature" of Walker's work, that aspect of Walker's work which, I think, explains the fact that Walker's work is seldom produced by the "official" theatres of the Canadian regional theatre system, and which often leads to an uneasy relationship between the plays and the audiences at the regionals on those occasions when they are performed there. "No dogma, no authoritarianism, no narrow-minded seriousness can coexist with Rabelaisian images," nor I would argue with Walkeresque images.

As I mentioned in Chapter One, when discussing Walker's work in a book such as this one, it's quite easy to lose sight of the fact that Walker is funny. Often, Walker comedy, and it's a decidedly non-literary sort, falls under the description of what Bakhtin calls "folk humour." There are times when my working-class background, thinly overlayed with nouveau middle-class respectability, is quite helpful. Directing a Walker play is one of those times. When the voices of my ancestral class and my acquired class set up a dialogue, the dialogism is more helpful yet, and one of the consequences of this class dialogism is an instability that is funny, irreverent, raucous, bawdy, "low," fartish comedy. You need the working-class to supply the fart, the middle-class to supply the rules that make the fart rude, and funny.

To take another tack for a moment, there is in Walker's comedy much of what Peter Brook describes in *The Empty Space* as "rough theatre." "It is always the popular theatre that saves the day. Through the ages it has taken many forms, and there is only one factor that they all have in common—a roughness. Salt, sweat, noise, smell ..." (65).

> Of course, it is most of all dirt that gives the roughness its edge; filth and vulgarity are natural, obscenity is joyous: with these the spectacle takes on its socially liberating role, for by nature the popular theatre is anti-authoritarian, anti-traditional, anti-pomp, anti-pretence. (68)

Walker's "roughness" comes from the East End, of course, and also, in its theatrical form, from its beginnings at the Factory Lab, in many respects the "roughest" of the Alternatives. (In other respects, in its populist bent, for example, Passe Muraille was the roughest in Brook's sense of the word.) If middle-class audiences at the Bluma Appel or the Manitoba Theatre Centre are reluctant to accept Walker's work, or tentative, excessively polite, and self-congratulatory in doing so, it is not because of the plays' intellectual difficulty or abstruseness, although the sudden shifts in style, strident hyperbole, and naked emotions may be disconcerting to an audience expecting lineal domestic realism. Rather, it is a response to the Factory Lab, working-class roughness: this stuff is rude, and has an energy that exceeds the bounds of decorum, not to mention an anti-establishment message and attitude that goes beyond slogans and is embedded in the nature of the world as Walker presents it on stage. The regionals' rejection of Walker's work is in part classist. Walker's "vulgarity" is certainly the superficial hook on which reviewers of the right-wing press often hang their counter-attacks, although, I would argue, their unease with Walker runs much deeper than that: "vulgarity" is an ingredient and emblem of a spirit and a worldview profoundly threatening to the establishment, but it is easy to identify and to repress through the application of "family values." Through attacks on four-letter words ("We now know what the 'F' in 'George F. Walker' stands for."), through pretended moral indignation, these critics can launch *ad hominem* reprimands and ridicule which they hope will weaken, discredit, and silence the spirit and the worldview, this challenge to the established order. In effect, these critics try to do with Walker what Inspector Clair does with Bernard in *Theatre of the Film Noir*.

Walker's work *is* vulgar, certainly, as those critics imply, using the meaning of the word most commonly in use today, according to the Oxford English Dictionary: "Having a common and offensively mean character; coarsely commonplace; lacking in refinement or good taste; uncultured, ill-bred." But Walker's work is also vulgar in a number of the other senses listed by the OED. "Common or usual language of a country; the vernacular." Applied to Walker's work, we here mean not only English in English Canada, but English as it is spoken here employed as the base and raw material for Walker's stage language, which takes that "vulgar" speech and through selective exaggeration, heightens it and gives it even more than its native energy for the stage. "Persons belonging to the ordinary or common class in the community; not distinguished or marked off from this in any way, plebian." "A person not reckoned as belonging to good society." (Note how classist all these definitions are.) These definitions of "vulgar" apply not only to many of Walker's characters, characters representing kinds of "common" people who rarely appear in conventional plays, certainly not in plays produced at the regionals, but also to Walker himself, or to Walker as he sees himself. These are characteristics, I would argue, that not only set Walker's plays apart from the usual run of plays, the North American equivalents of boulevard theatre, but contribute to the quality of Walker's plays, their uniqueness, the ways in which they compel attention in the theatre.

Thus Walker and Walker's work operate "outside the law," metaphorically at least. He comes from the "criminal classes" and certainly doesn't try to hide it. In the world of literature, he's a "crook," and certainly many of the reviews of the early work carry a moral indignation that he's breaking some law, trying to get away with something, a fraud, a con-man. These plays are bad cheques. Walker is also "outside the law," outside the usual order of things, in the carnivalesque quality of his work. Bakhtin discusses in Rabelais' books not only that great writer's use of popular source and expression, hitherto regarded as below the attention of literature, but also its use of the spirit of carnival.

There were, in the Middle Ages, occasions during the year, Carnival, Mardi Gras, the Feast of Fools, where normal rules were suspended. Frequently a principle of inversion is involved, the lowest made the highest, as when a novice or even a scullery boy is made bishop for a day (and Ken Gass wrote a play called *The Boy Bishop* about such an inversion in history). Nothing is sacred. Even the mass can be mocked. Sexual liberty is permitted, either real or verbal. The folk, and folk humour, rule. Bakhtin links to carnival a number of other features of medieval life, literature, and sub-literature which, he says, work with this carnivalesque disruption of hierarchal order in Rabelais' work: parody, the diableries of the mystery plays, familiar speech in the marketplace, and profanities and oaths. Consider, for a moment, Walker's talent for, and delight in, elaborate and profane insult: "You are a big stupid shit-spewing asshole. One of the world's truly pathetic empty spaces. An enormous nothingness on legs. At total waste of time. Vomit." "Social sexual single-celled creations of a cruel God." "I'll push your asshole through your brain until you're inside out in another fucking universe! The universe of the brainless assholes!" "... I knew you were stupid. And stupid's a thing I don't usually have a problem with in a man. But come on. There are limits. You've gone beyond the limits of tolerable stupidity. You're toying with a mercy killing here. I mean I was out there thinking 'They're too stupid to live. Just go on in there and put them outta their misery.'"

Bakhtin also explains what he calls the "grotesque realism" of Rabelais' work:

> It is usually pointed out that in Rabelais' work the material bodily principle, that is, images of the human body with its food, drink, defecation, and sexual life, plays a predominant role. Rabelais was proclaimed by Victor Hugo the greatest poet of the "flesh" and "belly," while others accused him of "gross physiologism," or "biologism," or "naturalism." (18)

> In grotesque realism ... the bodily element is deeply positive. It is presented not in a private, egotistic form, severed from the other spheres of life, but as something universal, representing all the people. (19)

> The essential principle of grotesque realism is degradation, that is, the lowering of all that is high, spiritual, ideal, abstract; it is a transfer to the material level, to the sphere of earth and body in their indissoluble unity. (19–20)

> Earth is an element that devours, swallows up (the grave, the womb) and at the same time an element of birth, of renascence (the maternal breasts). Such is the meaning of "upward" and "downward" in their

cosmic aspect, while in their purely bodily aspect, which is not clearly distinct from the cosmic, the upper part is the face or the head and the lower part is the genital organs, the belly, and the buttocks. These absolute topographical connotations are used by grotesque realism, including medieval parody. Degradation here means coming down to earth, the contact with earth as an element that swallows up and gives birth at the same time. To degrade is to bury, to sow, and to kill simultaneously, in order to bring forth something more and better. (21)

I don't think it would be pushing the point to describe Walker's work as "earthy" as well as "vulgar," "earthy" in the usual vernacular sense as employed today, and earthy in its association with Bakhtin's "grotesque realism," which itself is not a bad description of Walker's style in the eighties and nineties. Walker's work does make use of parody, parodic satire, if not quite in the central way it used to. It makes use of "familiar speech in the marketplace," oaths, and sometimes uses character types, especially villains, in the manner of the Vices of the medieval plays, the fooleries perpetrated by the devils in the diableries Bakhtin talks about. In many of Walker's plays the "abstract"—usually social abstractions, institutions which we customarily look up to—is "degraded," brought down to earth, by an examination of the institutions in the context of fundamentally human concerns, often of values as they are determined by the material body. And, it would seem, he wants to "kill" the abstractions "in order to bring forth something more and better," more human.

I would also say that Walker's plays are "carnivalesque" in that they operate in a carnival space in which the usual rules are suspended—the usual rules of theatre, propriety, perception, evaluation, and audience reception. It can be argued that because carnival and the carnivalesque are sanctioned disruptions of the status quo, in the long run they strengthen the dominance of mainstream society and its rules by providing a release from those rules ("letting off steam"), making those rules more bearable in other places and at other times of the year, rather than effecting permanent change. Ed Nyman takes such a position when he discusses *film noir* as "no more than a sanctioned disturbance that reinforced a dominant discourse" (59). Whatever—to use a vulgar expression currently in widespread use. The important point, at the moment, is that I think Walker's work does operate in this carnivalesque manner, and that Walker hopes with Kershaw that in the matter of the carnivalesque as in other ways "theatre may … influence, however minutely, the general historical evolution of wider social and political realities" (Kershaw 1).

As in other aspects of his work, there is a shift in the way Walker uses the carnivalesque between the plays of the seventies and the plays of the eighties, roughly speaking—again, 1982 seems to me to be the pivotal year. In the early plays, Walker more or less simply ignores the rules, because, he would say, he didn't know the rules well enough to follow them anyway, although I would say that this was also a matter of Walker, and Gass, having no respect for the rules in a way that made the Factory the Factory. (That's a generalization, but you know what I'm getting at.) The audience didn't always realize that it was supposed to be having a good time. The B-movie and *film noir* lenses signalled that we weren't to expect realism, that this was another sort of space, a carnival space, but the audience, and especially the critics, didn't always take the next step and appreciate the subversions of the subversions. In the East End plays, Walker develops further what I would describe as "grotesque realism" in his style, and in addition, uses plot devices which clearly create carnival spaces where the usual rules can be suspended, that in effect say "Pay attention audience, we're moving into another dimension now. Forget about the usual rules, you're free now." Thus, for example, William's eccentric manner, worldview and playacting, as when he impersonates the psychiatrist, suspend the usual rules, and, almost a match for Wineva's dark distortions, allow the forces of good to operate in flamboyant and carnivalesque defiance of the usual expectations of realism and probability. The absence of the father suspends the usual patriarchal rules at the beginning of *Better Living*, and we are taken into a matricentric society so unlike the one we're used to that it can function in a carnivalesque manner. One of Walker's favourite plot devices for effecting a carnivalesque inversion of the normal order is kidnapping; kidnappings occur in six Walker plays: *Bagdad Saloon, The Art of War, Love and Anger, Beautiful City, Escape from Happiness,* and *Criminal Genius.* Off-stage kidnapping is attempted, but fails, in *Problem Child.* Off-stage kidnapping succeeds, with terrifying results, in *Adult Entertainment.* Often in these incidents, the less powerful are temporarily made more powerful, and get to call the shots for a change. The initial breaking of the rules inverts power status, creating the space in which many other rules can be broken.

The pattern is perhaps clearest in *Love and Anger.* When Petie Maxwell and his gang of marginalized women kidnap Conner and put him trial for abusing his power, they put him in a situation where he is judged in the manner in which he is accustomed to judging and condemning others. In this trial, Petie is the prosecutor, Harris, Petie's old legal partner and Conner's legal adviser, is the attorney for the defence, and the schizophrenic Sarah is made the judge in a manner highly reminiscent of the "boy bishop" inversion. Sarah wraps herself in pink drapes to provide for herself makeshift judicial robes. She turns a waste can upside down, puts it on a desk, and sits on it: "I think I should be higher. In a position to look down on you all. I think the looking down thing is essential here" (*Love and Anger* 73). Gail says of her that Sarah looks like "a primitive warrior. A kind of furious but wise queen. Like someone in the Bible." Harris protests that there are "no rules"; Petie's advice is "Wing it. Speak from the heart, man." In Conner's world, he is "a citizen of some standing in this community"; in this inverted, carnivalesque world he is degraded to "a thieving, conniving, merciless, exploiting piece of sewage!" (*Love and Anger* 77), and when Sarah finds both Conner and Harris guilty, she sentences "them to death by drowning. In the toilet" (*Love and Anger* 81). It is Petie who disagrees with the verdict, says that in his weakened state he was unable to mount an adequate prosecution, says that Conner and Harris actually won by reinscribing the "normal" rules of the dominant society: "We've got to keep the momentum going. Let the slower people pick up the jet stream. That's our only choice. We've got to get richer. The only alternative is to get poorer" (*Love and Anger* 81). The carnival, it would seem, is over.

James Earl Baldwin also notes the carnivalesque state effected by the trial scene in *Love and Anger*. When Sarah presides at Conner's "trial," "normal" conventions and due process are suspended, and law and justice are subject to her rules: "There are no rules," says Sarah. Baldwin describes the result as "carnivalesque" in Bakhtin's sense, quoting *Problems of Dostoyevsky's Poetics*:

> All things that were once self-enclosed, disunified, distanced from one another by a noncarnivalistic hierarchical worldview are drawn into carnivalistic contacts and combinations. Carnival brings together, unifies, weds and combines the sacred with the profane, the lofty with the low, the great with the insignificant, the wise and the stupid. (60–61)

It's characteristic of Walker to create the carnival, and also characteristic of him to end it. He would like the marginals, what Baldwin calls the "centrifugal characters," to win, but knows that in life they seldom do. There is a conflict here between Walker the political partisan and Walker the observer of life. Life is not as simple as political dogma believes it is, or would like it to be.

But, in an inversion of the inversion of the inversion of the normal, Gail re-establishes the carnivalesque by producing a gun before Conner and Harris can leave.

> If you cross me or my husband again, I'll use it. If you make me mad again I'll find you and put it against your head and pull the trigger. Maybe because I think you're wrong about all the things you talked about. Maybe for ... some other reasons. We'll never know for sure why

I use it. I'll never know because I'll be too busy getting on with my life
to ask myself questions like that. And you'll never know because you'll
be dead ... (*Love and Anger* 83)

It is also characteristic of Walker that he does not romanticize carnival
by omitting its darker, more violent side, as above. Baldwin sees this darker
side in Sarah's "primal justice," the part of her she "likes the best," she
says, and that would throw Harris "to the floor, rip off his clothes and
pour battery acid down his rectum" (*Love and Anger* 67).

The freedom of carnival includes the freedom to commit violence, as
riots amply demonstrate. In the politically charged carnivalesque states
that Walker employs, the "good guys" confront the moral dilemma discussed in the previous chapter: is it morally justified to use violence against
violent oppressors? Gail in *Love and Anger* decides, in the speech above,
yes, violence under these circumstances is morally justified. In *Better Living*, Gail (another Gail, a different person) and Jack confront this problem
when Gail's gun gives her power over her father, inverts the normal power
status. Tom's reappearance at the end of the play indicates that their answer to the question was "no." In *Escape from Happiness*, Nora and Elizabeth kidnap Rolly Moore, use physical force on the man who held a gun
on them earlier in the play, and try to determine who his powerful em-
ployers are. Elizabeth herself sees the paradox involved: as part of her
campaign to end police brutality, she is herself brutalizing the sort of man
the police routinely brutalize:

> Believe it or not, a part of me hates doing this to you. You're a pathetic
> bastard. I see guys like you ever day. Messed up. Stupid. Defenceless.
> Beaten up by everything and everyone. You even get beaten up by the
> police. And that pisses me off. I'm truly pissed off that the police beat
> up pathetic bastards like you. They have no right, no right at all to
> punish you physically ... But this is different. I'm not the police. I'm
> not a representative of the state. I'm just a member of a family. A family
> you've fucked with! You see this is personal. A deeply personal thing.
> This is not sanctioned by the government. And therefore there's a limit,
> a restriction on the damage that can be done here. The only thing that
> can be damaged here is you. And basically, I think that's okay. I'm not
> enjoying your suffering or anything. But it doesn't really bother me,
> because really, all I'm doing is ... defending my family. (404-405)

This is Elizabeth's solution. Violence committed by an individual human
being for human reasons can be okay; violence committed in the name of
an abstraction is not.

Walker's ambivalence about and suspicion of authority and order are
reflected not only in the content of his plays, but also in his relationship

to them as the writer. Here, too, we have issues of authority, of course, the authority of the "author," the question of to what extent the plays are part of Walker, speak for him under his direction, and to what extent he allows freedoms to his own creations, freedom to function autonomously, taking them where their own interior logic takes them. Plays that avoid being definitive in this way also allow more freedoms to the audience, as more choices, more opportunities to interpret and create meaning, are left to them. One of the ways to consider these matters is through an examination of degrees of monologism and dialogism in a work. The question here, as we saw in Baldwin's discussion of *Nothing Sacred*, is to what extent a work is monologic, shaped by a single voice, or to what extent it is dialogic, where the presence of different voices creates a "space" between them, an opening up into many different possible meanings.

In "The Space Between Voices," Baldwin sees *Escape from Happiness* as the most dialogic of the three plays he examines (*Nothing Sacred, Love and Anger*, and *Escape from Happiness*) and thus the work least "finalized," the least monologic in that of the three, this is the play in which Walker's authorial voice and authority is least overtly present, and in which he is least inclined to shape the dramatic events into a conventional lineal form leading to a conclusion and a "moral." Baldwin says of this extremely complex, multiple plot, elusive play about elusiveness, crime, punishment, an East End family, and the complexity of life:

> Unlike either *Nothing Sacred* or *Love and Anger*, *Escape from Happiness* is almost entirely dialogic in its action. Unlike in either of the previous two plays, information is deferred in order to complicate and carefully contextualize each unfolding moment so that a character is seen to adopt different voices to suit each occasion. Since characters are derived from specific and differential contextualizing pasts rather than from simplified abstract universals or character types, there seems to be no collective or authorial consciousness directing their voices. Similarly, time and events do not define or finalize the characters; rather, characters situate events around themselves, seeing and understanding themselves and one another differently, with the result that the audience is never allowed to assume a superior knowledge of an overall "truth." (72, 73)

As information, or versions of information, are revealed in the course of the play, they re-contextualize earlier events in the play, thus revise the audience's opinion of the meaning of previous events, judgments, definitions, evasions, meanings which can only be provisional as still further revelations again re-contextualize and revise meaning. Thus, says Baldwin, no character, no voice, is deprived of "the power to mean" at any given moment. All "truths" are subject to negotiation. "It is in this state of imaginative flux, this position of contingent understanding, that the audience/reader, like the characters in the play, are placed" (77).

We proceed through the events of the play knowing no more than the characters know, having to revise our opinions of what is so or "true" as they do, and at the end, learn what they have learned, experientially, but know, as they know, that the process is far from over, that further revision and learning are required. When I was working on the essay on Walker for *Post-Colonial English Drama* (St. Martin's Press, 1992), Walker was working on *Escape from Happiness*. He said at the time that when he sat down to write, the voices he heard were those of the women from *Better Living*, and that suggests to me that he himself didn't know for sure where the play was going or what it "meant," but that he would have to live through these further events in the lives of Nora, Elizabeth, Mary Ann, and Gail as they did. *Escape from Happiness*, Baldwin says, is "a non-finalized demonstration of a family's communal being, rather than the linear demonstration of exemplary action" (98).

While I am in general agreement,[1] it seems to me that Baldwin might be in some danger of being seduced by the monologic myth of "progress," in this case, progressive "improvement" by Walker toward ever more dialogic work, and presumably, an ever more dialogic worldview. I think both he and Stephen Haff, whom he quotes, exaggerate the "absolutism," the monologism, of some of Walker's early work. The multiple identities and shape-shifting in the early and dream-like *Ramona and the White Slaves*, for example, certainly challenge concepts of unified subject, while *Zastrozzi*, to which both Baldwin and Haff refer, is far from a simple dialectical conflict of good and evil. Zastrozzi suffers from nightmares in which, as leader of the forces of evil, he confronts the leader of the forces of good, who is also him—an unforgettable image from the play is Zastrozzi struggling mightily to wipe from his face a smile, "the widest, stupidest, most merciful and good smile ever worn by a human being," a fragment from his dream that lingers on into his waking life. Zastrozzi is not absolute evil; he aspires to be absolute evil. It is part of his "process of simplification." When he seeks to kill Verezzi, he seeks to kill part of himself, the part that haunts his nightmares, perhaps falls in love with Julia, and sullies the purity of evil, "negative spirituality." Ultimately, he spares Verezzi in order to maintain the dialectic, but destroys the pragmatic, relatavist Victor, who complicates Zastrozzi's moral schema, first by seducing him into absolutism, then killing him. Still Zastrozzi fails to achieve absolute simplicity, and the play ends with two of his voices arguing with each other.

As I first said in Chapter One, through Walker's work I don't think we see so much a progress from monologism to dialogism as a series of adjustments and compromises as Walker looks for ways in which to present his worldview—which has always tended to dialogism—and to invite his audience's participation at a number of levels. On the other hand, Baldwin may be right in that as Walker became more experienced, and accepted and affirmed, he became more confident and better able to distribute authorial power to characters, actors, and audience. He became more generous in this regard, which doesn't always coincide with "generosity," as he uses the word, to describe audience accessibility. It could well be, too, that the huge success of *Nothing Sacred*, the first of the three plays Baldwin discusses, boosted Walker's confidence (and income) significantly, and that the result was a noticeable increase in "generosity" (or dialogism) in subsequent plays.

In addition to being a playwright, Walker is a self-taught stage director, and is now a rather experienced director, having directed eight of his own premières, or more, depending on one's definition of "première"—he says, for example, that he considers the Factory productions of *Problem Child*, *Criminal Genius,* and *Risk Everything*, which he directed, the "real" premières, rather than the earlier Rattlestick productions in New York, which were more workshop in nature. He has also directed many other productions of his plays, including the Factory's tenth anniversary revival of *Zastrozzi*. I was on sabbatical and living in Toronto in 1986–87, and Walker generously allowed me to sit in on rehearsals of the production as an observer. The results of these observations were published as an essay, "George F. Walker Directs George F. Walker," published in *Theatre History in Canada* in 1988. The essay belongs here, as a conclusion to our "cops and robbers" chapter, it seems to me, for two reasons. The character, Zastrozzi, is one of Walker's most important and well-known "justicer" figures, and the play, *Zastrozzi*, a striking example of Walker's order versus chaos stories and plots, with, of course, the characteristic ambivalence about issues of authority, order, and chaos. Secondly, I attended rehearsals because I wanted to see Walker in action as a director, not only to get a sense of how he operates as an interpretive and facilitating artist in the rehearsal hall, but to get further insight into Walker's attitudes to and misgivings about authority and power, as here was a situation in which Walker would be operating, or refusing to operate, from two positions of authority himself, that of director and that of playwright, "author."

George F. Walker Directs George F. Walker
(first published Theatre History in Canada 9.2, 1988)

George F. Walker hates directing George F. Walker. Or so he says. He may well hate directing, period, but as he has never directed a play by anyone else, he does not know for sure. Walker says he may have to do that some time, just to determine whether it is directing per se he dislikes so much.

Directing, says Walker, is socially embarrassing. The director is continually put in the position of having to say something whether he has anything to say or not, and whether or not the actors are listening (and often they do not listen because they are too busy doing their own work, inside), an experience Walker likens to talking to an empty parking lot. And in Walker's case, of course, directing is socially embarrassing because it involves talking about oneself. That is what made the prospect of sitting in on Walker's rehearsals for the tenth anniversary production of *Zastrozzi: The Master of Discipline* at the Factory Theatre in Toronto in April and May of 1987 a particularly attractive one.

I was interested in Walker's working relationship with his actors, to what extent he sees himself as an authority on his own work and to what extent he sees himself as a facilitator. Further, I wanted to know whether this relationship was influenced by past experience, whether Walker's theatrical language for actors experienced in the Walker mode is different from that which he uses for actors without that experience. I wanted to know if there would be rewrites, line alterations to accommodate any changes of mind Walker may have had concerning the script. We can deal with that one right away. No. A word was added here, deleted there, all in the service of business associated with this particular production, but there were no changes of substance. I wanted to examine Walker's theatrical statements as a director, and to examine ways in which this production illuminates the text, with particular attention to the manipulation of empathy and to the balance between serious and comic elements of the play.

The material for this article came from three interviews with Walker; less formal conversations with actors and audience members; notes taken by Catherine Smith, my fellow observer, who is preparing a thesis on Walker for the Graduate Centre for the Study of Drama at the University of Toronto;[2] and my own notes based on the observation of rehearsals. There is a gap in the latter two sources; George asked Cathy and I to stay away for four days during the second week of the three-and-a-half-week rehearsal period, as he was worried that in the presence of observers some of his actors were jumping forward to performance level too soon, with consequences destructive for reasons that I hope will be made clear by the following discussion of Walker's working methods.

For Walker the director, casting was one of the most important means of achieving his 1987 concept of the play. In pre-show publicity, Walker is quoted as describing the Factory cast as his "ideal cast" (Karastamatis 1). Flattery aside, it is clear that Walker's directorial objectives were furthered by the make-up of the 1987 cast: Michael Hogan as Zastrozzi, Michael McManus as Verezzi, Peter Blais as Victor, Robert Bockstael as Bernardo, Susan Hogan as Matilda, and Nicky Guadagni as Julia. One of the most frequently employed rehearsal notes was Walker's reminding the actors why they had been cast, reference to those qualities which they had already demonstrated and which Walker needed as ingredients for his vision of the play.

Zastrozzi himself is, as usual, the key. Walker specifically wanted Michael Hogan for the role, and Hogan's availability was a determining factor in Walker's decision to propose and direct the production. What Walker wanted was, in Walker's words, "a middle-aged, passionate actor" (interview, May 1987). That "passion" is necessary to a succesful production of Walker's work is now an accepted critical verity, but the reverberations created by the fact that Hogan's Zastrozzi was definitely fortyish were unexpected by many. They were anticipated, welcomed, and exploited by Walker.

Stephen Markle's Zastrozzi in the 1977 Toronto Free production was described by Bryan Johnson, then writing for the *Globe and Mail*, as "an impossible character, a mythical devil," "a fascinating, extraordinary evil dynamo" (17). Of Hogan's Zastrozzi, Robert Crew in the Toronto *Star* speaks of a performance "full of power and touches of humour but lacking a certain seductively evil suavity and charisma. This Zastrozzi shows signs of age and vulnerability" (Crew 4). Exactly. Hogan's Zastrozzi did show signs of vulnerability and age, but that is what Walker wanted, in 1987, without losing the character's persistent and perverse passion. Zastrozzi's vulnerability is integral to the script—his mind may be so powerful that he can have nightmares and observe himself having nightmares simultaneously, but he cannot prevent himself from having nightmares. And a forty-year-old's nightmares are not as easily dispelled as a child's, or even a thirty-year-old's. When Zastrozzi sees in nightmares glimpses of another self, he sees the possibility of good, and in Hogan's Zastrozzi, the commitment to evil was sometimes qualified in his waking actions: in the kinship with and compassion for Victor, clear at points throughout the innkeeper scene and at Victor's death; in the somewhat fatherly rough-housing with Bernardo; in the pedagogical quality Hogan gave to Zastrozzi's approach to all the other characters in the play, especially Verezzi. As Denis Johnston has pointed out in conversation, this was a Zastrozzi whose mind took precedence over his body. Ask questions first, stab later.

When Michael McManus auditioned for the part, he showed Walker a new way to play Verezzi, or so Walker says. McManus is a relatively inexperienced actor, but Walker saw in his energy and intensity the possibility for a Verezzi whose passion is a match for Zastrozzi's. Bryan Johnson describes Geoffrey Bowes' 1977 Verezzi as "a whining, silly weakling" and complains that this characterization renders insignificant the "deadly bond" between Verezzi and Zastrozzi (17). And in his 1979 *Scene Changes* interview with Chris Hallgren, Walker seemed not altogether pleased with audience reaction to Verezzi in early productions: "There is a tendency for people to think of him as moronic. I think that's just a reflection of our own age. We cannot accept God, obsession or goodliness, when, in fact, a Verezzi has his own power" (Hallgreen 24). Walker used McManus to give the 1987 Verezzi more substance and weight, and to attempt to redress what he sees as an imbalance in the Verezzi-Zastrozzi confrontation.

The attempt was not an unqualified success. There is some truth to the view that part of the difficulty lies in the script itself. Furthermore, there were times in rehearsal when it seemed to me that Walker worked against the larger strategy for the sake of a particularly effective and funny moment—Verezzi sight-gags are almost irresistable. Sometimes McManus could not take the stronger if still deluded Verezzi where Walker wanted him to go. In rehearsal, at the end of the play, McManus snatched up Victor's sword when made aware that Zastrozzi does exist and is present, but dropped the weapon on the line, "I'm immune. I am in touch with Him. Protected by Him" (*Zastrozzi* 109), putting himself wholly in the hands of God. A foolish man, certainly, but one whose faith is extremely strong. By the time the show opened, the moment had been abandoned—instead, Verezzi slashed desperately at Zastrozzi, and was instantly disarmed and flung to the floor for his final interrogation. Walker worried that his initial staging was a moment from his 1984 direction of *Zastrozzi* for the Nimrod Theatre in Sydney, Australia, which he was imposing on the Factory production and which was inappropriate for the actors involved. While the moment itself was strong as it stood in rehearsals, it seemed to Walker to provide insufficient impetus to take McManus into the final lesson on the nature of reality. While the change forfeited an excellent opportunity to express Verezzi's obsessive goodliness and inner strength, and, in my opinion, placed his transformation a few seconds too early in the scene, Walker's directorial decision to tailor the sequence to the needs and capacities of the actors involved is typical of Walker's approach as a director. Elsewhere, Walker and McManus between them did give us a Verezzi deluded but strong, substantial enough to convincingly motivate Zastrozzi's antagonism.

Because Hogan's Zastrozzi diluted elements of the "mythical devil" with garden variety cynical forty-year-old, the contest was further balanced; to the melodramatic opposition of good and evil, Walker, Hogan, and

McManus added the homely attributes of conflict based on a generation gap. The historical shift in values central to the text took on a human dimension. Critical comment on *Zastrozzi: The Master of Discipline* has often noted that Verezzi and Zastrozzi are both artists. Less emphasized is the fact that Victor and Zastrozzi are both teachers. In rehearsals, while helping Hogan define Zastrozzi's attitude to the other characters, Walker used the analogy of the grade-school teacher. Zastrozzi's teaching methods are somewhat extreme: his characteristic pedagogical tactic is to empty the victim-student's mind in order to replace the previously held belief with new thoughts of Zastrozzi's own choosing. Both Victor and Zastrozzi attempt to convince Verezzi that their vision, version of "reality," is the correct one. Because McManus was a stronger than usual Verezzi, in the 1987 Factory production, both Victor and Zastrozzi had to work harder on their lesson plans. In one of Walker's favourite phrases, "the stakes are raised."

Victor, of course, is already the most complex character in the play, making it up as he goes along, struggling with the implications of having a pragmatic relationship with God. Peter Blais added some complications of his own by taking and playing seriously Victor's very ordinariness. At the opening night party, Susan Purdy remarked that Blais' was the most genuinely ordinary Victor she had seen—often, the tendency for an actor playing Victor is to play a character of superior intellect (like the actor!) pretending to be ordinary. By being ordinary, Blais was free to do the unexpected, for instance, to be momentarily swayed by Zastrozzi's arguments. I believe Walker cast Blais knowing that Blais would be his most active collaborator in the re-exploration of the text.

Walker apparently wanted to play against stereotype with all the characters, to temper the dominant note with "realistic" or "wonky" inconsistency. Hence, Robert Bockstael's Bernardo was not the simple-minded, hulking henchman; to begin with, he is too physically small for the stereotype, much smaller than George Buza who played the part in the original production. In Walker's words, "Bernardo is not stupid, but lives in a narrow corridor—if he goes beyond that, he's lost." When Julia suggests in the prison scene that she and Bernardo start again, "develop a respectful attitude to each other. Eventually fall in love on just the right terms" (*Zastrozzi* 100), Bockstael's Bernardo considered the possibility for a moment, before violently rejecting it, terrified by the foreign impulse in himself. (This moment was an example of a minor line change, Walker the playwright adding a "No" to help Bockstael achieve the moment Walker the director wanted.)

Matilda was not the archetypal seductress. Susan Hogan gave a rather domestic quality to her scenes with Zastrozzi, and I do not think I am merely projecting biography onto production here. Walker is evasive when asked whether he had this effect in mind when casting the Hogans (who are married), but concedes that he is pleased that this Zastrozzi must still deal with this Matilda, that Matilda is to Hogan's Zastrozzi a real woman, a long-time partner, rather than the ghost of something he has already left far behind him.

Walker wanted Nicky Guadagni to be more than "virginal," instead an iron-willed individual determined to make the world conform to her "rosy coloured" vision; virginity is a symptom, not a cause. When, for example, Bernardo threw Julia into the prison, Julia exclaimed, under Walker's direction, "What is this place? I've never been here" (*Zastrozzi* 99), rather as one would comment on a smart little restaurant that has inexplicably escaped one's attention until now, instinctively reclassifying experience so that it fits comfortably within her "rosy vision." It seems to me that Guadagni had some difficulty transcending the stereotype and I agree with Ray Conlogue when he says of her first night performance that she was "acting her heart out but not quite hitting the right tone" ("A Triumph of Gothic Comedy"). Still, it should be pointed out that as the run progressed, Guadagni played the moments more and relied less on a preconceived notion of the part, demonstrating why Walker cast her.

Discussing Walker's casting has taken rather longer than I had anticipated, but as rehearsals progressed, I became more and more aware of how important that element was for this production. It has often been said that eighty percent of a production is in shrewd casting, and George F. Walker once said that a director's primary goal should be to mediate between actor and script, and to facilitate the actor's making full use of his own creative powers. Walker was clearly in an enviable position with regard to the script, and having chosen his actors very shrewdly, was in a position to undertake some very profitable mediation.

It became very clear very early in rehearsals that there is indeed a language for the Walker veterans, with Peter Blais at that end of the scale, and another for the Walker virgins, with Michael McManus and Nicky Guadagni at that end. Michael Hogan, who originated the role of Tom in *Better Living*, Susan Hogan, who has played Susan Scott in *Filthy Rich*, and Robert Bockstael, who had acted in three Walker plays in Ottawa, fall somewhere in between.

Blais has played eight Walker roles in the past twelve years, creating four of those roles: the King in *Rumours of Our Death* (Factory, 1980), Hank the American soldier in *Theatre of the Film Noir* (Factory, 1981), William in *Criminals in Love* (Factory, 1984), and Jack the Priest in *Better Living* (CentreStage, 1986). Blais and Walker barely talked to each other at all.

They smiled at one another occasionally. Most of their work together concerned blocking and timing. In the first scene between Victor and Verezzi, Walker and Blais were concerned with the focus on the painting: it was important that the conversation be not entirely confined to the painting, nor that it proceed immediately to abstraction. The conflict over the nature of reality must be precipitated by Verezzi's fury that Victor does not see how wonderful his painting is. When, then, is the precise moment when the argument should be about something else?

Blais' approach to the role of Victor in the Factory production is summed up in an interview published in the May 14th to 20th issue of *Now* magazine, appropriately titled "Playing Walker's *Zastrozzi* with passion and maturity." (Walker likes the piece so much he calls it "a little guide to acting in a Walker play" and recommends photo-copying it and handing it out to prospective cast members in future Walker productions.) In part, Blais says:

> As in any theatre piece, humour comes from conflict of interest. Once the reality and truth of a scene are established, the most remarkable things can happen. Without that reality, the humour can be slapstick, gratuitous or in poor taste. The best humour comes from character. Walker's writing is remarkably funny and lucid, though in rehearsal the actor has to find a heightened sense of truth in it. There's no joke to be built, constructed, or honed; if you build the character, the jokes will take care of themselves. (John Kaplan 35)

Blais and Walker obviously did not need to talk about what Walker wanted, so the work Walker did with the neophytes was much more helpful to an observer as an indication of the kind of world in which Walker's plays can live. A good deal of the early rehearsal time was devoted to finding the "heightened sense of truth" Blais speaks of. Because the situations in Walker plays are so grotesque, and because the characters themselves are often in the grip of monstrous obsessions, there is a tendency for actors to go immediately to a larger than life, operatic style, and that is what some of the 1987 Factory cast did. Walker had to take them back. That size, that heightening, is necessary, but does not work unless the reality of the scene is there first, becoming part of that which is heightened. Early in rehearsals, Michael McManus asked if one of his moments of revelation was too big, was over the top. Walker replied, "Go over the top. If you believe it."

The reality of the scenes was established through rather conventional, detailed script work. Walker seldom gave a meaning for a line, although he often paraphrased, more often to clarify the line's action or tone than to define meaning. Sometimes, he would paraphrase the situation in a scene to uncover the homely reality beneath the grotesque circumstances; hence, Bernardo and Julia's prison scene was a "first date." Occasionally, Walker would direct a line against its apparent meaning. Verezzi's reaction to Julia's telling him she will not marry him, "I'm depressed" (*Zastrozzi* 69), is not necessarily a depressed line. It could simply be a reaction to an interesting state of affairs; to Verezzi, all sensations are good. Again, immediately before Bernardo and Zastrozzi fight to the death, Bernardo says, "Sir, let me go" (*Zastrozzi* 104), but Walker blocked the moment so that Bernardo had a clear route for escape and directed Bockstael to deliver the line with elation: at last Bernardo is given his chance to supplant Zastrozzi.

At times, then, Walker is clearly the authority on the script, although his jokey style in the rehearsal hall usually undercuts any authoritarian tone. He is not at all a sit-behind-the-desk director, as he frequently plunges into the playing space, never to demonstrate how he wants something done, but often to create a force against which the actor can work, sometimes just to gesticulate encouragingly. But his sense of the script as he saw it was clear—curiously a bit distanced from this play in 1987: he points out that it is almost as though *Zastrozzi* were written by someone else, that in a sense the play was written by someone else. While we are noting the implications of Michael Hogan and Peter Blais' being forty, it is worth remembering that George Walker was about to turn forty when he was directing the Factory *Zastrozzi*.

Walker established the "truth of the scene" and the director's vision of that truth through establishing what he calls "marks," the dominant quality or issue of a sequence, or a particular moment, or even thing, that seems to Walker crucial or catalytic. The dislocation and abrupt changes in direction essential to a production of a Walker play are created by shifting the "mark." Around these points, Walker allows the actors a great deal of creative room, and confines his direction to finding the means of increasing that room, suggesting, for instance, a "productive state of mind" for the character at a particular point. Early in rehearsals, Guadagni began the first meeting with Verezzi in a state of indignation; Walker suggested that she try astonishment instead, not because it was necessarily preferable in its own right, but because it left the actress more places to go in the rest of the scene. Yes, Walker does call for emotional states in a way theoretically forbidden to directors working within "the Method."

Walker frequently accepts the opinions, preferably the instincts, of his actors. Many observers have noted the breakneck pace of the Factory production. Actually, Walker wanted it faster still; in Walker's dramaturgy, dislocation should also occur in the minds of the audience, and extreme pace is one way of achieving that effect. But the actors resisted, and Walker felt that they doubtless had good reasons for doing so. Even a week into performance, actors were still throwing away the ends of lines. While for obvious reasons Walker would have preferred having his lines completed, he suspected that the performers might have been concentrating on something more important to them, and was prepared to let them continue to work on developing the production unhindered, while of course still hoping that completing the lines would eventually become a priority too. For a playwright-director, Walker gives a great deal of weight to the actors' priorities while mediating between them and the script.

Once the "truth" of a scene was established, Walker would immediately "raise the stakes," intensifying that truth, sharpening the conflict, putting on additional pressure from within the dramatic situation, to get Walkeresque exaggeration and size. "We can build slowly. Or throw ourselves into it. Carefully." Scene seven, Matilda's seduction of Verezzi and Victor's subsequent attempt to convince Verezzi to flee, had never, in Walker's opinion, been taken far enough in earlier productions, had remained a declaration of ideas distanced from the audience. He used the act of seduction as the "mark," a concreteness to anchor the scene as he had used the painting in scene two. When McManus declaimed, Susan Hogan, with a little urging from Walker, re-established the mark, took it further, and "raised the stakes." One does not declaim when Susan Hogan is raising the stakes.

By the end of the week, Blais was indeed emerging as Walker's most active collaborator, not so much through anything he said to his fellow performers or through conversations with Walker, but by putting into practice what he has learned about how a Walker play works. He started small, worked doggedly at establishing the truth of the scene, and by doing so, compelled any actor who might be tempted to go for scale too quickly to play the scene at a level where the truth was not strained. Then, he raised the stakes, moving into the extreme close range Walker favours and jumping Victor's anxiety level astonishingly. Blais' work is contagious in a rehearsal hall.

Walker's directorial wit does not express itself in constructing jokes. He did engineer some exquisite comic business (the Byzantine complexity of Matilda's strangulation at the hands of a completely unwitting Julia was hilarious) but he made no attempt at all to time lines for a laugh, punch laugh lines, or build to a laugh. In Blais' words, "there's no joke to be built; if you build the characters, the jokes will take care of themselves."

Walker did give a good deal of attention to the characters' relationship with the audience, the next step in the rehearsal process. Only Zastrozzi was given direct address, only he played scenes with the audience, but all the other characters came close, must appear to be capable of doing so. When Blais achieved the correct balance in rehearsal, Walker gave the approving note, "He never speaks directly to the audience, but you always think he's going to." Walker, the director, was elaborating on the manipulation of empathy called for in the script. He wanted the audience to "share the responsibility with Zastrozzi; if you laugh at his jokes, you can't dissociate yourself from his actions."

During the first week, Walker was clearly having a good time, and later Walker conceded that this part of rehearsal period is an exception to his hatred of direction, "getting his licks in," working closely with actors and script. Then I was banished for four days. I understand that during this period, Walker concentrated on close, one on one work with individual actors. When I returned, the cast had moved from rehearsal hall to stage. George was no longer having a good time. Initial run throughs were quite discouraging, even more than is usually the case because of the extreme physical demands of the show. Walker was especially worried about retaining scene focus established in the rehearsal hall now that scenes were juxtaposed with the real fights. The fights in the Factory production were very intricate, and, incidentally, quite marvellous: they were not always perfectly executed, but fight director Robert Lindsay gave them fascinating dramatic content. They were conversations between characters rather than mere flashy business. In the second week of rehearsals, however, the fights worried the actors so much that their concentration on scenes immediately preceding fights suffered: you could see them starting to worry about the impending problems.

Reginald Bronskill's set was extremely effective and rather dangerous, as much of the action occurred on a platform ten feet in the air and on two curving staircases, one with a reverse curve part way down. John Roby's music not only bridged scenes, but underscored most of the fights and a number of speeches, creating precise timing demands.

Through all this, Walker allowed the show to rediscover the shape constructed during the first week, for it was during that initial stage that the production's underpinnings had been established. Most of his work with actors as previews approached consisted of re-establishing and reinforcing basics: calling an actor's attention to a lapse in character, or to an untruthful straining for effect; conducting a run through at conversational volume to re-establish truthful contact between characters; running a scene with no pauses, then running it again while letting pauses re-appear where they seemed truthfully necessary, not where they seemed theatrically effective.

Exploration continued. The final confrontation between Verezzi and Zastrozzi, the nightmare sequence between Zastrozzi and Matilda, were played in many, many variations right up to preview, with Walker allowing the actors to choose what was right for them. A few moments were changed when Walker apparently decided they could not work as they were, or were not worth the risk, either to truth, as in the case of Verezzi's abandoning his sword, or to the audience's safety: Zastrozzi, stage left, tossed a sword spectacularly to Matilda, stage right, until first preview, when the fumbled sword flew into the audience; the next night, Matilda entered stage left and was handed the sword, flamboyantly but safely. But mostly in the last week, Walker followed through on the choices he and his actors had made during the first week.

Walker's directorial methods appear to achieve the results he wants, and the Factory production was evidently a faithful reproduction of his 1987 vision of the play, like it or not. While he admires much of the original production, and while he unhesitatingly identifies William Lane as his favourite director, Walker found the 1977 Toronto Free Theatre production "a little too cerebral, a little too antiseptic." Walker's Factory production was visceral and quite nasty, human and playful. Not a little threatening. In the final moment of the production, Zastrozzi stepped down stage, isolated in light, directly facing the audience, and looked right at us to say, "I like it here." He did not mean in the prison, or in the world of the play. He meant out here in the auditorium with us, in our world. That, I think, is what Walker intended us to be left with from the 1987, Factory *Zastrozzi*.

***

As I worked on the above article, one of the things that most struck me about Walker in rehearsal in 1987 was the way in which his work with the actors and his collaboration with the composer and the designers— "getting his licks in" by setting the timing of the light cues and pulling together the sound, creating the moments—was a continuation of the creative process for him, composing a new performance text rather than "reviving" an old play. In rehearsals and prep for the 1987 *Zastrozzi* he demonstrated what he meant when he later told Robert Wallace:

> Originally, I started directing because I wanted to work with actors and make something—to enjoy theatre in the way that actors can. Playwrights often seem detached from the process of making theatre, as if they're just there to protect their own product. I think that my directing came mostly from trying to get closer to the fun of theatre, to the creativity of it. Before that, it was like I wrote a play on my own and

then went into the theatre essentially as a translator, a protector. That didn't seem to me a very creative thing to do. (Wallace, "Looking for the Light" 24)

Catherine Smith, who also observed the rehearsals for this production, notes both Walker's involvement in the process as co-creator rather than as authoritative authorial presence, and his discomfort with the role of director, as leader and as definitive interpreter, with both positive and negative results, on one hand leading to an unusual freedom for the actors to exercise spontaneous creativity, on the other, leaving some of them somewhat lost from time to time—it must have been a strange, even disconcerting, experience for actors more used to the more hierarchical structure of the "normal" theatre company.

Walker's notion of collaboration did not involve a large amount of verbal interaction with or guidance of the actors. Although he often had a keen kinesthetic awareness of the feel he wanted for certain moments, he would usually allow the actors to explore their own intuitive response to a situation rather than follow his direction because he respected their own creative processes so highly. With much of the rehearsal, Walker would offer an initial idea about the characters and situation and then allow the actors to take over, working, as he says, as a kind of "editor" to their process, rather than trying to impose something. In the early stages of the rehearsal he tended to alternate between sitting and listening to the actors and then jumping up and interacting with them.

This kind of collaborative approach to directing, while potentially capable of making everyone in the process feel part of the end product, also caused problems for some of the actors because they could not seem to develop clear channels of communication with Walker. In turn, Walker respected the contribution the actors made to the creation of the play to such an extent that he became uncomfortable giving them specific guidance when they got into difficulties. (Smith 159–160)

Of directing the six plays of the Motel suite at the Factory in 1997 and 1998, Walker says one of the things that pleased him most was discovering to what extent they are "actors' plays," plays in which Walker as director "doesn't come between the actors and the characters." He says he's learned from American productions of his plays that the stronger American emphasis on feeling is good for his plays in production, that he prefers a process in which the actor "feels his way to the light" rather than thinking about it, in a way he feels many Canadian actors do. He's also pleased that with the Suburban Motel plays he's reached a kind of theatre in which there is such a strong connection between characters and audience, that here, too, there's a sense that he doesn't have to intervene to the extent that he used to, and he likes it that way.

It's hardly surprising that the ambivalence about authority, about giving direction, that's evident in Walker's work in the rehearsal hall echoes (and/or is echoed by) similar ambivalence in the plays themselves. On one hand, Walker is a rebel, was initially attractive to the Factory for his rebelliousness, has made a career out of rebellion. "Ex-centric" in his origins, he has every reason to be suspicious of the "rules" which make him "Other." From this perspective, cops, the enforcers of rules, are more likely to be enemies than not. On the other hand, Walker is too much the anti-romantic to put much credence in the romantic myth of the outlaw hero, even when he's playing that role himself. Here the threat is that of "chaos," the danger that in the absence of rules, we can be overwhelmed by the "scum." More threatening still is the chaos within, and the infectious nature of scumminess. Rigid rules cannot contain the chaos, not without creating a "narrow corridor" so one-dimensional and constraining that its effect is to dehumanize. What Walker's good guy justicers, whether nominally cops or robbers, are left with, then, is righteous anger, and the power of Walker's careening, urgent, truth-seeking language.

Notes

1. Baldwin's dissertation is a provocative and helpful one, and I'm very cheered to see Canadian graudate students giving Walker's work this sort of serious and thoughtful examination.
2. A microfiche copy of Catherine Smith's thesis is on deposit in the National Library of Canada.

Chapter Five
Walker's Women and Sexual and Identity Politics
"Just basic fucking human beings"

> Why are we [women] always made to feel bad for trying to get them
> [men] to act like just basic fucking human beings! Sometimes I get the
> feeling they wanna suck my brains out and tie me naked to the nearest
> tree and fuck me to death. Because that's what they think I'm for. That's
> my purpose. To give them pleasure. Even if it kills me! Okay okay, I got
> that out of my system. (Jill in *Tough!* 490)

In Walker's earliest plays, female characters are often stereotypes, and
operate in polarized opposites: good mother/bad mother, good girl/bad
girl, *femme fatale*/loving wifeandmother, female female/male female, and,
of course, the classic Western male "one or the other" intellectual gender
trap, mother/whore. Before we dismiss Walker as a misogynist with a
superficial and limited understanding of women, it's important to point
out that in the cartoon style characteristic of the early plays, all Walker's
characters, male and female, tend to be stereotypes, cartoons, "masks,"
and that dichotomous structure and pairings of characters are prevalent
throughout the work, cartoons and melodrama depending as they do on
vivid contrast. If anything, at this stage in his career, I would say that Walker
is a misanthrope rather than a misogynist: *none* of his dramatic portraits
are flattering. Furthermore, Walker almost always turns the form against
the content of the form, subverting the stereotypes, and this is also true of
his use of cartoons of female types, thus interrogating and satirizing the
(usually masculine) assumptions which give rise to those perceptual,
dichotomizing categories. Quite early in his career, Walker adopted the
strategy of locating attributes of both pairs of a female polarized dichotomy
in a single character, one pole more evident than the other, but the second
nonetheless sufficiently present to cast doubt on the validity of the first,
indeed of the whole concept of cartoon dichotomy as a way of viewing

female people, or for that matter, any people. In the early plays, we not only see a picture of a world which is, in Walker's opinion, disintegrating, but also receive a critique of ways of looking at that world which prevent us from making it any better.

Walker's first female character is Mrs. Crane in *Ambush at Tether's End*, mother to Max, the philosopher who has hanged himself, leaving notes challenging his friends to follow his example with similarly "definitive action." Mrs. Crane and her husband are little more than plot devices whose refusal to claim the corpse thrusts the responsibility and decisions back on Galt and Bush. As a stereotyped neglectful mother and a satiric representation of the bourgeoisie, Mrs. Crane shows no emotional response to her son's death, and instead treats his suicide as an inconvenience: "You see, death is a touchy subject in some circles. Especially this kind of death. And so we'll have to decide if it's worth risking a scandal by claiming the body." The Cranes are rather reminiscent of Mommy and Daddy in *The Sandbox* (1959) and *The American Dream* (1961), and like Albee's cartoon parental figures, the Cranes address each other in terms of their family functions, "Mother" and "Father" in Walker, rather than "Mommy" and "Daddy" as in Albee. Walker's fictional parents are evenly balanced, two halves of the same character, rather than demonstrations of what Albee, following Philip Whylie and Erik Erikson, called "Momism" in American society, a dominant/submissive coupling in which Mommy is the "ball buster"; according to Wylie and Erikson, "the true nature of mothers [is] cunning, ruthless, and power-hungry" (French 134). Albee was extremely influential among young North American playwrights during the '60s and early '70s.

In *Sacktown Rag*, Miss Missus (shades of Joseph Heller, also very influential at the time) is another rather crude cartoon of a female type, the sexually repressed, secretly randy spinster school teacher who takes out her frustrations on her students, especially the male students. The girls in *Sacktown Rag*, Tina and Annie, pretty much keep to themselves, and when they do interact with the boys, they embarrass them by threatening to reveal that interaction ("I hate your guts Annie." "No you don't. You love me." "Stupid!" "Leave him alone. Look he's all red. [They smile.]"). Tina and Annie also side with the restrictive authority figures as tattle- tales, little Albee Mommies in the making. In this play, however, all opinions, including those negative opinions directed against girls and women, are qualified and subverted by the frame conversation between Brick and Jud as adults, strongly suggesting that the picture of Brick's East End childhood with which we are presented in the flash-back scenes is coloured by his self-pitying romanticizing of his working-class background.

There are three women in *Bagdad Saloon*, Dolly Stiletto, Gertrude Stein, and Sara, and this play is the first example of Walker's use of contrasting female stereotypes, and blendings of stereotypes, each ingredient commenting on the other or others. Dolly is gun-fighter Doc Halliday's mistress, and Gertrude Stein is the famous American writer; Halliday and Stein are among the American figures kidnapped by the Arabs Ahrun and Aladdin in their attempt to learn the secrets of the American method of manufacturing legends. Sara is Ahrun's adolescent daughter. Dolly combines attributes of "whore" and "mother," on one hand the stereotyped saloon girl, a manipulative seductress, on the other the devoted mother of Ivanhoe, the golfer, lounge singer, and grotesquely deformed representation of the "American dream" (and again there seems to be an echo of Albee here, and possibly of Sam Shepard as well). Devoted though she is, Dolly's placing her hope for the future in her son is clearly misplaced, mother-love blinding her to the ugly truth. Stein, while "mannish," is also a mother figure in that she treats all the men like little boys, reprimanding and correcting them in a fussy "mother hen" manner (rather like Mrs. Crane and Miss Missus, or, for that matter, Albee's Mommy) and makes much of her devotees' estimation of her as "Mother of all art." However, brilliant and perceptive as she apparently is, she proves incapable of communicating her wisdom, indeed takes pride in her refusal to be coherent:

> My emotions have survived in a neutrality of sincere indifference. For my country—which I left when I was young and returned to when I was younger still, I feel nothing except an obligation to confuse its citizens. By being both progressively obscure and traditionally literate. (*Bagdad Saloon* 59)

Because she refuses to nourish, she fits the category of "bad mother," or, through her sterility, is really no mother at all. Sara, the rebellious teenager, seems through her independence and defiance of her father's orders, made all the more obvious (and comic) through their context, a culture in which female subservience is automatically expected, seems the best hope for a female avenue to the future, even for an escape from the despairing conundrum in which all the characters in the play find themselves. However, Sara is seduced by Doc, becomes pregnant, and by the end of the play, seems to be headed in the same direction as Dolly. Motherhood, the traditional literary emblem for humankind's stake in a future, is in this play represented as futile.

Contrasts and subversions of female images are somewhat different in *Beyond Mozambique*, although the manner in which Walker is developing the good-girl/bad-girl, mother/whore duality, one which he uses in many of his subsequent plays, right up to those of the Suburban Motel cycle, is becoming clear in this work. The women involved are Olga and Rita. Olga is the wife of the mad scientist, Rocco, and is so devoted to the ideals of European high culture that, in the midst of the jungle, she believes she is Olga from Chekhov's *Three Sisters*, the eldest of the Prozorov sisters and the one most devoted to duty, most loyal to memories of the dead father and Moscow. Walker's Olga is obsessed with appearances, and with fulfilling the duties of housewife and hostess. Rita is a porn movie star with aspirations to legitimate film stardom; her identification is with Rita Hayworth, an unbuttoned blouse and cleavage sex symbol and pin up girl of her day, and Walker's Rita escapes the dangerous reality of the jungle by reframing her experience as a romantic, African adventure movie. In addition to an emblematic "good girl" and an emblematic "bad girl," we have here two women as representations of art, one high, the other low. At first, Rita and Rita's art would seem to be the more vital and vigorous of the two, the worldview which still allows for action, however ill-advised that action may be. But finally, Rita's Rita Hayworth fantasy doesn't work much better than does Olga's Olga Prozorov fantasy: Rita meets an end only somewhat better than Olga's—Rita is raped, but Olga is raped and killed, and thus she suffers both the "fate worse than death," as the source movies have it, as well as death itself, not to mention posthumous desecration of her corpse. Neither motherly devotion and attention to domestic detail nor seductive manipulation are efficacious, and Olga and Rita are ultimately equally naive in believing that what works in "civilization" will work in the jungle. In *Beyond Mozambique*, none of the European responses, including the two presented as specifically female, suffice to fend off the cataclysmic chaos which ends the play.

The title character in *Ramona and the White Slaves* is "bad mother" personified, a "mother" and "whore" in one person, like Dolly Stiletto, as she is the madame of a brothel in Hong Kong during and immediately after World War I, and a mother who enslaves her actual and surrogate children, and who severs their limbs in order to prevent them from leaving home and becoming independent—this takes "mother henning" a lot further than fussy correction and instruction. In his introduction to *Three Plays*, Ken Gass describes Ramona as:

> a man beyond morals, a vicious bitch goddess, supreme manipulator, whose torments to others are not designed for pleasure or even personal gain. Unlike Olga [in *Beyond Mozambique*], she achieves no secret sexual twinges from others' pain, and, despite an overwhelming Catholic background, shows no traces of guilt. In fact, she has moved beyond guilt, through punishment, and into oblivion. She is a Medean figure,

a cannibal, who devours her children to keep them at home, and who slices apart the men who have failed her ... a woman who doesn't much like herself, yet who uses drugs to help herself remember her own scars. But she is charming too, articulate and seductive, mirroring too well the society around her. (14)

This is a complicated maze of a play, one which Walker says he now doesn't entirely understand himself, and one which its first audiences certainly didn't understand. Drugs, recreational and prescription, are frequently referred to in Walker's plays, especially the early ones, but none of the other works are as imbued with drugs and drug-induced states of mind as is *Ramona and the White Slaves*. Characters frequently use drugs in the course of the action, primarily opium and mescaline, and in the first scene of the play, we are taken into Ramona's opium nightmare in which she is raped by a lizard. In any case, drugs and hallucination are certainly important components of the maze, and serve structurally to confuse both characters and audience, and to contribute to the difficulty of distinguishing between "realities." They also serve as possible explanation, and hence a way of reducing the distance between Ramona and members of the audience, of short-circuiting our desire to dismiss her as a monster—if she is drugged, she may simply be experiencing hidden desires, hostilities, hatred of spouse and children, which lurk unacknowledged and even consciously denied within the shadows of many people, those darker corners into which we glimpse only through drugs or nightmare. Monstrous though she is, she is also, as Gass points out, "seductive," and part of the seductiveness is the possibility of kinship.

"Motiveless malignancy" does not adequately describe Ramona; while she herself may have passed into oblivion as Gass suggests, possibly drug induced, possibly the consequence of moral numbness, and is consequently no longer consciously aware of what drives her, Walker nonetheless gives us numerous clues as to how she got where she is. The lizard of the opium nightmare is identified with the priest who accompanied Ramona to Hong Kong when she was a young nun; the priest molested and assaulted her, later married her, fathered her son Friedrich, and subsequently, we are sometimes told, died. At other times, we're told Miguel is Mr. Sebastian, the pimp, who apparently enslaves Ramona, Friedrich, and her two "adopted daughters," but who also tries to right Ramona's wrongs, giving prosthetics to the children who have been deprived of limbs, legs for Friedrich and a hook to replace Leslie's missing hand, a golden hook she assiduously polishes throughout the action, and often uses as a sex toy. Or Sebastian may be merely a device, the "bogey man," which Ramona uses to enslave her "family." Sebastian, in yet another turn, is identified with

Cook, the police detective who is investigating a series of murders which occurred outside the brothel, an investigation which frames the play proper, and moves the action back and forth between the present and the recent past (in character notes, Walker specifies that Sebastian and Cook "must be played by the same actor"). And finally, Cook is identified with Ramona herself, as they trade places in the interrogation which constitutes the penultimate scene of the play—Ramona is still wearing the suit with which she played Cook's role in the previous scene during the long monologue which concludes the play, in part:

> No one is safe. Behaviour is not what it once was. Oh this nightmare is real. It tells the story of—Christians? Cannibals? The story of a family and Miguel's deterioration and how small he became and how he changed disguises. Priest to poppa to pimp, not that it was his idea, by the time he'd sunk to poppa he had no ideas and his mind was—(*She observes herself in the suit for the first time*) Oh look at this then. Very smart. Very strong. Oh yes this will do. (*Stops suddenly. Sniffs*) The lizard again. (*Looks over her shoulder*) Where? (*Blackout*) (*Ramona and the White Slaves* 190)

Leslie and Gloria, the "white slaves" to whom Ramona is both mother and madame, although both "bad girls" from one point of view, are good-girl–bad-girl from another. One of the first signals we get that this is so is a visual one, as obvious and crude as white hat/black hat technique: while both are dressed in black and white schoolgirl uniforms, with all the kinky and potentially titillating dualities that implies, Leslie's appearance is "very neat" while Gloria's uniform is "ripped and soiled"—within the iconography of eroticized pop art and police detective soft-core pornography, a "messy girl" or "dirty girl" is almost always a "bad girl," thus available. In this context, the schoolgirl uniform signals chastity and taboo, unavailability, while the disarray signals the opposite, setting up an erotic and moral tension. Personalities as well as appearances are, at first glance, opposites: Leslie is submissive and acquiescent in a stereotyped "good girl" way, while Gloria is sullen, lethargic, and ultimately defiant. However, Leslie has evidently been the more independent in the past, as it is she who is missing a hand, the hook hidden by a fur muff when we first see her, and it is also Leslie who, in the course of the play, develops, against her "mother's" wishes, a romantic relationship with Mitch, the German aviator. (Who may also be Friedrich, Ramona's son. Perfectly clear?) Gloria remains defiant throughout, arming herself with a knife and threatening to kill anyone who obstructs the family's escape from the brothel, but evidently never does see that it is Ramona who is the primary obstacle to her freedom. Furthermore, by defying the expectations placed upon her in this situation, by rebelling against the rules of the brothel, Gloria refuses to acquiesce to the conventions of an essentially evil fantasy world. And doesn't this rebellion then make her the "good girl"?

Among the melodramatic dualities Walker employs in *Zastrozzi* is, again, a good-girl–bad-girl contrast, here between Julia, "an aristocrat. A fair-haired beauty," and Matilda, "a gypsy. A raven-haired beauty"—in B-movies, blonde and brunette are frequently the female equivalent of white hat/ black hat, or moustache versus clean-shaven. In his review of the New York Public Theater production of *Zastrozzi*, Frank Rich sees Matilda and Julia as "two hideously caricatured women" and "the butts of the jokes" (Conolly 216). He evidently misses the function of stereotype in Walker's strategy, which requires that all the characters, male and female, be stereotyped if the audience is to be lured into making the easy assumptions on which melodrama depends. Further, Rich evidently doesn't see the ways in which Walker manipulates those assumptions, and that to this end, all the characters, including the women, exhibit characteristics and undertake actions which deconstruct those assumptions along with our conventional, dichotomized categorization of good and evil. Zastrozzi has nightmares about being good. Verezzi is a saintly hero with a murder in his past. Victor is a pragmatist who is killed when he succumbs to the temptation of absolutism. Bernardo is a thug, but also, often, a lonely little boy. (To be fair to Rich, it should be pointed out that Walker himself disliked this production, finding Andrei Serban's direction much too serious, indeed, apparently oblivious to the comic dimension of the play, hence I would assume, to many of the subversions effected by the comedy.)

So Matilda is not entirely the two-dimensional, cartoonish bad girl, as vivid and compelling as this aspect of the character is. A student of mine, Anne Ross, pointed out to me that there is an exchange of some of the expected attributes between Matilda, the *femme fatale*, and Julia, the "virgin bride." While Matilda appears to be, and in many respects is, a strong, confident, and independent woman who defies convention and plays by her own rules, she is nonetheless dependent on a man, Zastrozzi, for her sense of identity, and her devotion to that man, however perversely expressed, is what ultimately destroys her. On the other hand, Julia, the stereotyped "good girl," goes against type in that she refuses to allow any man to possess or control her. There is a toughness in Julia; Walker directed Nicky Guadagni to play her as a woman who expects the world to conform to her expectations, without reservation.

T. M. Power's progressive disintegration through the Power Plays trilogy is initiated, in part, by a woman and by unrequited love, by the demands Margaret makes for intimacy on her terms, long and probing conversations, while refusing intimacy on his terms, sex. Cynical and hard-bitten reporter, albeit in *Gossip* still something of a romantic, meets New Age woman (spinny in a way Smith says is meant to refer to Margaret Trudeau, very much in the news at the time of *Gossip's* writing and first production):

> MARGARET: You promised me we'd spend some time alone together, Tyrone. In a relationship a person has the right to make certain demands.
> POWER: We don't have a relationship.
> MARGARET: Yes we do! Just because we don't go to bed together doesn't mean we don't have a relationship.
> POWER: It does to me!
> MARGARET: Just because I don't love you doesn't mean that you can't love me.
> POWER: They call that unrequited love, Margaret. It's a disease. People wither away from it. They move into rooming houses and die, staring at the little triangles on the linoleum floors.
> MARGARET: Romantic garbage. (45)

Margaret is dangerous to Power not only by virtue of her being a woman and sexually attractive, but by her class, as her money insulates her from reality; by her avocation as a poet, as her dilettantish high art distances her still further from reality; and by her mental instability, which contributes to Power's difficulty in retaining *his* tenuous grasp on reality. Margaret is stereotypically feminine in her willingness to use her appearance and her frailty to get her way; she complains often of the "tension" in her life, especially when the conversation takes a turn she finds threatening, and she finds the talk most threatening when it approaches her relationship with her brother, Paul, with whom she is having an incestuous affair, or the possibility that Paul, a federal cabinet minister, may be involved in some political wrongdoing. Later in the play, Margaret disguises herself, badly and transparently, as the expensive call girl, Susan Long, in a futile attempt to put Power off the trail, and as an expression of her own alter-ego, again a good girl/bad girl dichotomy. At the end of the play, when it is revealed that Paul is indeed the source of most of the corruption Power uncovers, Margaret leaves the stage to be committed to a mental institution. Among other things, Power's investigation destroys any chance he may have had of bedding the object of his sexual desire (and this is the last time in the Power trilogy that we see Power expressing any sexual desire whatsoever; in *Filthy Rich*, it is Jamie who is almost misled by lust and romance, confusing the *femme fatale* Scott sister for the "good girl").

In his investigation of Walker's subversion of gender roles, Ed Nyman first refutes the idea that *film noir*, in and of itself, is a subversion of dominant American values:

> The two streams merely appealed to different desires in the audience: A-movies to the desire to affirm the national narrative and the B-movies, the desire to be titillated by the (containable) disturbance of that narrative. B-movies and *film noir* were the carnival space within the dominant American ideology and, therefore, despite their seemingly subversive effects, no more than a sanctioned disturbance that reinforced a dominant discourse. (59)

If that is so, then, Walker cannot simply reflect B-movies and *film noir* in order to effect subversive art, but must subvert the B-movies themselves, and their conventions and conventionalized view of life, including the "good girl/bad girl" classification of women. Nyman quotes John Tuska's *Dark Cinema: American Film Noir in Cultural Perspective* to the effect that in *film noir* there are *femmes fatales*, "interesting, intelligent, and often powerful," and then "wives and mothers" who are "dull and insipid." Since wife and mother is the ideal role prescribed to women by these movies, says Nyman, "no matter how subversive the very existence of a woman such as a *femme fatale* is, she is nonetheless proscribed as that which is to be avoided and punished" (60). Nyman notes the many women in Walker plays who appear to have the characteristics of the *femme fatale*: Rita in *Beyond Mozambique*, Ramona from *Ramona and the White Slaves*, Brigot Nelson and Margaret in *Gossip*, one of the Scott sisters in *Filthy Rich*, Matilda in *Zastrozzi*, Lilliane in *Theatre of the Film Noir*. But appearances are deceptive, and that's the point.

> Though the plays do put women in dangerous, seductive roles, the *femme fatale* identification remains an unstable category; and even when a female character is genuinely dangerous, she is not punished for her gender-transgressions. Women such as Margaret in *Gossip*, who appear to be the loving, safe, domesticated women that *film noir* valorises, turn out to be neurotic and dangerous ... Brigot Nelson, on the other hand, turns out to be less of the *femme fatale* that she appears and more of a crank. In *Filthy Rich*, the difficulty of distinguishing which of the Scott sisters is faithful and which is a *femme fatale* suggests the absurdity of the convention. Walker's play consistently blur the two roles for women that are so clearly demarcated in *film noir*. (Nyman 61)

In *Theatre of the Film Noir*, Lilliane, the only woman in the play, appears to be a *femme fatale*, but she does not serve as an object of sexual desire for the men in the play, most of whom are more interested in each other, but as a means of concealing their identities, sexual in the case of the homosexual Jean, national in the case of the German soldier Erik.

> Rather than being lured to their doom, the male characters flock to Lilliane for the protection that her sexuality offers them … Her sexuality is not a threat but a haven. Indeed, at the end of the play, Lilliane is not punished for her independent sexuality—both unlicensed and incestuous—but is brought by the inspector's influence into the American *film noir* industry to become, perpetually, the very *femme fatale* she has not been in the play. (Nyman 62)

Other gender issues in the play are, of course, raised by Bernard's homosexuality, and here Nyman argues that the play fails to

> De-essentialise, de-hierachlise, and de-sacralise … the heterosexuality of [the] patriarchal order. The *film noir's* typical reinscription of compulsory heterosexuality is not perverted in the same way that its binary gender categories are. Indeed, the play contradicts its own trope of perversity by making the overtly homoerotic … an image of decay and distasteful perversity. (62)

Nyman is made particularly uncomfortable by the play's presentation of homosexuality as co-symptomatic with "incest, fraternisation, necrophilia, murder, and the moral decay of post World War II culture." What Nyman doesn't say is that these associations come from one of the play's source works, Jean Genet's *Funeral Rites*. Genet *wants* the reader (whom Genet always imagined as a heterosexual male) to be uncomfortable. In this regard, Walker is following Genet's lead, for I believe *Theatre of the Film Noir's* debt to and use of *Funeral Rites* goes far beyond the "general setting and situation, the names and personalities of some of the characters, and the perverse, sexually obsessed tone of one of the characters, Bernard," which Smith identifies as Walker's borrowings from the novel (98). Indeed, Walker has described the play as his "*hommage* to Genet" (interview, June 1998) although here, as in all his "borrowings" and adaptations, Walker is selective in what he takes, builds more from the impression the work made on him than from the work itself. In the case of *Theatre of the Film Noir*, nonetheless, I'm convinced he stays quite close to Genet in the use of the central character as a "social saboteur" and as an assault on the audience's or reader's sensibilities. The *last* thing Genet wants to do is "recuperate" homosexuality as an acceptable alternative to "compulsory heterosexuality," as for him (and for the semi-fictional "Jean Genet" who is the novel's narrator and the model for Walker's Bernard) his homosexuality is an essential part of the difference which sets himself apart from and in opposition to "normal" French society, which he hated. In a similar vein, hence Genet's well-known celebration of murder as the distinguishing characteristic of contemporary "saints." Nyman's concept of "perversity" is not perverse enough to encompass Genet's social and moral inversions, nor Walker's use of those borrowed inversions to assault the audience and its values, its supposed capacity for the tolerance of difference. While, of course, making them laugh at the same time. As Nyman himself says when he concludes his essay, "perversion has no *telos*; it simply goes on, always desecrating what has been made or left sacred" (65), including, I would suggest, homosexuality itself, or, for that matter, "recuperation." But I would say that for the most part, Nyman's "queer reading" of *Theatre of the Film Noir* doesn't make it a better play, nor more complex and challenging, simply more fashionable, and thus perhaps less challenging, in 1981, the date of the play's first production, or 1998. As we saw from his first play, *The Prince of Naples*, nothing is sacred to Walker and safe from debunking, including rebellion in its various forms, particularly given rebellion's tendency to romanticize itself and to construct its own version of the sacred. Genet said of the Palestinians, whom he championed, that as soon as they formed their own state and acquired their own flag, he would betray them. I suspect that Walker is similarly inclined.

While Walker follows Genet, he does not follow him exactly, of course. For one thing, Bernard is much more anxious than either of the two Genets, much less assured and strong in his differentness. There is a strong American presence in the play, none at all in the novel, for in a North American, late-twentieth-century play, the American soldier, Hank, and the profusion of American gum, cigarettes and chocolate bars serves much more effectively to represent a return to "normalcy" than does the re-establishment of French bourgeois values in Genet's French, mid-century novel. Perhaps most importantly, Bernard is killed before the play ends, shot dead by Inspector Clair, while Genet's Genet lives on. It is here that I think Nyman's queer reading is most helpful and illuminating, for in Clair's eyes and according to the values of "normalcy," which of course includes the patriarchy to which Nyman refers, Bernard *had* to die. "Clair deliberately re-constructs the fiction of a heterosexual patriarchy at the end of the play, making Bernard the necessary sacrificial goat to achieve it" (Nyman 64). Or, as Clair has it, Bernard had to die because he was sad and unpredictable: "How could the rest of us survive and prosper with him out on the streets making other people sad and unpredictable too" (*Theatre of the Film Noir* 159). Bernard's unpredictablity, dangerous to men like Clair because difficult to control and possibly contagious, is manifested in all Bernard's "anti-social activity," his anxiety, his resemblance to Genet, not just in his homosexuality.

Once again in discussing Walker's plays, we have reached that border in Walker's career, ending the extremely cynical phase, and moving into the more autobiographical, politically committed phase. But, I would argue, Walker is still Walker, enough the pragmatic skeptic, to continue to question his motives for choosing sides even while he chooses sides, and sufficiently anxious to remain alert to the dangers of accepting any set of values without question, the dangers of "social romanticism." In the matter at hand, he chooses more and more often to valorize women and their perceptions. Walker has often spoken of the importance of women in his life; in his interview with Carole Corbeil, he mentions the effect of growing up in a household with three older sisters, and, significantly, he dedicates the East End plays to his daughters, of whom he has three. I think the increased attention to women, their place in the world, in Walker's work has a good deal to do with Walker's being the father of daughters. Nonetheless, Walker being Walker, he often interrogates his own valorization. For example, in *Escape from Happiness* he pokes fun at the pop-psychology, pop-feminism mix so much in evidence in magazines and on television talk shows, it itself another form of "social romanticism." Mary Ann, mixed up, neurotic, timid, is at a "crossroads"; influenced by her therapist, Clare, Mary Ann wants to "share some important information" with her family, and "outs" her older sister, Elizabeth, a tough, no-nonsense lawyer.

> MARY ANN: Elizabeth is a lesbian.
> ELIZABETH: What.
> MARY ANN: You're a lesbian. And you're proud of it. And I'm proud of you for being proud. And now Mom and Gail can be proud of you, too.
> ELIZABETH; Mary Ann, what are you doing.
> MARY ANN: I'm outing you.
> NORA: What, dear?
> MARY ANN: I'm outing her. She's been in the closet. I'm helping her get out. She's a lesbian. Say it loud and clear. She's a lesbian. She's a lesbian! Clare told me to do it. Someone did it to Clare, and it was the best day of her life. So I'm doing it to you, Elizabeth. You're a lesbian. You have sex with women. Lots of women. Lots and lots of women. Right?! (*Escape from Happiness* 374)

Mary Ann learns that everyone in the family but her already knew, and had known for a long time. Later, Mary Ann is disillusioned, devastated, when Elizabeth tells her "I sleep with women *and* men if you must know. I sleep with anyone I like. I find nice, sexy people and I sleep with them." Mary Ann replies:

... You were supposed to be a lesbian. You were supposed to have made a choice. But no. You sleep with anyone just because they're nice! What kind of choice is that. That's not courageous. That's not politically ... important. Anyone can do that. Even I can do that. (392)

In her M.A. dissertation, "Walker's Women in the East End Plays," Mary Pat Mombourquette examines *Better Living, Criminals in Love, Beautiful City* and *Love and Anger* within a feminist-materialist framework, "feminist in that it examines Walker's depiction of the social construction of gender and the relationships of power between men and women," and materialist "in its examination of those relationships in the context of other power relationships, specifically those between social institutions and the individual" (Abstract), and to this end, employs the psychoanalytic theories of Lacan and the linguistic theories of Derrida.

> Walker explores the social being who desires to recreate the remembered plenitude of the pre-Oedipal state. This desire acknowledges the matriarchal realm, as opposed to the patriarchal realm. Yet just as the patriarchal realm is based on the transcendence of the phallus, the matriarchal realm is based on the transcendence of plenitude. Neither the Mother's plenitude nor the Father's phallus can be given anything but symbolic value in society; they can be represented but never made present. (Mombourquette 6)

Thus the individual's social experience (our experience after we have acquired a knowledge of "Other" and after we have acquired language) is based on "lack," lack of the undifferentiated, all-caring world of the womb and of nursing on one hand, lack of the "phallus" (not the penis *per se*, but the power of the patriarch, the Father, in the social, linguistic world) on the other. In consequence, the individual's primary motivation is one of "desire," desire for that which cannot actually be attained in a post-Oedipal state, for in society "they can be represented but never made present."

Thus, according to Mombourquette, the female characters in Walker's plays are important in two ways. To the male characters, they often represent the "Mother," the "lost matriarchal realm."

> Tom in *Better Living*, Junior in *Criminals in Love*, Paul in *Beautiful City*, and Maxwell in *Love and Anger* look to women to take the place of the mythical other, the Mother, who will reinstate their universality. They view women as the site of plenitude and therefore able to deal, better than they, "with the complex nature of reality." (Mombourquette 26)

The men try to "recapture the illusion of plenitude that the women represent" (15). Secondly, the women, because they are excluded from structures of power, are better able to see those structures as constructs, and are thus better able to maintain a sense of who they are as individuals.

> In Walker's plays the terms of empowerment are problematic because the women are not part of society's institutions (a fact they acknowledge) and thus, paradoxically, they are able to maintain a sense of self; in contrast, the men believe (often erroneously) that they will find a place for themselves within society's institutions. Because of this belief the male characters risk surrendering their selfhood to the demands of social institutions of which they are not part. Walker creates a space on stage in which the problems of identity, imposed by institutions and their laws, can be repeatedly experienced by the characters. Within this space women, because they are socially marginalized, raise the most fundamental problems of the psyche within the social dimension of the theatre. (Mombourquette 2)

In *Criminals in Love*, then, Junior turns to Gail both as "the site of plenitude" and because he thinks she is better able to deal "with the complex nature of reality."

> [Junior] does not capture Gail; he captures the position Gail will fill in this world as his "salvation." Junior defines what he desires Gail to be in order to fill some void in his own world. The identity he gives Gail is thus based on some lack within himself. (Mombourquette 22)

Elsewhere, I have argued that the shifts in convention and theatrical scale in the play are a function of Junior's point-of-view, and that the world of the play is the world seen through Junior's eyes, or through the eyes of a *naif* like Junior, as the magnifications and distortions apply whether or not Junior is present on stage ("'I put it in terms that cover the spectrum'"). Thus the older characters, Junior's father, Henry, his aunt Wineva, and William, the philosophical bum and "wise guide" figure, are, to Junior, "primal forces" over whom he has no control, thus "larger than life" on stage because they are larger than life to Junior. The young women in the play, his girlfriend, Gail, and her friend, Sandy, are also subject to the colouring of Junior's perspective, and early in the play, he naively sees women as either "mothers" or "whores," the polarized dichotomy which categorizes so many of the female caricatures in early Walker plays. Thus, when Sandy turns a trick to see if she could do it "in an emergency," Junior tries to forbid Gail to see her anymore: "if she's going to be a hooker, I don't think you'll have much in common" (*Criminals In Love* 1988, 42). Sandy is another of Walker's working-class pragmatists, and her tests of her own ability to survive are presented simply as an extension of the sort of practical common sense we also see in Gail, but which Gail is unwilling to exercise in this particular way. "She's [Sandy's] just looking for security. Other people invest in bonds" (*Criminals In Love* 1988, 85). In this respect, Sandy resembles Jamie in *Filthy Rich* and *The Art of War*. Through the course of the play, as Junior comes to know Sandy as an individual, he goes beyond his initial, fearful stereotyping of her towards a fuller understanding of her human complexity.

Similarly, but in a more involved way and in a way more central to the development of Walker's protagonist, Junior eventually moves away from a fearful stereotyping of Gail as a substitute mother to a recognition of her as an independent human being, complete with weaknesses and her own fears, and begins to love her not out of his dependence on her but for who she is. He begins to pay attention to what he can give her rather than concentrating entirely on what he needs from her, whereas early on his desperate need, the insistence of what Mombourquette would call a void within himself, results in his projecting onto Gail super-human capabilities. Having lost his real mother at an early age, and being completely cowed by his inept criminal father, Junior experiences "lack" even more so than do most men, and, as his name suggests, remains infantilized. *Criminals in Love* is in large part about Junior growing up, a little, about the much delayed process of separation from Mother, the mother in his imagination and the persona of mother he has projected onto his girlfriend.

At the beginning of the play, we see Junior with his head up Gail's sweater, quite literally suckling at her breast. Gail gets bored with the activity because "it keeps [her] passive" and asks, "Were you breast fed." Junior reacts defensively: "I have no problem about breasts. I've never had a breast thing in my life. I just like yours … that's all I can say really" (*Criminals In Love* 1988, 16). Obviously Junior protests too much, and obviously he does long to be taken care of as if he were a child, a fact the clear sighted Gail herself recognizes: "He [Junior] thinks I can do anything. He has this picture of me in his head about twenty-times the size of life" (*Criminals In Love* 1988, 57). When he speaks of his own mother, Junior longs for the security she represents in his imagination, of the remembered, paradisal absence of individuality and responsibility: "I wish my mother was still here. We could have a little talk. I could get really scared and she'd understand. She's the only person I could let myself get totally scared in front of. I get close with you, Gail. But with her I could lie down on the floor and pretend I was jello" (*Criminals In Love* 1988, 79). At least by now (scene seven) Junior is able to recognize that Gail is *not* his mother, although he still hasn't progressed to the point where he is really capable of action independently and on his own initiative.

Fearing that it is his "destiny" to become like his criminal father, unless Gail saves him, and encouraged by Gail and William, Junior visits his father in prison and tries to "end our relationship." He fails. "What are you talking about you dumb fuck. We're father and son. That's not a relationship. It's destiny" (*Criminals In Love* 232). Henry uses a combination of physical force and appeals to filial loyalty to coerce Junior into storing stolen goods, saying that Uncle Ritchie will arrange to have him (Henry) killed unless Junior co-operates. By agreeing, in order, he thinks, to save his father's life, Junior falls under the influence of Ritchie's wife, Wineva, who leads Junior into a life of crime, taking Gail, Sandy, and William with him.

According to Mombourquette, Wineva adds a second female dichotomy to the exploration of male-female relationships and their dynamics of lack and desire. If Gail is the "good Mother," Wineva is the "bad Mother"; after meeting Wineva, and being frightened by her, Junior ruefully mentions that when he was a child he had always wanted an aunt, evidently an earlier expression of his desire for a substitute mother. Mombourquette says, "By dividing the attributes of the mother into two separate categories and having each category personified by a different character, Walker is able to illuminate both the attraction and the fear that underlies the power of mother" (55)—a central issue for Junior in his struggle to grow up. Wineva smothers her victims with hugs and kisses (William says she is a "truly terrifying kisser") and imprisons them within "family," denying everyone she thus incorporates any sense of individual identity. If Wineva is bad mother to Gail's good mother, William is the good father battling Junior's bad natural father for Junior's soul or identity. "In effect Junior externalizes the demons and angels of his unconscious onto the playing space" (Mombourquette 58).

Near the end of the play, the demons appear to be winning. Henry Sr. betrays the whereabouts of the "Junior Dawson Gang" (the original, working title of the play) to the police, who have surrounded Junior's house. Gail recognizes their plight in language that both echoes and transcends the pulp-novel romanticism with which she had sometimes earlier viewed their relationship, in contrast to her usual commonsense: "We're going to jail. Young lovers doomed, taking the plunge. This is that cliff, Junior. That one I read about in a dozen books ... In the books it was a bit romantic" (*Criminals In Love* 1988, 114). After the others have left the house to surrender to the police, Gail and Junior are left alone. They reaffirm their love for each other, and try to help each other come to terms with, to fully understand, the reality of their situation. On one hand, they might be going to jail, separate jails at that. On the other,

GAIL: ... Tell me this isn't the start of something bad. Just the beginning
  of a bad life, you know?
JUNIOR: It's not ... Now you tell me.
GAIL: It's not.
JUNIOR: You're sure?
  Pause. GAIL shrugs.
GAIL: No. And that's what really scares me. (*Criminals In Love* 280)

There are no guarantees, either way. This isn't *necessarily* the beginning
of a "bad life," the fulfillment of Junior's "destiny" and the consequence of
William's "hanging shadow," but the possibility of a "bad life" is definitely
real, especially for people marginalized as they are, and while their love
might see them through, and while this is a comfort for both them and
the audience, it can't be counted on to do so.

Junior goes on to say that what scares him is the realization that he
could "get really mad" and kill someone—he probably has his father and
Wineva in mind. He places the possibility of the "bad" within, sees that
that is part of Gail, whom he had previously thought of as his Good Mother,
as well. Indeed, at this point in the play, near the end, Junior sees that the
"bad within" is part of being human. The "bad" is no longer external, no
longer some outside force threatening to ruin his life, but something over
which he might at least have some control.

The young lovers decide to wait for the police to come inside for them,
and in the meantime, kiss and embrace. Gail invitingly holds out the bottom
of her sweater; Junior is putting his head slowly inside as the lights fade
for the last time, and the play ends with the image with which it began.
Mombourquette sees this concluding image in negative terms:

> The final image of the play echoes the opening scene; however, now it
> takes on darker overtones. It is a visual image of a tragic yet absurd
> solution, that place of transcendence where death and desire merge. It
> is also the essence of Walker's paradoxical stance. *Criminals in Love*, like
> *Better Living*, discloses Walker's fear of the world as a social unit as well
> as his anxiety about the condition of the individual psyche. (74–75)

Here I think I disagree with Mombourquette, and see in the concluding image, particularly given the exchange which has just gone on before,
much more of Walker's "possibility" than Mombourquette evidently does.
True, the young lovers have discovered that the "world as a social unit" is
indeed a fearful place, and true, their "individual psyche[s]" have been
sorely tested, and true, Walker is not about to give us a sentimental, happy
Hollywood ending in which young love conquers all. But *Criminals in Love*
is a comedy, not a tragedy, and love and life might win ("might" rather
than "will" because this is a Walker comedy). Gail and Junior understand

themselves, the world, and their love better than they did at the outset of the events depicted in the play. Junior has finally "ended [his] relationship" with his father, and sees the necessity of trying to break out of the script that Henry and the sociologists have set out for his life. In the matter of love, Junior has moved beyond the hysterical separation anxiety we see at the beginning of the play, and has recognized his responsibility for Gail, a fallible human being, as well as hers for him. Their love for each other has matured, only a little, but too much would fall into the sentimentality and romanticism Walker so dislikes and finds so destructive. Gail, who was earlier dissatisfied with a physical relationship that imaged them as mother and child, and which had reduced her humanity, can now offer comfort to Junior, and probably to herself, by inviting the intimacy of "nursing" him because that act no longer constitutes the whole of their relationship—it is just one part of something now larger and more complex which requires them both to exercise human responsibility. I think Walker repeats the image to invite comparison between the meanings of the image before and after its transformation by the effect of intervening events and discoveries. That, certainly, is the meaning the audience took from the image when I directed a production of the play for the University of Manitoba in 1988. What is clear is that the image is a very rich and disturbing one, as many of Walker's images are, and that it both insists on attempts at interpretation and allows a wide variety of readings.

Better Living, a "prequel" to *Criminals in Love* in that we see Junior and Gail at an earlier stage in their life, is one of Walker's most complex and intricate examinations of women, different kinds of women, ways women use to communicate with each other. At the center of this examination is one of his most complex character studies, Nora, the mother of the family. It is a measure of her complexity that I can't think of another Walker character to whom I have such mixed, and such violently mixed, responses. On one hand, one can't help but like her—she's flaky and funny, but she's also the very embodiment of working-class determination, a woman who will stop at nothing to make things "better" for her family, whether they want her help or not. On the other hand, her need to talk, incessantly, in order to avoid both thought and reality, her evasiveness, drive me crazy (and because *Better Living* is one of the Walker plays I've directed, I've spent quite a lot of time living with Nora). Hearing from Jack that Tom is alive, in the city, and coming to visit, she replies: "He's dead, thank God. I saw him die. In my dreams. Hundreds of dreams. Hundreds of deaths. Cruel, slow, painful" (290). When Elizabeth says she'll kill Tom, Nora elaborates the defensive fantasy:

> Good. We could all kill him. That would be nice. If your father was
> alive he'd need killing, we all know that. But he's dead. He died in Swift
> Current, Saskatchewan. Five years ago. Run over by a runaway tractor.
> Crushed both his legs. He lay in the hospital for five days. In agony.
> Out of his mind with pain. And then he died. They buried him in Swift
> Current. (*Better Living* 295)

Mary Ann is temporarily taken in; Elizabeth knows immediately that
Nora "just made it up." When Tom actually does show up at the house,
and subsequently moves in, Nora says he's a burglar, then a stranger, Tim,
who lives in her house and whom her daughters inexplicably refer to as
their father.

I have a very similar mixed response to Madame Ranyevskaya in
Chekhov's *The Cherry Orchard*, a woman who, like Nora, embraces the
world with a warm generosity, and simultaneously energetically avoids
reality. The other, inevitable comparison from the modern classical repertoire is, of course, Nora from *A Doll's House*, Ibsen's play about female liberation (or, as he would have it, human liberation).

Unlike Ibsen's, Walker's Nora does not leave home—when she slams
doors, she does so in order to hide herself safely in the underground room
she is busy digging. Essentially, she stays, and tries to make things better
where she is, if she can, avoids reality entirely if she can't. In *Better Living*,
it is the husband who has abandoned home and family, leaving Nora to
try to sort out her life by herself, raising three wildly disparate daughters
with the assistance only of how-to books, and with the somewhat ineffec-
tual help of her brother, the priest, Father Jack. The woman in *Better Living* and *Escape from Happiness* who leaves her husband and abandons her
child in search of self is Mary Ann, but Mary Ann's anxiety is so intense
and neurotic that she can neither definitively leave her marriage nor find
herself. (The other echo from *A Doll's House* that I see in *Better Living* is in
the father's use of diminutive endearments to belittle the females of the
household; Elizabeth tells Tom: "You called Mary Ann honeybunny. You
called me baby doll. You called Gail pumpkin, puddin, peaches, puddles
and precious. It was sickening then. It's disgusting now" [*Better Living* 305].)

This household has become, of necessity as well as by preference, a
matricentric society, to use the term as Marilyn French uses it, arguing
that a "matriarchal" society has never existed, and cannot exist. Almost
like an anthropologist, Walker investigates the consequences and significance of bringing together and into conflict two systems of social organization, or, in Mombourquette's terms, by imposing a "social world" of
naming, ordering, and alienating on a "natural," non-hierarchical, maternal world of immediacy and the senses. When the prodigal husband and

father, the "wandering male," returns ten years later, claiming not to be the "Bad Father" of the past but someone else entirely, the matricentric structure and vaguely feminist values, demonstrated but never specifically defined, which Nora has used to reconstruct her life, are quite literally besieged and tested by patriarchy and its sociopolitical assumptions. Mombourquette says of this contest:

> Walker presents both these experiences [maternal and paternal] in a comic light, with Nora (an eccentric mother) representing the maternal realm and Tom (the prodigal father) representing the paternal realm. Both characters are larger-than-life personifications of the realm that they help illustrate. Nora's existence is based on the continuation of the female line while Tom's existence is based on destroying the feminine line, by attaining power over it and thereby making it his own. By creating two such opposite characters Walker is able to make statements about the absurd quality of our society, which gives preference to death over life. Thus Walker's comedy is subversive, illuminating and focusing on the illusion of our society. (26)

Better Living has been one of the plays closest to Walker's heart, and for many years, was the play to which he returned most often to rewrite and revise, "warming up," he said, for work on new plays. Nora is the centre of the play, the focus of male-female conflict and half of each of the mother-daughter relationships which reach toward a female social structure, or, perhaps more accurately, mode of living, as an alternative to patriarchy. Walker has said of this character:

> Nora, in fact, is the first east end positive character I wrote because, chronologically, I wrote *Better Living* before *Criminals in Love*, even though it was produced after. Nora is my first clear response to what we've talked about as the change in my writing, the focussing on my past, what I'd been avoiding. All Nora is doing, really, is taking everything she possibly can and trying to make it better. She has no space in the house, so she tries to create space; this is typical of her response to any problem that comes up in the family; she turns it into something good or, at least, she tries to. She doesn't give up even when she gets a mad man for a husband: she tries to turn him into something better. She is the first of what we've talked about as a "possibility" character. Because it was important for me to test this type of character, I put her under a lot of pressure, to test the possibility, to see how far she would go. What was important was that she held up. The worse things got, the better she got in some way; she took all that stuff and translated it into "betterism," as I call it. Sometimes that meant not exactly hearing the way the other characters speak, or not looking as if she knew what

she was doing; but this was only part of her process of turning things into something better. (Wallace, "Looking for the Light" 30)

But *Better Living* isn't a simple morality play, woman=good and man=bad, anymore than *Zastrozzi* is. While our sympathies are tilted towards Nora's "maternal world," and while that world is clearly morally superior to Tom's, it too exacts a price from its inhabitants.

> The maternal space in *Better Living* is the realm of pure need. According to Lacan, need, which by definition cannot be articulated in demand, predates the social. Nora's love of her family is in excess; in over-investing her desire in her daughters and her daughter's daughters she threatens to annihilate any distinction between the women. As Nora appropriates her daughters' lives she acknowledges no rigid dividing line between self and other. Therefore Walker, with his characterization of Nora and her daughters, creates a realm which like the maternal space described by Doane has "the potential to destroy the very notion of identity." (Mombourquette 32)

Looked at from another point of view, that of systems psychology, Nora's feminine family can be seen as dysfunctional, and in pursuing this line of thought I'm indebted to my wife, Lillian Esses, a clinical psychologist. On seeing a tape of the University of Manitoba production of the play, Lillian first noted how "over the top" the characterizations are (evidently on the part of both Walker and the actors), but after a brief discussion of ways in which Walker is trying to achieve a "reality" other than that of photographic realism, Lillian pointed out that here, the dramatic "types" isolate and dramatize psychological "types," types representative of members of a family with abuse in its past (and that, indeed, is the family secret we discover as *Better Living* progresses). From this point of view, then, the male is still the "bad guy," as Tom, and the abuse he inflicted on his family in the past, is responsible for many of the difficulties the women in his family are encountering in the present.

When a parent betrays his or her parental role through abuse, or abandons the family entirely (and Tom has done both), one of the children, typically, takes on a parental role as "the protector," and usually the child who assumes that role is the eldest—in *Better Living*, Elizabeth, the lawyer. But, of course, such a role is beyond the power of a child, and the strain of assuming more responsibility than a child is capable of does damage, and the role separates the individual from her self. Elizabeth takes on the task of protecting the family from Tom (and, perhaps, also wants to prevent him from usurping her parental role), and, at the end of scene three, does shoot at him, whether with the intention of hitting him or of scaring him to death we never discover. In another variation on the mother-whore dynamic we've seen Walker employ in a number of earlier plays, we learn that Elizabeth prostituted herself in order to put herself through law school, to look after the family, thus using prostitution to support her parenting, her ability to nurture, and to facilitate her entry into the "masculine," and patriarchal, world of the law. That the prostitution in Elizabeth's past is fact rather than a lie meant to intimidate Tom is one of the matters clarified in subsequent rewrites of the play. After Tom has imposed his regime of "consumer socialism" on the family, things come to a head between Elizabeth and Tom, starting with a disagreement about who could do a better job of fixing the floor, a man's household chore.

> ELIZABETH: I think you're primitive. You've got ideas but they're primitive. They don't go far enough. They lack intelligence.
>
> TOM: I'll fix the floor. It'll be fixed. That's intelligent enough.
>
> ELIZABETH: I could fix the floor. If I thought it was important I could fix the floor, design a new floor, make the floor do things.
>
> TOM: Whatya mean make the floor do things. A floor doesn't have to do anything except be there. And be level.
>
> ELIZABETH: I could design a floor that did things. A floor that cleaned itself. A self- cleaning floor. Or a floor that provided heat. I could run electric current through the floor that would heat this whole room. I could put burglar alarms in the floor. I could put trap doors in the floor. I could put mirrors in the floor that would reflect light so you could use this room as a greenhouse. I could do anything to that floor. I could take your basic primitive idea of a floor and make something really amazing out of it.
>
> TOM: So what?
>
> ELIZABETH: So you have to deal with me. (*Better Living* 335–336)

Tom and Elizabeth are rather alike, a fact Tom sees, and one which Elizabeth probably sees, but doesn't want to admit.

The argument proceeds to the future, what Tom calls the "total shit future," and who can protect the family in the future. Finally the argument comes down not to who would kill, as Elizabeth would if she had to, but who would *want* to kill, and Tom would:

> I can kill. With my bare hands. I can rip flesh. I can take a knife and cut throats. I can put it in bellies. When the total shit of the future comes, I can look it in the eye and keep it out of this fucking house. I can take anyone who tries to invade this house and rip his eyes out. I can cheat. I can lie. I can steal. I can beg. I can sneak and grovel and betray and murder and burn things to the ground to protect this family. I am the soldier of the total shit future. I am the provider of the total shit future. I am the basic ingredient for survival. (*Better Living* 337)

We believe him. We also believe Elizabeth when she replies, "You're insane," and we also believe her a little later and shortly before she flees the room, defeated, when she says "You've brought insanity back into this house" (338). The scene moves abruptly and disconcertingly from the hilarity of the floor contest to a mixture of scary and creepy, as Tom swings back and forth between threatening Elizabeth, in our production, with a knife, implying that Elizabeth is one of the invaders he would be prepared to kill, and apparently trying to seduce her in a way that is sexual as well as persuasive.

It is characteristic of the parent-child that she cannot admit to weakness, that she must keep up the front no matter what, and that itself, of course, requires tremendous effort. Shortly before her confrontation with Tom, Elizabeth starts to come apart at the seams under the strain of playing her parental role under extremely difficult circumstances, and of a situation which seems to threaten her authority in that role:

> ... What's going on here. I don't understand a thing. Barbed wire. Organized work projects. A thousand cans of tomatoes. Some strange man digging a bomb shelter in the basement. You [Nora], talking about sex. Listen, I'm overloading here. I've had a hard day. I lost two cases. You know what this is? A letter from the senior partner. You know what she says? She says I'm messing up. And she's right, the jerk. My mind isn't on my work. My mind is on my family and my family is—well my family is—really fucked up it seems to me. Maybe I'm wrong. If I'm wrong I'll just go away, divorce myself from the whole thing, let you get on with it, whatever it is, and I'll just step back, try to get some objectivity. But it's hard, you know. I need an aspirin. Have you got an aspirin. Never mind. I'll just lie down. Can I go upstairs and lie down. I think I'm overloading. It's just too much. Too much. (*Better Living* 326)

After losing her challenge to Tom's authority and leadership, Elizabeth comes apart completely, trades roles with the middle sister, Mary Ann, who, in the schema of systems therapy, is the "lost one," the "lost child." It is one of the most striking characteristics of *Better Living*, and one of its most daring departures from conventional wisdom about what an audience will accept, that Walker gives to each of the characters, men as well as women (except Junior who, as an adopted member of the family, is doing his best to make himself as small as possible, to "blend in"), at least one, big, extravagant anxiety aria, like Elizabeth's above. These obviously provide glorious opportunities for actors, chances to take everyday emotions and follow them as far as they will go, into an emotional intensity and flamboyance usually reserved for opera. They also provide "reference points" for the actors, journeys into the characters' deepest selves and fears, around which the actors can construct Walker characters, "real" and what Walker would call "connected" to the real, but not necessarily "realistic." Mary Ann's aria, a great favourite as an audition piece among my students, goes as follows:

> I'm worried. About my future. I'm worried that my past didn't prepare me for any future. I'm worried about a basic failure to understand how the world operates. I'm worried that I won't bring my baby up right. That I can't teach her how the world operates. I'm worried about the world. Even though I don't understand it entirely I'm worried that something is deeply wrong with it. With life in general. I'm worried that there's a general lack of faith and security in the world and in life. It's too much. Maybe it's all too much. I don't understand it but maybe that's because it's too much, too complicated. Yeah. Money. Love. Responsibility. Family. Work. Crime. Food. God. Children. Insanity. Friends. Sickness. Death. Shopping. Traffic. Teeth. Pollution. War. Poverty. Oil. Infidelity. Ignorance. Fear. Shoes. Hats. Nuclear power. Cats. Winter. Sex. Elevators. I worry about all those things and more. All the time. It's awful, really … I had this dream once. I was outside somewhere with a whole bunch of people. It was a fantastic day. Everyone was happy. Birds were singing. There was an incredible rainbow on the horizon. All of a sudden the air was filled with beautiful music. And God appeared in the sky. Smiled down at everyone. Everyone smiled back. Then God beat me to death with a hammer … I think I understand that dream. You see I've always believed I'm prone to bad luck. And bad luck is just a slap in the face from God. (*Better Living* 311)

Nora is the parent whom Mary Ann resembles, a fact that terrifies Mary Ann when Elizabeth points it out, but Nora buries her anxieties under torrents of speech while Mary Ann exposes hers quite openly. Everything terrifies Mary Ann, especially questions and complexity, and it is a rule in the family not to ask Mary Ann questions, nor to supply her with details. It is Mary Ann who submits most abjectly, almost, it seems, with relief, to the restrictions and requirements of Tom's "consumer socialism," but it is also Mary Ann, whose anxiety provides her with something like an early warning system, who sees most clearly the dangers of authority (which she expresses in the "murdered in our sleep" speech quoted in Chapter Three). The exchange of roles between Mary and Elizabeth, their need to trade functions of leader and led for a while, is one of the areas of the play expanded in the rewrites which occurred between the publishing of the play in *The East End Plays* (1988) and in *Shared Anxiety* (1994).[1]

> At the beginning of scene ten, the play's last scene, when the sisters enter carrying a beam for the underground room, Walker makes much more of the role exchange between the two, going so far as to ask that

Elizabeth be wearing one of Mary Ann's dresses. On one hand, Elizabeth seems more damaged by the encounters with her father than was previously the case, less able to cope with current stresses, and genuinely in need of someone else, even Mary Ann, to take charge ... On the other hand, Elizabeth, by withdrawing, seems to be trying to force Mary Ann to be decisive, a change in Mary Ann underlined a page later by new speeches given to her: "What's wrong with me. What's wrong with me! It's so easy isn't it. So easy. What's wrong with me. Well, listen to this. (*To JACK*) What's wrong with you! (*To ELIZABETH*) What's wrong with you! (*To NORA*) What's wrong with you!" [346]. (Johnson, Review of *Shared Anxiety* 113–114)

This inclusion of traits opposite to that which we would expect of the character's dominant "type" is consistent with Walker's practice in earlier plays; the effect, as Smith says, is that "the character is not a closed entity but is a dynamic created by the clash of these opposing traits" (153). In the case of *Better Living*, this emergence of contrary, unexpected facets of the personality also represents a journey on the part of each character, a discovery of aspects of the self concealed by the "masks" or "roles" the dysfunctionality of the family had compelled each to adapt. These discoveries are forced on the characters by the recurrence of the crisis that had led to the creation of the roles in the first place, the reappearance of the abuser. In effect, Tom's return brings "repressed memory" to the surface, and each character recovers a version of who she might have been in the past. Mombourquette says of the roles the daughters play:

although Elizabeth turns her emotion outward and Mary Ann turns her emotion inward, both emotions have the same effect of uniting the family against a common enemy, the father. Elizabeth's and Mary Ann's roles therefore bring into question the terms for defining passive and active, masculine and feminine.

Gail's role is both passive and active and she is the member of the family they all unite to protect. (37)

In this version of the family's story, Gail, the youngest, is the "baby." In the "systems story," she is the "delinquent." She goes out with Junior, a Protestant who rides a motorcycle and is the son of a criminal, and whom her mother suspects of being a criminal as well. She has "sex outside the church." She is going to drop out of school and become a hair dresser. In the opening scene of the play, she does everything she can think of to elicit her uncle's disapproval, because, paradoxically, she wants his approval. In the course of the play, she leaves home. But, most "delinquent" of all in the context of this family's dynamic, history, and story—the story the family tells about itself—Gail sides with Father against her Mother. (Indeed,

Nora convinces herself that Gail is possessed by Tom's spirit, and early in the play in a very funny seance scene, tries to exorcise it.) The rest of the family has conspired to hide the truth of Tom's brutality from Gail, and as she was too young to remember the facts when he left, or so everyone thinks, she has created a heresy, a counter version of the family story that insists that Nora wrecked the marriage and drove Tom from the house (the last part of Gail's story is partly true, as Nora and Jack did, in fact, scare Tom away, in self defence after Tom tried to burn down the house while the rest of the family was asleep in their beds).

Gail returns to the house, now a fortress complete with barbed wire, in scene nine, having remembered something that happened to her when she was a little girl:

> … I saw a face. It belonged to a man I knew. I recognized his voice, and the way it gurgled and spat out things that weren't real words. And I recognized his shape. Stooped over. His arms making circles in the air. And I knew this man was really mad. Then I saw me with this man and I knew it was me he was mad at. And I got so scared I couldn't believe how scared I was. (*Laughs*) … When I saw my father's face, at first I thought he'd raped me. The look in his eyes! Excited. It was confusing. Then I remembered the beating. I remembered hearing my arm break. Hearing it crack. I remember being kicked. I remembered bleeding. Was he drunk. (*Better Living* 341)

Jack tells Gail the rest of the violent family history, and she and Jack confront Tom in the gun and sandwich climax I discuss as an example of a Walker "wonky bit" in Chapter Three. Indeed, the confusion of gun and sandwich as a daughter and her uncle, a priest, determine to kill the girl's father is the "wonky" pinnacle of a play whose overall concept is the height of wonkiness: *Better Living* is, after all, when all is said and done, a comedy about child abuse.

Scene nine ends with Jack pointing the gun at Tom, but before he shoots (if, indeed, he does). Thus in scene ten, the last of the play, we don't know whether Jack is lying when he tells the others that Tom has "gone away." Elizabeth and Mary Ann have traded roles, apparently. Gail reveals that she is pregnant. Nora tries to assimilate these changes into the old feminine order, and into Walker's "betterism," and to find value in the family's recent experience with having a "man in the house" again (Jack and Junior don't really count):

> We tried to deal with it by making it into a second chance I guess. A new Tom. A new way of talking. New things to talk about. Some of them crazy. A more positive kind of crazy though. He actually had ideas. Progress was taking place. Nothing important. Just practical things,

mostly. I took it all as a kind of atonement. A gesture. Things occurred. Systems. Ideas. Rehabilitation. Intimacy occurred. Looking back maybe it wasn't all that good. But it was better ... Well these things are all relative of course. But it's my job to help this family by keeping a positive outlook on life. (*Better Living* 1988, 177)

Nora's locus of dysfunction is in her denial: in effect, the role of Nora is one long anxiety aria, and habitually, she deals with her anxiety by denying the seriousness of the anxiety's cause, as she seems to see in the preceding speech. While Tom of the present may not put his violence as directly into action as does the Tom of the play's antecedent action, the violence is still there, as Nora herself sees the morning after she and Tom have sex.

Power. And dominance. And violence. I think if you take the hugging and kissing and the orgasm away that's what last night was really about ... I think I made a mistake becoming intimate with Tim [what Nora calls Tom, insisting that he's a friend of her husband, not her husband]. I felt it was expected. I wonder now if it's too late to stop. You see, I don't like looking into his eyes in bed and thinking he could kill me. (*Better Living* 333)

And Nora, although at the end of the play she tries to deny it, also sees in the above speech, the hierarchy and authority Tom brought with him in the form of "power" and "dominance."

The change [brought by Tom] is one of interpretation; the natural must now be understood within the terms of the social—being is replaced by knowledge of being. Something is lost. Because the cultural construction of the women's femininity is based on Tom's look and being watched is a central issue of paranoia, the women lose sight of their essence and see themselves only as a reflection of Tom's malevolence. (Mombourquette 49)

The play ends with one of Nora's long speeches, an aria of denial or "betterism," perhaps both, in which she tries to restore the mutable feminine order and encourage feminine self-reliance by elaborating on tips from her how-to and self-help books: "In the meantime here's a helpful hint. No, here's two helpful hints. One about happiness. And another one about wallpaper" (*Better Living* 351–352). Unseen by the others, Tom appears at the back door, carrying a television set. End of play.

We see the same family, some months later, in *Escape from Happiness*, a play written some years later (1991). The Tom we see in *Escape from Happiness* is much more sympathetic than the Tom of *Better Living*, or at least much less menacing, much less the domestic fascist. He's still very much a "guy" and into "guy things," creates a good deal of trouble and unhappiness by viewing problems through male eyes and, without consultation, applying male solutions to what he perceives as male responsibilities, as when he undertakes to protect his family from the dangerous conditions of their deteriorating neighbourhood by attacking local criminals and making them think the attacks were the responsibility of other local criminals, thus pitting different criminal individuals and factions against each other, theoretically neutralizing them. Clever and devious, in a cunning sort of way we recognize from *Better Living,* but still ultimately dependent on violence, even at one remove, and as usual, violence begets violence. Still, the play seems to be moving toward a balancing of male and female energies. Nora finally recognizes Tom as her husband, admits that she knew all along:

> I know he really is your dad. I'm not insane about that. That's good news isn't it, Elizabeth. So far so good. And I actually had a very good reason for not acknowledging him. For the first time in years I had something he needed. Needed badly ... Do you want to know what it was. Recognition! The power of simple recognition ... Of course, I just stumbled across this power. I came to it accidentally. But once I had it I used it without remorse. (*Escape from Happiness* 420)

At the beginning of the play, Tom feigns illness and helplessness in order to persuade the women to let him stay in the house (another male ploy, an obvious attempt to regain "maternal plenitude"). Towards its end, he asks the family outright if he can stay. In the last moments of the play, Nora is giving Tom very long, very complicated advice about what sort of work he might be suited for and what sort of work might be good for him. Still pragmatic and practical, as she was when she pretended Tom was someone else, Nora now tries to integrate Tom and his male energies into her family system in ways that are destructive neither to it nor to him.

Nora, too, has changed somewhat since *Better Living,* and in *Escape from Happiness,* while still pretty flaky, she demonstrates a sort of pragmatic toughness. She has managed to control her denial, and to direct it in order to protect her family and the individuals in it. That denial can be paradoxically a virtue, even heroic, is demonstrated in the first scene when Nora and Gail, Gail carrying the baby whose conception was announced at the end of *Better Living,* enter the kitchen to find Junior lying on the floor, badly beaten. She insists that he get up. By denying death, like the heroes of ancient myth, Nora defeats it:

> NORA: Junior! Junior! Can you hear me. This is Nora. This is your wife's
> mother. This is your child's grandmother. I want you to do some-

thing for your wife and child. Junior! You have something to do. If you don't do it the people you love will be destroyed. You'll be destroying your young, innocent family. Junior! Here's what you have to do. You have to get up.

GAIL: Mom!

NORA: Don't distract me, dear. Get off that floor, junior! Get off that floor!

GAIL: Mom, please. He's bleeding to death. He's probably got internal injuries. He's—

NORA: Get up, Junior! You're killing us here! You're killing us with your misery. We need you to get up. Your baby wants you on your feet. Hear her crying for her daddy? (*She pinches the baby. The baby cries.*)

GAIL: What did you just do.

NORA: (*whispers*) I pinched her. (*She pinches the baby again*)

GAIL: Stop that! Stop doing that. What's wrong with you.

NORA: Junior, do you hear your baby crying! She's crying because she wants you to get up. She's saying, "Daddy, Daddy please get up. Daddy, please, please don't die on that floor!" (*Escape from Happiness* 358–359)

Junior eventually gets up. How could he not? Sometimes denial prevents one from dealing with reality, and sometimes denial enables one to defeat it. At least temporarily. "Betterism" here is Nora's version of Life Force, and in this scene, like Gina Mae in *Beautiful City*, Nora is a wonky Great Mother, taking on the forces of darkness and death and defeating them. "Defeat that floor!" is her battle cry, because "the floor is for dying."

Escape from Happiness is a long play, over three hours as first produced and published, although somewhat shorter in the version printed in *Shared Anxiety*. It's also extremely complicated, a "domestic epic" in its size, its complexity, its bringing together of domestic and social realms. As well as the characters from *Better Living* (and, in a sense, Gail and Junior from *Criminals in Love*), *Escape from Happiness* brings back other Walker characters from other earlier Walker plays, Rolly and Stevie Moore and Dian Black from *Beautiful City*. Through the reappearance of characters, and through relationships that cross between plays, we begin to get a sense in this play of a Walker world, an East End for the stage, drawing on but not duplicating the real neighbourhoods to the east of downtown Toronto. The play is also epic and complex in that Walker is trying not to describe but to *demonstrate* patterns of communication as they occur within a family (which we've already seen in *Better Living*) and also the patterns of communication, and attempts to block communication, that occur between the individuals in the family and a larger, social world beyond that family. In the attempts to determine what is happening (Who beat Junior up?

What are Rolly and Stevie looking for when they break into the house and hold everyone at gunpoint? What do the police really want? Who planted the drugs in the basement?), we see the family, led by Nora, trying to survive and stay together in the face of increasing pressure from a complex and apparently hostile outside world.

As we saw in James Earl Baldwin's analysis of the play, we in the audience have to experience the play moment to moment, as do the characters, as do the actors, and must adjust our sense of what is happening accordingly. It's as though we see the events of the play through the eyes of the members of a "matriarchal family" as described by Mombourquette:

> ... all members share a pool of raw material, a collective unconscious. They use language to attain their desires and to express themselves but not to give each other a structural identity. It is not the linear language of definition by opposition. Their language is cyclical. The craziness, violence or love expressed by each character is not used to elicit an answering action or emotion in the future tense. All actions and emotions are grounded in their immediacy ... (40)

It's as though the people in the audience become members of such a family during a performance of *Escape from Happiness*.

However Walker may sympathize with most of his East End women, and however he may tend to privilege feminine vision and values in the plays of the eighties, he still doesn't succumb to the excessive simplicities of male-female melodrama, with white hats automatically going to the women. Just as a working-class upbringing is no guarantee that one will have responsible and generous political opinions, clearly not the case with "Babe" Conner in *Love and Anger*, so neither does being born female guarantee "good guy" status. Mary Raft in *Beautiful City* (1987) is a ruthless real estate developer and, apparently, boss of an organized crime syndicate. She personifies unalloyed class and economic power: "... don't assume that the people around here, your so-called victims, were put on this earth for any other reason than to serve the needs of the powerful ... this natural state of affairs ..." (*Beautiful City* 320). Also, significantly in this play which is often seen as Walker's personal angry response to the destruction of his city, Mary Raft is an American, someone foreign and oblivious to the value and nature of that which is being taken over and transformed, for the worse in Walker's opinion.

But, while the primary "bad guy" in *Beautiful City* is a woman, so too is the primary "good guy," Gina Mae Sabatini, a cashier at Bargain Harold's described by her daughter as a "witch." The conflict here, as in *Better Living*, is between patriarchal and matriarchal visions of family; in *Beautiful*

City, Walker moves outside the home into a larger society and includes conflict between families and concepts of family and community, the Mafia-like "family" of the Rafts on one hand, and the local, grounded, Life Force Sabatinis on the other, both, as it happens, led by women. Between these two families, and, in effect constituting the battle ground, are two male families, the architect protagonist Paul Gallagher and his brother, Michael, and the petty crook, Rolly Moore, and his son, Stevie, who are also Gina Mae's brother-in-law and nephew.

Once again, as in *Criminals in Love*, we have a "good mother" and a "bad mother," a mother who provides but who also encourages and empowers her "children" to take responsibility for their lives versus a mother who demands obedience, kills (or orders killed) those she finds dispensable, gives approval only on her terms, who requires the sons to surrender individual volition. The names Walker gives "bad mother" and "good mother" in *Beautiful City* are significant. Mary Raft's Christian name is just that, a Christian name recalling the Virgin, a central figure in a patriarchal religion, indeed the only female persona embedded in that religion's hierarchy, and Walker's Mary is indeed a very "manly" woman, a Mother who possesses many attributes of the Father, in the authoritarian, patriarchal, phallocentric sense. As Mombourquette has it:

> ... she caters to the social being's desire for an identity. The sustenance Mary offers is not milk but money. Tony, Michael and Stevie do not look to Mary for life (the position of the pre-Oedipal child) but for economic value. (102)

> Mary shows all the viciousness of one who recognizes no obligations to an other; she is self-centered, a narcissist. Knowledge of the other only goes as far as an understanding of what he or she can do for her; beyond that s/he ceases to exist. In this way she positions herself as part of the elite class—that class which dominates society's values, beliefs and morals for the benefit of this one class. (104–105)

Gina Mae's initials could stand for "Good Mother" but also, I think, signify "Great Mother," the nature goddess represented by the female figurines found throughout Europe and dating from the upper Paleolithic period on, "the most sacred figure of prepatriarchal eons. She ruled over both life and death and was worshiped simultaneously as Mother Goddess, mistress of the animals, and receiver of the dead" (French 44). These goddess figures "beatify mother love and nutritiveness for sons" (French 46). Gina Mae is concerned with sheltering and nourishing, recommends food not only healthy for the body but for the inner, emotional self. Her vision of a city is "a throbbing, connecting, living, creative neighbourhood" (*Beautiful City* 314), an extended family and hence matricentric society.

The title of the play itself recalls Utopia and aspiration to Utopia, not just a physical city but a manifestation of a perfect, godly society so central to Western myth and thought; I'm specifically reminded of William Blake's New Jerusalem. Here too in Walker we strive for, progress towards, a place, a state of mind and spirit, to be realized in the future, not a future whose existence is guaranteed but one dependent on our striving.

Beautiful City opens with a scene between a real estate developer and an architect. Tony Raft, the developer, is trying to solve a problem: how to convince prospective customers that buying a condo is a good investment, a good buy, a good life, the site of "better living":

> A million five. A million five. Is this place worth that much money. Forget the southern exposure, the state of the art security system, the pools, the sauna, the weight room, the diet room, the committee room, the convenience store, the liquor store, the personalized parking space. Forget the Italian tiles in the bathrooms. Forget the fucking bathrooms altogether. All three of them. Forget the Samurai kitchen, the generationally conceived bedrooms, the solarium, the atrium. Forget everything except the primary living space. Because that's the ticket, that's where it happens, that's where you ... live. So ask yourself, are you going to be pleased, are you going to feel good about spending one and one half million dollars on what is essentially four bare eggshell-surfaced goddamned walls?! (*Beautiful City* 229–230)

Paul Gallagher, the architect and Walker's protagonist, also has a problem: throughout the conversation, Paul is sickening, perhaps dying, protesting, groaning, eventually curling up from the pain and collapsing on the floor. Raft persists in pursuing the conversation, demanding a solution to his problem, dismissing Paul's illness as an anxiety attack.

In the next scene, Paul is in the hospital, but the doctors can find no physical cause for his sickness. His sickness, of course, is a sickness of the soul, of the inner self, and comes from a betrayal of that self through, among other things, the prostitution of his artistic gifts and professional skill to serve the market place, to serve the Rafts in particular. He meets Jane, a volunteer in the hospital, who says she will take him to her mother to get help, for her mother is a witch: "... a real witch. She's descended from witches. I was one too but she took my power away at birth. My father made her do it. I'm kinda glad. It's awesome. The power is awesome but it kinda removes you from the rest of the world. Puts you in opposition" (*Beautiful City* 236). Paul seeks out Gina Mae at Bargain Harold's so she can tell him his "simple ugly truth," the key to understanding himself. As Paul aligns himself with Gina Mae in her struggle with Mary Raft for control of the city, control of the future, and also in her struggle with

Rolly Moore, Gina Mae's pornographer brother-in-law, Paul's health improves.

Gina Mae, like William in *Criminals in Love*, is a wise guide, a magician figure here specifically linked to the female religion of wicca. In addition to the presence of a witch, a good witch, the shape of the plot, the search for the secret, the restoration of health, the promise of marriage at the play's conclusion, are all strongly reminiscent of the fairy tale, a point Mombourquette pursues:

> As the audience views Paul's metamorphosis from victim to hero, they cannot fail to notice the similarity between Paul's story and that of a fairy tale. Like a fairy tale, *Beautiful City* seems deceptively simple. Its plot illustrates the agonies of self-knowledge, the delight of wishes coming true and of the humble being elevated, the recognition of true merit and poetic justice. And as in fairy tales, this overt content conceals material of a more complex nature, which plot alludes to just enough to trigger the spectator's memories. (78)

In fact, Walker himself has called *Beautiful City* "a fairy tale for adults" (Joel Kaplan 47). Note that at this stage in his career, Walker does not parody fairy tales, nor employ fairy tales as the vehicle for parodic satire, nor use the fairy tale as the "lens" through which to view the dramatic action, but rather alludes to fairy tale, uses it to amplify the resonance and significance of everyday life (at Bargain Harold's!) and thus transgresses and makes us question the usually accepted boundaries between the real and the imaginary, and external and internal.

In Mombourquette's reading of the play, Paul's profession, the way he practices that profession and the interests he serves, the persona he created to fulfill these social functions, have severed the connection between inner and outer lives. The inner life, denied the opportunity to seek its desires and express itself in Paul's social life, makes him sick. "Instead of the unconscious being represented by some form of desire in his social reality, Paul manifests a disease, guilt" (Mombourquette 79). He looks to Gina Mae in his search for the "memory of maternal plenitude," free from the pressure of social Others, like Tony Raft or the people who will live in his condos. "She [Gina Mae] does not operate in the internal/external dualism of society. She has direct contact with the internal being; she can 'come visit you in your brain' and therefore does not need to depend exclusively on the external symbols of society for communication of knowledge to occur" (Mombourquette 86).

Nonetheless, Gina Mae does not simply give Paul what he wants; rather, she teaches him how to find what he needs. The key is "the simple ugly truth." Everyone, according to Gina Mae, has a simple ugly truth, a core truth about his or her personality. For example, Gina Mae's daughter, Jane, has as her "simple ugly truth" the fact that she will "do just about any-thing to keep people happy." Paul's is "There's life right here on earth and you're not part of it!!" (*Beautiful City* 267). Jane expands:

> You've been living like a fool … You've lost touch with the genuinely complex nature of reality. All your friends think alike, talk alike, want the same things … … You're dying from a kind of simplicity … It's like you've taken the huge throbbing life force and turned it into a piece of thread … and it's not enough to hold you together. (*Beautiful City* 266)

Immediately after hearing these truths, Paul "for some reason" feels better, realizes he feels better.

I've cited Jane's speech before, in Chapter Three, where I discussed Walker's right-wing villains' need to control and to simplify, to contain the complexity of life and of the politics of life, within simple, absolutist rules. As Paul is not a right wing villain, chooses not to become a villain nor to follow the example of his brother Michael and become an unquestioning dupe of the villains, the Rafts, the energy required by the tasks of simplification and control is directed within, and makes him sick. Gina Mae's formulation of Paul's "simple" truth points, paradoxically, to com-plexity and the need to embrace complexity.

In Gina Mae, gender politics and right-left, class, and social politics come together. One of the first things Gina Mae does with Paul in his education as to the nature of reality, after she dresses him warmly in a very motherly fashion, is take him foraging through garbage bins for per-fectly good food that has been discarded. When Paul refuses some of the good bread she's found, she replies "Okay, but if you don't taste it you don't get the purest kind of outrage. You just get it second hand. *(takes a bite)* This stuff is edible! I'm mad as hell!!" (*Beautiful City* 257). When, having kidnapped Tony, Gina Mae makes demands of Mary, her list is pri-marily concerned with social justice:

> I want a community centre. I want two new parks. I want low cost housing. I want a shelter for the homeless and the mistreated. I want big bright wonderful stores where people get useful products at reason-able prices. [like Bargain Harold's] I want halfway houses for people who are trying to re-enter the world from the unfortunate darkness of their circumstances." (*Beautiful City* 314)

As a "wise woman," Gina Mae knows what is needed for health, for the individual inside and out, and for the community. A healthy individual needs to live in a healthy community in order to maintain his/her health, and a healthy community is designed to accommodate the needs of individuals, of the healthy who need to stay healthy, and of the unhealthy who need to become healthy. Thus the need to create a healthy, integrated individual and the need to create a healthy, integrated community co-incide and interact.

To the still somewhat skeptical Paul, who wants to know what she means by his "sliding into hell," Gina Mae explains the connection between external and internal health, the health of the body and the health of the spirit, the material circumstances of want and death, by two kinds of starvation:

> If you don't get better you won't be able to work, you won't have any money, soon you won't have any friends. You'll be on welfare. They'll cut you off welfare. You won't be able to eat properly. You won't have a place to live. No clothes. You'll sleep in doorways … In the winter you'll freeze. Being naked and freezing and starving is hell. The simple ugly truth is metaphysical. Get the difference? I mean they can both lead to death. Sometimes the same death by their combined forces. But essentially they're different problems, connected by circumstance. (*Beautiful City* 267)

Gender politics (and female "magic") and the politics of social justice are both needed, and the boundary between them is one of many transgressed by *Beautiful City*. At the same time, Walker subverts some of the stereotypes Paul (and many of us) attribute to women, wise women, and witches.

Gina Mae works at Bargain Harold's, and the conjunction of the mystical world and a discount store is not only absurdly funny in that very Walkersque way, but, by presenting Gina Mae with her feet firmly on the ground, a proponent of good quality, reasonably priced clothing for people with "low to moderate incomes," Walker questions the nature of "magic," of "fairy tales," of the difficulty of achieving social justice—far from being so difficult, so complex and arcane, so intractable that magic is required to effect a difference, some of the "answers" to questions and issues of poverty and class injustice are remarkably simple, practical, and easy to achieve. Paul makes assumptions about Gina Mae, such as her not eating meat (she does) based on what he assumes are her "spiritual beliefs"; Gina Mae resists his definition and stereotyping, resists being "finalized" in Bakhtin's sense:

> You keep referring to my spiritual beliefs. I think you're confusing me with someone else. Maybe one of those mother earth types. I don't have much in common with them. Truth is, I don't have much in common with anyone. I'm an original. Get used to it. When you've come to terms with my originality you'll be on the road to recovery … (*Beautiful City* 291)

Because when Paul "comes to terms" with Gina Mae's originality, he will be abandoning stereotyped over-simplifications, a monologic view of life, and will instead encounter the complexity of the life in which he finds himself, i.e. polyphony. What he (and we) call "reality" is in fact a delusion/illusion, and a dangerous one at that.

Gina Mae is attributed with the magical power to turn a cat into a raccoon; Gina Mae replies that maybe "the cat did most of the work" (258). Later we see her transform her nephew, the repulsive Stevie Moore, into a crow, but that, we're led to believe, has more to do with Stevie's nature and state of mind than with Gina Mae's magic.

> I'd like to take responsibility for that. But I think he did it to himself. The man has such low self-regard it's possible his subconscious just couldn't deal with the idea of him winning at anything and took the necessary steps to prevent it. I mean if anybody was wondering. (*Beautiful City* 313)

Gina Mae does not set out to achieve magical mastery over the natural world; she works with nature. The acts we call "magic" are perhaps more natural than we think, or perhaps it is our concept of what constitutes the "natural" that is at fault, that confuses us in this way, and ultimately separates us from our "natural" selves.

Walker subverts and discredits some of our stereotypes about female "mysticism" and folk wisdom, thus making it impossible for us to dismiss Gina Mae as a cackling old hag with a pointy hat and a broom, or even as a "crystal sucking" New Ager solving the world's problems with positive thoughts. At the same time, Walker subverts some of his own subversions; the last thing he wants is for the audience to abandon one set of stereotypes simply to fall prey to another. For example, he doesn't want us to leap from the assumptions of patriarchy and monologism to the easy assumption that "woman" automatically equals "good." Hence the "bad mother," Mary Raft. And hence niggling little "wonky bits" that remind us that even while we come to admire Gina Mae, and are surprised by her down-to-earth and extremely convincing revelations about how things work, she is nonetheless human and fallible. Four of her five daughters, we are told, have had virtually no contact with their mother since they left home. "Jane's best. The others all left home. I never see them. And they're really young. They all got away from me as soon as they hit puberty" (*Beautiful City* 254). This detail is not necessary to the plot, and not necessary to a characterization of Gina Mae, not if we're satisfied with a simple, straight-forward characterization. The detail niggles, and it asks questions. Were all the daughters but Jane unable to deal with Gina Mae's honesty and "power"? Who was responsible for the apparent, effective endings of mother-daughter relationships? Was it the "father" who convinced Gina Mae to take away Jane's power at birth? What happened to these female bonds? Does "got away" suggest that Gina Mae in some way tried to prevent them from "getting away," that she attempted to control her daughters? If she's so good at intuiting what is happening inside other people, why was there evidently a breakdown in communication between mother and daughters?

Gina Mae, by herself, is unable to overcome Mary Raft and the forces Mary represents. Instead, the conflict is "resolved" by the unconventional and mysterious policewoman, Dian Black, and she is the biggest and most disturbing "wonky bit" of all in *Beautiful City*. As in *Zastrozzi*, we're given not two poles, but three; the dichotomy, the Lacanian melodrama, is disrupted, and both plenitude/lack and "good mother" versus "bad mother" conflicts or schema are problematized. The "resolution" leaves many questions unanswered, and at all its levels, *Beautiful City* avoids closure and easy conclusions.

From her first appearance, at Bargain Harold's interviewing Gina Mae about her brother-in-law Rolly's pornography distribution network, Dian Black is an enigma. Gina Mae says of her that she sends "out very confusing signals. You have the manner of a policewoman but the brainwaves of a politician" (*Beautiful City* 251). When next we see Dian, she is at the police station interrogating Rolly, or playing mind games with him, apparently trying to extract information about the Rafts and their illegal activities. She doesn't, Rolly says, talk like a cop. "Go get me a cop who talks like a cop." Dian replies, "They're all dead ... All the cops who talk like cops. They died" (284). Rolly tries to make sense of the interview and of the situation in movie terms; Dian might be a "rogue cop," "magnum force." No, she has a supervisor. Rolly is nervous "on a whole new level now." She tells him "I'm single. I'm thirty-five years old. I have a degree in sociology. I'm not afraid of death" (285). Now, Dian is "weirding" Rolly "right to death"; she's a "space monster." Letting Rolly believe that there is poison in his coffee, a slow acting poison leaving time to administer an antidote if he co-operates, Dian calls for a stenographer as Rolly is apparently ready to tell her what she wants to know, although what that "something" is she has revealed neither to him nor to us.

The penultimate scene of the play is a showdown between the forces of "good" and the forces of "evil." After Rolly and Stevie blow up Gina Mae's house, hired to do so by Mary, Gina Mae kidnaps Tony and holds him at gun point (although he likes being with Gina Mae, and enjoys her visits within his brain). Gina Mae demands from Mary five million dollars in ransom or "compensation," money she intends to use to restore the health of her neighbourhood as described above (but nonetheless kidnapping and threatening violence seem rather *un*-wisewoman things to do). The transaction goes wrong, Stevie tries to make off with the money, turns into a crow, and Gina Mae and Mary struggle for possession of Stevie's gun. Enter Dian. Dian likes Gina Mae's plan: "It has scope, Courage. And it seems deeply connected to a kind of popular fantasy" (315). Here Walker flirts with the kind of "reference point" he employed in early plays, alluding to the fairy tale patterns he uses in *Beautiful City*. Dian sees the problem essentially as a conflict between families. "I mean if you simplify it. Let's do that. Let's simplify it, so we can all find a way out" (318). There's a Walker warning bell here—a desire to simplify and impose order, remember, is almost always a characteristic of a "bad guy." In Dian's view, Gina Mae's solution is incomplete.

> It needs clarification. The money is the problem. If the money just goes haphazardly from that family to that family and then that family … helps to build all those wonderful facilities well, you can imagine the questions. The public revelations. Any solutions? … I've got one. A foundation. A legal beautiful philanthropic foundation. The Raft Foundation … The money will pass from the Raft family to the Raft Foundation to the Sabatini family to the Sabatini Rebuilding Fund. It's a beautiful solution. Trust me. (*Beautiful City* 318)

Dian is able to enforce her solution because, evidently, she has the power to do so. She tells Mary:

> You will do it [establish the Foundation] under amazing and relentless duress. You will do it. Or you will be dispossessed of all your holdings in this city. I speak with authority here. It was given to me. I'm using it. Understand? (*Pause; goes to MARY; hands her a piece of paper*) There's a telephone number on that paper you could call to confirm my authority. I know you recognize that telephone number … Do you understand now? (*Beautiful City* 319)

We never do discover the identify or significance of the mysterious telephone number, the source of Dian's authority. There is a kind of fairy tale or folk tale rightness about this "resolution" of the conflict, certainly a high degree of wish fulfillment, the return and restoration of the rightful king, the absolution and rehabilitation of Robin Hood. Furthermore, her name, in a play in which names seem to assume unusual significance, links her with the moon, the virgin goddess, and a feminine world valorized as more likely to be "good." But again there's a "wonky bit": the name lacks an "a," or even the more usual "e," and furthermore her surname is "Black" (as in "black hat"?). The *deus (dea) ex machina* sets everything to right, restores balance, and along the way, reunites families, returning Tony to Mary, Michael to Paul, and Rolly to Gina Mae, who is to reform him. But Euripides and Molière used the device of the *deus ex machina* for ironic purposes more often than not ("Life isn't really like this; there aren't really any miraculous divine interventions; the Tartuffes often win") and I have a pretty strong suspicion that Walker too is being ironic here, with Dian Black's timely appearance and "simple" solutions near the conclusion of *Beautiful City*.

Mombourquette, however, sees Dian's intervention as entirely benevolent:

> Dian is set up as the mediator. She is in sympathy with Gina Mae's desires and she has the authority to dispossess Mary of all her holdings in the city.
>
> This situation sets up a metaphor for acquiring desires in society because it is only through Dian's mediation that either Mary or Gina Mae can satisfy her desire. Desire and satisfaction do not have a direct connection within society; language, the mediator, must be used to represent that desire to another, and because language is not a transparent medium of desire it distorts desire. Gina Mae wants a home, a better neighbourhood, which Mary understands in economic terms. Mary desires money but that desire is represented as the authority to make money. (319)

I'm not convinced that Dian as facilitator simply represents language as a mediator of conflicting desires. What is this mysterious power that permits Dian to act. Surely not simply elected government—"hurray for democracy." What power is there that can control the political and economic forces represented by Mary? Are philanthropic foundations really as benevolent and constructive as Dian seems to assume they are, or do they too have their role to play in the machinations of social politics? Is this what they're really about, laundering dirty money and spending it on good works to buy public approval? And provide tax benefits? What's "real" and what's public relations here? My response to Dian is that I'm more disturbed by the implications of her and her intervention, the bothersome questions left unanswered, than I am comforted by the fairy-tale results. This suggests to me not liberation and individual responsibility for the communal good, but yet another level of control, one that I can't identify, much less control or influence. I'm anxious, and I think Walker is too.

In *Escape from Happiness* (which in fairness to Mombourquette had not yet appeared when she wrote her dissertation), Dian who at first appears to be the good cop component of a good-cop–bad-cop duo, turns out to be the bad cop, responsible for extra-legal activities and much of the threat to Nora's family. In that play, Dian is ultimately defeated by Elizabeth, Nora's lawyer, ex-prostitute, bi-sexual daughter, who says to Dian "My family is made up of human beings. You're loyal to an institution [the police department]. I'll visit you in the asylum some day and explain the difference" (438). Dian falls to pieces. She applies lip balm furiously.

> I'm the only one with vision! With imagination. I see the big picture. I see the big picture with details. Details that contradict what *you* see in the big picture. You think that's easy?! It's scary! It makes you do scary things sometimes! (*Escape from Happiness* 439)

Indeed. I don't think Walker expects us to trust this woman. If we're tempted to trust her in *Beautiful City* it's because of a vestigial need to be taken care of, first by Gina Mae, then, when shown that even Gina Mae's power has limits, by someone, anyone, who can protect us from the Mary Rafts of the world. And surely one of the most important things that Gina Mae has to say is that only we can do that. Surely one of the most important things that Walker has to say in this fairy tale about wounded heroes, families, male and female principles, and beautiful cities is that trusting anyone else to build our cities for us, whether Big Daddy or Big Mom, is dangerous.

But *Beautiful City* is not quite over; there's one more scene, a couple more dips of the roller coaster, to go. Two weeks pass. We're back in Bargain Harold's. Paul enters, ostensibly to buy socks. He buys all the socks in the store. Gina Mae can no longer "read" him. He's still dirty, and wearing the same clothes he was wearing two weeks previously when last she saw him. Paul doesn't want to feel better yet. "You see there's still something … sort of … missing. (*pause*) Help me" (328). He kisses her, gently, on the cheek. Gina Mae still can't read him.

> You just kissed me like I was your aunt or something. What's your problem. Have you got something you want to say or not. I'm busy here. This is my job. And I've got a life to get on with. One of my five children actually loves me and needs me. That's something to build on. I don't need any problems from you. If you've got something to offer me, it can't be a problem. It's gotta be something positive. (*Beautiful City* 329)

Paul kisses her with more conviction.

> GINA MAE: Okay. The truth is I'm not entirely surprised by this event. (*He kisses her again. She kisses him back. Then breaks it gently.*) And I'm not entirely against it either. I mean I have feelings too you know. I have needs. It's just that we never talked about mine because we were so busy dealing with yours. Kiss me again. Let's see what this

thing going on here really is. (*He does. Then steps back.*) … This thing
has … potential.

PAUL: I have to be … with you … I want you to … I guess I want you
to marry me. (*pause.*) So will you … Will you marry me.

GINA MAE: So what are you saying here? You don't want the socks?

PAUL: Do you want me to take the socks.

GINA MAE: You can take some. But they're a real good buy. So you should
leave some for other people.

PAUL: Okay. I'll leave some.

GINA MAE: Okay. I'll marry you.

> *Pause.*
> *PAUL smiles weakly. GINA MAE shifts from one foot to the other.*
> *Lights are fading.*
> *They look at each other. Look away. GINA MAE shrugs. PAUL shrugs.*
> *Blackout.*
> *The End.* (*Beautiful City* 330)

Isn't that sweet? It really is. The fairy-tale ending, the "happily ever after."
Completion. Male and female principles/principals together. But this is a
Walker play we're talking about here, and the sweetness does not go
unqualified, and the completion is disrupted—closure, however sweet, is
opened up with work socks and shrugs. The work socks are a wonderful
and entirely Walkeresque touch, a classic wonky bit, very funny, effectively undercutting the potential sentimentality of the moment, and at the
same time reintroducing, very lightly and deftly, the issue of social justice
into the romance. Gina Mae simply wouldn't marry a man who took all
the socks. The shrugs could mean many different things, the same or different things to each of the "lovers": lack of certainty, relief, self-consciousness (and all that *that* implies), embarrassment, or recognition that "happily
ever after" is not guaranteed. Doubtless the shrugs mean different things
to different performers, different things to performers at the conclusion of
different performances, and certainly mean different things to different
members of the audience. A happy ending, but a happy ending with a
difference, and the consequence, on stage and in the auditorium, is many,
many differences. Several Walker plays end with shrugs, metaphorically
or, as here, literally. Mombourquette says of the ending of the play:

> The promise of marriage at the conclusion of the play symbolizes a state
> of true independence in which Paul feels as secure, satisfied and happy
> as the infant felt in his most dependent state, when he was truly taken
> care of in his world of fantasy. With the successful resolution of the
> positive Oedipal complex, Paul emerges from his state of dependency
> to a social construction of independence. With Paul's new found inde-
> pendence he gains a new world, a "beautiful city."

> In *Beautiful City* the entire city returns to renewed life the moment
> Paul does. Just as Paul comes to terms with his inner desires and exter-
> nal pressures, so Gina Mae comes to terms with the inner city problems
> and external forces that feed upon them. (92–93)

All well and good, and, as I said, an excellent and penetrating reading of
this and other Walker plays, but here I don't think Mombourquette comes
to terms with either Dian Black nor the shrugs.

In his introduction to *Love and Anger*, Robert Wallace sees in Petie
Maxwell a possible persona for Walker himself, like Paul Gallagher in *Beautiful City* "who Walker has acknowledged expresses many of his own ideas
about life and work" (8). Wallace goes on to point out that both characters "turn to women in an attempt to find the answers they seek—women
who offer them a way through the morass of anger, guilt and moral confusion they have created in their lives" (9). In *Love and Anger*, the hope for
the future is female. So, apparently, is God: to Eleanor's "God help us,"
Petie replies "Sure. If she has the time" (*Love and Anger* 42).

While Petie is one of a long line of outsider, crusading males taking on
the establishment in Walker plays, Petie's allies are all female, and vital to
his cause, whereas the "bad guys" are both male, indeed in some respects
caricatures of the worst characteristics associated with the stereotyped,
aggressive male personality. In an ending very reminiscent of the conclusion of *Nothing Sacred*, where the possibility is held out that the peasants
may be the hope for the future, Petie dies, and in so doing holds out the
possibility that the marginalized women, Gail who is black and Sarah who
is schizophrenic, and their new friendship may lead to a new world. Just
before he is stricken, Petie says of Gail "She is your leader. Follow her to
the ... promised ..." (*Love and Anger* 83), but is cut off, just as Bazarov is
at the end of *Nothing Sacred*. Walker sets up the tensions and ambiguities
of the end of his play by earlier introducing a sequence in which Sarah is
apparently able to help Petie recover from another stroke by "zapping [him]
with positive negative ions" (60), making him all right by concentrating
on thinking that he's all right. When Petie later dies, the audience is torn
between hoping that the women will once again be able to heal and save
Petie, and dreading that the ending of Walker's play is about to become
hopelessly sentimental in a New Age sort of way. Petie stays dead, and
while we go to blackout with the women still looking at Maxwell's body
and concentrating, and while the possibility of yet another rebirth for Petie
is thus still open, it's the Gail-Sarah friendship, and the female virtues that
friendship embodies, that is the real vehicle for Walkeresque "possibility"
in this play.

Tough! (1993) is Walker's "battle of the sexes" play, but while it has the wit, in this case street-wise wit, usually associated with the sub-genre, it certainly does not have the romantic, happy-ever-after resolution required by tradition, a resolution in which the female almost always submits to the male, with only minor reservations to qualify the strictures of marriage, and those usually cosmetic only. *Tough!* was commissioned by Green Thumb Theatre in Vancouver, a theatre which plays to young audiences, although Walker insists that this is not a play exclusively intended for young audiences—its three characters are young, nineteen, but they're human, after all, and experience problems that can be as dramatically interesting as the problems encountered by any people.

While it can be said that the play is "about teen pregnancy," it is not the sort of admonitory, didactic "issues" play too often offered to young audiences. Walker subverts this formula, as he subverts the "battle of the sexes" formula, by opening it up, inviting questions, avoiding closure, and interrogating matters of allegiance and identification.

The setting is a city park where Tina has asked her boyfriend, Bobby, to meet her after she gets off work selling jewellery in a department store. She brings her friend, Jill, with her, "for support." *Tough!* begins in the middle of a heated argument, Tina yelling at Bobby:

> It's all lies. Everything you ever told me was a fucking lie. You said I could trust you. That's a lie. You let me think I knew you. What did I know about you. Lies. I knew your lies. Ah shit, aren't you going to say anything. Are you just gonna sit there like a dog. A lying dog. (451)

Jill sits nearby, writing in a notepad. It becomes clear that Bobby was caught coming on to another girl, "You had your hand up her fucking shirt." When Bobby tries to suggest that that's only a story going around, Jill says she saw the incident, at a party at her place. Bobby accuses Tina of trapping him, says the only witness in his "trial" is Jill, who has always disliked him, disliked him since kindergarten. Then he claims he was drunk. Tina feels betrayed, says her heart has been ripped out, reminds Bobby that he had said they were forever. Bobby is taken aback: "Forever. Jesus. Forever is … What's that mean. I mean, come on. I'm only nineteen. I've got a whole life to live" (*Tough!* 454). Tina hits him and storms off, leaving Jill and Bobby alone together. Jill tells Bobby that Tina is pregnant. Bobby is stunned, then disbelieving. "No way." Tina rushes back on. "I heard him. I was hiding behind a tree. I knew he'd deny it" (*Tough!* 455).

The "I'm pregnant" scene has begun, a scene in which the majority of us have participated, in reality or in the imagination, contemplating the possible, and which those of us who teach Theatre have seen our acting students improvise countless times. With the "I'm pregnant" scene comes the central conflict of the "battle of the sexes," and it covers all the issues at the core of that battle: the question of paternity, commitment, responsibility, identity, life goals, expectations, gender based values, failed communication, and of course, last but not least, sex. As the pop anthropologists and sociologists on Arts and Education television would have it, Tina wants a "mate" to share the responsibility of raising their offspring, and Bobby wants to spread his genes around as widely as possible.

This play is extremely intense and high energy, even by Walker's standards, never letting up, except for a few minutes near the end of the play when Bobby leaves for awhile, and the two young women are left alone to try to sort out the meaning of what has happened. For most of the play's eighty minutes, no intermission, the pace and pressure are relentless, "fierce and uncompromising":

> What makes *Tough!* compelling is that the connections between the characters' brains and tongues is direct and uncensored. They struggle to find the words that they hope will capture and tame unfamiliar and difficult emotions, but their attempts to communicate are foiled by an unrelenting velocity of feelings and thought that language alone can never contain. (Armstrong 45)

In structure and effect, *Tough!* is Walker's most "realistic" play. Elapsed "real" time is equal to the running time of the play, and the play as a whole is the most extended scene anywhere in Walker's work. In earlier treatments of adolescents in Walker's plays the adolescents' subjective view of older characters as "primal forces," William, Wineva, and Henry in *Criminals in Love* for example, brings to those plays larger than life elements, what Wallace has called a "manic, grotesque theatricality." In *Tough!*, however, "the adolescents ... struggle not with the uncontrollable, outside forces represented by their elders, but with problems of their own making, issues of their own responsibility" (Johnson, Review of *Shared Anxiety* 111). And this world of teenagers dealing with their selves, and with each other, is a relatively realistic one. When looking at the relative realism of the dialogue, I point to Jill's condom speech (I could equally well have pointed to the "fuck me to death" speech which I quote at the beginning of this chapter) to observe:

> Jill's dialogue has the wise-ass, street-smart, colloquial punch and aggressiveness so typical of Walker, but there's nothing inherently outrageous here, nothing we couldn't imagine a real adolescent saying. More to the point, there's nothing a real adolescent couldn't imagine herself

saying, or even wishing she had said, and Walker's unusually "realistic" and consistent approach makes this '90s battle of the sexes, and issues of sexism, gender based values, and failed communication more readily accessible to the audience to whom it is aimed, their acceptance of or resistance to drama influenced so strongly by the conventions of television realism. (Review of *Shared Anxiety* 112)

When I started rehearsals for the University of Manitoba's 1994 production of *Tough!*, I had pretty well concluded that the young women in the play were right, and that Bobby was irresponsible and wrong. And indeed, when Bobby tells Tina, after he learns that she is pregnant, that he had been planning to break up with her, "I found myself looking around at ... others ... and thinking, hey, they look nice" (462), our audiences, mostly teenagers, squirmed and groaned. Bad timing guy. This seemed yet another familiar situation in which the women are "better able to deal with the complex nature of reality," more attuned to the subtleties of interpersonal interaction, and thus completely out manouevre the man, often leaving him defenseless and speechless. Further, it seemed to me that young women in general have it "more together" than do young men, and that young women mature sooner emotionally and intellectually as well as physically. Bobby tells Tina: "I'm a child! And you're an adult! You're all grown up. I mean, come on. That's the problem. You're a hundred years old to me. You might as well be. You've just got it all figured out"(464). Late in the play, Jill, in an unusually reflective moment, says:

> ... maybe they [men] just need more time and instruction. Time and instruction through those dangerous stupid years between about fourteen and twenty-six. Maybe it's that simple. Maybe we have to help them. Maybe that's part of our purpose here on earth. Not all of it. Not all of it by any shot. But part of it ... (*Tough!* 490)

Indeed if often seems to me that women are more grown up than men over our entire live spans. So I was quite surprised to discover that the young women involved in our show, Holly Longstaff, who played Tina, Leigh Anne Kehler, who played Jill, and the associate director, Andrea von Wichert, didn't see *Tough!* that way at all. They felt that Tina and Jill are "wrong" or "in the wrong" almost as often as Bobby is. The women do outnumber Bobby, and they do gang up on him. They've had time to assimilate the information, and Bobby hasn't; they expect Bobby to come through with the "right answers" right away. For most of the play, they don't give him credit for sticking it out and trying to do the right thing which, often, he does, nor for telling the truth, as damaging as those truths may be to him They do "talk down" to Bobby and treat him as if he were a child. There may be some truth to Bobby's contention that Tina has a plan, a list, "A man to love. Some kids. A few good friends. A nice place to live," and that Bobby is part of that plan. According to Holly, Leigh-Anne, and Andrea, Tina and Jill have picked up some ideas from the air, from the *zeitgeist*, and apply them to the immediate situation without really understanding or internalizing them themselves. There are two particularly tricky points.

There does seem to be some internalized classism in Tina's dismissing and mocking Bobby's admittedly vague ambitions as unrealistic because of their working-class background (Bobby's dad drives a cab). "You've got dreams or something. Big ones. Is that what you're telling me. You've got *ambition* all of a sudden?" (*Tough!* 465). "Maybe he's been watching too much television. Maybe he's got us all confused with those kids on those shows who live near a beach. And drive nice cars. And whose parents have big houses. He's pretty … you know … impressionable" (*Tough!* 469). Bobby is groping towards some sort of social justice in this matter: "What's that got to do with anything. I mean if you're saying you can't want stuff because your parents don't have stuff, I don't get it" (*Tough!* 470).

Secondly, there is the question of physical violence. When Bobby tries to prevent Tina from leaving by holding her by the arm, Jill rushes back from getting them soft drinks and beats Bobby up. He is not allowed to use any force at all in his dealings with Tina. "If she wanted to go, she should have been able to go. And no one should have tried to stop her! Get it?!" (*Tough!* 468). Jill uses physical force on Bobby many times in the course of the play, sometimes on Tina's behalf, sometimes, it would seem, simply to express her own anger. Is Jill an instance of a character on the whole sympathetic who reaches a point where violence is morally justified, as we've seen in a number of Walker plays? Does the prohibition of violence apply only to male violence against women? Or are Jill's professed values in hypocritical contrast to her actions? Bobby doesn't fight back. Is he a coward? Is it because of his medical condition, which sometimes causes him to faint? (A wonky bit.) Or has he taken to heart, as many men do, the fundamental belief that he must never, ever, under any conditions, hit a woman? Jock Martin chose the latter in our production.

Again, *Tough!* is not a simple morality play, and questions and gaps such as these make it a much more interesting and involving play than I originally thought it was. There are, to be sure, many moments where women in the audience do identify with the young women on the stage, where they are encouraged to nudge their male companions and give them a somewhat accusatory "isn't that just like a man" look—I saw that many times during our production of the play, and Walker, too, says he's often seen this kind of interaction between male and female members of an audience for *Tough!* But there are enough moments in which we question the women's motives, or fairness, or honesty about themselves, and enough moments in which we feel for Bobby, that our sympathies do move back and forth between the characters, whether we ourselves are male or female. Once again, Walker has thwarted the easy answers, and however much he may agree with his female characters on many issues, and however much we may sympathize with Tina in her difficult situation and be angry with Bobby on her behalf for failing to give her what she needs, we aren't permitted the easy out of siding with "good guys" against the "bad guy."

Finally, Tina tells Bobby that he can go. "… *we* were special to me. And anything less than special is shit. Pressure's off. Go home. Go on" (*Tough!* 481). Tina has reached the realization that Bobby can be of no practical use to her.

> BOBBY: You're just saying that now. Because of how I am now. But how I am now isn't necessarily me. I mean I'm under pressure and—
> TINA: You handled the pressure okay. You protected yourself okay. You didn't commit yourself to anything here. You told me about the things you needed. The time. You told me about your dreams.
> BOBBY: Ah, don't start with the dream stuff. I never said anything about dreams. That was you.
> TINA: No. It was you. It was all about you. You you you.
> BOBBY: Ah, Jesus. That's just how it sounded. Come on. I was under attack.
> TINA: No, that's just how it sounded. I gave you opportunity. You could have said some stuff. You could have gone forward. Made a move. Got involved in the possibilities.
> BOBBY: What. You saying it was a test or something.
> TINA: I didn't mean it to be a test. But maybe it was. Maybe it was a test.
> BOBBY: Yeah. And I failed. (*Tough!* 485)

Bobby leaves. The girls have their talk, about men, women, life, Bobby—a lovely, quiet, girl-talk scene. Tina is not entirely alone. She has Jill. Female friendship takes the stage, and seems to point toward a kind of solidarity, a kind of hope. Just as they are preparing to leave, Bobby returns, to everyone's surprise—Tina and Jill's, the audience's, probably Bobby's.

> BOBBY: … So … I came back.
> TINA: Yeah …
> BOBBY: You see, I've … It's just that … well, I've been … I've been thinking …

TINA: Good for you. Keep it up.
   (*TINA walks past JILL , and leaves*)
JILL: She means that.
   (*JILL winks. Turns and leaves. BOBBY watches them. Pause.*)
BOBBY: Hey! ... Hey, I ah ... I ah ... (*to himself*) Hey. Hey ... (*sits down.
   Gestures a couple of times. Shrugs. Scratches his ear*)
   (*Blackout*)
   (*End*) (*Tough!* 491)

Hardly "happy ever after," but it can be read as a tiny little bit hopeful, for men and women, for their getting along. In fact, because there's more honesty, less sentimentality, there's really more hope here than there is at the end of most conventional "battle of the sexes" plays.

Walker, especially the later Walker, writes well for women, and gives female actors access to aspects of their personalities, aspects of the female experience, in a way not often found in contemporary drama, especially contemporary drama written by men. In both his interview with me in late June and with Corbeil, he talked about ways in which the women in the motel plays get angry, really angry, in a way not often seen on stage, and in a way which actors find strange, at first even a bit disorienting.

> I'm not used to women who think of themselves as victims. You start writing strong women and you come across a whole generation of women actors who have been asked to play victims for a long, long time. I remember doing this early on, with some of these actors, going, I still don't understand why, when your script says you're angry at him, it comes across like you're angry at yourself. What's this all about? It's okay to be angry at yourself sometimes but sometimes it's just okay to be angry at someone else. That was a big thing. So the actors worked that out. Now I think they know. If the woman in a Walker play is mad, she's *mad!* She's not feeling like she's a victim, she can be mad. You don't have to carry the weight of the world with you—you can just be pissed off. (Qtd. in Corbeil 60)

Notes

1. Actually, those rewrites must have been completed before 1990, as we were asked to use the version subsequently published in *Shared Anxiety* in the University of Manitoba's production of that year.

Chapter Six
Suburban Motel

> A man who murdered his wife while depressed about rumours of downsizing at the hospital where he worked has been sentenced to life imprisonment.
>
> The behaviour of Keith Bruce Woodland, normally a peaceful and decent citizen, was completely "inexplicable," prosecutor Phil Perlmutter said yesterday. He said Woodland was "the last person you'd expect to behave in such a way." (Oakes A25)

I had been wondering for some time when someone was going to write this play, the play about what these stingy, mean-spirited times are doing to ordinary people; I guess what I was anticipating was something along the lines of *Death of a Salesman* for the nineties. I should have known that it would be George F. Walker who would write it. When I told him about my admiration for *The End of Civilization* in these terms, for its timeliness and for the way in which it expresses the fears of many in its middle-class audience, Walker said that he thinks he is able to write plays of this kind, that connect to what people are experiencing right now, because he's "attached to what's going on out there," to the gritty and fearful world around him, rather than to theatre, what's happening in theatre, what's theatrically fashionable, what, supposedly, will "sell" (interview, June 1998).

The End of Civilization is one play of six, a "suite" or "cycle" which also includes *Problem Child, Adult Entertainment, Criminal Genius, Featuring Loretta* and *Risk Everything*, all set in the same "slightly rundown motel room" on the outskirts of a large North American city—Walker sets all his urban plays in this generic location, but I persist in believing that at some level in Walker's psyche and experience, this city is Toronto, which, conveniently, can stand in for any number of other North American cities, as in fact it does in many of the movies and television shows shot there. "Everything I have written is about Toronto, and no matter where I am, in some way everything I will write will also be about it" (Conlogue C4). The plays can stand independent of each other, and several of them are to be produced that way in some of the many North American productions scheduled for the 1998–99 theatre season. At the same time, they complement each other, thematically, tonally, even though some are "serious" dark comedies, and others, flat-out farce. Some characters appear in more than one play (and some characters make reappearances from earlier Walker plays). There is an additional structural commonality in that all are full-length, one act plays designed to be played without intermission, each with a running time of around an hour and twenty minutes. They can be seen, in fact, as one big mega-play about contemporary urban life, and having seen the productions of the plays at the Factory, where they were presented in rep in two sets of three, over a period of a few months, my inclination is to think of them in that way. The Factory productions were all directed by Walker during the 1997–98 season, and while *Problem Child*, *Criminal Genius*, and *Risk Everything* had been given workshop productions by Rattlestick Productions at Theatre Off Park in New York in 1997, directed by Daniel De Raey, Walker has said that he considers the Factory run as the "real" premières of all the plays.

All six plays were written in a period of "about ten months," some in Toronto, some in Vancouver, where Walker and his family lived during 1996–97. It had been some time since a new Walker play had appeared; *Tough!* premièred in 1993, four years earlier. Some people (among them, me) were wondering what had happened to George, and Walker, going through one of his periods of disenchantment with the theatre, had thought "in some part of [his] brain" that he had given up the theatre.

The "cycle" did not start out as a cycle, but when he finished the first, *Problem Child*, "the door opened, and someone else came in." He found the single setting

> … incredibly liberating. Because I don't have to recreate the world. The world is that room, and there's nothing between me and the characters, no narrative pressure, because the story is only what happens in that room. It can't be anything else. (Posner D3)

Furthermore, the motel is a kind of neutral space: virtually *anybody* can walk through that door. But the sort of neighbourhood in which Walker's motel is located is not a vacation spot, and this is not the sort of motel to which vacationers would go, for a holiday, or to stop between home and a resort destination. This is the sort of motel where one can find hookers (Sandy in *The End of Civlization*), porn movie producers (Michael in *Featuring Loretta* and *Risk Everything*), crooks doing a job (Shirley, Rolly, and Stevie in *Criminal Genius*), people looking for work (Henry and Lily in *The End of Civilization*), people having an extramarital affair (Jayne and Max in *Adult Entertainment*). For most of the characters, the motel's detachment from the usual routine, from either home or place of work, makes it "carnivalesque" in that behaviour which would not be "allowed" elsewhere is permitted here. All the characters regard the place they are in as the locus of a temporary state of affairs, and almost all come to the motel because they are looking for futures better in some way than their desperate presents. They all fail. They are all "on the edge," on the outskirts of life as well as of the city.

> In this deceptively unremarkable place, a drab, camouflaged circle of hell with an ice machine, we meet people, blue collar people, standing toe-to-toe with life; groping it, throttling it, pulling it closer or fending it off, and in the process coming to some greater self-awareness that usually scalds as it enlightens. Can any of this be funny? Yes, very. (De Raey 5)

At the same time that these plays are funny, they are also all rather dark, darker than the "looking for the light" East End plays of the eighties. Even the funniest and most farcical, *Criminal Genius*, ends with all five characters dead—Walker hasn't left such a pile of corpses on stage at the end of a play since *Zastrozzi*. Yes, the way Walker presents it does make this macabre *denouement* absolutely hilarious, but, to me at least, simultaneously rather disturbing. A little part of *my* brain was sad—I'm going to miss Rolly (although as Walker points out, there can always be a "prequel"). There seemed to me to be in the motel plays a shift in Walker's work as significant as the shift toward "possibility" which Walker and Wallace discuss in their 1988 interview. This impression was strengthened by my reading Walker's 1997 interview with Carole Corbeil in *Brick*:

> ... I was looking for the light [in the East End plays], I was actually searching for it. In *Escape from Happiness* it was important to me to look for some kind of resolution in that family. I was looking. So that got in. And then to let all that drop away, if you're going to let that drop, then everything has to drop away. Then you just write it from the character's point of view, and god knows what their point of view is going to be about certain things. So I have no point of view, I wasn't looking for anything. And it's that way in all six plays ...
> When you get to *The End of Civilization*, which is about this middle-class couple from the suburbs and they are fucked—they can't be saved, they are economically fucked. He's frustrated. And it ends with bleakness, with the wife sitting on the bed for ten minutes, in silence, because she can't find anything to say. I wanted to give the audience a feeling of what that would be like. I don't know if we can do that, but it felt not necessarily a healthy thing to do. I wanted to be healthy, for

> a long time, in and around *Love and Anger*, I wanted to contribute, to be
> the good citizen. Now I suppose it's okay to say, I don't give a fuck. I'm
> that way. So I'm in this thing where I'm not responsible for saving the
> world, or making it better or anything else. (64)

In his interviews with me, he explained that he was in a sense freed by being relieved (in his mind) of the responsibility to look for "possibility," as that responsibility had created "expectations" he didn't want and that interfered with his current work. Anyway, he said, his looking for the light "finally doesn't cure the world." Abandoning the felt need to impose optimism on the world as he sees it, or more accurately given the preceding quotation, as his characters see it, doesn't necessarily preclude the possibility of light in future Walker plays: "If light is there, it is." In the Suburban Motel cycle, it seems strongly to me, it isn't.

It can be argued, and probably will be argued, that in letting go of a responsibility to "look for the light," Walker is also letting go of the more explicitly political activism associated with the East End plays. I would argue, though, that while Walker might no longer be trying to "save the world," the plays of the Suburban Motel cycle still make a very strong political statement. All the plays have a social dimension, all the plays are the consequence of Walker's "attachment" to what's happening around him, and if the vision of contemporary society that emerges is more pessimistic than was earlier work, that can be seen as direct and honest reporting of the quality of life as experienced by the people who frequent the suburban motel in the late '90s. That, in turn, has clear political implications, and probably ought to be heeded as a warning. One of the impressions that emerges most strongly from the six plays is that there isn't as much distance between us, seated in the audience, and Walker's "marginal" characters as we would like to think there is. Walker's approach in Suburban Motel doesn't allow us to distance ourselves from his crazies, nor to protect ourselves with the comforting thought that what's happening on stage couldn't possibly happen to us. Donny, the cop I quote at the beginning of Chapter Four, is coming apart because his attempts to distance himself from the unfortunate people and desperate circumstances he encounters in his work have failed: living, in effect, two lives now seems to him hopelessly dishonest and fraudulent. In other words, Donny is failing as a cop, and disintegrating as a human being, in part because, in some part of himself, he's a "good guy," a good man too sensitive to the misery of others to be immune to it himself (not unlike William in *Criminals in Love* and Petie Maxwell in *Love and Anger*). Or, as Walker tells Corbeil about Donny:

> I had a feeling like that, walking through Parkdale [one of Toronto's
> poorest neighbourhoods]. How can you separate those lives? How long
> can you separate life with a family and our big, long Toronto streets full
> of debris and homeless, fucked-up people? How long can they be really
> separate? How separate are they now? How are they going to get en-
> twined, finally, down the road? They can't do it, can't have all these
> parallel lines, it's wrong in some way. I don't know if it's a moral, but it's
> wrong. (66)

The honest anger is still there, and the conviction that it's "wrong," and
both come through in the motel plays. The straightforward presentation
of these stories, the dramatic strategies which make it difficult for us to
separate our lives from the lives of the social casualties, to abandon *our*
responsibilities, seem to me "political" in a very profound sense, different
from ways in which Walker was political in earlier plays.

Problem Child, the first play in the cycle, begins with R.J. watching a
talk show on television, getting upset over a guest's humiliation. Denise is
trying to persuade him to go out for something to eat; they can't go out,
R.J. says, because they're waiting for a phone call. R.J. continues to get
upset over the talk show; he's going to write a letter to the producer. Denise
wants to know why he's getting so worked up; it is, after all, a TV show,
not life. R.J. disagrees:

> Hey, that's no more disgusting than life, that show. Life is disgusting
> like that. Life is the place where dopes like that guy get to be humili-
> ated ... Life is the place that fucks people like you and me up. Life is
> just like that show. (*Problem Child* 10)

When R.J. tries to phone the producers, he discovers that the phone is
broken—no wonder they didn't get the call they were waiting for. "What
is this. Is this fate. Is this a kick in the face from fate. What is it. What"
(11). The hanging shadow again, bad luck dogs those who are already
down. Phillie, the alcoholic motel manager, arrives to tell them their phone
is broken. After a self-excoriating, self-pitying monologue about his drunk-
enness, Phillie passes out. The scene ends with R.J. and Denise waiting for
Phillie to come to so he can fix their phone.

Scene two raises the stakes. The awaited caller is there in person, Helen
the social worker. She's there to interview Denise and R.J., ex-hooker drug
addict and ex-con respectively, as she sees them, to determine whether
they've reformed to the point where their baby, now in foster care after
being seized on a complaint from Denise's mother, can be returned to them.
Again marginal Walker characters are having to cope with the expectations and definitions of an abstract social institution. Denise is extremely

agitated, as she thought Helen would be bringing the baby with her, and now finds herself dealing with yet more questions and paper work. Helen jumps to the conclusion that Denise is "on medication." Helen is the "cop" in this play, the imposer of order. She is also, as Kate Taylor suggests in her review of the Factory production, a bit too much the caricature of the officious bureaucrat, "her judgmental attitude simplistically unattractive" (Taylor, "Motel cycle a gritty triumph" C3). "Denise, what's that expression on your face supposed to mean. All that ... attitude. You think that's helpful? I'm just doing my job" (*Problem Child* 14).

> DENISE: We need our baby back. It's not gonna work if we don't get Christine back. I won't make it.
> HELEN: What do you mean by that, Denise. Do you think you'll start back on drugs, Denise. Do you feel that's a possibility.
> DENISE: Of course it's a possibility. Everything is a possibility. I'm not a new person. They didn't throw out the old Denise and make a new one. It's a repair job. I'm just ... repaired ... (*to R.J.*) She doesn't get it. (*Problem Child* 15)

Precisely. Helen doesn't "get it," cannot connect to the reality Denise and R.J. are experiencing because the requirements of her social role, the prejudices of her professional class, prevent her from doing so. Denise is another of Walker's "mother whores"; in fact there are four such characters in the Suburban Motel cycle. The "mother" half is infinitely more important to Denise. When she was absolutely broke, she turned a few tricks, but to her, it's no big deal. It's a very big deal to Helen; it's the half of the paradox that seems to her the most significant, the category into which she slots Denise, and to Helen, these two aspects of Denise are mutually exclusive.

> DENISE: I was never a prostitute. I turned a few tricks, and even if I was a prostitute, who says a prostitute can't raise a child.
> HELEN: I do.
> DENISE: You do?
> HELEN: Yes I do.
> DENISE: Is that an official position there Helen.
> HELEN: More or less. Yes.
> DENISE: And one you agree with.
> HELEN: Oh, yes.
> DENISE: Is this getting personal here, Helen. It sounds like you take this personally. (*Problem Child* 26)

Helen, the societal spokesperson, cannot distinguish between "doing her job" and the values, the middle-class moral constructs, she has so internalized that she takes them for the way of the world, simply the way it is.

During this exchange, in which Denise learns more or less up front that she will not get her daughter back, Denise holds Helen by the hand, refusing to let go, forcing the issue. Helen had previously cut her hand on a broken glass, and Denise's squeezing it causes the blood to flow faster. Things now get very wonky. Helen goes into the bathroom, faints, falls, and hits her head on the toilet. She's unconscious, but Denise thinks she's dead, and, sure that she will be accused of murdering Helen, panics. She enlists Phillie's help. It's not hard. "He's one of us ... Scum of the earth. So he knows. He knows about getting screwed ..." (32, 33). Denise and Phillie take Helen and bury her in a patch of wasteland behind the motel. Denise then sends Phillie to kidnap her baby from her foster home. R.J. is very upset when he discovers what has happened. "We could've gotten a law-yer. We're trying to be the kind of people who get lawyers in circumstances like this, Denise" (34).

Some observers have opined that Walker gets the dark comic effects he does by taking ordinary people and putting them in absurd situations. Others say he takes absurd characters and puts them in ordinary situa-tions. I myself think he uses a combination of these approaches, some-times one, sometimes the other. In the situation at hand, I think he uses the former. Denise is hyper and emotionally wired through much of the play, certainly, but Walker makes it clear that in most important respects, Denise is very much like many of the people in the audience. As Kate Taylor asks in her review, "How far would you go to win back your child?" ("Motel cycle a gritty triumph" C3). My honest answer to that question would be "pretty damn far"; with stakes that high, I would certainly be capable of extreme behaviour, perhaps even killing someone, and if one can entertain the idea of killing someone under those circumstances (the issue Gail and Junior debate at the end of *Criminals in Love*), hiding the body of someone I didn't in fact kill doesn't really seem all that extreme. Here, as often in the Motel plays, Walker reduces the distance between people in the audience and characters who under other circumstances we might be tempted to dismiss as marginal, crazy, or outrageous.

Scene seven begins with R.J. and Denise in the room, looking tense; the bathroom door is closed, and we hear the sound of someone shower-ing. The door opens. Helen comes out, wearing one of R.J.'s shirts. A truly remarkable *coup de théâtre*.

Helen is extremely indignant, her self-righteousness multiplied many fold by the experience of being buried alive, and gives Denise a lecture on politeness, civilized behaviour, and moderation. The exchange between the three is quite extraordinary and extremely funny, even by Walker stand-ards.

HELEN: So as I was lying in that mud under that pile of leaves and debris under the billboard out back afraid to move, not knowing if I were paralyzed, how seriously injured I was—I thought about your lack of education. Why didn't Denise call for help. Why has she taken the criminal route in this. Why hasn't she taken the reasonable moderate—yes, even polite approach and called an ambulance. And then of course I remembered all my training and everything I've been taught about people like you and I decided you just don't know any better.

R.J.: Are you going to call the police.

HELEN: I don't know yet. Probably. I mean it is the reasonable thing to do. I was just buried alive.

R.J.: You see, what happened was, she panicked.

HELEN: I was buried alive! I had to claw my way up through garbage and leafy smelly muddy things because I was buried alive in a deep hole.

DENISE: (*To herself*) Not deep enough.

HELEN: I heard that.

R.J.: She didn't mean it.

HELEN: Oh, she meant it.

R.J.: (*To DENISE*) Tell her you didn't mean it.

DENISE: (*To HELEN*) I didn't mean it.

HELEN: Yes you did! You meant it. What's wrong with you. Don't you have any civilized instincts left in you. Have they all been dulled or killed by your senseless self-indulgent life style.

DENISE: Look, I'm sorry. Don't start … with that judgement crap. I can't take it.

HELEN: Well look who's going on the offensive. I mean talk about inappropriate responses. I mean who buried who alive. (41–42)

At the end of *Problem Child*, Denise comes down stage, sits on the edge of the stage, and speaks directly to us. At this point in the production, I was a little frightened, for Walker, the character, the actress—this sort of moment, this kind of abrupt shift in convention, is so hard to pull off. It is the kind of moment that asks for language that soars, to justify the violation of convention, to pull everything together by taking the play to an entirely different level. Denise calmly tells us what has happened since the events we have seen. Phillie has made several attempts to kidnap Christine, and all failed. Denise and R.J. wait in the motel room for another six months. Denise goes through the motions of being the sort of person Helen, society, wants her to be. Denise gets more and more desperate. The speech, in part:

I'm in hell. I'm more desperate that anybody I hear on those [TV talk] shows and I'm trapped in a sadness and an anger so deep I know I'll never get out. Because I'm just slipping deeper into the sadness. And deeper into the anger ... I have horrible thoughts about doing horrible things to people. If I were on one of those shows and I told people how I really felt and what I really wanted to do ... they wouldn't be able to give me any advice ... they wouldn't even be able to talk ... Maybe they'd just cancel the show ... If I leaned over in bed and told R.J. what I felt about everything ... about life ... about our life and everyone else's life and how really useless and stupid it all is ... he'd die probably. He'd give up and die ... So I don't tell him. I tell him I'm waiting. I'm being a good girl. Seeing if things work out. I tell him maybe there's still a chance we'll get Christine ... But I know ... things don't work out ... Not for people like us. They just get worse. (*Problem Child* 48)

As with the confession speech by Henry in *The End of Civilization*, there is nothing "literary" about Denise's monologue, and nothing ostentatiously theatrical. It is, Walker said, "a cry from the character to the audience" (interview, June 1998). Ordinary words arranged to convey deep grief beyond that we're used to seeing on stage, even in classical tragedy. The Walker language, here and elsewhere, allows the actor direct contact with the thoughts and feelings of the character. When Walker directed the Factory production, he says, he put off work on Denise's monologue until well into rehearsals. Finally, he asked Kirsten Thomson if she felt ready to do it, she said "yes," and did it, perfectly, with no need for further direction from Walker; Thomson subsequently performed the speech with such utter conviction that both she and the audience were devastated. Walker's simple eloquence of ordinary language used to express a sadness of more than ordinary intensity is in fact enough to take the play to a whole new level, without literary pyrotechnics, and projects out into the audience through direct address. The "cry" works and is of a piece with the rest of the play.

The speech reaches the emotional intensity it does in part because it follows immediately on and contrasts sharply to the hilarity of the exchange between the resurrected Helen, R.J., and Denise on "civilized" behaviour. In his seminal work on the genre of dark comedy, J. L. Styan says "The dramatist who can swing between the extremes of tragedy and farce within the same framework is today the man to sting us" (282). "The unity of a play is not to be conceived narrowly as a matter of forms, as unity of 'action', but as a final tone and climate, a 'fourth' unity in which opposites may flourish together in the audience's mind" (283). It is in this "fourth unity" that *Problem Child* leaves us at its conclusion.

The issues of "fairness" and "justice," "justice and a fair heart" to quote the apt phrase used by Walker in the play, which are raised by the story of Denise and R.J. and their child are further pointed by two other elements in the play. One is the character of Phillie, who so quickly sides with the couple. Justice and injustice in the world are of obsessive interest to Phillie, so much so that they threaten his stability; he thus tries, unsuccessfully, not to think about them; when he comes to vacuum the room, he and R.J. discuss the talk shows, "Fair behaviour for fair behaviour. You know? Even breaks for everyone."

> No, no ... Don't take me there, man. I can't get into that. Next thing I'll just get upset. I'm capable of some pretty self-destructive behaviour. I gotta concentrate on doing my job. I'm lucky to have this job. If it wasn't for my cousin Edward ... No ... No I can't get into that justice shit. The lucky and the unlucky. The haves and the have-nots. The fuckers, the fuckees—oh man. Let me just suck up some dirt. Let me just do what I can do, and suck up what little dirt I can here. (*Problem Child* 18)

The second is the television shows themselves, an ongoing motif throughout the play as R.J. maintains his obsession with them (he became addicted to talk shows while in jail). We hear R.J. talking back to the TV, R.J. talking to producers on the phone. R.J. projects his anger and anxiety onto the talk shows because he can't cope with their application to his own life. He's right, of course, when he sees parallels between the way the guests are treated on the shows, and the way in which he and his wife are treated in life. In *White Trash*, a writer raised in trailer parks says of TV talk shows:

> Nowadays, trailer park folks still try to get out by playing games—not as TV game show contestants, like our neighbors in the fifties who made fools of themselves for prizes, but as "guests" on so-called "trash" talk shows, like Geraldo, Richard Bey and Jenny Jones, who "win" celebrity—but no prizes—if they can act out the real dramas of their lives as trashy stereotypes, reassuring viewers that it's someone else who's really on the bottom. (Berube 38–39)

R.J., Denise, and Phillie can't reassure themselves in this way. And, as I've been arguing, neither can we by the time George Walker's finished with us.

I think that television is a presence throughout the Suburban Motel plays, either explicitly, as in *Problem Child* and *Risk Everything*, or through connotation. It is certainly an ongoing presence: often in the plays, the characters, when they momentarily have nothing to do, turn on the TV for a while, watch, or half watch for a few minutes, then turn it off again. On the Factory's set for the cycle, the room was at an angle, protruding into the auditorium, and in the corner of the room closest to the audience, the one with invisible walls, was the TV set, its back facing us. In effect, then, the image of the television set intervened, I would say "mediated," between us and most of the action on the stage. The plays, then, are television shows, distortions of television shows, variations on television shows. When I raised the possibility with Walker, and asked whether this latest work for the stage wasn't incorporating his work in network television, he was, at first, a little skeptical. He said that whatever he had been doing, whatever work he was doing, was bound to get into his stage writing, and that the work he had been doing immediately prior to writing the Suburban Motel plays just happened to have been script work for television (interview, June 1998). If the work had been something else, what was incorporated would have been something else. He did allow, however, that there may be some similarities between many of the characters in the cycle and TV "types"; the plays go where TV does not because they spend more "in depth time with the characters" and because the scenes are extended past the point where TV would break for a commercial, the scenes are "played out" as far as they will go.

I think the plays can be regarded as "perversions" of TV show formulae and dynamics. *Problem Child* perverts the trash talk show, and provides a "reference point" while doing so. We are drawn to the play and its world in part by the kind of voyeurism and gratifying feelings of class superiority that draw us to the television talk shows. But we get ambushed. Denise's final speech, initially, provides a point of reference and of comparison, referring to the sort of shattered, sad lives we've seen on Ricki Lake and the others, then it goes beyond that, and perhaps adds to Styan's "fourth unity" a degree of guilt that we ever found such spectacles entertaining. Through the strategies I've been discussing, we're taken into shared feelings ("How far would you go ...") that eliminate the distance required for voyeurism. The social reassurance Berube mentions is "perverted" in Richard Paul Knowles' sense of the word: the form intended to reassure becomes in Walker's hands very threatening indeed. One of the reviewers of the Suburban Motel cycle says of its characters that if we're honest, we would admit we "wouldn't want any of them as neighbours" (Chapman, "Walker's dramatic return" E5). The point, it seems to me, is that they not only *are* our neighbours, they're us.

If the talk show is perverted in *Problem Child*, the formula perverted in *Adult Entertainment* is that of the TV cop show, especially the recent, supposedly "gritty" variety. The formula is so well known to us that no character needs to refer to television for us to find connections (and besides, that television set is still sitting there). Later in the Suburban Motel suite, in *Risk Everything*, R.J. does specifically refer to *Columbo, McCloud, Hart to*

Hart, and *Cagney and Lacey*: he remarks that all the "detective shows" after *Columbo* are "crap."

The beginning of *Adult Entertainment* is relatively unthreatening, gives the title of the play a reassuring if *risqué* meaning, and draws us into its world through voyeurism and titillation—a couple is in bed, having sex, noisily. Walker fulfills our expectation of the cheap motel, the sleazy connotations the venue takes on through the North American folklore of dirty jokes and sly winks. The phone rings. After a farcical scramble in which the couple tries to determine whose cell phone is ringing, the woman answers the room phone. The man's partner, his police partner, is playing a practical dirty joke, phoning to see how they're doing. The mood is broken, on stage and off.

We learn that the man is a policeman, the woman a lawyer, and that they are not married to each other—this is, as we had suspected and hoped, extramarital, sleazy sex. He is married, she is not. They've had an affair some time in the past, and for some reason, are here this afternoon for a reprise. Jayne starts to take the conversation and the play somewhere other than where we, or Max, had expected: "This was a mistake. It was better when it was over. A thing in my past. I felt better about you. I even started to have fond memories … But looking at you now I'm remembering how much I hate your guts" (*Adult Entertainment* 53). She starts to put a wider meaning on this moment of post-excitement disillusionment.

> You're here because you've given up. Just like me. We sensed that about each other. When we first met we sensed it, and we sensed it even stronger today. We're both finished. Two people of a certain age done like dinner. Done being useful citizens and lawyers and cops and husbands. (*Adult Entertainment* 56)

They are, Jayne says, "turned on" by each other's "deadness." Max and Jayne are both middle-aged, and have reached a point where neither really believes in what he or she is doing.

We learn more. The wife of Max's partner, Donny, has left him, and she and her eleven-year-old daughter, Emma, have been living at Jayne's apartment for two months. Jayne wants a favour from Max: she wants him to "persuade" a young man, "scum," to take the blame for an offence one of her female clients, perhaps salvageable, is charged with. Max, too, wants a favour: he wants Jayne to find out where her client's sister's boy friend is hiding. Neither they nor we know whether the wanting the favours or going to the motel room came first; they talk about it. They resume sex.

Scene two. Donny and his wife, Pam, are in the motel room, Pam dressed like a prostitute. Donny is the "infected" cop who can no longer live one life at home, another at work. He's a drunk. Later in the play he says of his life:

> I want this. I like this. I like ... wanting this. *(Laughs)* Want to live in
> a cheesy apartment hotel. Have rough sex with professional ladies, drink
> vodka samplers, go prowling for criminals at night and kick the shit
> out of them. That's my life. It's not a good life by normal standards. But
> I've become fond of it. (*Adult Entertainment* 82)

Donny and Pam are in the motel room to, what? They're not sure. Attempt a reconciliation? Have rough sex, with Pam pretending to be one of Donny's hookers? Talk about how lonely and sad their lives have become? They start to have rough sex, Pam grabs Donny's revolver, says "Let's just get it over with for both of us," and, in the blackout, there's a shot. When the lights come up, Max and Jayne are looking at the bodies.

> JAYNE: Oh my God. Oh my God ... Look at them. It's—Why am I dressed
>   like this ... Why are we in our underwear.
> *MAX is leading her back to bed, sleepily.*
> MAX: Because it's a dream.
> JAYNE: A dream ... Oh well that explains it.
> *They are getting into bed.*
> MAX: It also explains why there are two bodies and there was only one
>   gun shot.
> JAYNE: Oh ... right. (*Adult Entertainment* 72)

End of scene.

There is, I think, a perversion here of a television formula and a "reference point." Ever since *Dallas* kept much of the world holding its breath over "who killed JR?' in 1980, then answered the question with the "it was all a dream" twist (the event is even recorded in *The Timetables of History*), the dream resolution has been a staple of TV script writing, and is now a cliché. Walker perverts it by first allowing us relief and a laugh that it wasn't "real," nobody died, then, later, by not ending a nightmare when someone *is* killed, and demonstrating that in the suburban motel, as opposed to prime-time television, there are no easy, sleight of hand resolutions.

Donny, drunk, has gone beyond finding out where the kid who is to be coerced is located, picks him up, and takes him to the motel in an unmarked police car. Jayne, fearing she will be disbarred and left destitute, leaves after rehearsing Max in saying "Jayne had nothing to do with it" (and remarks that while he may be a failure at everything else, Max is a "world class liar"). Max beats Donny up for "fucking up" so badly, and goes off in the car to take the kid to a secluded place the policemen have evidently used in similar situations in the past to "scare" him into confessing to a crime he didn't commit in order to get Jayne's client off the hook.

Later, Max returns, badly wounded in the stomach. He has been stabbed. Donny was evidently too drunk to search the kid properly, the kid had a knife, and stabbed Max; Max shot the kid dead, buried the body as well as he could, returned to the motel.

The bare facts as outlined might, just might, show up in a television show about good cops gone bad. But *Adult Entertainment* ("adult entertainment" indeed, for the meaning of the title is changing as the play progresses) goes past that, and eventually "perverts" the formula, in two ways. This isn't TV, it's theatre, so when Max shows up bleeding profusely, especially given that this occurs in a play which up until this point had largely been comedy, it has an impact well beyond that which might occur if a similar event occurred on television. Further, we spend more "quality time" with these people than we would if we encountered them on television, and scenes are "played out"—a "real" encounter between Donny and Pam, with real discussion of what is happening in their fucked up lives, and the extended attempts of Jayne, Pam, and Donny to sew up Max's wound (he can't go to the hospital) are both excruciating in their different ways, and drawn out well past the audience's "comfort zone." Still further, this is a Walker play, and even after the "turn," there are many comic moments, many laughs, so just when we think we're becoming accustomed to the new turn of events and the new tone, we're knocked off balance again.

> Dark comedy is drama which impels the spectator forward by stimulus to mind or heart, then distracts him, muddles him, so that time and time again he must review his own activity in watching the play. In these submissive, humiliating spasms, the drama redoubles its energy, the play's image takes on other facets, the mind other aspects, and the spectator "collects the force which again carries him onward." But now progression is more cautious, and he is on guard. He is charged with a tension as a result of which he is a more alert and therefore responsive participant. This tension is one of dramatic irony. (Styan 262)

In *Adult Entertainment*, the dramatic irony takes the play and the audience into a hard and unguarded look at the nature of "justice," at the implications of what happens when police, thinking they're serving a larger justice, or maybe just beyond caring about justice, or, strangely, a combination of the two, go themselves outside the law. Pam, who is encountering the really nasty, not just sleazy, side of her husband's life for the first time, is aghast, and in effect voices our horror. "We have a child, Donny. She lives in this world … You're making the world she lives in worse"

(98). Jayne tries to explain to Pam the empty place she has come to in her life:

> JAYNE: ... Most people think life ... life itself, is pretty important. I used to think that ... I was ... nicer when I thought that ... You know this all started because I was trying to do a young woman a big favour. I thought she had potential ... I don't know that she does, for sure ... But I do know she has a lot more potential than that "kid" in the field ever had ... Because well ... because he was basically scum.
>
> PAM: And ... that's all you feel about him.
>
> JAYNE: Yes. I think it is.
>
> PAM: So feeling someone is scum doesn't ... kinda make you feel like you're scum too.
>
> JAYNE: No, Pam it doesn't. It makes me sad and kind of disappointed in myself. But not like I'm scum. I've met scum, Pam. Lots of it. Scum doesn't have conversations like this with people like you. Scum grabs people like you by the throat, drags you into an alley then rapes and kills you. (98)

Adult Entertainment is one of the three Suburban Motel plays which end, or almost end, with a demanding (of both actor and audience), emotionally supercharged monologue. Max's monologue concerns the first time he killed someone in the line of duty. He and Jayne are alone on stage; Donny and Pam have left to go to the field where the killing occured, to try to dispose of the evidence. Max tells about the time he shot an old man who was beating up his wife with a baseball bat, then came after Max with the bat. Walker, and other writers, have taken me to the place where I can recognize that, under some circumstances, I would indeed kill. I'd like to think that afterwards, it would bother me more than it evidently bothers Max, after he sobers up:

> And I'm thinking "When I get up tomorrow morning my life will be changed ... I'm gonna have trouble living with this." ... But when I get up ... that's not how I feel. I look around at my kids and what I feel is ... I was doing my job ... And anybody who ever comes at me and threatens my life, carrying a bat, a knife, a gun, a saw, a fucking stick ... is gonna die ... That's just what has to happen ... *(shrugs)* *(Adult Entertainment* 103)

But I don't know for sure that I would feel more. Walker says that this revelation, this monologue, its matter-of-factness, is "chilling" and of course, he's right; Max is, or has become, a kind of "monster," a term applied to Donny and Max in the play by Pam (us). At the same time, whatever our liberal protestations about deprived childhoods and so on, "part of our brain" knows that Jayne is right when she says that scum is out there, that scum doesn't have conversations, that scum rapes and kills. And we expect the police to protect us from that scum. The way in which *Adult Entertainment* "perverts" the TV cop show is that it uses the formula to take us to a place where we recognize not only what our expectations and needs do to the "scum" who get killed, but what they do to those whom we expect to do our killing for us, and that's certainly not where "crime fighter" entertainment on TV takes us. We are implicated. We are involved in the fight between "good" and "evil," and telling the good guys from the bad guys is just not as easy as it is on TV.

According to Annalee Newitz, popular film and television, like TV cop shows, like "reality TV" programs such as *Cops*, the latter even while "sympathetic" to the police, have constructed white brutality, especially white police brutality, as the province of the lower classes. Thus, for example, middle-class viewers can dissociate themselves from responsibility when they watch the infamous Rodney King beating videotape—they can't distance themselves by relegating the police officers involved to a racial "other," but they can nonetheless construct and relegate the police to a classist "Other" using the white trash stereotypes developed through films like *The Hills Have Eyes*, *Kalifornia*, *Deliverance*, *Evil Dead 2*, *Copycat*, and *Cape Fear* (both versions), movies which, Newitz says, direct white self-hatred onto "low-class, monstrous, or criminal whites."

> Since many police officers come from lower-class white backgrounds, images of violent police culture could be said to grow out of already-existing stereotypes of a brutal, ignorant white working-class and to feed back into real social relations between the police and the poor as a catalyst for more white violence and frustration. (137)

I would say that most of the Suburban Motel plays pervert TV formulae to defeat and short-circuit the assumptions and values, in part formed and certainly reinforced by TV, which under normal circumstances allow us to distance ourselves from what one reviewer of the cycle called "scary characters from society's under-belly" and "members of the victim class" (Chapman, "Walker's dramatic return" E5), or, I suppose, in the case of the police, the "violent, aggressor" class, "monstrous" or "monsters," to follow up on both Newitz and Walker.

Adult Entertainment takes the issues concerning the "fucking, wonderful, goddamn scum" from Mike Dixon's speech in *Escape from Happiness*, and pushes them much, much further. At the same time, we can't dissociate ourselves from Max and Max's lack of feeling for his victim as much as we would perhaps like to. Early in the play, he's likable enough (and played with great charm by Layne Coleman in the Factory production). He's funny. He's having an affair with a lawyer (our class), a smart, beautiful woman (Karen Robinson), and apparently getting away with it: wish fulfillment. His middle-aged disillusionment is certainly familiar to many. He's pretty honest and straightforward about many things. I think many of us, certainly middle-aged men, are likely to identify with him, as once before we identified with the pragmatist Victor in *Zastrozzi*, especially when Max lets us see him in his underwear. We know too much about him to stereotype him, to place him in that classist "Other" that Annalee Newitz discusses. So we're still a bit attached to him when he takes us to a place where, like Walker, we'd rather not be:

> Maybe we should listen to these people, who are sending out warnings about this stuff. Maybe that's what it was, acting out the fears of these things. It's interesting when you come across a character who says something alarming, that alarms you, you go, No—where did that come from? You go searching for it in yourself ... I'd just as soon not go there, but I went there. (Qtd. in Corbeil 66)

Walker and his family recently moved into a new apartment in Toronto, and in the new apartment there is a (non-working, he was careful to stress) fireplace. The big interior decorating problem here, of course, is deciding what is important enough to put in a focal point as obvious as the space above the mantel. Walker chose a blow-up print of the Marx Brothers "because looking at it makes me feel good." I'm willing to bet that Walker, like many of his generation, developed his affection for the Marx Brothers by watching their films on late-night television. It's out of this "feel good" response to the Marx Brothers, the love of clever but raucous comedy and what he calls his "deep roots in vaudeville," that *Criminal Genius*, the next play in the Suburban Motel cycle, comes. This is the funniest, most farcical play of the cycle, the one that Walker went back to see himself several times because it makes him "feel good."

The play begins with an extended "routine," an unabashed comic crosstalk routine, its heritage clearly showing, involving forty bucks, a watch, and a pair of shoes. The participants are Rolly and Stevie Moore, the father and son team of petty crooks who earlier appeared in *Beautiful City* and *Escape from Happiness*, and Phillie, the alcoholic motel manager back from *Problem Child*. It's past checkout time and Phillie wants them to leave or give him forty bucks. Rolly and Stevie can't leave, they are evidently supposed to meet someone regarding some criminal activity they're involved in and fear for their lives if they don't keep the appointment, but they don't have forty bucks. Rolly tells Stevie to give Phillie his watch. Stevie doesn't want to give Phillie the watch; its was a gift from Rolly, the only thing his dad ever gave him. Even when Rolly tells Stevie that he got the watch "off a dead guy," Stevie will not change his mind and tells Rolly to give Phillie his shoes, also formerly the property of a now deceased fellow criminal. Phillie doesn't want the shoes, at first, he wants the forty bucks. And round and round they go. Walker clearly had a wonderful time writing it; he says it's as though Rolly, Stevie, and Phillie had been looking for him: "Where's that guy who's going to let us talk about forty bucks, a watch, and a pair of shoes for ten minutes?"

Phillie eventually decides he will take the shoes, and leaves. Shirley, "Shirl the Pearl," bursts into the room and starts berating Rolly and Stevie, "the two biggest fucking morons in the universe." We're now into the hierarchical "master servant" status game of the sort Keith Johnstone discusses in his book *Impro* (67), pecking order as slapstick farce: Rolly abuses Stevie, Shirley abuses Rolly who abuses Stevie. The Three Stooges did it all the time, as did the Marx Brothers, more selectively and with more finesse. There is a Walker wrinkle here. Rolly has been reading self-improvement articles: "I didn't know about … caring. Then one day I picked up one of those magazines and I read 'Having Trouble Caring?' and I thought 'Yeah'" (*Criminal Genius* 128). Thus Walker adds a little parodic satire to the Marx Brothers routine.

Shirley has hired Rolly and Stevie to burn down a restaurant. The problem is that the Moores are against violence, and if they had burned down the restaurant, someone might have been hurt. "I've lived a criminal life for thirty-five years and no one ever got hurt in my endeavours" (*Criminal Genius* 116). So they kidnaped the cook instead, and have her gagged and bound in the washroom. Shirley is simultaneously enraged and terrified: the man who hired her to hire someone to burn down a rival restaurant is Mike Castle, an off-stage gangster who's got more "status" in Johnstone's sense and more power than anyone we see on stage—who knows what he'll do to our three stooges for screwing up. The cook is Castle's daughter, Amanda. Rolly, feeling a bit stupid about not following Shirley's orders, unbeknownst to Shirley, returns and burns down the restaurant. Amanda escapes and, furious with her father who keeps killing her boyfriends and has now been responsible for burning down the restaurant she established across the street from her father's with the intention of putting his out of business, burns down her father's restaurant. Now everybody's really in trouble.

Amanda returns, and engages in a power status struggle with Shirley, which she wins, thus taking over the "gang," such as it is. She has decided that's she's going to have to kill her father to prevent him from hiring anyone to come after them, and that while she's at it she may as well take over his criminal empire. Phillie regains consciousness (he had returned to the room because Rolly's shoes didn't fit him and had then passed out). Amanda enlists him as well. Phillie will fit right in: "Are you a fucked-up pathetic individual with a bleak past and almost no potential" (*Criminal Genius* 133). Furthermore, Phillie's too drunk to know any better:

> Well I gotta say and you have to understand that everything I hear think and say is filtered by a very thick alcoholic fog but I gotta say nonetheless that if there's only one person that you kill in your life I think a dominating murderous criminal father with gangland connections is a good choice. (*Criminal Genius* 137)

Walker thus adds another step to the master-with-a-servant-with-a-servant-comic pecking order, now very complex and capable of many permutations as it has four basic levels with Phillie as "wild card" stumbling drunkenly up and down through the status hierarchy as well as in and out of consciousness.

In scene three, the conspirators return to the motel room, first Rolly and Stevie, then Phillie, then Amanda and Shirley. The men fled at the first sign of violence; the women fought ferociously, killing seven of Castle's twelve guards, but having failed to kill Castle himself. The men are in trouble, and we go into another round of blame, recrimination and insult while the women prepare to kill the men. Because the women are "hot" after killing the guards, they confuse Stevie mightily: "I'm gonna die. I'm gonna die but I'm listening to you talk to each other about sex and I'm getting excited. So I'm gonna die but I'm excited and I'm fucked up by that … Help me, Dad. I'm confused! Really confused!" (*Criminal Genius* 148–149). Phillie is in the bathroom, refusing to come out. The internal bickering is suddenly made irrelevant when a car pulls up outside the room and a volley of bullets shatters the window and wounds Shirley before the vehicle speeds off into the night. Our inept criminals try to come up with a plan for what they should do when Castle and his thugs return. They fail. The thugs return, there's another volley of shots, and Rolly, Stevie, Amanda and Shirley are all killed, leaving Phillie alone, alive, in the bathroom; the Marx Brothers meet *Reservoir Dogs*. Again, a Walker Motel play ends with a long and revealing monologue, here delivered by Phillie, sitting, unseen, in the bathroom.

> Hey! What's happening out there. Were those gunshots … Well? … Well? Ah the hell with you all … I'm sorry I ever met you … You're just like everyone else … You take advantage … You see that I'm a not-well man, that I'm addicted to alcoholic beverages, prone to bad luck, you see that I'm not a very strong person and you take advantage. Get me involved

in something I'm too impaired to fully understand. Whatever happens to me, I'm blaming you. You thought you were gonna blame me, well I'm blaming you. The forty buck thing, the shoes thing, the running thing, I'm not taking responsibility for any of it. Who said we were bound together ... That's crap. We're not bound. It's every man for himself. Dog eat dog. Fuck you. Did you hear me. Fuck you. Talk about bad luck. Bad luck loves me like I'm its mother. (*Criminal Genius* 155)

I've quoted another section of this very long monologue previously when discussing the role bad luck plays in Walker's political analyses. Near the end of the monologue Phillie sees a man at the bathroom window with a gun, "some other demented idiot in my life for no good reason and this one is going to shoot me. Well go ahead, asshole. Shoot me. Why not. Who cares. (*A gunshot*) Great. (*Sound of body falling.*)" (156). End of play.

This is an extremely "perverse" way to end a farce, and perverse in a number of ways. Conventional farces do not end with all the characters dead; Marx Brothers movies do not conclude with mass slaughter; pratfalls are not fatal. Indeed, the standard classroom story to explain comic distance and objectivity goes something like: Fat man comes on stage, slips on banana peel, falls. Big laugh. Man doesn't get up, doesn't get up, doesn't get up—he's either dead or badly injured. We thus feel sorry for him, and "comic distance" disappears. Laughter dies. Not funny anymore. But when Walker does it, it is funny. And isn't. At once.

Second perversion. There's no one, alive, on stage to look at while we listen to the long monologue. This is the only play I can think of that ends with a monologue delivered by a character who is off-stage. This puts the audience in a state of mind and in confusion unusual in a theatre. Part way through Phillie's speech, it occurs to audience members that there's really no point in looking at the stage anymore. They start looking at each other instead, perhaps have little discussions. The dislocation and confusion experienced by the characters are projected into the auditorium; we're a bit uncomfortable, and probably a bit amused by our discomfort. This is simply not the normal relationship between audience and play.

At about the same time, we realize that this monologue, given the extent of Phillie's self-pity and his loquaciousness and given that George Walker wrote the play, could go on for a very long time, indeed, theoretically, all evening. We thus begin to simultaneously anticipate the expected shot and dread it, want it to release us from this uncomfortable state, and don't want it, because it will mean the end of a wonderfully entertaining monologue, a delightful character, and an extremely funny play.

At the end of *Criminal Genius*, Phillie is what Styan describes as a "comic-pathetic hero," a traditional comic "type" (here the drunk) to whom the

playwright gives other sides, in a manner more often associated with tragedy. The contradiction calls up a complex of responses, rather than one,
and these are set in opposition to each other:

> This kind of double response arises when your initial recognition of
> the clown in his traditional role of wit and joker is denied and contra-
> dicted, when he is shown as capable of suffering the pains of mundane
> life, pains which would not have mattered to him or to us in his artificial
> character. (Styan 270)

What could be more mundane than death? Especially this death, sitting
on a toilet waiting for a stranger to blow one's brains out because one was
in the wrong place at the wrong time, at the end of a life of being in the
wrong place at the wrong time. In this play, it seems to me that Walker
has gone beyond dark comedy to dark farce. Maurice Charney speaks of
the "tragic farces" of Joe Orton and Tom Stoppard. "Everything evokes
contradictory impressions, so that the audience might eventually think
that it is the victim of the playwright's practical joke—that it is being had
or put on" (106).

Walker might think that *Criminal Genius* is entirely light, and entertaining, but then, being the practical joker himself, he would. I will also
admit that there were many in the audience the night I was there who
took the play in that way, "pure entertainment." But I'm not alone in seeing some darkness in the play. "Despite their antics, these are really tragic
characters, standing beyond the pale and completely unable to figure out
what has put them there" (Coulbourn, "Walker's Criminal Genius" 45).

> ... its railings about the misfortunes of the desperate losers with bleak
> pasts and no potential, is a prodding reminder that smug flagwavers
> touting the virtues of places like, for example, Toronto the Mega-Good,
> always ignore the grim and grubby lives many have to endure.
> (Chapman, "Mostly non-stop fun" C5)

Phillie's impending death, then death, as well as the deaths of the others, certainly brought home to me the darkness noted by both Coulbourn
and Chapman, but I was not as ready as they evidently were to distance
myself from Phillie, his "standing beyond the pale" and "grim and grubby"
life were not for me, at least, the province of the "Other." I think I feel in
Phillie's predicament, and in the way Walker "perverts" the farcical presentation of his predicament, obliterating objectivity and detachment in
the way that Styan attributes to the comic-pathetic hero, the sense that
Phillie's life (and death) is not without relevance to ours, mine. It has been
noted of farce, especially the plays of Georges Feydeau, that in their structure, which places an ordinary human being at the mercy of a mechanistic

universe, a plot made up of impossible coincidences, mistimings, and bad luck, farces can be seen as models of the human condition. What Stoppard and Orton (and I think Walker) do is pervert the traditional farce so that rather than hiding this frightening vision under uncontrollable laughter, they bring it out into the open in their "tragic farces." With the metatheatrical manoeuvre at the end of *Criminal Genius*, Walker dumps it in our laps.

Since *The Mary Tyler Moore Show* pioneered the format, the single career girl making her way in a complex, male dominated, and often zany world has become a staple of the television sitcom, with *Murphy Brown*, *Sybil*, and *Suddenly Susan* continuing the trend, obviously aimed at a target audience of which single career women constitute a significant portion. This is the type of sitcom Walker perverts in *Featuring Loretta*. When Walker is finished applying "Walker twists" and "wonky bits" to the formula, the "situation" goes something like this:

Loretta has come to the big city to find her fortune after her husband has been eaten by a bear. She's a couple of months pregnant by her dead husband's best friend, the result of her retaliating against her husband's cheating on her. She's living in the motel while working at Buffalo Bob's steak house, and when we first see her, is wearing her abbreviated cowgirl waitress costume complete with holsters for the mustard and ketchup. The career options open to her, other than cowgirl waitress, would seem to be white slave dancer in Tokyo, porn film actress, and "high end call girl." She's currently beset by two controlling men, Dave, a casual date who has become infatuated with her and now has fantasies about the domestic delights of going shopping with her, and Michael, a hyperactive, sunnily optimistic wannabe porn movie producer who wants her to star in a series of sex movies. She's also beset by phone calls from her sister, who on their mother's behalf urges her to go home, from her in-laws, who think the unborn child is their grandchild, and from the actual father of the child, with whom Loretta wants nothing more to do.

Loretta is another of Walker's working-class pragmatists. She sees her situation clearly, and in the dilemma in which she finds herself, realizes that her body is really her only asset, her "product," and that it doesn't make sense that only Buffalo Bob should be profiting from it; her position is not unlike the one Mrs. Warren puts forward early in Shaw's *Mrs. Warren's Profession*. If she's going to be exploited, she's determined to be the one doing the exploiting and getting the profit. In a very hard-nosed, unsitcom speech, she spells out her position to Dave, who is trying to forbid her from performing in Michael's movies:

> I can do whatever I want. What I want to do right now is make as much money as I possibly can. Money is the only thing that expands your options. No matter what anybody says, it's money. Only money. It's not love and respect and intelligence and hard work. The world doesn't give a shit about any of those things if they're not also connected to the ability to make money. (*Featuring Loretta* 185)

Thus the plucky single girl sitcom formula is neatly perverted; those sitcoms often do say that "love and respect and intelligence and hard work" count, but of course they say those things in order to make money. Realistically, we have to admit that Loretta is right, and, that being the case, we really have no right to judge Loretta's choices, any more than do Dave, Michael, or her in-laws.

Michael, too, is something of a pragmatist; while he also has feelings for Loretta, lust more than Dave's romantic longings, he is quite prepared to accept that the attraction is not returned, and to concentrate on "business." He adds a Rabelaisian touch to the play through his celebration of the senses, his enjoyment of everything; the quality he sees in Loretta, the quality he wants to market, is her ability to give men instant erections (another Rabelaisian and very Walkeresque "wonky bit," as it were). In a very carnivalesque scene, Dave is recruited as Loretta's partner for the first sex movie: Michael sets up camera and lighting gear and the scantily clad Loretta waits while Dave undresses in the bathroom. The two male perspectives, each controlling, each intimately linked to male phallic fantasies and egos, are brought to the point of conflict; as Michael tells Dave: "We don't need a mushy romantic erection. We need a big hard nasty erection" (*Featuring Loretta* 205). The attempt to shoot the movie fails. The young men seated near me in the Factory audience were obviously hoping the scene would get even more carnivalesque and explicit than it was—Walker's use of titillation to bring the issues down to their most basic level (Bakhtinian "degradation") was obviously a successful strategy.

The only support Loretta gets in this situation is from Sophie, a Russian immigrant working as a chambermaid in the motel her father owns while she studies physics, at her father's insistence. Sophie's story parallels Loretta's in some respects, and reinforces the "battle of the sexes" aspect of the play, with women trying to free themselves from controlling men. Sophie's father is an ex- KGB man who "yelled [her] mother to death" in Russia, and who is now controlling Sophie by yelling at her. "He screams like when he was KGB screaming at dissidents" (*Featuring Loretta* 173). Later in the play, Sophie's father dies:

> My father is yelling this close to my face. Usually Father is yelling farther away. But this time this close. I'm scared. I tell him I'm scared. He

yells louder. He yells and yells. And then he dies. He dies yelling. He dies on his feet. Standing up. Yelling … He falls. But he is already dead. (196)

Sophie experiences many intense emotions simultaneously. She is shocked, and suddenly feels alone, but she is also liberated, as she no longer has to study physics, which she hates, and she will no longer be yelled at. She laughs and cries at the same time, then goes into the bathroom to vomit, something you don't often see in a sitcom, but certainly in keeping with Walker's take on moments of personal and emotional crisis. (People throw up quite frequently in these plays, and because the washroom's so handy, we know about it.)

The women establish a bond in the course of the play, and achieve insights into each other's dilemma. By the end of the play they seem to be moving toward the sort of feminine community of marginalized women whose embryonic beginnings we saw at the conclusion of *Love and Anger*. However, here as before, Walker is not about to give us a simple male-female contrast, and Sophie, too, tries to make decisions for Loretta, insisting that she not have an abortion, projecting onto Loretta her own lonely fantasy in which Loretta works at Buffalo Bob's, makes sex movies, dances in Japan all for the sake of the baby to come. While being a woman, and a woman controlled by men, gives Sophie some insight into Loretta's situation, Sophie, as a romantic, finally cannot understand Loretta's pragmatism and realism. Similarly, Loretta's pragmatism and realism, and the reality of the social situation and of the gender traps in which she finds herself, elude and ultimately subvert the "plucky career girl" social romanticism of the TV sitcoms.

> I've got lots on my mind. Its like *The Grapes of Wrath* out there. It's a disaster area. People walking around like they're victims of some huge cataclysm. They've got the eyes of wounded dogs. It's fucking horrible. (*The End of Civilization* 225)

So Henry Cape describes the experience of looking for work when there is no work. It is the end of civilization. Henry and Lily have sent their kids to her sister's and come to the city while Henry, laid off from his old job a couple of years ago, looks for work. They're staying in the motel, and they're desperate, on the verge of losing their home, their self-respect, their marriage, everything. Of all the plays in the Suburban Motel cycle, I think *The End of Civilization* goes the farthest in reducing the distance between the middle-class characters on stage, and the middle-class people sitting in the audience. Walker speaks of the experience of sitting in the balcony at the Factory, looking down at the audience below, and seeing women bent over, their hands covering their eyes, while their husbands rubbed their backs to comfort them. I myself have seldom seen an audience as upset as was the audience at the end of *The End of Civilization*. Toronto *Sun* critic, John Coulbourn, has reservations about this play, precisely because of the bleakness of its conclusion:

> Still, in the end, this is a flawed work, at least for my money. Certainly, the scenario Walker paints is almost hopeless—and anyone who doesn't squirm in his or her seat at the realization that this could happen to any one of us is living in a fool's paradise. But in leaving his characters and his audience without hope, he abandons us in the very place where we need the strength of his playwrighting, and not his preaching voice the most. A place without hope is indeed the end of civilization, but few of us are willing to pay to see it. ("Down at the End" 44)

Other critics, like Vit Wagner of the Toronto *Star*, see *The End of Civilization* as the strongest play of the cycle ("The End of Civilization best yet of cycle" D15). As our culture's ranking of writing for the stage does privilege "serious drama" over comedy, it does seem likely that the two plays of the cycle with the highest proportion of the valorized tone, *Problem Child* and *The End of Civilization*, will be the most highly regarded. I myself would certainly place *The End of Civilization* among Walker's highest achievements. The play is an extremely dense and rich one, interweaving a number of Walker's ongoing concerns and sharpest anxieties, the political implications of power imbalance and marginalization, justice and injustice, the conflict between men and women, motherhood, stereotyping, and demonstrates the ways in which these issues and conflicts interconnect with and influence each other, while all the while managing to be bleakly funny.

The play's engine, the force that drives all the concerns and the anxieties, and its hook, the issue that activates its audience's anxiety and empathy, is the issue of unemployment, the ways in which economic developments in the nineties are marginalizing people who thought themselves safe and secure. Henry's response is rage.

> ... a bunch of greedy pricks can't put any fucking limits on themselves. It's because every asshole who runs a large company can smell these enormous profits, and he knows the only thing between him and these profits is a little human misery. A few ... layoffs. A little downsizing. Just a little cutback here and there. A prudent reduction in the labour force. And no one's trying to stop any of this ... Because no one cares. (*The End of Civilization* 227)

Note the phrase, "greedy pricks," the same phrase that other extremely angry man, Petie Maxwell, uses in *Love and Anger*. "Greedy pricks" uses the scatological language of the street to cut through the bullshit, to "degrade" the self-serving mumbo jumbo of the economists and the schools of business management, to call "a Nazi a Nazi," and to precisely identify the real cause of the problems. What's at risk here is the social contract, the agreement that we do have responsibilities to each other, and this agreement, the play says, is the foundation of civilization.

> All the rules of the game are suspended. I went to school. Worked hard. Paid my way as a useful citizen. I made a contract with the world and I obeyed the rules and stipulations of that contract. But if the contract is null and void ... if I can just be discarded, thrown away like garbage then okay ... okay ... Anger! Yeah. I've got anger. You don't know what kind of anger I've got. It's got nothing to do with depression. And you know what, not just anger, contempt. I've got a shitload of contempt for a lot of fucking things, and if the rules are suspended then fuck it. (*The End of Civilization* 258–259)

Henry's rage is the anger behind the currently popular saying, "going postal," the rage that sends the laid off worker back to his place of work with a gun. It's the despair behind cases like that of the unfortunate Mr. Woodland and the even more unfortunate Mrs. Woodland, to whom I refer at the beginning of this chapter.

Henry kills people. Not management, as Lily first assumes when she learns that her husband is suspected of murder, but men looking for work, men who express their despair and desperation through grovelling; Henry calls it "mercy killing."

The police are looking for him, and since the policemen on the case are Max and Donny from *Adult Entertainment*, we can be sure that the concept of "justice" at work here is a slippery and mutable one. Time is also slippery and mutable, in *The End of Civilization* and, in some respects, through the Suburban Motel cycle as a whole. So it's important to note that although *The End of Civlization* follows *Adult Entertainment* in the cycle, that doesn't necessarily mean that the events of *The End of Civilization* follow the events of *Adult Entertainment* chronologically. That, in turn, means that Max's appearance in *The End of Civilization* doesn't necessarily mean that he survives his wounding in *Adult Entertainment*, a point Walker explicitly confirmed when asked. When the plays are presented in rep, theatre goers choose the order in which they see the plays. The plays are designed to be self-contained and to stand independent of each other, and will often be produced in this way. Walker doesn't specifically tell us whether Max lives or dies; each audience member will create a fiction which goes in one direction or the other, perhaps one way on one occasion, the other on another. In any case, as in *Love and Anger*, the "perversion" of the neo-Aristotelian convention is such that the "death of the hero" *per se* (or his survival) is beside the point—the real point at the end of *Love and Anger* is the birth of a kind of hope, and the real point at the end of *Adult Entertainment*, where there is no connection between the two characters left on stage, Jayne and Max, is the death of hope.

Donny, the "infected" cop who now lives a drunken and dissolute life in both *Adult Entertainment* and *The End of Civlization* went to high school with Lily of the second play, and has a thing for her, in part a longing for a time in the past when they were as yet unspoiled, when there was still hope. "It's like we knew each other when we were both … you know … still complete human beings" (240). Donny has also been defeated by the "shit of the world," the state of mind he also suffers in *Adult Entertainment*.

> The shit in the world gets in the pores of your skin and in your brain. And it just gets really hard to think in an orderly normal way when you have shit in your brain, Max. That's my defense. "Your honour, I have shit in my brain. I'm not responsible for my actions." (*The End of Civilization* 250)

Motivated by both his feelings for Lily and "the shit in his brain," Donny plants evidence and frames another man in order to take the heat off Henry. In a world so patently unjust, Donny will construct his own version of justice, a "primal justice" similar to Sarah's in *Love and Anger,* in which those who commit evil at arm's length are to be dealt just such violent retaliation as Henry's; Donny proclaims: "If the fucking world is so fucked up and evil and uncaring and harsh that it creates these poor sick bastards then the fucking world has to suffer the consequences of their actions!" (*The End of Civilization* 249). In Walker's production at the Factory, Daniel Kash, playing Donny, wrapped a bedspread around himself, like a mockery of judicial robes, and stood on the bed looking down at Max and Lily, pronouncing his "verdict" in a mock "official" voice—it was a carnivalesque moment, an inversion of authority, the fool as king for the holiday, similar to Walker's perversion of the format of the trial in *Love and Anger* with Sarah, wrapped in drapes and enthroned on an inverted wastepaper basket, presiding as judge.

In off-stage action, Donny gives Henry three thousand dollars to go away, perhaps so Donny can have Lily for himself, or so he thinks, or perhaps so that Henry can get a fresh start, get back on his feet; Lily's life will thus be restored to her. Either way, it's a romantic gesture. In the version of the play published in *Suburban Motel*, that's the chronological end of

Henry's story, although not the end of his involvement in the play, as we'll see in a few moments. However, during rehearsals for the Factory production, Walker made a major change to the script as published. He added a scene, the penultimate scene of the play as produced. Henry returns to the motel, finds Donny alone there, and produces a gun. He has concluded that Donny is trying to bribe him with the three thousand dollars, get him out of the way so that Donny can have his wife, yet another humiliation for Henry. Henry wants to show Donny that he's "not the kind of guy who can be fucked around like this." Donny warns Henry that if he doesn't put down his gun, he will slowly draw his own gun. Henry responds, "Then we'll both have guns. That'll be exciting. You know, intense." Very Walker, a grim little metatheatrical joke at the moment of greatest tension. In his anguish, Henry demands that Donny look at him and "see the man I used to be." There is an echo here of Donny's seeing in Lily someone who knew a former self, a self that was still "complete." Henry refuses to put down his gun until Donny, who by now does have his gun out, sees Henry's former self. After a stand-off in which Walker cranks the tension up to the maximum, Donny shoots and presumably kills Henry.

There is more disruption of time-line in *The End of Civilization* than there is in any other Walker play, as several times we go back to see events which precede events we've already seen, the future colouring the past in a way not unlike that used by Quentin Tarantino in *Pulp Fiction*. Walker as both playwright and director manages these transitions between scenes and time periods through very elegant manipulation of the semi-hidden bathroom playing space—a character in a two-hander can go into the washroom, leaving his or her scene partner on stage who can then, as lighting shifts, play a scene set in another time with a character or characters coming in through the motel room door. While the play's scene structure is very complex, *The End of Civilization* is largely continuous as it plays—there are only four scenes in the play as published, and in production, we go to black only three times during the running of the play, greatly increasing the audience members' sense that they are perceiving fluid time, which helps disarm the defense mechanisms we might otherwise rely on to establish distance between ourselves and the characters. Framing human experience within a time sequence that fractures lineal time but is presented to the audience in a continuous flow of theatrical time involves us in a way that simultaneously allows us to view events through dramatic irony, as we know where the characters are going and they do not, and makes us more vulnerable to sharing Henry and Lily's dilemma, for we are forcefully reminded that we do not understand the forces shaping our lives any better than do the characters. The play is an experiential model of the human inability to see the future coming, a future in which we could be moved from the centre to the margins as catastrophically as Henry and Lily are. The most radical time shift in the play occurs at the beginning of the play's last scene, which is chronologically the first event in the story which has already unfolded by the time we see the scene depicting that event—Henry and Lily arrive at the motel for the first time, move their belongings into the room, and unpack their luggage. At the beginning of their quest, they still hold out a little hope, although we can see in what is happening between them the beginnings of the events that constitute the play we've just seen; the sense of impending doom and the tension of dramatic irony are intense throughout the scene, even more so in the play as produced than in the play as published, as in the former case we watch this scene knowing that Henry is going to die, that the disintegration of Henry and Lily's lives is even more catastrophic than it was in the earlier version of the play.

Henry and Lily are both clearly under a lot of pressure, and it starts to show in their many disagreements, most about money, small amounts of money. Lily thinks they should have rented a housekeeping room so they wouldn't have to eat in restaurants; Henry thinks that's "demeaning." Lily thinks Henry should accept any job that's offered to him; Henry is still holding out for a little self-respect. Lily wants to phone the kids; Henry wants her to wait until the rates drop; Lily counters that by then the kids will be in bed. Henry wants to know if they're "pulling together." Lily loses it. "No, Henry. We're not pulling together. Because I'm right behind you. I can't 'pull' from behind you. I can only watch you 'pull'" (*The End of Civilization* 257). As often in Walker plays, pathetic characters aren't simply the victims of an unjust society, or even of bad luck; they are allowed the dignity of contributing to their own sad states. The relationship between Henry and Lily is not a healthy one, a fact that is revealed under the pressure created by Henry's being unemployed. In fact, that relationship contains within it the same sort of power imbalance that afflicts Henry in the larger world outside the family.

Henry and Lily's marriage is traditional in that Henry is the "bread winner" and Lily is "mother and housekeeper." While many couples have successfully managed an arrangement in which one partner stays home and one works, the "traditional" structure has become more and more difficult to maintain through social and economic changes in the larger world. For one thing, it is difficult to avoid a power imbalance in which the stay-at-home partner, usually the woman, is "dependent" in a way psychologically harmful to both partners, and destructive to the relationship in that equality between partners is virtually impossible, especially in hard economic times, as Henry and Lily's case demonstrates. Henry feels helpless because he is unable to meet what he regards as his responsibilities; Lily feels doubly helpless because her dependence makes her a passive observer and it is thus impossible for her to "pull together" with Henry—Henry is dismissive of her speculation as to whether she might be able to find a job in order to save the situation, and Lily herself admits that she has been at home so long she wouldn't even know how to go about looking for employment, and that, so she thinks in the theatrical present, she has no marketable skills. Henry's "tortured male soul," to use the phrase Walker used under other circumstances, feels compelled to "lead" even when circumstances make it apparently impossible for him to do so. Lily's major discovery in the last scene of *The End of Civilization* is the "big lie" of their traditional relationship, the hollowness of Henry's assurances that "it'll be okay." This is the "mark" around which this scene is structured, and, in a way that "perverts" conventional recognition, and retrospectively, motivates many of the choices we've seen Lily make in previous theatrical time, subsequent "real" or depicted time.

> Oh I can be supportive. I can "pull" along with you. But basically it's your rope we're pulling on. And if there's nothing on the end of the rope worth anything then well that's it ... We might as well gather up the kids, go home, lock the doors, make up some Kool-Aid with arsenic in it and have our own little Jonestown. Are you saying that. (260)

The scene and the exchange between the characters illustrate two important points about Walker's work, especially Walker's recent work. The first is the "nakedness" of the characters, a nakedness that required similar nakedness from Walker as playwright, and from the actors playing the roles, at the Factory, Brenda Bazinet and Michael Healey. Walker says that in rehearsal, at this point in the play Healey wanted to know if Henry knows that what he is saying is incredibly stupid. The short answer is "yes," stupid in a way with which we are all familiar, seldom admit to, and rarely see on stage. Henry does know that "it'll be okay" is a very stupid thing to say, knows it's stupid even as he says it, but when he opens his mouth, stupid things fall out because he can't think of anything better to say. Healey recognized the personal experience of knowing something is stupid even as you say it, and recognized that men often feel this particular sensation while in conversation with women, but had never been asked to play such a moment before. Walker says of the kind of exposure, the abandonment of ego, needed to write the motel plays:

> ... you have to be able to feel like an idiot, in theatre, the way actors have to—you're going to go out, totally exposed: I'm an asshole. This

is it—the feeling of coolness falls away—I never felt a great cool, but the little cool I felt continued to fall away. (Qtd. in Corbeil 60)

The second point is the anger, the rage, that Lily feels during this exchange, and the way in which Walker as playwright and director encourages the expression of female rage, anger directed outward rather than inward. Walker women, especially female characters in recent work, can be "pissed off" rather than self-blaming in the way that we often see in social interactions and drama involving male-female emotional conflict. "It'll be okay" is the biggest, most destructive lie Lily has ever been told, and she's angry at Henry, not the company that fired him, not the personnel managers who won't hire him now, because it's Henry, playing the traditional male role, who has perpetrated the "bullshit" with which she has now come face to face: "It's already not okay. All the savings gone. House remortgaged. Kids in someone else's car going out with someone else for dinner. None of that's okay with me" (*The End of Civilization* 257).

Earlier in the play, later in "real time," Lily decides to solve her immediate financial problems by turning a trick, earning some money as a prostitute. This "option" is revealed to her through her meeting Sandy, a prostitute who works out of one of the other rooms in the motel. The Sandy we see in *The End of Civilization* is the older self of the Sandy we saw in *Criminals in Love*, then the pragmatic working-class teenager who tests herself by trying prostitution as a form of "insurance," as William of that play puts it. This Sandy is still the pragmatist, a survivor, a businesswoman, in many respects the healthiest and certainly the happiest character in the play, a Loretta who has successfully established her independence. That in itself can be read as a social comment. The two systems depicted in the play, business and justice, have both failed, and the character who has remained outside the systems, the one who is theoretically most marginalized, is the character who can see the whole most clearly, and who has retained the most control over her own life and self:

I did the street. Just to see if I could. But I didn't ever feel comfortable ... It's ... not me ... I'm more comfortable in bars. Hotels. Escort work. You know, meeting people through contacts. It's a more controlled situation ... (*The End of Civilization* 229)

When Lily first meets Sandy, Sandy is to her an exotic being, the subject of curiosity. But Lily is alone and lonely. Sandy is friendly, and invites Lily out to a club, just for a good time. At the end of the scene, there is a flash of recognition and fellow feeling between the two women when they discover that each has two kids. The *femme fatale*/wife and mother bifurcation collapses in the exchange of glances. Walker interrogates the "mother/whore" dichotomy again, and as in the case of Denise in *Problem Child*, the mother half emerges as the most important, the other merely a means to an end. If Sandy is no longer an exotic being but a fellow mother, Sandy's way of life is no longer an impossible curiosity to Lily but a real "option" for her, particularly given her desperate circumstances, as by that point, it seems to her that her husband is not only unemployed, but possibly mad and possibly a killer. She justifies her "bizarre choice" to an accusatory and progressively possessive Donny:

> I had no money. I had forty dollars. Now I have two hundred and forty dollars. I'd like to have a few hundred more by the end of the week. I choose to have money. I choose to have enough not to worry about it for awhile. So I can send some back for my kids … Okay? (239)

> … Henry feels that he has been demeaned and he's very very mad about that. And so he's going to rip everything apart. Including what's left of our lives … And so okay, that just leaves me to protect the kids … To, you know, get some money together and get away from here. Far far away. So they don't have to hear about anything their father has done. Ever. So … I'm really just making plans. Getting prepared. And I know I'll need money. (240–241)

I think it could be said that here, as elsewhere in his work (*Criminals in Love*, *Better Living*, *Escape from Happiness*, *Problem Child*, *Featuring Loretta*), Walker does tend to romanticize prostitution, although not nearly to the same degree nor in the same dishonest way as does, say, the film *Pretty Woman*. In *The End of Civilization*, the dangers of the occupation are mentioned only in passing and in the abstract. No mention of drugs, criminal coercion, rape, sexually transmitted diseases, social marginalization, and so on. Prostitution is simply a choice, an "option," a means of achieving financial independence, and perhaps more a cause for female optimism than it actually is in "real life." The control it offers in several of Walker's plays is often illusory in life.

Nonetheless, it is the choice Lily makes; it is her choice to make, and one of the points of the play is that this is so. In the play and under the social and economic circumstances the play depicts, it is not an unreasonable choice to make, or so Walker convinces us. "I'm not going into a shelter with my kids. And I'm not doing that humiliating crawl through social service hell. I had a life! I want it back! I need a substantial amount of money to get it back!" (*The End of Civilization* 240). Kate Taylor suggests that the "rapidity of Lily's transformation" might be "absurd," and "thus the source of some comedy," but adds that the context of the transformation forces the question "What else would you expect a woman in these circumstances to do?" ("Falling deeper into motel hell" D6). As in *Problem Child* and *Featuring Loretta* our inclination to judge and distance the "whore" is short-circuited.

Meanwhile, back in the last/first scene of the play, Henry and Lily struggle to establish a sort of peaceful equilibrium after Lily's exploding with anger at Henry's "it'll be okay" betrayal. The tension and pressure are so great, however, that the peace cannot last, and the next frantic and anxious exchange of hostility is set off by underwear, an absurd and in this case extremely touching Walker "wonky bit." Henry has forgotten to pack his underwear. He says he will go out and buy some more. Lily says they can't afford new underwear. Henry says that Lily usually checks his luggage to make sure he didn't forget to pack anything, puts in anything he forgot, but this time, Lily didn't. Lily is upset. They've become so accustomed to each other, have so blended their lives, that Lily wasn't even aware that she looked after Henry in this way. "Pathetic. I'm pathetic."

> HENRY: Well I wouldn't worry about it. I mean you didn't do it this time, Lil. So I wouldn't be worried about a habit you've already broken ... I mean it's okay.
> LILY: What's okay.
> HENRY: The underwear. It's okay that you didn't pack some for me.
> LILY: Oh ... thanks. (*The End of Civilization* 261)

The dramatic irony arising from the fact that we know what is going to happen to these two is truly heart-wrenching; no wonder so many couples found the last scene in the Factory production so difficult to watch. In the final few moments of the play, we learn that Henry is on prescription drugs whose nature and effect he doesn't really understand, prescribed for "depression" by his home-town physician, a possible retrospective instrumental explanation for Henry's behaviour during the play. Henry goes into the bathroom for a shower leaving Lily alone in the motel room. She tries to phone her kids. Gets no answer. She sits on the bed. "Lost in thought." For a long time. Again, Walker as both playwright and director uses the strategy of stopping visible action on stage so that a great deal of activity can occur in the auditorium. As a director, he chose Credence Clearwater Revival's "Some Day Never Comes" (a very familiar and haunting song from the youth of those now middle-aged, like Walker) to play during this extraordinarily pregnant and provocative pause. Lights fade, music continues, end of play.

Walker describes the response of the audience at the end of *The End of Civilization* as "That's me. Now you've got me scared." He also says that when he completed the scene, he was somewhat concerned that it might be rather too revealing and that friends might see in the scene, especially the sequence concerning Henry's underwear, too much of him and his wife. Susan assured him that friends in the audience would be too busy dealing with the scene being about them to pay much attention to it being about George and Susan.

As the distance between stage and auditorium is much reduced, even eliminated, at the conclusion of *The End of Civilization*, so too is the distance between the personal and the political. At the same time that many in the audience see themselves in the small intimacies and hostilities on stage, they are also aware of the closing economic trap, the apparently hostile world outside the motel room.

> The whole country looks more like a trailer park every day. As our lived economy gets worse, more jobs are becoming temporary, homes less permanent or more crowded, neighborhoods unstable. We're transients just passing through this place, wherever and whatever it is, on our way somewhere else, mostly down. (Berube 38)

For "trailer park," read "motel," and you get something of the social component whose recognition Walker adds to the mix of emotions experienced when the lights go down on *The End of Civilization*.

If *The End of Civilization* "perverts" a TV formula, that formula would seem to me to be that of the issue-based, "disease of the week" made-for-TV movie (in many respects, the nineties version of the "B-movie"). We have the "people next door" stock characters, on the surface at least. In Henry we see the "nice guy with a monster hidden inside" type with which such productions frequently concern themselves, in Lily, the "nice normal housewife turned prostitute" (or secret drug addict, or lesbian). In this case, the fashionable issues, of course, are unemployment and controlling husbands, but *The End of Civilization* is anything but reassuring in the "tie up all the loose ends in an hour or an hour and a half" style common to the superficial "issues" docudrama we've become accustomed to seeing on TV. We don't so much feel for Henry and Lily, for pity is ultimately self-serving and certainly a way of establishing distance, as feel with them. *The End of Civilization* goes beyond establishing a resemblance between characters and members of the audience. Made-for-TV movies use this resemblance as the hook to make the production "relevant," but then let their audiences off the hook by introducing the element of the "Other" (the monster within, the secret prostitute, whatever). *The End of Civilization* follows the source form to the extent that it also introduces the "Other," the elements foreign to a normal, middle-class existence, but through devices such as the manipulation of time, and the association of "foreign" with a personal calamity which could occur to any of us, ensures that we are not let off the hook. Instead of stimulating anxiety and then diffusing it, Walker stimulates anxiety then projects it into the audience. The "other" is us, right up to and beyond the end of the play, and we are left in a state of acute anxiety, the "place without hope" about which John Coulbourn complains.

> DENISE: It's fucking television!
> R.J.: It's fucking … better.
> DENISE: Better than what!?
> R.J.: Better than this!
> DENISE: This is life!
> R.J.: Life sucks!! (*Risk Everything* 306)

Given that during this dialogue, R.J. is wired with explosives that may go off at any moment, R.J. may have a point. R.J. and Denise from *Problem Child* return in *Risk Everything*, and Michael the cheerful pornographer is back from *Featuring Loretta*. The fourth character in the play is Carol, Denise's mom, the off-stage character from *Problem Child* whose complaint to social services led to Denise and R.J.'s child being placed in foster care in the action antecedent to that play. Carol is a tough, old race-track harridan, an inveterate gambler, and the ultimate manipulative and controlling mother. She is also, paradoxically, quite likable, even admirable, dauntless and gutsy, sort of a Mother Courage for the nineties.

Risk Everything is much "lighter" than *The End of Civilization*, and with *Criminal Genius* and *Featuring Loretta*, represents the lighter half of the Suburban Motel cycle. Critical response to the Toronto production seemed to suggest that some of the critics regarded *Risk Everything* as disappointingly insubstantial. Kate Taylor says "What is missing from *Risk Everything*, however, are the more seriously examined themes of some of the earlier plays" ("*Suburban Motel* finale" C10), and John Coulbourn calls it "a bit of a dud," "It's funny but it also leaves a loyal audience with the lingering feeling that *Suburban Motel* is not really finished, but simply suspended" ("Speed puts play at risk" 107). I would say, however, that those themes are there, if not as foregrounded as they are in the more "serious" plays of the cycle, and that as in the case of *Criminal Genius* and *Featuring Loretta*, darker tones both qualify and heighten the comedy which Walker privileges in these works. These tones are darker still when *Risk Everything* is regarded as part of a larger whole. While *The End of Civilization* does not necessarily follow *Adult Entertainment*, *Risk Everything* is specifically located by internal references to a time following that of *Problem Child*. That, in turn, confirms Denise's pessimistic prediction at the end of *Problem Child* that she and R.J. will not get their child back, and that for people like them things "just get worse." These are, as Taylor notes, "always unabashed, ever sympathetic low-life characters who are victimized both by society and by their own worst impulses" ("*Suburban Motel* finale" C10), and that in itself carries darker implications.

This play, like *Escape from Happiness*, begins with the revelation that one of the characters has been badly beaten, and as in the earlier play, the question of who is responsible for the beating, and why, is one of the primary means of moving the story forward. Carol first tells Denise and R.J. that her live-in is responsible, and they take her to the motel to hide her. In a long series of revelations, we learn that an off-stage thug, Steamboat Jeffries, was actually responsible, and that Carol had "borrowed" $35,000 of his money in order to place a bet. The thug wants the principle, and Carol's winnings, back, for a total of $68,000. By suggesting that R.J. is now somewhat boring, watches too much television, is not as willing to "risk" things as was the old R.J., Carol persuades R.J. to act as a go-between. Consequently R.J. ends up wired to the aforementioned explosives, and conveys to Carol and Denise the threat that if Steamboat's money is not forthcoming by midnight, R.J. will be blown up. In the meantime, Michael, who comes to the room to apologize for the noise his movie-making next door is creating, jumps into bed with Carol and becomes infatuated with her. When he attempts to help out, he too ends up wired with explosives. As Taylor points out, when you have two characters wired with explosives sitting on a bed discussing classic comedy in general and *I Love Lucy* in particular, you can be pretty sure you're watching a George Walker play.

It is the long-suffering, continually frantic Denise who must cope with the combination of Steamboat's threats, R.J.'s short attention span (he watches TV through much of the play), and her mother's lies and manipulation—Carol wants to hold out, to dicker and manouevre so that she ends up with at least some of the money. Going to the police is out of the question: "Our family hasn't gone to the police in, what, three generations?" (*Risk Everything* 282). When Michael enters the picture, Denise is pretty much at the end of her tether: "Oh look. Mommy's in bed with a total stranger ... Now there's a blast from the past" (*Risk Everything* 286).

As we get to know Carol better, it becomes clear that the money isn't really the issue, and it's not the money for which she's risking her own life and the lives of Denise and R.J. It's the gambling itself, the "risk." "Look, all I'm saying is feeling like you're taking a risk can make life ... okay ... That's all I'm saying. Because life isn't really okay at all. So it's good if you can feel that it is ... sometimes" (*Risk Everything* 278). This willingness to risk is probably the characteristic that contributes the most to our inclination to like Carol, for all that she is a liar and a manipulative and controlling mother. This quality is central to one of Walker's most important "ideas":

> ... there are no *ideas*, per se, worth exploring in theatre. I don't have any great ideas. I don't know anyone who has great ideas or has come across a great idea. The only time I came across an idea that made any sense to me was that we're all really, really pathetic, but we should try anyway! And I thought, well, that's enough. It's the trying anyway part that was the active part of that, and that's all you need to hold onto in theatre—try anyway. (Qtd. in Corbeil 60)

In this regard, then, mother and daughter are really quite alike. Carol "tries anyway" in her attempts to outdo Steamboat Jeffries, and Denise "tries anyway" in that, despite the formidable odds against her and the very real dangers confronting her, she tries to preserve the lives of the people close to her, while at the same time pursuing the larger goal of achieving "normal lives" for her and R.J. and, one senses, even though Carol says its hopeless, getting her child back. Even the deep sadness from which we see Denise suffering at the end of *Problem Child* is not enough, finally, to stop her trying.

If gambling keeps Carol going, and, finally, "love" keeps Denise going, for R.J. the thing that makes life seem "okay" is television. "Life sucks" but "TV is better." Of the Suburban Motel plays, *Risk Everything* contains the most references to television, and here, in the last play in the collection, and the last of the plays to be written, it seems to me that Walker is providing "reference points" as he did in the old B-movie days, points of self-referential identification which apply not only to *Risk Everything* itself, but which retrospectively cue us to the media "perversions" which occur throughout the cycle.

Television is the thing that has mellowed R.J. out, that has converted him from the criminal risk-taker to the quieter, more docile R.J. we now see, the R.J. who just might possibly conform to the "rules" and be regarded as a normal, responsible citizen (this in itself constitutes a Walker comment on both television and social expectations). In the Walker "aria" which begins scene two, R.J. explains his philosophy of television, his evolution as a television connoisseur. R.J. begins with a description of the agonies of commercials. "It's like God has all of a sudden stopped everything and what are you supposed to do. Just wait?" (276). This problem, he says, was solved for him by the sit-com, when the networks started to program "a whole evening of funny shows together. I mean how strung out can you get watching lighthearted family entertainment. It's like taking a pill."

The shows, he says, were not from "any golden age of television comedy." Rather, "These ones were mostly about families and everybody talked too loud and only a few of the jokes ever worked." *Risk Everything* is about a family, albeit not the sort of family you would normally encounter in a TV sitcom, and everybody does talk very loud indeed most of the time; although I think that most of Walker's jokes do work (even though, as a director, Walker seldom "constructs" jokes as jokes). I also think this line is not only a "reference point" but a bit of an in-joke, a little dig at the critics who have often complained that Walker productions are too fast and too loud, too big. It's ironic, then, when critics from all three Toronto papers make this complaint about the Factory production of *Risk Everything*.

> ... Walker, the successful playwright, is undone again by Walker, the director, whose track record isn't nearly so good. As a director, he seems to have adopted as his credo three simple words: Faster, faster, faster. (Coulbourn, "Speed puts play at risk" 107)

Risk Everything is, when all is said and done, a family sitcom, and a perversion of a family sitcom, with a thoroughly bizarre situation, and a family that makes even the Bundys of *Love and Marriage* seem genteel and normal, certainly formulaic.

R.J.'s next phase was reality, "I turned into a reality fan," starting with the talk shows to which we saw him addicted in *Problem Child*, but it was "too much": "I got too emotional. Sometimes I couldn't sleep, thinking about those people" (*Risk Everything* 277). So he moved onto cooking and maintenance shows, the "'life' channels." Ironies proliferate. Finally, he became attached to his current obsession, wildlife shows. Earlier, in the midst of one of the play's many crises, he argues passionately and longingly about a show he is missing, "The Lions of the Serengeti" and its star, Leila. In the aria in scene two, he describes as a spiritual experience a show he saw about a snake.

> ... by the end of it I felt like I knew this snake personally. I mean, sure I knew where it lived, and what it ate, how much venom it could inject into its victims, but really I think I knew how it felt, what made it tick. That show was awesome. It changed my life. I'm sure it did. I don't know how. But I feel better than I did before I saw that show ... I mean a snake ... A snake ... (*Risk Everything* 277)

Later, when he is wired with explosives, he defends his preference for wildlife shows and television over life by pointing out that long horned goats don't wire other long horned goats with explosives.

He regrets the difficulties he and Denise have in communicating. He wishes they could have watched more television together, like the sitcoms, one of which we're watching at that very moment, of course.

> They're funny! We could have shared a lot of comic moments. Or we could have watched a lot of miniseries together and shared in the longing and the fears of a lot of really interesting characters. (*Risk Everything* 306)

Miniseries like "Suburban Motel," perhaps. John Coulbourn also makes the connection:

> Having invented—or, at the very least, perfected—serial theatre, playwright/director George F. Walker has now come face to face with the problem that has faced the creators of serial television for decades. ("Speed puts play at risk" 107)

That problem, according to Coulbourn, is how to end it, how to "check out of here." Walker has often been accused of having trouble ending his plays.

> There's a critic at the *Washington Post*—who's actually a big fan—who has problems with my endings. A friend of mine got tired of hearing about it. He said, The same stuff you liked about his work is why he's having a hard time ending his play—don't you see that? They're all part and parcel! There are no endings, he's saying that, you can't do that—have that emotional mess—and then go, Aha! But here's the satisfactory ending. (Qtd. in Corbeil 63)

"The satisfactory ending" as in TV show. For all that the plays of the Suburban Motel cycle do have relatively decisive endings (Walker notes gleefully that killing all the characters off at the end of *Criminal Genius* certainly solved the problem), Walker still seems, constitutionally perhaps, anxious to avoid closure—he says of ending plays that he often gets to what he thinks is the end, then finds there's more, then another moment he thinks may be the end, then still more, and so on. In *Risk Everything*, the lack of closure is, I think, "part and parcel" of a number of things Walker is doing in the play, perverting television formulae for one, and asserting the need to "risk everything," to "try anyway," even if we are "really, really pathetic." The last moment of the play is Michael pointing to the erection he has maintained out of his lust for Carol even while undergoing the delicate ordeal of Steamboat's removing the explosives. This is not just a "crude sight gag" as Taylor asserts, but Michael's priapic (carnivalesque, Rabelaisian) victory over life as "an ocean of shit." He's trying anyway, or at least part of him is.

Chapter Seven
Walker and High Art, Walker Versus High Art

> George was a wonderful contradiction ... His roots were very much working-class. Yet he was extremely well-read. And because he hadn't been educated in theatre, he was able to give free reign [sic] to his imagination. (Ken Gass, qtd. in Posner D4)

Two of my favourite stories about Walker himself:

Somewhat inebriated, and making audible and rude remarks about the production and the performances, Walker was once ejected from the Festival Theatre at Stratford, Ontario. A little sheepishly, Walker admits that the story is true. As well as demonstrating his celebrated irreverence for the established rules of art and conduct, the incident reveals some of the anger Walker feels about a Canadian art establishment which devotes so much attention and so many resources to art from the past, and so little to the art that is being produced in Canada in the present. In the Corbeil interview, he tempers the anger but remains grounded in his discontent when he quotes Paul Thompson in describing the current artistic directors of the regional theatres in Canada as "The Gentles":

> ... perfectly fine people, but I don't feel any kind of passion. To put new work up requires a commitment, and an ability to take a risk that I don't think they're willing to take. So I think it's worse now than it's ever been, on those stages, because these people are gutless ... They're all pleasant people, but they should not be running the flagship theatres of these towns. (67)

In his most recent interview with me, he was very irritated when discussing the current state of theatre and arts funding in Toronto, the lack of provision for extended runs which might make it possible for theatre artists, especially playwrights, to make a decent living in Toronto; he was particularly irritated by a pastiche show of excerpts from Shakespeare jammed together out of context, primarily for cheap laughs, which has been running for months, in part because it sold itself to many local school boards as "Culture"—it must be "good for" students because it has "Shakespeare" in the title. Here, his indignation seemed partly on behalf of Shakespeare the playwright, as opposed to Shakespeare the cultural institution, travestied and exploited in the interests of commercial theatre—without too much of a stretch of the imagination, the same could be said of many productions at Stratford, which some have described as a "theme park for adults."

Second story. When the Factory was preparing the production of *Theatre of the Film Noir*, it was put out that the play was not a Canadian play by George Walker, but a translation and adaptation of a long lost play by the obscure "post-existentialist" French writer and film-maker, "Henri Bernard Berger." Legend has it that Walker went so far as to put fake cards into the card catalogue system at the Toronto Metro reference library to give additional credence to Berger's existence. Later, Factory admitted to the ruse, and claimed that it was simply trying to "get into the spirit" of the Festival. However, I think the whole business was also, at least in part, an elaborate practical joke on the critics, especially Gina Mallet from the Toronto *Star* whose "acid commentaries and anglophile reputation so infuriated the smaller theatres" (Johnston, *Up the Mainstream* 194). Mallet was especially hard on the new Canadian theatre and what she regarded as its pretentions, and probably hardest of all on the Factory and Walker. Walker felt that Mallet would be much more generous in response to the play if it was given a European, intellectual pedigree. She was. The ambush worked.

Walker's ambivalence towards high art and culture are clear in the early plays. *The Prince of Naples* is derivative of Ionesco (even self-consciously so) and draws on Nietszche, but doubt is cast on the authenticity and sincerity of intellectual challenges to established ways of thinking and perceiving at the same time that Walker questions the *status quo*—Walker both stands with his rebellious generational peers, and makes fun of *their* pretentions. In *Ambush at Tether's End*, Beckett is the mentor. Max, the dead philosopher, is influenced in his actions and attitudes by Rimbaud, and in the play, Walker makes fun of philistine Bush and Galt's ignorance and fear of poetry at the same time he demonstrates the inadequacy of Rimbaud's decadent *fin de siecle*, "bad boy" romanticism as a response to that philistinism.

In *Bagdad Saloon*, Walker mixes figures from popular culture, like Doc Halliday, and the show biz fatuity represented by Dolly Stilleto, the Masonettes, and lounge singers like Ivanhoe Jones with high culture representatives like Gertrude Stein and Henry Miller, who eventually prove equally vapid. At the same time, by depicting the futility of Ahrun and Aladdin's attempts to manufacture a mythology to fill the "cultural desert," Walker also seems to be making fun of one of the professed aims of the Canadian alternative theatre movement of which he himself was a part. *Bagdad Saloon* metatheatrically discusses the creation of art, a mythology, at the same time that the play's structure, and deviations from conventional structure, demonstrate, first, that such a thing is a construction and second, that it is difficult to create such a construction in a cultural vacuum, and, furthermore, using icons lifted from someone else's mythology. The play begins with "Cacaphony. Shadows. Trumpet calls. Arabian pop music. Singing. Banging. A great din. The entire cast taking part." Ahrun enters, wearing a business suit. He sits, calls "action," the din abruptly ceases. Ahrun speaks directly to us:

> Action. Call it a through line. One man. Me. Wanting to be the hero of the piece. Wanting to act and act well. Or failing to act, act that well as well. Hero. Anti-hero. Failed hero. Action. Acting. Actor. (*Bagdad Saloon* 20)

Thus, it seems to me, *Bagdad Saloon* demonstrates processes involved in the creation of art, failed or successful, at the same time it discusses them, in a manner similar to the way in which Dorothy Hadfield, in an essay I quote later in this chapter, argues that the plays of the Power trilogy demonstrate as well as discuss the difficulty of determining what is "true" or "real."

As well as bringing the good-girl–bad-girl dichotomy to *Beyond Mozambique*, Olga and Rita represent high art and low art in this parable about the decline of Western civilization. Finally neither Olga's treasured Renoir and her identification with Chekhov, nor Rita's identification with Rita Hayworth and dream of making a "sex movie with class" can survive the chaos and the beating drums. Walker concludes the play by giving Olga, and Chekhov, the last word, in a way, by quoting directly the final speech from *The Three Sisters*:

> "The music is so gay, so confident. And one longs for life! Oh, my God! Time will pass, and we shall go away forever, and we shall be forgotten, our faces will be forgotten, our voices and how many there were of us. But our sufferings will pass into joy for those who will live after us, happiness and peace will be established upon earth, and they will remember kindly and bless those who have lived before. Oh dear sisters our life is not ended yet. We shall live! The music is so gay, so joyful, and it seems as though a little more and we shall know what we are living for, why we are suffering … oh. If only we could know. If only we could know?!" (*Beyond Mozambique* 49)

Olga and Chekhov have the last word only "in a way" in part because the context in which Walker places the quotation "perverts" (in Knowles' sense) the original, its wistful hopefulness and its irony, so spectacularly. Olga is dead by this time. Having been raped by Tomas' "monumental erection" in the rectum, Olga says "Good taste died immediately." Olga decides to follow, and does, with no further explanation from either character or playwright. While everyone else on stage hums "Swan Lake," Rocco seats Olga's corpse on his lap, like a ventriloquist's dummy, and "manipulates her vocal chords" to compel her to speak Chekhov's words "in her own voice, but distorted and unbearably erratic," while he silently mouths the lines. *Beyond Mozambique* is one of those Walker plays I have not had the opportunity to see produced, but even in the "theatre of my mind" this moment is one of the most grotesque and shocking attacks on the assumptions of "high art" I have ever encountered anywhere, in Walker's work or anywhere else. "Good taste" does indeed die immediately, but what replaces it is much more memorable, and much more artistically important.

Like *Bagdad Saloon*, and like the Power plays, *Beyond Mozambique* metatheatrically projects the issues of art and "reality," and here, disintegration and decay, into the auditorium. As the world of the emigrés distintegrates, the characters become more and more aware of the audience, and the audience is identified more and more with the drummers in the jungle. Near the end of the play, Corporal Lance stumbles out of the jungle, missing an arm; a note pinned to his sleeve reads "Entertain us." After the on stage characters read the note, "*there is a distinct tendency for everyone to play outward*" (47). At the very end of the play, after Olga's Chekhov speech, we are again drawn into the action and implicated:

> … OLGA's mouth is still moving as if there were more to say. But all we hear are groans and mutterings. ROCCO is smiling at us obsequiously. The others are staring in disbelief at OLGA. TOMAS looks at them. At us. Raises his arm and beckons. The drums explode. Sudden violence and activity from the bushes, getting closer and louder. Everyone on their feet now, edging toward the door of the house, looking at us in confusion and growing anxiety—backing up slowly. Blackout. (*Beyond Mozambique* 49–50)

Why are we placed in the jungle, and/or aligned with it? Smith suggests that the "self-conscious theatricality" makes the audience aware of its role, and also "wittily underscore[s] the way many actors think of their audience as an enemy that needs to be carefully handled" (62). Maybe our demands and expectations threaten the "art" on stage, and Walker is playing with the balance of idiosyncratic artistic vision and "generosity." Maybe it is we, the play implies, who have been "colonised" by both Chekhov and Tarzan movies, and who are now breaking free of the bonds and exacting our revenge.

In *Ramona and the White Slaves*, the telling of the Tannhauser story lulls the inmates of the brothel, and this romantic high art prevents them from either seeing their situation clearly or, in the early part of the play, planning a real and effective, as opposed to imaginary, escape. On the other hand, popular art, in the form of the detective story frame, also fails to make sense of Ramona and her world, instead succumbs to the chaos they embody. In *Zastrozzi*, the arch-criminal pursues Verezzi in part because Verezzi is an "*artiste*," an insincere dilettante who pursues many arts, all of them superficially: "Verezzi the poet … Verezzi the painter … before that Verezzi the dramatist. And before that Verezzi the dancer. His vocation makes no difference. Always changing. Always pleasantly artistic" (58). Verezzi's playing loose with "truth," what some would call dishonesty, is one of the characteristics that qualifies his "good guy" status in Walker's perversion of the melodramatic structure. Verezzi's "art" blinds him to what his going on around him, and prevents him from taking action to save himself. In scene two, Victor holds an umbrella over Verezzi while Verezzi paints.

> VICTOR: How can you paint a German landscape when you have never been to Germany?
> VEREZZI: My father was in Germany. He told me all about it.
> VICTOR: That's silly. You present a false image.
> VEREZZI: Perhaps. But my heart is in the right place.
> VICTOR: Unsuspecting people will look at your art and think they see the truth.
> VEREZZI: Perhaps my Germany is the real Germany. And if not, then perhaps it is what the real Germany should be.
> VICTOR: What's that supposed to mean?
> VEREZZI: I'm not quite sure. Yes I am. Perhaps Germany is ugly. Or perhaps Germany is bland. What is the point of creating bland or ugly art?
> VICTOR: To illustrate the truth.
> VEREZZI: Art has nothing to do with truth.
> VICTOR: Then what is its purpose?
> VEREZZI: To enlighten.
> VICTOR: How can you enlighten if you don't serve the truth?
> VEREZZI: You enlighten by serving God.
> VICTOR: Then God is not serving the truth. (*Zastrozzi* 60)

In this exchange, we can hear Walker the ambivalent artist siding with both characters. On one hand, we can hear Walker the pragmatic working-class boy from the East End siding with the pragmatist Victor in questioning the point of art that apparently has nothing to do with the "truth" of observed and lived experience. From this perspective, "ugly art," which Victor champions and which certainly has its place in Walker's body of work, does serve a purpose because it "illustrates the truth," even when the "truth" in question is one that many in the audience would rather avoid. On the other hand, we can also hear Walker, and another set of Walker's values, in what Verezzi has to say about art's duty to "enlighten," even when the route to enlightenment is through the "heart," the world as the artist sees it expressed in his own voice, even when both heart and voice stand apart from that which is conventionally regarded as "reality."

It is this second Walker who was speaking when he told me of the determination, the persistence, required to keep going early in his career, when critical response to his first seven plays (except *The Prince of Naples*) was luke-warm at best, and often hostile. He quoted Robert Woodruff, the American director responsible for many of the early productions of Sam Shepard's plays and who directed Walker's *Filthy Rich* for the Northern Light Theatre in Edmonton in 1983, to the effect that like Shepard, Walker had to "wear down" that early, negative response from the mainstream press, to overcome the suspicious response to a radically different voice by persisting and thus "showing that you mean it. I'm actually here. This isn't a mistake. I'm doing what I'm doing on purpose." What kept Walker going, he says, is that regardless of the critics' opinions, there seemed to be an audience for what he was doing. There is, then, yet another set of contradictions which occur when, on the one hand, Walker tries to stay true to what he sees, how he sees it, and what he is doing, and on the other hand tries to reach the broader audience in a way that is clearly important to him. He said that perhaps the best compliment he's ever received was the observation that he may well be "the favourite playwright" of people who for the most part "don't go to and don't like theatre." These are people usually turned off by conventional theatres' artistic and social conventions; Walker's plays are different, something else. Walker is pleased that his audience is as diverse as it is, perhaps more diverse than any other audience he's seen in terms of age range and class (and from observing the Factory audiences during the run of the Suburban Motel plays, I would agree with him that his is an unusually diverse audience). He regrets that there still "aren't enough poor people," but then "poor people have other things to worry about." This need to reach a "diverse" rather than an "elite" or coterie audience, this urge to democratize theatre, is behind his efforts, with regard to *Gossip* and *Zastrozzi*, to achieve a "generosity" while at the same time he was trying to maintain the Walker "voice" and all that goes with it. Walker had to deal with that same combination of dynamics, and apparently contradictory forces, when he moved into the autobiographically "real" world of the East End plays, and, I would suggest, yet again with the writing of the Suburban Motel plays, and the refusal to "look for the light" that characterizes this latest body of work.

Nonetheless, I would also suggest that Walker's ambivalence toward Art (and the connotations carried by the upper case "A"), and toward the art establishment, is in part, a consequence of political conviction, or at least political instinct—art, as it is practiced, funded, and consumed in Canada, indeed much of the Western world, is often co-opted by and involved with political issues of class, power, and economics. Consequently, many of Walker's childhood East End neighbours would share his suspicion that theatre, most North American theatre, is "elitist," and that literature is too often the exclusive province of the "U of T thing." These suspicions are revealed and explored in a number of his plays, perhaps most explicitly in the plays of the Power trilogy.

In *Gossip*, the worlds of elitist art and power politics are closely intertwined. When society woman and art patron, Bitch Nelson, is murdered by poison at a gallery opening, T. M. Power, a political journalist, is taken off his regular beat by his editor, and assigned the task of finding the killer. The goal, ostensibly, is to sell newspapers, but at the end of the play, in the obligatory detective story conclusion in which all the suspects are assembled at a dinner party by Power, as detective, to listen to him more or less unravel the story and accuse the guilty, we learn that editor Baxter has had personal motives all along for assigning Power to the case. In the course of his impossibly Byzantine investigation, Power uncovers immensely complicated corruption and two more murders, and finds that the source of most of the wrongdoing is a federal cabinet minister, who is conducting an incestuous affair with his sister, Margaret, neurotic poet, with whom Power is also in love, unrequited of course. Along the way, Power interviews a number of people who were at the opening at which Jane "Bitch" Nelson was killed, and this collection of characters constitutes a caricature and satire of the amalgam of high society and high art as Walker saw it at the time.

The opening image of the play is a tire hanging from a rope, with a crowd of people staring at it, drinking champagne, and "smiling stupidly." Bitch Nelson then toasts "minimal art," and falls dead through the tire, a thoroughly grotesque and vivid comment on the vacuity of the society with which the play is about to concern itself. With the possible exception of poetess Brigit Nelson, Bitch's sister, none of the characters understand or value art, for all that they call themselves artists or patrons of the arts: for them, art is simply an excuse for gathering in exclusive groups in which they can conduct their vicious political, personal, and sexual intrigues. Brigit's problem, in contrast, is not that she doesn't understand art, but that she doesn't understand life. In all cases, there is no real connection between art and life; each seems to have very little to do with the other, except when art is used as a vehicle or weapon to further personal or political ambitions.

Power's first interviewee is Peter Bellum, a British stage director. His nationality, of course, is very significant, given Walker's dislike of British pretension and social hierarchy. His nationality is also significant given the Toronto alternative theatre movement's ongoing quarrel with the importing of British talent to run Canadian theatres and the perpetuation of Canada's status as an artistic colony. We first see Bellum in rehearsal, coaching a male and a female actor through a spatial exercise: "Keep moving. Claim your space. Define it ... Don't stop. Keep moving. Look for your space. Create activity ... Good. Very good, indeed. Now verbalize your imperative. So that Allan must respond" (*Gossip* 20). Having determined that the "aesthetic is domestic violence," Bellum coaches the actress to "create an activity," so Anna grabs Allan by the crotch, Allan screams in pain, and the improvisation stops. Bellum is unsympathetic to real pain, "I'm not interested in your pain unless you define it in the context. Break!" (*Gossip* 21), and complains to Power that one of the problems of working with non-Equity actors is that they have very little "technique." Power wants to know if there's a technique for having your crotch grabbed. "Certainly. Brando wouldn't have flinched. He would have just internalized the whole thing and turned it into one of those magic moments in theatre. Tea?" (*Gossip* 21). Technique, control, is what is important here. "Magic moments." And tea. The niceties of social ceremony. Walker may be ambivalent in his attitudes to theatre, but he is actively hostile to "theatah."

Bellum's "art" is art operating in a vacuum, with little connection to either the reality of the performers or to any "reality" they may be attempting to create—real pain has no place in this kind of art. The preoccupation with "technique," with style, was anathema to Walker, and indeed to many of his co-workers in the Toronto alternative theatre of the '70s; the importance attached to production values, or not, and the attention paid to conventional dramatic form, "technique," or not, were the issues which distinguished the rivalry between Ken Gass and the Factory on one hand, and Bill Glassco's Tarragon Theatre on the other. The Stratford Festival's preoccupation with form, both artistic and social, is certainly one of the reasons Walker dislikes that institution as much as he does.

Bellum claims not to be part of the art gallery crowd, admits to "putting the bite" on the bank book of Bitch Nelson, an admirer of his, ironically claims to be fascinated by Power's lack of irony, distinguishes between British faggots (of which he is one) and North American faggots on the basis of "upbringing," claims that William Blake and Augustus John were "queer" and hints that Elvis Presley may have been, and finally agrees to supply "speculation" as to the identity of the murderer in exchange for Power's using his influence with the newspaper's drama critic to secure good reviews. In the final scene of the play, he is revealed to be relatively free of the web of corruption (although he has been impersonating one of the murder victims in order to maintain the fiction that the man is still alive), is killed in order to reveal a killer, then revived when a witness is required, all in good pulp fiction, and pulp fiction send-up, fashion.

There is a rigid class system in Bellum's theatre, and in the social milieu of which that theatre is part. The actors are the peasants. Powerless and willing to do anything for money or an Equity card, Anna and Allan are co-opted to play their parts as pawns in the intrigues of the power players; in this way, they prostitute not only themselves (Anna literally) but also their art for, as actors, they are ideally suited to impersonate others and to deceive, fitting right into the larger patterns of deception and corruption. In Allan's mind, life and art merge; art, theatre, is so important to him, in fact the only thing that's important to him, that art is invoked to precipitate life, or death; ordered to shoot Baxter, Allan uses lines from plays to psych himself up: "Oh, what a rogue and peasant slave am I ... Stella! Stella!" (*Gossip* 48). Anna's toughness gives her some insight into her situation; she calls the stage work she was doing for Bellum "Garbage. Everything I do is garbage. Eventually I'll have to take my sweater off. Then it will be called garbage with tits" (*Gossip* 24). But she never uses her toughness to try to effect fundamental changes to her situation, and instead revels in the illusion of power provided by her participation in the endless round of gossip and innuendo in which all the characters indulge.

Brigot Nelson, a "cross between Gertrude Stein and Jane Fonda," resembles Power in both her misanthropy and her idealism. Like Bellum, she separates herself from Bitch Nelson's crowd, distinguishing between their superficiality and her work, her poetry, which she describes as pragmatic and concerned. Be that as it may, her work is also detached and unworldly: "In order to create an artist closes off what is of no consequence. Milk deliveries. Heavy snowfalls. Sisters" (*Gossip* 27). Her detachment from mundane realities, her claims to prophetic vision, her desire for a "better world" all contribute to a naivety which is her undoing. While she tries to participate in the intrigues which surround her sister's death, despite the disclaimer above, she is no match for the real power players, and in the end is revealed to be more victim than victimizer.

The real evil-doers in *Gossip* are the politicians, the lawyers, and the editor, Baxter, who killed Bitch Nelson in order to instigate the whole investigative process whose revelations serve to exact his own personal revenge for the death of his father. The artists are for the most part innocent of sins of commission, but they have all been party to the intrigues by allowing themselves to be used as accomplices and stooges. "Civilization is sinking into the slime and I'm running around interviewing the fringe elements," says Power (*Gossip* 29). The artists' sin of omission is their involvement in art which has no impact on or connection to real life, and certainly has no chance of changing or even commenting on the corruption of the social world which surrounds them and which, after all, nurtures and tolerates their art, for high society's own purposes. The artists have no real power except that small amount given to them, allowed to them, by their masters. All the artists in *Gossip* are, at best, prostitutes or dupes.

Art, or rather a particular kind of art, is also associated with power, this time specifically right-wing power, in the third of the Power plays, *The Art of War*. The villain of the piece, Hackman, a retired general and ultra-conservative power broker in international politics and arms dealing, uses as his cover his position as adviser to the Minister of Culture. T. M. Power has gone to Nova Scotia to spy on Hackman's seaside retreat, convinced that Hackman is up to something "evil, dangerous, and destructive." Power's sidekick, Jamie McLean, learning that this is not the paid job of observation he was led to believe it would be, accuses Power of being obsessed with Hackman and what he may stand for: "That generation of yours. Scandals in every corner. Corruption on every level" (*The Art of War* 169). There is some truth to Jamie's accusation with regard to Power's being obsessed, but Power's suspicions and anxieties are justified, and Hackman turns out to be every bit as nasty as Power feared and hoped he would be. The situation inevitably leads to a little "war" between Hackman and Power, and the issues, including the political, revolve around style, aesthetics, reality, and the function of art.

While his role as adviser to the Minister of Culture is just a cover, Hackman does make a number of pronouncements about the nature of art in the course of the play, and there is no reason to believe that he doesn't actually hold these beliefs, as they do accord with his larger views on life. Hackman is something of an aesthete who loves his garden and looks for beauty, even in acts of violence: he remarks to his henchman who has just murdered an intruding journalist, "You just have to take time to appreciate things. A lovely night. A lovely killing" (167). To Hackman, art is good because art is control, his kind of art is control, and control is good; he justifies war as merely "a way of taking temporary control" of the "vast darkness" that's coming anyway (179). Hackman defines art as "The leisurely reflection of an elite society" (195), and on another occasion, as "the leisurely reflection of a discriminating society" (211). On the other hand, according to Jamie, "Power hates art. He thinks it's 'the leisurely reflection of a dying society'" (192). There is a similarity in thought here that goes beyond verbal repetition. Hackman values art because it is useless; "The best art is the art of superficial spectacle which demonstrates the beauty of art for art's sake" (211). Power despises art because it is useless (and probably because he is unable to complete the novel on which he has been working for fifteen years). In his first statement, Hackman links art and social status, art being the concern of the upper strata of the hierarchy which can afford to concern itself with useless things, and in that sense an expression and affirmation of power, and in his second statement, as a means of judging and ranking, of control. Power sees art as a symptom, as an irrelevant distraction which society uses to take its mind off its own decay. But there is a strong and important similarity in that both men agree that art is "reflection" rather than action, and in the fact that both value action over reflection.

As in *Zastrozzi*, characters who appear to be opponents are in some respects rather similar, and as in *Zastrozzi*, there are not two poles but three to this argument. The character who sees the possibility of a more grounded art is the working-class Jamie, although he also admits that this possibility has not been realized: "They say this country has no real working-class art. And I think that's because it's always presented by a bunch of middle-class academics who patronize the shit out of the working-class with a lot of romantic bullshit" (*The Art of War* 198). (And how do you think that makes me feel!)

The challenge to Jamie's position, of course, is the play *The Art of War*, the work of art containing the argument about the nature of art—the work was commissioned as the keynote address at a Conference on Art and Reality at Simon Fraser University in Burnaby, B.C. All of Walker's plays, in fact, demonstrate that there is working-class art in Canada; I would argue that Walker's choosing substance and passion over form contradicts both Hackman's and Power's definition of art. William Lane, director of the première production of *Filthy Rich*, sees parallels between Walker and Jamie, and between Walker and Power. Further, he sees in the form of *The Art of War*, or rather in the play's disregard for smooth and conventional form, a representation of the Power-Hackman argument:

Power's life is not homogenous. He's a creature of impulse and misdirection, candour and accidental emotion. As a result, the plays are not homogenous. In a successful production of any of them, scenes of hysterical comedy are followed by scenes of strained seriousness. The only way to level out these plays, or to give them a conventional external shape, is to send them up. But that would be to make them into Hackman's kind of theatre, rather than Power's—to make them into art for "a discriminating society." Hackman's favorite words are nouns like "beauty" and "style," adjectives like "tasteful" and "arrogant." These are not Power's kind of favourite words. And the "art" they conjure up has no place in these plays. In performance, the Power Plays demand to be bumptious and fractious, calling up a whole range of reactions in no predictable order, rather than smooth and efficient, like Hackman's insidious "art of war." (Lane 13)

Dorothy Hadfield rejects the view of the Power plays as variations on the whodunnit formula.

This unsatisfactory focus on Power as detective intent on exposing wrongdoing or corruption obscures an important structural and thematic anxiety that all plays do share, about the relationship between art and reality, the power of art in shaping reality, and the question of whose power controls art. (67)

Pointing out that Power does not unravel the mysteries with which he is confronted, Hadfield argues that the Power plays are not really conventional detective mysteries at all, and refutes the view put forward by Denis Johnston and Tim Wynne-Jones that the ways in which the first two plays of the trilogy deviate from the formula are structural flaws. Instead, she looks to Marvin Carlson's book, *Deathtraps*, for a new kind of play, "the postmodern comedy thriller" of the 1970s and '80s to establish theatrical kinship for Walker's plays. According to Hadfield, the Power plays are related to the "postmodern comedy thriller" in that in both cases, the plays try to keep a step ahead of an increasingly sophisticated audience's ability to predict the outcome of a formulaic genre, and to do so "create 'a machine for increasing destabilization of generic givens and creating their replacement by ludic experimentation'" (69)—which is something that some of us have been saying all along applies to Walker's treatment of all literary, theatrical, and cinematic formulae.

Hadfield then goes on to discuss metatheatrical elements of *Gossip* and *Filthy Rich* which confuse matters of characters' identities, whether indeed some mimetic and diegetic (off-stage) characters exist at all or whether they're merely being impersonated by other characters or, in the case of off-stage characters, are the creations of lies and rumours; these elements also raise questions of what is "real" and what is not, of what is "truth," and finally, of who has the power to decide what "truth" is. Walker's plays, Hadfield says, are constructed in a way that not only makes it difficult for the characters to determine what is "real" and what is not, but difficult for members of the audience as well, which in turn leads us to question our notions of what "truth" is. One of the matters Hadfield cleverly investigates is the identity of the murder victim in each of the Power plays: Bitch Nelson, whose death at the gallery opening precipitates the action in *Gossip* and whose murder Power keeps forgetting he is trying to solve when sidetracked by numerous other mysteries; Fred Whittaker, Power's friend, whose corpse comes crashing through Power's office window at the beginning of scene five in *Filthy Rich*, bringing with it a briefcase full of money and incriminating evidence against city officials; and Paul Reinhardt, murdered while looking for evidence of Hackman's illicit activity at the outset of *The Art of War*.

In examining production programmes for productions of the three, *Gossip* and *Filthy Rich* at the Toronto Free Theatre, and *The Art of War* at the Factory, Hadfield can find no reference to the actor playing any of these three (tiny) parts—obviously, though, someone, some human body, had to be there to give each of the victims a theatrical reality. On the other hand, the Free Theatre programme lists an "Ian Beckthorpe" as the actor playing Norman Lewis, but "Mr. Beckthorpe" couldn't have appeared on stage because in the play proper, the role of Norman Lewis doesn't exist; in the "reality" of *Gossip*, Norman Lewis has been dead for some time, and has been impersonated by the character Peter Bellum, who was played by Stephen Markle in "our reality" at the Toronto Free Theatre. "… the program and its cast list has been co-opted into the theatrical performance" (Hadfield 71). In these ways, Hadfield argues, questions of identity and reality in the texts of the plays (Does Pedro Puchinsky, the artist who created the hanging tire, actually exist? Which Scott sister is the "good one"?) are metatheatrically projected into the audience's "reality" in the auditorium. The characters' difficulties in "reading" each other and of determining what is "real" are thus made our difficulties as well, and we are compelled "to engage in exactly the same type of interpretive activity [we witness] the characters perform onstage" (Hadfield 75). What a glorious shell-game!

In the interior realities of the plays, the power to determine what is "real," or what is to be taken as "real" and thus for all practical purposes is real, is frequently ascribed to money and to those who have money. Thus, for example, Jamie in *Filthy Rich* is inclined to give "the benefit of the doubt" to the Scott sister who is Power's client, the one who is paying him. As it turns out, he was wrong, but Jamie has remained enough the pragmatic cynic to resort to the good old, time-honoured "put a blank bullet in the suspect's gun" routine. (Walker laughing up his sleeve, doing the expected, the very expected, in the midst of the unexpected thus making the expected unexpected.) This in turn, as Hadfield says, leads us to ret-rospectively reinterpret the events leading to the revelation that Jamie is not dead but still very much alive, i.e. to re-evaluate our ideas of what is "real" and what is not. Power himself nearly succumbs to the power of "filthy money" when he is tempted to keep the cash he finds in Whittaker's brief-case, and in this state is prepared to forgive everyone, and abandon the mystery. Only when he throws the money out the window, in a fit of idealism and in order to save Jamie from corruption, is Power in a posi-tion to piece together a definitive "truth" about what "really" happens on stage and off in the course of *Filthy Rich*. It is strongly implied throughout the play that money usually wins, that money and economic power are usually the forces that determine what the "truth" is. But Power is still sufficiently the hero to defeat that power, in this case, provisionally at least, and relatively speaking, since the good guys aren't all that good.

Hadfield then brings together her analysis of the Power plays and some theatre history: neither *Gossip* nor *Filthy Rich* did well at the box office during their first productions, a fact which Hadfield, citing a Free Theatre letter to its "preview club" and the theatre's distributing of free tickets to *Filthy Rich*, ascribes to dismissive reviews from Toronto's theatre critics, and their exercising *their* economic power—in a sense, then, life imitates art. In turn, Hadfield ascribes the critics' hostility to their applying to the first two Power plays standards which do not properly apply to those plays, asking the works to be conventional whodunnits when, as Hadfield has already argued, they are not, but plays whose analyses of "truth" and the construction of "truth" are conveyed as much by the plays' disconcerting, unconventional, deliberately bewildering structures, or anti-structures, as by what the characters say about the difficulty of determining what is "real." Thus, through Walker's sleight-of-hand dramaturgy which projects the questions into the auditorium, the audience experiences as well as ob-serves what the play is about. Hadfield quotes an Ann Wilson article about theatre reviewing in Toronto, and the influence of Toronto reviewers with particular attention to Gina Mallet, and to Mallet's reviews of theatre of social action:

> Apparently, only intelligence defines Gina Mallet's imaginary theatregoer. Just as she replicates the stance of the New Critics when she suggests that reviewers must evaluate each production as a self-contained entity,

she indicates that position when she identifies theatregoers as among the company of "educated individuals." This position renders her (or anyone operating from these assumptions) virtually incapable of discussing theatre which doesn't aspire to the standards of "high art" … (Wilson, qtd. in Hadfield 80)

The Art of War fared better at the box-office, Hadfield argues, because in it Walker "lays his cards out on the table, much to the apparent relief of the critics" (78). Issues of power, art, and "reality" are explictly discussed—I would argue that explicit discussion occurs in the other two as well, but that in *The Art of War* there is less of the structural demonstration that apparently bewildered the Toronto critics in response to the first two Power plays, bewildered them in a way that irritated them rather than in a way that involved them in Walker's playfulness. Furthermore, *The Art of War* is obviously not a "whodunnit"—the audience knows right from the start of the play who killed Paul Reinhardt, and Power arrives at his conclusions regarding Hackman more through intuition than through any process of deduction—but is, rather, a "howdunnit," to quote Hadfield quoting Carlson, or, I would add, a "whydunnit," containing as it does the examination of evil and right-wing power I discuss with regard to the play in Chapter Three. Since *The Art of War* is clearly not a "whodunnit," it wasn't condemned for failing to meet the expectations created by "generic givens."

> The first two skirmishes apparently go to the critics: Power gets his murderer, but Walker fails to get his audience. The third battle resembles more of a negotiated cease-fire, with Walker giving up the playful superiority of Power in exchange for connection with a wider audience …
>
> Carlson notes that comedy thrillers almost invariably end in death, usually the death of the "trickster protagonist" who has been responsible for the mayhem and disorder in the play. In the Power plays, where the play worlds leak into the world of the audience, it is not farfetched to consider Walker himself as the trickster protagonist. (Hadfield 81)

But, of course, neither Power nor Walker die.

In Walker's work as a whole, there are relatively few characters who are artists. Those who do appear are seldom either happy or effective. They are seldom better able than are other Walker characters to see through the chaos around them, and while they may be "good guys," insofar as any Walker characters are good guys, they are ultimately as helpless when confronted with dark forces as are most other characters in the Walker plays. Again, Walker the artist seems somewhat ambivalent as to the value of "Art."

In one of its plots, and on one of its levels, *Science and Madness* pits the visions and truths of art against the visions and truths of science, a twentieth-century "morality play" if ever there was one. Set on the Isle of Mull in Scotland in 1900, *Science and Madness* draws on Mary Shelley's *Frankenstein*, and on that novel's pop art descendants, such as Boris Karloff films and the Hammer Studios horror films of the fifties. It does this in the same way Walker's earlier melodrama draws on Mary's husband's novella, *Zastrozzi*, and the way the early plays in general draw on cartoons, B-movies, and *film noir*—or even as *Theatre of the Film Noir* draws on a combination of Genet and French *film noir* movies which in turn draw, rather self-consciously, on American *film noir* movies. What's important here is not so much "allusion" and literary "debt" as ways in which Walker uses, and subverts, the iconography established by these works, high and low, as it has made its way into the popular imagination. And this includes Walker's imagination, or at least part of it. For the time being at least, this body of artifacts serves as a warehouse of images and ideas from which we all draw, and which we can use as a medium of exchange, rather as the Bible served in times past, as Northrop Frye would argue. Or, at least, we try to make the "media garbage bag," which includes transmogrified "high art," indeed the Bible itself, serve in this fashion, because it's all we've got.

Benjamin Heywood, a medical doctor now involved in scientific experiments involving operations on the mutilated brain of a hapless half-wit, Freddy, is challenged as to the morality of his work by his sister, Lilliane, a poet. By the time the play begins, Lilliane, like Verezzi in *Zastrozzi*, has reached a point where artistic vision and religious vision are closely intertwined, indeed virtually interchangeable. Although an "avowed atheist" for most of her life, Lilliane has been reading the Bible again "for the poetry." "Then something else caught my attention. A warning maybe?" (*Science and Madness* 3). It is this recent vision or warning that tells her that in pursuing his experiments, her brother is working for the "Prince of Darkness," and that "There are forces in the world that will destroy love. Be careful what you do, or you'll bring them upon us" (3). Heywood rejects Lilliane's observation that he studies "the unknown." "You can't study the unknown. I study fact to decrease the sphere of the unknown." Lilliane's blurts out: "When you deal with the unknown you tamper with the devil's domain" (3). She surprises herself, as the words seem to come unbidden. She adds, "I'm sorry. I don't know what's come over me. Sometimes I find myself half believing some of these things I say. I mean I usually just say them to get your attention, but lately I ... (*laughs abruptly, puts the Bible away*)." As the play progresses, she is less self-conscious, less apologetic about her religious declarations, unabashedly calls evil "evil," the devil "the devil." ("If it looks like a Nazi, call it a Nazi," as Petie Maxwell says in *Love and Anger*.)

Lilliane's position is quite similar to the views on good and evil expressed by Walker in an interview with Robert Wallace published the same year as the first production of *Science and Madness* 1982.

> ... evil makes the world spin out of control. Well, by "evil" I mean destructive elements, seductive destructive elements. It's there. It's an obsession of mine. I can close my eyes and say that I do see the world in terms of good and bad. I have a very simplistic, moralistic vision. Evil is the threat that I put in the plays, the threat that I feel and therefore must express in moral and spiritual corruption and people trying to fight their way out of it, or else succumbing to it. (Wallace & Zimmerman 220)

In giving Lilliane the position he does, Walker is in tune with a widespread lay, popular, and inexpert conviction and suspicion regarding science and the limits of science. This suspicion is rooted, in turn, in religious convictions and suspicions going back as far as Greek tragedy, *hubris*, and the sense that it is dangerous to meddle with that which properly belongs to the gods. There are good reasons why *Frankenstein* and its progeny have come to constitute one of the most widespread and most deeply rooted "myths" of the technological twentieth century. From Dada's rejection of the contributions science and technology made to the battlefield horrors of the First World War, to the meanings attributed to the sinking of the Titanic, to all the monster films inspired by the atomic bomb and fears of the atomic bomb, there is in art and popular art (and I would argue, a fear in the popular imagination as well, or these works of popular art would not be so popular), a heretical argument against the twentieth century's official religion, science and scientific method. All too often, the priests, the experts, are fallible: why is it that DDT and PCB's were once okay, then all of a sudden, a few years later, they're not okay? Now we wonder about irridated meat and hormonally enhanced dairy products, despite all the scientific (and corporate) assurances to the contrary.

At the same time, however, as we are inclined to sympathize with Lilliane's position, and to intuitively accept her religious and artistic vision, we are also made uneasy by some of her statements, like "When you deal with the unknown you tamper with the devil's domain." To begin with, we don't really believe in the devil. Do we? Furthermore, there is in Lilliane's expressed fear of the unknown, and rejection of the human drive to discover, to expand human knowledge and consciousness, something of the "medieval superstition" of which Heywood accuses her, or "Rubbish from the dark ages" as another character has it. There is something here both antique and repellent, dogmatic. Again, Walker successfully projects an ambivalence, a set of conflicting responses, into the auditorium.

At the same time that there is an ambivalence within Lilliane, there is an ambivalence within Heywood. Some part of him questions the rightness of what he is doing, and he experiences a repeated nightmare in which he unbandages a patient who has been mutilated by a botched experiment, and is assaulted, in some way, by that patient. The nightmare enters waking life when, eventually, Heywood is attacked by Freddy (who identifies closely with chickens), and reaches its climax in the sleeping world when the patient is revealed to be Heywood himself. This occurs shortly before Heywood commits suicide by setting both his laboratory and himself on fire in the approved Hammer Studios fashion.

There is, in the play, a conflict larger than Heywood versus Lilliane and even science versus art. In this larger conflict, *Science and Madness* enters the realm of the supernatural, perhaps of what Walker calls the "spiritual" in his 1982 interview with Wallace, and that realm, finally, is once again good old-fashioned, melodramatic morality play Good versus Evil. The mysterious Medeiros is Heywood's mentor, a "technician," an advocate of science and inquiry given to aphorisms and definitive proclamations rather like those of Rocco in *Beyond Mozambique* or of Zastrozzi in *Zastrozzi*. "All poets are wasted human beings," and "Learn dedication. Humility is anticreative" (*Science and Madness* 7).

> It is 1900, Ben. The first year of a new century. A time for an adventurous but rational mind. Discard the notions of the past. Your sister will talk to you about evil. It is a concept from a darker age. Your sister will talk to you about science and say it will kill romance. But romance is the invention of an artistic mind. And there is only emptiness in the mind of the modern artist. Because it is a sorry state of limited possibilities we have in our world and the artist can do nothing about that. Only the scientist can fill the emptiness and change the world. Remember that. You will have to be cruel sometimes. But you will change the world! (*Science and Madness* 18)

Science places itself above Good and Evil, note the echoes from *Zastrozzi*. Medeiros sees in the emptiness of the coming age not a vagueness to be fought against, ordered, and resisted, but opportunity.

> You must be big! Do not allow the sky, the world or men to keep you small. That is the conspiracy . The function of religion. The function of government and poetry. All conspire to keep men obedient to the myth of a fate out of their hands. Resist them. Or there will be no future. Or worse, the future of the banal and the timid. (*Science and Madness* 29)

Again, Walker characters battle for the future. In another telling scene Medeiros, who has telekinetic powers and the ability to read and enter minds, comes into Heywood's mind while Heywood is staring at his scalpel, Freddy lying unconscious on the operating table before him:

> Ben. Listen to me. This is information for your subconscious. Trust it ... Let it rest deep in your mind. Then let it rise. Slowly. As you need it. Now basically there are two kinds of science. Experimental. And theoretical. In the case of Freddy's brain it is not really important if the experiment succeeds. Only that you get over the fear of performing it. Freddy was my gift to you. Your road to a better kind of knowledge. Because passing through the experiment to the theory is like coming into a new world. The world of godless imagination. Where the scientist is the real poet. (*Science and Madness* 32)

Finally, what Medeiros offers Heywood is abstraction, theory, the biggest temptation and the ultimate apple, for here science can claim to be beyond good and evil, and by this means, the individual scientist escapes human responsibility.

A hunger for power as big as that of Medeiros, and an imagination dark enough and abilities incomprehensible enough to serve that hunger, need an opponent larger than Lilliane, even larger than art. Medeiros finds his opponent in Mary, who appears at first to be a simple village girl and who, we later learn, is Freddy's sister. She seems to Heywood to have "the power to create," is elsewhere identified as "the positive spirit of youth," and elsewhere again, is associated with revenge and "the power of anger." She sees Medeiros as a "magician," "a devil," and urges Heywood to kill him. Finally, she allies herself with the power of an approaching storm, which she uses to confront Medeiros, zapping him with its lightning. Mary seems, in fact, to be a "white witch," and we see someone like her again in Gina Mae in *Beautiful City*.

The battle between good and evil does not go well for the forces of good. Medeiros uses his powers to seduce Lilliane, who afterwards appears "dressed like a tart." Freddy kills Lilliane and Heywood kills Freddy. Mary loses the duel of magical forces, and is compelled to flee the stage, leaving Medeiros on stage alone: "All gone. The weak. The self-doubting. The possessed. The frightened. The superstitious. The sentimental. All dead and gone. Except me ... Because I am the reasonable man" (53). Medeiros seems even to have won the battle for Heywood's soul. Heywood returns from the grave, badly burned by the laboratory fire, and pleads to Medeiros "Help me." Medeiros replies, "Sure." End of play.

Rather pessimistic, at least on the surface. My description of *Science and Madness* makes the play sound much more serious and solemn than it is: the play is very funny in that dark and wonky way we can now call "Walkeresque," and for Walker, laughter is a means by which we confront chaos and the dark forces. But again it's important to remember that in performance, this play, like other Walker plays, works metatheatrically as well as in terms of its explicitly expressed content.

In *Science and Madness*, as in the Power plays, the "play worlds leak into the world of the audience," as Hadfield has it. After Heywood sees the light, with Mary's help, temporarily at least, and of course too late, he says of Medeiros: "I don't like the future! I've seen it. It's him. He's the new man. Intrepid. And cruel. And seductive. No I don't like the future at all!" (51). But, of course, Medeiros is not science, "the raven on the shoulder of the anti-Christ," or anything as essentialist as that: he is an *artistic representation* of the power of science, or of science unrestrained by morality, or of a cruel future. He wins because Walker lets him win, is afraid that what Medeiros represents might win, and Walker wants to warn us about the possibility of that victory and what it might mean. And to laugh at it, thus preserving our sanity. Ultimately, then, the play, *Science and Madness*, is itself a triumph of art, even if it depicts the victory of evil science. The play contains a number of Hadfield's "leaks" which remind us of this structural meaning, hence of construct and structure, hence of the "possibility" of structuring a future. Medeiros, Lillian says, reminds her of characters from "Mr. Edgar Allen Poe"; Medeiros, Heywood replies, claims to be the model of the Poe characters. Maybe so, on the stage, but in the auditorium, we know that Walker modelled Medeiros after the Poe characters for whom Medeiros claims to be the model. Throughout the play, in the flamboyance, the hyperbole, the arch references and "points of reference," the campiness, the extreme demands placed upon the special effects department, the really real reality of the theatre in which the play is being produced is kept in the audience's minds. Above all, the laughter maintains the presence of that reality; here as in all the other Walker plays, there is always laughter during the performance of a Walker play, and through that laughter, the audience always participates in the created world, and always reminds itself of its existence and of its own reality.

The play's most spectacular metatheatrical slippage, and one of its funniest (and scariest) moments occurs at the beginning of scene twelve. Medeiros is onstage alone, in a spotlight. "Staring out at us. Smiling benignly. For a long time." Walker likes those long pauses, in which nothing apparently happens on stage, because, invariably, a good deal happens in the auditorium instead. Now, remember that Medeiros can read minds. "Finally he looks at one of us in particular."

> I heard that. And you're wrong. I am not the villain. I am not the mad scientist. I am not the manipulator of weak men. I am not the seducer of vulnerable women. I am not the devil's right arm. I didn't bring on this chaos. I didn't bring on this storm. (*Science and Madness* 47)

Medeiros is right, of course, on two levels. Within the interior reality of the play, Mary is bringing on the storm. Within the exterior reality of the theatre, Medeiros is an actor (at the Tarragon, Steven Bush) speaking Walker's words, Walker brings on the chaos, and we're Walker's collaborators. Medeiros' collaborators too, for that matter, as we've agreed to play the game with him. *Science and Madness* argues that art cannot win this struggle, and demonstrates that it can.

In general, *Science and Madness* is not highly thought of relative to Walker's other work. It has never been reprinted, and is available only in the Playwrights Canada Press mimeographed edition of 1982. Walker himself has said that in this play he feels he was "repeating" himself (interview, May 1987), and we've already noted ways in which it strongly resembles *Beyond Mozambique* and *Zastrozzi*. Significantly, this is the last exotic locale, heavily referenced, strongly parodic play he wrote before moving on to the East End plays. I used to agree with this generally low opinion of *Science and Madness*, and while it's still not among my favourite Walker plays, I found, rereading it in 1998, that I admire and enjoy it much more than I used to. Partly, my change of mind is the result of Hadfield's help in seeing a metatheatrical dimension I hadn't much noticed before.

There has long been an argument whether architects are primarily artists, or whether they are primarily engineers. And in *Beautiful City,* the protagonist, Paul, an architect, is the closest Walker has yet come to a "portrait of the artist." That Paul is Walker in some significant respects has been noted by a number of observers, not least among them, Walker himself.

There is, first, the metatheatrical irony of Walker's being made "homeless" shortly before the play's writing by the very forces of development and real estate speculation *Beautiful City* attacks and satirizes. The owner of the house Walker and his family were renting wanted to sell it, and, unable to buy the house (the 1980s were a period of enormous increases in the price of Toronto housing), Walker felt compelled to move his family to Sackville, New Brunswick, wife Susan Purdy's home town. "I'm not confused by the fact that we moved there (to New Brunswick). I'm confused by the fact that we *had* to move there" (Wagner, "Curse of the Shopping Class" E1). The Walker family lived in Sackville for a year, *Nothing Sacred* was a huge success in the U.S. and made a lot of money, they could afford to move back to Toronto, did, but still couldn't afford to buy a house. The play, then, arises from Walker's feeling "out of place" in that regard, and from what he sees as the destruction by developers of his "home city," a betrayal by his own generation, now "yuppies." "Toronto is a delicate city. It never had much soul, and it is now selling what little it has for glamor and glory. And nobody is thinking about it." "I'm thinking of what my neighbors say when houses are flipped on their street. These are people who would no more flip a home than they would flip a child. And it's *our* generation that's doing it. And then you see the deep sadness this arouses in people who don't understand it and are not part of it." "When did shopping become the major cultural event in this city? When did this generation turn away from complexity and decide to go with a simple narrative: acquisition?" (Conlogue, "Walker has left the city ..." C1). Walker feels out of place in time, too, as there seems to be here a hold-over of sixties idealism, as Denis Johnston suggests in his commentary on the Power plays. More importantly, though, and more to the point in this discussion of high art, low art, is the possibility that in Paul we see a portrait of Walker feeling vocationally out of place, questioning his life as an artist, once again going through a period of disenchantment with the theatre, and with his role and work in it.

In our interviews, Walker said that the problem with *Beautiful City* is that there's "too much" of him in the play, that at the time he was feeling sick and in need of healing in the same ways that his protagonist experiences in the play. I think he was experiencing particularly acutely the effect of the contradictory forces I discuss earlier, the need to reach a relatively broad audience and to stay true to the Walker voice and vision at the same time. Given the financial difficulties he was also experiencing at the time, I think the "broader audience" side of the equation was more strongly coloured with matters of commercialism than Walker is comfortable with; he was feeling "uneasy" and ill. I think Walker was feeling the pull of commercial theatre (that end of the spectrum represented by *Cats*, *Les Miserables*, *The Phantom of the Opera* and other mega-musicals was increasingly a force on the Toronto theatre scene at the time) in the same way that Paul feels the pull of developers like Tony Raft. At the same time, like Paul, Walker was repelled by it, and felt that that kind of theatre would separate him from his self, his artistic self, in the way that Paul's attempting to function in Raft's world severs the relationship between Paul's inner and outer selves. Like Paul's, like Petie's, like Toronto's, Walker's "soul" was in danger. If I'm reminded of an Ibsen play in this case, it's *The Master Builder*, at least to the extent that the work of architects and playwrights are placed in parallel, and that the issue is truth to the real self, the real self represented by a younger, "purer" self.

At the time, Walker says, he was also working on *Nothing Sacred*, one in the morning, the other in the afternoon, the only time he has ever worked on two plays simultaneously. The work on *Nothing Sacred*, he says, "healed" the sickness expressed in *Beautiful City*. Interestingly, *Nothing Sacred* is one of the Walker plays in which the writer most satisfactorily reconciled the contradictory forces—it reached a very broad audience indeed (and, incidentally, made a lot of money), and yet, while it is in some respects quite unlike anything else he has written, it is very much a Walker—a Walkeresque—play, with Walker voice and vision both entirely intact.

Just as it is difficult to "place" Walker within any particular "school" of playwriting or style of theatre, and just as it is difficult to identify his political opinions within the doctrine of any clearly definable party position, so is it difficult to place him and his work in the theatrical mainstream, or even on the theatrical continuum with the dominant culture at one end, and the radical, subversive, "ex-centric" (in the sense that it is produced by and for communities away from the centres of power) at the other. He began his career as a playwright with the Factory Theatre Lab, established as an alternative to theatres of the Canadian regional system. While some elements of the idea of "theatre centre" as envisaged by the creators of the system, John Hirsch and Tom Hendry at the Manitoba Theatre Centre, could be regarded as radical at the time, the late '50s, by the time Ken Gass and Paul Thompson and Co. came along in the early '70s, the regionals were regarded as mainstream, establishment, and frequently imperialist in their reliance on imported American and British plays and directors. In those days, a theatre like the Factory Lab or Passe Muraille could be regarded as peripheral and subversive just on the strength of its producing Canadian plays and collective creations.

At the same time, while its repertoire was exclusively and defiantly Canadian in that the plays were all written by Canadians, the Factory was probably the most internationalist of the Alternatives in theatrical outlook, in its relative indifference to whether a play had specific and identifiable Canadian subject matter, in its attachment to an internationalist avant garde form and set of assumptions which could be described as late modernist. From the beginning, there is a tension in the Factory's work, and in Walker's, between imperial cultural centres and "colonial Toronto," between "High Art" and the observed experiences and lived imaginations of young Canadians in Toronto in the early '70s. It's here that we find that odd mix of the concrete here and now (a theatre above an autobody shop on Dupont Street, for example) on one hand, and media and pop art (frequently

American, frequently imperialist in its effect) on the other—a mix that so characterizes the Canadian experience.

In *Up the Mainstream: The Rise of Toronto's Alternative Theatres 1968–1975*, Denis Johnston points out that the creation of an alternative theatre in Toronto was itself a political act, paradoxically using American counter-cultural models in an attempt to subvert American (and British) cultural imperialism. In explaining some of the inter-theatre rivalries, and the aesthetic and political arguments between the companies closer to and those further away from the cultural centre, here measured by presentational priorities and material amenities, Johnston says:

> While Tarragon's comparatively high production standards made it more attractive to some writers, the sheer volume of opportunities available at the Factory fostered a group spirit among others who held naturalism in contempt, notably George Walker and Gass himself. (158)

Walker's avoidance of naturalism does not arise from his participation in a theoretical debate, as Johnston's statement would seem to suggest. Walker refuses to write in a naturalistic mode because to him it's useless, and doesn't serve at all to convey a picture of the world as he sees it. Naturalism doesn't provide opportunities for arias or wonky bits. "I have an unholy aversion to naturalism on the stage now. I think television and movies do it so much better than theatre can possibly hope to do, and after a while you come to see that there is a basic denial of theatricality in it" (Fraser 23). Furthermore, for Walker, naturalism's politics are suspect. The Factory, and Walker, then, by their existence perpetrate two political acts: they are, in the seventies, in and of the alternative, and secondly, they deliberately reject a definition of Canada based on neo-realistic ruralism: "Not many wheat fields in Walker," Gass remarks; "What do I know about the farmer and his wife?" says Walker. For them, Tarragon's approach is an inadequate alternative to the colonialism imposed by exclusive reliance on British and American plays, and in fact, represents simply another form of colonialism. All this, however, is notwithstanding the High Art, modernist, and internationalist aspects of the work being produced by Walker and other Factory playwrights early in the seventies, impulses that connect the Factory to its own cultural power centres in its affinities. Once a colonial, it's very hard to stop being a colonial.

As the Alternatives moved through the '70s, they all moved closer to the "mainstream," led by Bill Glassco's Tarragon Theatre, which always was more mainstream in its outlook, packaging, and preference for the well-made, neo-realistic play. Even the Factory moved into a new era (more "stable" or more "cautious," depending on your opinion) in 1978, when

Ken Gass resigned as Artistic Director and was replaced by Bob White. At the same time as the Toronto theatre scene itself seemed to be shifting towards the centre, Walker's work underwent a change from the earlier eccentric, "ex-centric" plays to work more accessible to a broader audience, more "generous" to use Walker's word, and arguably, then, more "mainstream." Significantly in 1977, *Gossip* and *Zastrozzi*, the first of Walker's more "generous" plays, were premièred not at the Factory, as all other Walker plays had been to that point, but at the Toronto Free Theatre, which despite its early experiments with free admission policies, theoretically universal access, and cheerful, some said sensationalist, exploitation of on-stage nudity, was more "mainstream" than was Factory in its production values and in the comfort of its venue. In a relatively short time thereafter, Walker rose to what passes as prominence in Canadian theatre and drama, became what could be called canonical if there were a dramatic canon in Canada.

Walker, rather like Jamie in *Filthy Rich* and *The Art of War*, is direct and honest about his desire for the material rewards of success—he often says of his work "It's just a job," and he himself was primarily responsible for forming the organization that produced *Nothing Sacred* as a commercial venture. There is, nonetheless, still a tension between mainstream and alternative in Walker's work. When I saw the première of *Better Living* at the Bluma Appel, the mainstage of the Canadian Stage Company, a regional, and when I saw the Manitoba Theatre Centre production of *Filthy Rich* and the Vancouver Playhouse production of *Nothing Sacred* (with Vancouver *avant garde wunderkind* Morris Panych as Bazarov) I sensed an unease in the mainstream audience, an uncomfortable unwillingness to accept or even acknowledge the subversive elements of these plays: they "didn't get it." They wanted the sugar coating without the pill, and in Walker's case, they couldn't have that because the relationship between the comedy and the social issues is not that superficial, and the two are not that easily detached from each other. The plays, for all their appeal, seemed out of place in an upscale venue. I concede that nostalgic sentimentality and memories of the Dupont Street Factory Lab may have had something to do with the way I felt ("my Walker" was being taken away from me), but others have noted similar phenomena when watching a mainstream production of a Walker play. Walker, discussing his plans to direct a production of *Better Living* at the Factory in the spring of 1999 said of the CentreStage première of that play that it was seen as a "sort of anthropological exhibit" (interview, June 1998). Gregory Sinclair says of that occasion, "The audience, mainly well-heeled and neatly dressed, take their seats and chat about the Bourgogne they had with dinner. Every here and there is a beret or a topknot of garish hair, but there are vastly fewer of these" (6), and "The house lights have come up. *Better Living* is over, the cast have taken their bows. There is great excitement among the few colourfully clad. Many of the neatly attired leave the theatre shaking heir heads, wondering what it was all about" (10). Both Richard Paul Knowles and Robert Nunn have written about the effects of moving "alternative" Canadian plays from "alternative" venues and conditions to mainstream ones, including the transfer of *Love and Anger* from the Bathurst Factory to the Bluma Appel, and both feel that the subversive and transgressive elements of the play were transformed and hegemonized by the move.

> … something changed after the moves to more opulent surroundings. Apparently containment occurred in the new settings: what had been empowerment devices in the first productions [of *Love and Anger*, and of *Goodnight Desdemona (Good Morning Juliet)* by Anne-Marie Macdonald and *Dry Lips Oughta Move to Kapuskasing* by Tompson Highway] became ways of constructing a kind of unity and universality that effaced difference. In any case, the focus of reviewers after the transfers was on the uproarious comedy and aesthetic quality of the productions. While the anticapitalist diatribes of Petie Maxwell in *Love and Anger* had been greeted with cheers at the Factory Theatre … the same production at the Bluma Appel Theatre … was read as being more polished and contained, and was greeted more with sympathetic laughter than with cheers. (Knowles, "Reading Material" 278)

It seems to me that one of the things that is happening here is that Walker is being detached from "his" diverse audience, people who for the most part "don't go to theatre." At the Factory, especially for Walker's plays, there is such a diverse audience, whereas at most Canadian regional theatres, the audience is drawn from a rather narrow segment of society. Many of the audience members who contribute to the diversity of the Factory audience would feel uncomfortable and unwelcome at the Bluma Appel (or the Manitoba Theatre Centre or the Vancouver Playhouse or the Neptune). Removing a Walker play from this diverse audience disrupts the reciprocity which seems to me to generate much of the energy experienced at a Factory production of a Walker play. Nunn, too, notes a decline in energy.

> Some of the stuffing seemed to leave the play. Its attacks on the mainstream seemed to meet with a lukewarm response far removed from the electrifying atmosphere of recognition and complicity at Factory. To Dian English [then managing director of the Factory], this was due to the commercial producers' decision to market an award-winning hit, not a play that was passionate about social issues. (220)

Nunn makes the telling observation that the tuxedos worn by the villains in scene four of the play, which make them look like "Nazi vampire machines" to Sarah Downey, look bizarre and threatening to the audience as well at the Factory, and "signify ... the casual arrogance of power," whereas the Bluma Appel is a building where such clothes might actually be worn. The insider/outsider polarity of the moment is reversed. Indeed the meaning of the play as a whole is changed by the new context. Knowles says "The coming together at Petie's death of the play's three marginalized women, which at the Factory had been an empowering image of solidarity, became at the Bluma a sentimental gesture, invoking a conventional closure ..." ("Reading Material" 279). Walker becomes safe, unified, and a safe Walker isn't really Walker.

Nunn also points out that while the old alternatives became more mainstream than they were, they're still not as mainstream as regional theatre, or as the new commercial theatre of *Phantom* and *Les Miserables*, which threatens to marginalize even the old, regional mainstream in Canada. He thus helpfully identifies an intermediate step and modifies Wallace's view of an Alternative theatre that betrayed its principles and lost its ability to "produce marginality," by positing "a difficult and complex middle ground" between mainstream and radically subversive in Canadian theatre. Nunn thus problematizes the simplistic dichotomy of dominant versus subversive:

> These theatres [like Factory] are ex-centric simply by virtue of their choice of producing Canadian work, and by their modest and out-of-the-way venues. More importantly, they are ex-centric by virtue of a counter-current that resists the pull towards the mainstream. The fact that some of the mainstays of these theatres have been works by playwrights like John Gray, John Krizanc, George F. Walker, and Judith Thompson reinforces my point. These are only mainstream in comparison with an extreme avant-garde, only politically conservative in comparison with the more *engagé* "popular theatre." It is a matter of continually shifting positions on a continuum: the location of a company like Factory Theatre on the continuum between mainstream and fringe shifts, sometimes drastically, with each successive production. In comparison with the imports that take the place of boulevard theatre in this country, however, companies like Factory Theatre are ex-centric indeed. (219)

It is in Nunn's "complex and difficult middle ground" that Walker's plays seem to live and function most dynamically and productively; indeed, I would argue that Walker's plays, starting with *Gossip* and *Zastrozzi*, were more than a little responsible for creating this complex and difficult middle ground in Canadian theatre in the first place. Walker continues to exploit this site for the production of a marginality that, while it speaks to a broader audience than did the earliest Walker plays, is certainly far removed from the worlds of *Phantom of the Opera* and Neil Simon. Or even from the relatively staid work of most other published and produced English-Canadian playwrights, especially those of his generation.

Nonetheless, the "difficult" aspects of this "middle ground" tend to marginalize Walker in two ways. Obviously, he's not mainstream, the successes of plays like *Nothing Sacred* notwithstanding; he sure ain't *Anne of Green Gables*. On the other hand, though, as Nunn points out, there is now an avant garde more extreme, a political theatre more *engagé*. And theatres loyal to one identity politic or another and more "ex-centric" and "marginalized" than Walker's theatre. Walker is no longer in the canon of the anti-canonicals, and not "fashionable" (or perhaps even "politically correct") in those circles (not that he much cares). In other theatrical cultures, a playwright like Walker, having written as many plays as he has, having persisted as long as he has, having achieved the acclaim and the wide-spread production that he has and having demonstrated the talent he has, would probably be quite wealthy and an "old fart" by now. (He even became a grandfather last February.) It is here, I think, that we must take into account the "Canadian" factor; Canada is a country in which theatre is so marginalized that even its leading practitioners remain marginalized as well.

Also germane to the question of the degree to which Walker is, now, "mainstream" or "alternative" is the matter of critical reception. While critical acceptance of, indeed praise for, Walker's work is much more common and widespread than it was in the early days, Walker's work is by no means universally respected in the mainstream press even now, and well into his career, he was still being called to task for, in effect, not writing conventional plays. In a single review written in 1986, Jamie Portman calls Walker a "backwoods philistine," a "talented primitive," and an "also ran" relative to Pinter and Shepard. He says of *Better Living*, "Untidily constructed, lacking a cohesive dramatic style and sagging under the combined weight of its scrambled metaphors and contrived eccentricities, it has all the hallmarks of a rowdily original but ultimately undisciplined talent" (E9). He attributes Walker's by then considerable success to the "doting members of the George F. Walker fan club." Portman says, flat out, that Walker did not deserve to win the Governor General's Award for *Criminals in Love*.

> It's sort of like music [Walker says], not worrying about where it's going. There's some kind of narrative—he wanted this, she wanted that,

that's what happened and that's it, I can't do any more. I'm not trying to create great art. I'm not trying to create *any* art, actually, but I want something very alive in the room. That's all. (Qtd. in Corbeil 62)

Everyone who comments on Walker's work is struck by the startling quality of Walker's language, its size, presence, and energy. Everyone has to work hard, to struggle, to find the words capable of describing the effect of Walker's words. Often critics themselves resort to Walkeresque rushes of words, chopped chunks of language, exclamations, in attempts, apparently, not only to describe Walker's language, but to demonstrate it. Furthermore, its energy and nervousness is infectious, and I've found that working closely with it energizes and dares one to enter into its directness and its visceral rhythms; when things go well in the rehearsal hall, actors find that too.

In his excellent introduction to *Shared Anxiety*, Stephen Haff calls Walker's dialogue "a desperate kinetic poetry of directness" and "Spoken Opera" (and I think here he refers to the rush, the immense emotional power of the word amplified and driven higher into the reaches of passion by music in romantic opera). Haff says:

Walker puts his speakers into a primal relationship with language so that everyday words are suddenly re-discovered and applied to shape the world with intense, almost physical, power. Because his words are active—searching, seizing, beating, tearing open, hanging on—the body of the speaker must speak too. The characters' acts of communication— of speaking and listening—are so urgent that they demand the engagement of the entire person. Walker's language tells the actor: listen with your whole body; never take your eyes off the person you're speaking with; breathe each other's air; need every word the other speaks as if it were a vital drop of desert rain and let it come alive in you. His language issues directions: speak to *send* words out; send the energy through, *past* the end of the lines, so that the lines give *outward*; expel the words from the very soles of your feet. What results is Spoken Opera in which the actor must turn him or herself inside out as the characters do. ("The Brave Comedy of Big Emotions" xiii)

See what I mean about infection? Earlier in the introduction, Haff says:

In these plays speech is thinking out loud, and it's desperately matter of fact. Nothing is decorative, oblique, circuitous, hinted at, hidden, subtextual or vague. In this absence of clutter, speech is relentless, a rush of crucial word upon crucial word, revelation revising revelation, a terrifying and exuberant momentum of essential things spoken without preparation or regard for consequences. Be it a solitary word, a rapid exchange of epigrams or a dam-burst of an aria, there's no wasted space in this speech; no pockets of relaxation for retreat; no leisure time. The characters speak with volcanic abandon, yet they are clearly committed to every utterance. (xii)

I think Haff might be going just a bit too far when he says there's no sub-text in Walker, although as a general rule, this is true. There is often in Walker's dialogue that quality of good Country and Western music, straight talk about strong emotion. Sometimes, however, Walker characters do lie, and sometimes something meant to be hidden slips out; Piotr concludes his explanation of the rules of duelling delivered to the nihilist Bazarov in *Nothing Sacred* "That should be the end of you ... it" (91). Characters do assume false identities in order to deceive others: Victor in *Zastrozzi*, William in *Criminals in Love* and Sarah in *Love and Anger* come quickly to mind. Elizabeth and Tom aren't really arguing about floors in *Better Living*.

In discussing the plays of Judith Thompson, a Canadian playwright often compared with Walker, and with good reason, George Toles says:

Perhaps the most distinctive, and consistent, quality of her characters is their lack of a public, social self that monitors and limits the exposure of the private self. Thompson often establishes ... a familiar social context ... whose properties are generally understood, and then shows one character after another doing violence to decorum as images from their unconscious force their way into speech. (116.)

In Walker, too, characters voice thoughts as soon as the thoughts occur to them with absolutely no mediation, and consequently, are frequently ambushed by their own thoughts. Bobby in *Tough!*, about to abandon his pregnant girl-friend, tells her:

Shit. That's right. You're right. I'm a coward. Holy fuck. How'd you know that. She told you, didn't she. Jill told you. That's the thing she knows. And she told you. And she's right I'm a fucking coward. Holy fuck. I don't even care about you I'm so scared. I want to, I want to care about you. But really I don't. Holy fuck. I'm scum! (460)

In his essay, "Slashing the Pleasantly Vague: George F. Walker and the word," Haff extends his analysis of Walker's aggressive, "in your face" stage language to make some conclusions about the acting style demanded by this kind of extreme, present-tense dialogue:

Walker's writing calls for boldness of performance style to match the absolutism of his language, the fury of the fight it indicates. The absolutism is both form and subject of his dramaturgy. Believing that the characters say exactly what they mean, and mean exactly what they say, is the necessary starting point from which to build the stage-life of the play. From there, the words can also take on power as mere utterance because they can be given the kind of physical attention (enunciation, projection) proper to incantation. The actors' clarity of delivery is exceptionally crucial because so much rides on the characters' precise word choices. (65)

In his introduction to *Suburban Motel*, Daniel De Raey, who directed the premières of three of the six plays at the Theatre Off Park in New York, also explores the demands Walker dialogue makes on actors:

Actors intuit that, in the playing, Walker is more akin to basketball than chess. It's a verbal workout. These characters don't talk for talk's entertainment value. They're far too busy for that. With serious decisions hanging on the balance, they are desperately trying to make sense to each other or to themselves. Even their emotional states are largely dependent on the success or failure of these attempts at sense-making. This involves in-the-moment, intense dealing from the hip and the heart, from which emotions will surely follow. (5)

All stage language, of course, works within the convention of the perpetual present (except perhaps in Japanese Noh plays and the plays of Bertolt Brecht), but Walker's is more present than most because, performed with full conviction and courage, it not only gives the illusion of being spontaneous, it is spontaneous, paradoxically—while it is, of course, written stage language, and while the actor knows in advance which words of the English language will be spoken in the course of the performance, the actor does not know precisely what those words will mean that night, nor where they will take him or her. The result is a state of anxiety which can and must be shared with an audience if a Walker play is to have its full effect in performance.

Walker dialogue builds thoughts, re-creates a way in which people actually think by talking. First, a statement, an approximation, something to get the ball rolling. Then expansion, possibly elaboration and refinement. Often a key word in the initial statement is repeated as more details are added to the thought contained in that word, so the word acquires additional meaning through repetition and the accompanying elaboration. Sometimes a line of thought is abandoned, and a character starts again from another angle. Sometimes the character conducts a dialogue with him/herself, and often, as in Bobby's speech from *Tough!* above, and as in Henry's speech from *The End of Civilization* below, characters ambush themselves with a sudden, unexpected, usually frightening insight not so much revealed by the words as created by the words.

There's a change in how people think about these things. They don't think it's important to have people working ... They don't think it's the most important thing. I'm not sure what they think is important. It can't be … just profit. It'd be totally depressing to think these companies were only thinking of profit. (*The End of Civilization* 254)

Walker's dialogue is distinguished by the "colloquial eloquence" Baldwin ascribes to Junior in *Escape from Happiness*. Often characters, using the most familiar of colloquial language, its rhythms, its vocabulary, nonetheless express a sharpness of insight and an inventiveness of expression not commonly encountered in everyday life; as Walker once used popular art forms to express ideas beyond the capacity of the source form, so now he uses popular speech and idiom to express a character's reality and his/her opinion of that reality with a startling eloquence (another form of ambush, this time ambushing the audience) that one doesn't expect to find in everyday, "realistic" speech and thought.

In *The End of Civilization*, Henry, unemployed, desperate, confesses to his wife, Lily, that he is guilty of murdering some of his fellow job applicants. Not management, as Lily first thought when she heard that her husband was suspected of murder. And not to reduce competition for jobs, as we might first suspect, but because

> They were disgusting ass kissers. They had to die … They were … depressing. Everywhere I went there was a guy or two sucking up in the worst way. Totally desperate. Totally fucking pathetic. Those three were the worst. Desperate and dangerous. It's bad enough when management fucks you over. But when you see your colleagues degenerating like that it's … well demeaning in a way you just can't stand … They were mercy killings in a way … I'm chemical free, Lil. There's nothing wrong with me. I just got very annoyed with a certain kind of behaviour. And well let's be honest, life hasn't been all that great lately. So maybe I'm a bit stressed … Yeah definitely I'm stressed. I mean I totally forgot about killing those guys I've been so stressed by other things. No money. Running out of places I could apply for meaningful work. My wife becoming a prostitute. Stressful stressful things really … Look I guess I better go turn myself into the police. (144–145)

Very ordinary words, ordinary language, but in context, startlingly eloquent, taking us into a mental state, part desperation, part anger, part compassion, whose existence we may have suspected, but which we had never before seen on stage with such sudden clarity.

Walker's approach often seems to be to overwhelm his audiences, with the size of the characters and their emotions, the "here and now" effect of the language, the sheer speed of the production when he himself directs. To these ends, Walker has become progressively concerned with producing his plays as an uninterrupted rush, overwhelming the audience's senses and minds and leaving no time for retreat, pause, regrouping of accustomed defences. When he directed the Shared Anxiety Co-op revival of *Theatre of the Film Noir* at the Factory's Studio Cafe in 1993, he staged the play with no intermission. When *Criminals in Love* and *Escape for Happiness* were revised for publication in the anthology, *Shared Anxiety*, both plays were shortened, *Criminals in Love* so it could be staged without an intermission, while *Escape from Happiness* was reduced from three acts to two. His seven most recent stage plays, *Tough!* and the six plays of the Suburban Motel cycle, all dispense with intermissions entirely, each playing for about an hour and twenty or twenty-five minutes.

Recently, I had one of those rare opportunities to see something through someone else's eyes, in this case, George F. Walker's work through the eyes of someone who had never experienced Walker's work in the theatre before. These are good eyes too, the eyes of one of my most promising students, Anna Brierley; eyes simultaneously innocent: not a lot of preconceptions about what theatre is or should be, and sophisticated: she's an Honors English student, an accomplished actress, and very articulate. She can describe the experience of seeing a Walker play for the first time with precision, sensitivity, and honesty. The play in question was Walker's own production of *Problem Child*, one of the Suburban Motel plays, at the Factory in the fall of 1997.

First, I was amused and, I'll admit, gratified by Anna's response to being in the Factory—"Oh my God, here I am in the Factory Theatre!!" That's the kind of awe and reverence (and sort of disbelief) I can remember the first time I was in the Theatre Upstairs at the Royal Court, or the Traverse, or der Brakke Gronde. Pretending I knew what I was doing at the King's Head. Or seeing Peter Brook's *A Midsummer Night's Dream*. Maybe even Epidaurus, which was, as they say, a "religious experience." (In that respect, then, maybe Canadian theatre has come a long way in the last twenty-five years.)

Anna was also dazzled by the overall quality of the production, not one role played excellently and the rest just so-so, but all of a quality, and all excellent: Nola Augustson, Shawn Doyle, James Kidnie and Kirsten Thomson—indeed Thomson won a Dora Award for best actress for her performance of Denise. Here, then, was theatre as Anna felt and sensed it should be, but seldom is. She talked of the immediacy of the experience, the world of the stage insisting through both its completeness and energy that she accept it and become involved in it without reservation, even though she knew that this wasn't quite realism as she understood realism from Chekhov and Ibsen. This was a motel room all right, a realistically convincing motel room, but at the same time, more than a real motel room, the quintessence of motel rooms. Of how moved she was by Denise's final monologue, even while "in a part of her brain" as Walker would say, she knew that sudden shifts of convention, like this move into direct address, were not to her taste. She was, genuinely, shaken, and very excited.

Interestingly, Anna was accompanied at the Factory by her sister and a friend, neither of these other young women were as interested in or as involved in theatre. They were not as positive about the experience as Anna was, and they were of the opinion that *Problem Child* was "too much," too aggressive, too "real," too connected with a real and sad world, "connected" in George Walker's sense of the word. A couple of days later, the trio went to see *Rent*, and positive and negative responses were reversed. In our conversation, Anna and I regretfully came to the conclusion, more's the pity, that Walker may indeed be a minority taste among theatregoers.

But that's Walker, a playwright with ambivalent feelings towards the theatre, or at least some theatre, and an artist suspicious of high art, or even capital "A" "Art itself," but who who nonetheless draws heavily on a wide range of high art as well as popular art to inspire his own work, to communicate to an audience steeped in art of all sorts as is he, sometimes to frame his own work and to establish "points of reference." At the same time, as he himself has pointed out on several occasions, when he started to write plays, he was sufficiently innocent of the theatre's traditions and expectations that he was free to make it up as he went along. In his most recent work, he seems to be trying to reclaim this state of innocence, reducing as much as possible the layers of interpretation and predetermined expectation between his subject and the resultant work of art, trying to get back to a state of artistic innocence in which he is again free to make it up as he goes along, or in which, in a state of informed innocence following twenty-five years of experience as a playwright, his characters are free to make it up as they go along. In this ambivalent relationship with established art, as in many respects, Walker is a fascinating set of contradictions.

Appendix
Significant Productions
of Plays by George F. Walker

Jul 1971 (première)	*The Prince of Naples,* Factory, directed by Paul Bettis
8 Dec 1971 (première)	*Ambush at Tether's End,* Factory, directed by Ken Gass
Apr 1972 (première)	*Sacktown Rag,* Factory, directed by Ken Gass
28 Mar 1973 (première)	*Bagdad Saloon,* Factory, directed by Eric Steiner
1973	*Bagdad Saloon,* Bush Theatre London Factory tour
9 Apr 1974 (première)	*Demerit,* Factory, directed by Ken Gass
11 May 1974 (première)	*Beyond Mozambique,* Factory, directed by Eric Steiner
13 Jan 1976 (première)	*Ramona & the White Slaves,* Factory, directed by George F. Walker
Feb 1977	*Sacktown Rag,* Factory, directed by Patricia Carroll
21 Apr 1977 (première)	*Gossip,* Toronto Free, directed by John Palmer
2 Nov 1977 (première)	*Zastrozzi,* Toronto Free, directed by William Lane
Jan 1978	*Beyond Mozambique,* Factory, directed by George F. Walker
1978	*Gossip,* Empty Space Theater Seattle, directed by Jeff Steitzer
1978	*Gossip,* Williamstown Festival, Mass.
1978	*Zastrozzi,* Wakefield Tricycle at the King's Head Theatre London
20 Jan 1979 (première)	*Filthy Rich,* Toronto Free, directed by William Lane
Feb 1979	*Zastrozzi,* Centre Stage Theatre London Ont., directed by Ken Livingstone
Apr 1979	*Gossip,* Arts Club Vancouver, directed by Brian Richmond
1979	*Beyond Mozambique,* National Institute of Dramatic Art Australia
1979	*Gossip,* Cricket Theater Minneapolis
1979	*Gossip,* PAF Playhouse Long Island
1979	*Zastrozzi,* Australia
12 Jan 1980 (première)	*Rumours of Our Death,* Factory, directed by George F. Walker
1980	*Zastrozzi,* Court Theatre New Zealand
1981	*Zastrozzi,* New York Public (Walker playwright-in-residence), directed by Andrei Serban
11 May 1981 (première)	*Theatre of the Film Noir,* Factory for the Toronto International Theatre Festival, directed by George F. Walker

Aug 1982 (première)	*The Art of War,* Simon Fraser U Conference on Art And Reality
30 Sep 1982 (première)	*Science and Madness,* Tarragon, directed by William Lane
1982	*Beyond Mozambique,* Nimrod Theatre Sydney Australia
1982	*Filthy Rich,* Empty Space Theater Seattle
1982	*Theatre of the Film Noir,* Williamstown Theatre Festival
Feb 1983	*Filthy Rich,* Great Canadian Theatre Co. Ottawa, directed by Paul Hanna
Feb 1983	*Filthy Rich,* Neptune Halifax, directed by Peter Froehlich
Feb 1983	*The Art of War,* Factory at TWP (first professional prod after SFU premiere), directed by George F. Walker
Apr 1983	*Filthy Rich,* Belfry Theatre Victoria, directed by James Roy
Oct 1983	*Filthy Rich,* Kam Theatre Thunder Bay, directed by Peter Raffo
1983	*Filthy Rich,* Northern Light Theatre Edmonton, directed by Robert Woodruff
Sep 1984	*The Art of War,* Great Canadian, directed by George F. Walker
Sep 1984	*The Art of War,* Kam Theatre, directed by Maureen McKeon
7 Nov 1984 (première)	*Criminals in Love,* Factory, directed by George F. Walker
1984	*Theatre of the Film Noir,* English tour
1984	*Zastrozzi,* Nimrod Theatre, directed by George F. Walker
Jan 1985	*Theatre of the Film Noir,* Great Canadian, directed by Patrick McDonald
Apr 1985	*Le theatre du film noir (trans. Louise Ringuet),* Theatre d'la corvee Vanier Ont., directed by Alain Fournier
May 1985	*Filthy Rich,* Theatre Calgary, directed by George F. Walker
Oct 1985	*Filthy Rich,* Double Image Repertory Co. New York, directed by Max D. Mayer
Mar 1986	*Criminals in Love,* Theatre Calgary, directed by William Lane
Apr 1986	*Filthy Rich,* Manitoba Theatre Centre Winnipeg, directed by Linda Moore
15 May 1986 (première)	*Better Living,* CentreStage, directed by Bill Glassco
Jan 1987	*Ramona & the White Slaves,* Dark Horse Theatre Vancouver, directed by Robert Garfat
May–Jun 1987	*Zastrozzi,* Factory 10th anniversary revival, directed by George F. Walker
30 Sep 1987 (première)	*Beautiful City,* Factory, directed by Bob White
Nov 1987	*Criminals in Love (as L'amour en deroute)* trans. Anne Nenarokoff, Théâtre français de Toronto, directed by Gilbert Lepage
1987	*Better Living,* New York Stage & Film Co. at Vassar College

1987	*The Art of War,* New Theater of Brooklyn, directed by Stephen Katz
8 Jan 1988 (première)	*Nothing Sacred,* Canadian Stage, directed by Bill Glassco
Jan 1988	*Filthy Rich,* Grand Theatre London Ont., directed by Martha Henry
Jan 1988	*Nothing Sacred,* Mark Taper Forum Los Angeles, directed by Michael Lindsay-Hogg
11 Oct 1989 (première)	*Love and Anger,* Factory, directed by George F. Walker
1989	*Better Living,* Matrix Theater Hollywood
1989	*Nothing Sacred,* American Conservatory Theater San Francisco
1989	*Nothing Sacred,* Arena Stage Washington
1989	*Nothing Sacred,* LiveEnt at Bluma Appel Theatre Toronto (commercial run)
1989	*Nothing Sacred,* National Arts Centre Ottawa
1989	*Nothing Sacred,* Seattle Repertory
Dec 1990	*Love and Anger,* New York Theatre Workshop, directed by James C. Nicola
1990	*Nothing Sacred,* Australia
1990	*Nothing Sacred,* Israel
1990	*Nothing Sacred,* Sweden
1990	*Zastrozzi,* Oxford University Dramatic Society
Jul 1991 (première)	*Escape from Happiness,* NY Stage & Film Co. Powerhouse Theatre at Vassar College, directed by Max Mayer
1991	*Love and Anger,* Round House Theater Maryland
Feb 1992	*Escape from Happiness,* Factory (Cdn. Premiere), directed by George F. Walker
1992	*Criminals in Love,* TriBeCa Lab NYC, directed by Lee Milinazzo
1992	*Gossip,* Artists Repertory Theater Portland Ore.
1992	*Love and Anger,* Actors' Theater of San Francisco
1992	*Nothing Sacred,* Atlantic Theater Co. NYC, directed by Max Mayer
1992	*Nothing Sacred,* Hong Kong Rep.
1992	*Zastrozzi,* Shakespeare Institute Warwickshire UK
4 Feb 1993 (première)	*Tough!,* Green Thumb Theatre for Young People Vancouver , directed by Patrick McDonald
1993	*Beyond Mozambique,* Chicago
1993	*Criminals in Love,* Round House Theater
1993	*Escape from Happiness,* Center Stage Co. Baltimore
1993	*Escape from Happiness,* Yale Repertory Co.

1993	*Theatre of the Film Noir,* Shared Anxiety Co-op at Factory Studio Cafe, directed by George F. Walker
1993	*Tough!,* New York Stage & Film Co.
Sep 1994	*Nothing Sacred,* Nothing Sacred Corp. at Winter Garden Theatre Toronto, directed by George F. Walker & Patrick McDonald
1994	*Escape from Happiness,* Round House Theater
1994	*Tough!,* Factory, directed by Patrick McDonald
15 Jun 1997 (première)	*Risk Everything,* Rattlestick Productions at Theatre Off Park New York, directed by Daniel De Raey
13 May 1997 (première)	*Problem Child,* Rattlestick Productions at Theatre Off Park New York, directed by Daniel De Raey
19 May 1997 Park (première)	*Criminal Genius,* Rattlestick Productions at Theatre Off New York, directed by Daniel De Raey
1997 (première)	*Adult Entertainment,* Factory, directed by George F. Walker
1997 (Canadian première)	*Criminal Genius,* Factory, directed by George F. Walker
1997 (Canadian première)	*Problem Child* , Factory, directed by George F. Walker
24 Apr 1998 (première) Walker	*The End of Civilization,* Factory, directed by George F.
7 May 1998 (première)	*Featuring Loretta,* Factory, directed by George F. Walker
17 June 1998 (Canadian première)	*Risk Everything,* Factory, directed by George F. Walker

References

Armstrong, Gordon. Review of "Tough!" [Green Thumb production]. *Theatrum* 33 (April/May 1993): 44–45.

Bakhtin, Mikhail. *Rabelais and His World*. Trans. by Helene Iswolsky. Bloomington: Indiana University Press, 1984.

Baldwin, James Earl. "The Space Between Voices: Dailogics in the Late Plays of George F. Walker." M.A. dissertation, University of Guelph, 1994.

Barris, Alex. *Stop the Presses!: The Newspaperman in American Films*. New York: A. S. Barnes & Co., 1976.

Berube, Allan, with Berube, Florence. "Sunset Trailer Park." In *White Trash: Race and Class in America*, edited by Matt Wray and Annalee Newitz. New York: Routledge, 1997. 15–39.

Brook, Peter. *The Empty Space*. London: MacGibbon & Kee, 1968.

Chapman, Geoff. "Mostly non-stop fun." Toronto *Star*, 17 Nov 1997, C5.

———. "Walker's dramatic return." Toronto *Star*, 27 Oct 1997, E5.

Charney, Maurice. *Comedy High and Low: An Introduction to the Experience of Comedy*. New York: Oxford University Press, 1978.

Cohen, Leonard. "Nancy." *Leonard Cohen: Live Songs*. Columbia Broadcasting System, 65224.

Conlogue, Ray. "A Triumph of Gothic Comedy." *The Globe and Mail,* 14 May 1987, C3.

———. "Walker has left the city but the city hasn't left him." *The Globe and Mail,* 19 Sep 1987, C1, C4.

Conolly, L.W., ed. *Canadian Drama and the Critics,* revised edition. Vancouver: Talonbooks, 1995.

Corbeil, Carole. "A Conversation with George Walker." *Brick: A Literary Journal* 58 (Winter 1998): 59–67.

Coulbourn, John. "Down at the End." Toronto *Sun*, 4 May 1998, 44.

———. "Speed puts play at Risk." Toronto *Sun*, 19 Jun 1998, 107.

———. "Walker's Criminal Genius is pretty smart." Toronto *Sun*, 17 Nov 1997, 45.

Crew, Robert. "Zastrozzi Returns in Splendid Form." Toronto *Star,* 14 May 1987, F3.

De Raey, Daniel. "Chords: Lost and Vocal, an Introduction." Introduction to *Suburban Motel*, by George F. Walker. Vancouver: Talonbooks, 1997.

Duchesne, Scott. "Our Country's Good: The export market favours Walker, Tremblay and Thompson." *Theatrum* 38 (April/May 1994): 19–23.

Esses, Lillian M., Ph.D., Conversation with the author regarding the characters of *Better Living* as "dysfunctional family". 12 Jul 1998.

Esslin, Martin. *The Theatre of the Absurd*. Garden City, NY: Doubleday, 1969.

Filewod, Alan, ed. Introduction to *The CTR Anthology: Fifteen Plays from Canadian Theatre Review*, xi–xx Toronto: University of Toronto Press, 1993.

Fraser, John. "Walker Turns to Murder With Comedy." *The Globe and Mail*, 19 April 1977, 23.

French, Marilyn. *Beyond Power: On Women, Men, and Morals*. New York: Summit Books, 1985.

Galloway, Myron. "George Walker—Resolving the World's Chaos." Montreal *Star*, 3 Mar 1979, 18.

Gass, Ken. Introduction to *Three Plays* by George F. Walker, 9–15. Toronto: Coach House Press, 1978.

Genet, Jean. *Funeral Rites*. Trans. by Bernard Frechtman. New York: Grove Press, 1969.

Glassco, Bill. Introduction to *Nothing Sacred*, by George F. Walker. Toronto: Coach House Press, 1988.

Hadfield, Dorothy. "The Role Power Plays in George F. Walker's Detective Trilogy." *Essays in Theatre* 16.1 (November 1997): 67–93.

Haff, Stephen. "Slashing the Pleasantly Vague: George F. Walker and the Word." *Essays in Theatre* 10.1 (November 1991): 59–69.

———. "The Brave Comedy of Big Emotions: An Introduction." Introduction to *Shared Anxiety: Selected Plays, George F. Walker*, by George F. Walker, xi–xvii. Toronto: Coach House Press, 1994.

Hallgren, Chris. "George Walker: The Serious and the Comic." *Scene Changes* 7.2 (March/April, 1979): 24.

Hay, Peter. Introduction to *Sunrise on Sarah*, by George Ryga. Vancouver: Talonbooks, 1972.

Horenblas, Richard. "Playnotes." *Scene Changes* 3.10 (October 1975): 8.

Houpt, Simon. "Therapeutic anxiety: Walker's *Beautiful City*." *The Varsity*, 1 Oct 1987.

Hutcheon, Linda. *Irony's Edge: The theory and politics of irony*. New York: Routledge, 1994.

Johnson, Bryan. "Zastrozzi Wields a Satanic Rapier." *The Globe and Mail*, 3 Nov 1977, 17.

Johnson, Chris. "George F. Walker." In *Post-Colonial English Drama: Commonwealth Drama since 1960*, edited by Bruce King, 82–96. New York: St. Martin's Press, 1992.

———. "'I put it in terms which cover the spectrum': Mixed Convention and Dramatic Strategies in George F. Walker's *Criminals in Love*." In *On-Stage and Off-Stage: English Canadian Drama in Discourse*, edited by Albert-Reiner Glaap and Rolf Althof, 257–269. St. John's: Breakwater Books, 1996.

———. Review of *The Canadian Dramatist, Volume Two: Playwrights of Collective Creation* by Diane Bessai. *Theatre Research in Canada* 16.1–2 (1995): 151–153.

———. Review of *Shared Anxiety: Selected Plays*, by George F. Walker. *Theatre Research in Canada* 18.1 (Spring 1997): 111–115.

———. "'Wisdome Under a Ragged Coate': Canonicity and Canadian Drama." *Contemporary Issues in Canadian Drama*, edited by Per Brask, 26–49. Winnipeg: Blizzard, 1995.

———. "Wooing Winnipeg: The Manitoba Theatre Centre and the Community." *Canadian Theatre Review* 66 (Spring 1991): 13–19.

Johnston, Denis W. "George F. Walker: Liberal Idealism and the 'Power Plays'." *Canadian Drama* 10.2 (1984): 195–206.

———. *Up the Mainstream: The Rise of Toronto's Alternative Theatres, 1968–1975*. Toronto: University of Toronto Press, 1991.

Johnstone, Keith. *Impro: Improvisation and the Theatre*. New York: Routledge, 1990.

Kaplan, Joel. "Walker's Toronto harbours hope." *Now*, 1–7 Oct 1987, 47.

Kaplan, John. "Playing Walker's Zastrozzi with Passion and Maturity." *Now*, 14–20 May 1987, 35.

Karastamatis, John. Factory Theatre press kit for the 1987 production of *Zastrozzi*.

Kershaw, Baz. *The Politics of Performance: Radical theatre as cultural intervention*. New York: Routledge, 1992.

Knowles, Richard Paul. "Reading Material: Transfers, Remounts, and the Production of Meaning in Contemporary Toronto Drama and Theatre." *Essays on Canadian Writing* 51–52 (Winter 1993–Spring 1994): 258–295.

———. "The Dramaturgy of the Perverse." *Theatre Research International* 17.3 (Autumn 1992): 226–235.

Lane, William. Introduction to *The Power Plays*, by George F. Walker, 9–14. Toronto: Coach House Press, 1984.

———. Introduction to *Zastrozzi: The Master of Discipline*, by George F. Walker. Toronto: Playwrights Co-op, 1979.

Little, Paul. Untitled article. *Maclean's*, 25 Feb 1980, 27.

Lowe, David. *Turgenev's Fathers and Sons*. Ann Arbor: Ardis, 1983.

Milliken, Paul. "Walker's Living Theatre ignites the imagination." *Performing Arts in Canada* 18.3 (1981): 45.

Mombourquette, Mary Pat. "Walker's Women in the East End Plays." M.A. dissertation, University of Guelph, 1990.

Mullaly, Edward. "Waiting for Lefty, Godot, and Canadian Theatre." *The Fiddlehead* 104 (Winter, 1975): 51–54.

Newitz, Annalee. "White Savagery and Humiliation, or a New Racial Consciousness in the Media." In *White Trash: Race and Class in America*, edited by Matt Wray & Annalee Newitz, 131–154. New York: Routledge, 1997.

Nunn, Robert. "Marginality and English-Canadian Theatre." *Theatre Research International* 17 (Autumn 1992): 217–225.

Nyman, Ed. "Out With the Queers: Moral triage in George F. Walker's *Theatre of the Film Noir*." *Australasian Drama Studies* 29 (1996): 57–66.

Oakes, Gary. "'Downsizing' fear drove him to kill." Toronto *Star*, 16 May 1998, A25.

Olson, Gust. "From Page to Stage: The transformation of I. S. Turgenev's *Fathers and Sons* into George F. Walker's *Nothing Sacred*." *Germano-Slavica* 9.1–2 (1995–1996): 21–40.

Penley, Constance. "Crackers and Whackers: The White Trashing of Porn." In *White Trash: Race and Class in America*, edited by Matt Wray and Annalee Newitz, 88–112. New York: Routledge, 1997.

Porter, Thomas. *Myth and the Modern American Drama*. Detroit: Wayne State University Press, 1969.

Portman, Jamie. "Playwright hasn't proved he deserved award." *Calgary Herald*. 11 Jun 1986, E9.

Posner, Michael. "Strange voices from a motel." *The Globe and Mail*, 4 May 1998, D6.

———. "Strange voices from a motel." *The Globe and Mail*, 23 Oct 1997, D3–D4.

Russell, Frances. "Fraser Institute's agenda." Winnipeg *Free Press*, 20 Mar 1998, A12.

Saul, John Ralston. *Voltaire's Bastards: The Dictatorship of Reason in the West*. Toronto: Penguin, 1992.

Sinclair, Gregory J. "Live from Off-Stage: Playwrights Walker, Walmsley and Thompson shout from the street." *Canadian Forum* 66 (August/September 1986): 6–11.

Smith, Catherine Mary. "Parody in the Plays and Productions of George F. Walker." Ph.D. dissertation, Graduate Centre for the Study of Drama, University of Toronto, 1991.

Sontag, Susan. *A Susan Sontag Reader*. New York: Farrar Straus Giroux, 1982.

Stoppard, Tom. *The Real Thing*. London & Boston: Faber & Faber, 1984.

Styan, J. L. *The Dark Comedy: The Development of Modern Comic Tragedy*. Cambridge: Cambridge University Press, 1968.

Taylor, Kate. "Falling deeper into motel hell." *The Globe and Mail*, 4 May 1998, D6.

———. "Motel cycle a gritty triumph." *The Globe and Mail*, 27 Oct 1997, C3.

———. "Suburban Motel finale is more raucous than risky." *The Globe and Mail*, 19 Jun 1998, C10.

Toles, George. "'Cause You're the Only One I Want': The Anatomy of Love in the Plays of Judith Thompson." *Canadian Literature* 118 (Autumn 1988): 116–135.

Wagner, Vit. "Curse of the Shopping Class." Toronto *Star*, 25 Sep 1987, E1.

———. "The End of Civilization best yet of cycle." Toronto *Star*, 1 May 1998, D15.

———. "Never write another play? Here are six more." Toronto *Star*, 18 Oct 1997, J1, J16.

Walker, George F. *Adult Entertainment*. In *Suburban Motel*. Vancouver: Talonbooks, 1997.

———. *The Art of War*. In *The Power Plays*. Toronto: Coach House Press, 1978.

———. *The Art of War*. In *Shared Anxiety: Selected Plays*. Toronto: Coach House Press, 1994.

———. *Bagdad Saloon*. In *Three Plays*. Toronto: Coach House Press, 1978.

———. *Beautiful City*. In *The East End Plays*. Toronto: Playwrights Canada Press, 1988.

———. *Better Living*. In *The East End Plays*. Toronto: Playwrights Canada Press, 1988.

———. *Better Living*. In *Shared Anxiety: Selected Plays*. Toronto: Coach House Press, 1994.

———. *Beyond Mozambique*. In *Three Plays*. Toronto: Coach House Press, 1978.

———. *Beyond Mozambique*. In *Shared Anxiety: Selected Plays*. Toronto: Coach House Press, 1994.

———. *Criminal Genius*. In *Suburban Motel*. Vancouver: Talonbooks, 1997.

———. *Criminals in Love*. In *The East End Plays*. Toronto: Playwrights Canada Press, 1988.

———. *Criminals in Love*. In *Shared Anxiety: Selected Plays*. Toronto: Coach House Press, 1994.

———. *The End of Civilization*. In *Suburban Motel*. Vancouver: Talonbooks, 1997.

———. *Escape from Happiness*. In *Shared Anxiety: Selected Plays*. Toronto: Coach House Press, 1994.

———. *Featuring Loretta*. In *Suburban Motel*. Vancouver: Talonbooks, 1997.

———. *Filthy Rich*. In *The Power Plays*. Toronto: Coach House Press, 1978.

———. *Gossip*. In *The Power Plays*. Toronto: Coach House Press, 1978.

———. Interview with the author. June 1998.

———. Interview with the author. May 1987.

———. *Love and Anger*. Toronto: Coach House Press, 1990.

———. *Nothing Sacred*. Toronto: Coach House Press, 1988.

———. *The Prince of Naples*. In *Now in Paperback: Canadian Playwrights of the 1970's*, edited by Connie Brissenden. Toronto: Fineglow Plays, 1973.

———. *Problem Child*. In *Suburban Motel*. Vancouver: Talonbooks, 1997.

———. *Ramona and the White Slaves*. In *Three Plays*. Toronto: Coach House Press, 1978.

———. *Risk Everything*. In *Suburban Motel*. Vancouver: Talonbooks, 1997.

———. *Rumours of Our Death*. In *The CTR Anthology: Fifteen Plays from* Canadian Theatre Review, edited by Alan Filewod, 107–131. Toronto: University of Toronto Press, 1993.

———. *Sacktown Rag*. Toronto: Playwrights Co-op, 1972.

———. *Science and Madness*. Toronto: Playwrights Canada Press, 1982.

———. *Theatre of the Film Noir* [souvenir edition]. Toronto: Shared Anxiety, 1993.

———. *Theatre of the Film Noir*. In *Shared Anxiety: Selected Plays*. Toronto: Coach House Press, 1994.

———. *Tough!* In *Shared Anxiety: Selected Plays*. Toronto: Coach House Press, 1994.

———. *Zastrozzi: The Master of Discipline*. Toronto: Playwrights Co-op, 1979.

———. *Zastrozzi: The Master of Discipline*. In *Shared Anxiety: Selected Plays*. Toronto: Coach House Press, 1994.

Wallace, Robert, and Zimmerman, Cynthia. *The Work: Conversations with English-Canadian Playwrights*. Toronto: Coach House Press, 1982.

Wallace, Robert. Introduction to *Love and Anger*, by George F. Walker, 5–10. Toronto: Coach House Press, 1990.

———. "Looking for the Light: A conversation with George F. Walker." *Canadian Drama* 14.1 (1988): 22–33.

———. *Producing Marginality: Theatre and Criticism in Canada.* Saskatoon: Fifth House, 1990.

———. Preface to *Shared Anxiety: Selected Plays, George F. Walker*, by George F. Walker, vii–x. Toronto: Coach House Press, 1994.

Wasserman, Jerry. "'Making Things Clear': The *film noir* plays of George F. Walker." *Canadian Drama* 8.1 (Spring 1982): 99–101.

White, Edmund. *Genet: A Biography.* New York: Vintage Books, 1993.

Wilson, Ann. "Deadpan: Ideology and Criticism." *Canadian Theatre Review* 57 (Winter 1988): 11–16.

Woodman, Ross. *James Reaney.* Toronto: McClelland & Stewart, 1972.

Index